HIDE
AND
SEEK

ALSO BY SHERIDAN ANNE

Broken Hill High
Haven Falls
Broken Hill Boys
Aston Creek High
Rejects Paradise
Bradford Bastard
Haunted Love
Darkest Sin
Midnight Stage
War Games
Boys of Winter
Depraved Sinners
Empire
Kings of Denver
Denver Royalty
Rebels Advocate
Play with Fire
Until Autumn
Remember Us This Way
Slayer Academy
Pretty Monster

HIDE AND SEEK

SHERIDAN ANNE

Podium

So, asking for a friend . . .
Is it just me or is the buzzzzzzzzzzzzzzzzzzzzz so much better than the buzz buzz buzzzzzzz?
IYKYK. But also, if you don't know, what the hell are you still doing here? Get busy, girl!

Cover design by Catherine Imbeault

ISBN: 979-8-3470-3619-6

Published in 2026 by Podium Publishing
www.podiumentertainment.com

Podium

CONTENT WARNING

Hide and Seek is a dark stalker romance novel that contains graphic scenes of a sexual nature, explicit violence, and assault. It features a morally gray MMC and dubious and nonconsensual sex. Additional themes that some readers may find triggering include self-harm, bondage, weapon play, corpse and organ mutilation, and psychological torment. It is intended for mature readers.

HIDE AND SEEK

CHAPTER 1

HARPER-RAYN

Quick question. If I said that I enjoy chatting with rotting corpses, just how quickly do you think I'd be sedated and put in a strait-jacket? I'm not crazy, I swear. But a few nights in an asylum kind of sounds like fun.

Crap. That's the type of shit that crazy people say.

It's not like I'm talking to dead people in a weird way. Nobody needs to call me a witch and chase me through town with pitch-forks and torches. And no, I'm not some messed-up ventriloquist who's shoving her hand up dead people's cold asses and using them like puppets just to have someone to discuss conspiracy theories with.

I'm a forensic pathologist at Blackstone Private Hospital. Well, almost. Okay, that's a lie. I'm only twenty-eight and in my second year of residency. I still have another two to go and then another year of fellowship after that before I can officially claim the title. But I'm well on my way there.

In short, I perform autopsies for a living.

To be honest, it's generally a lonely job. Well, for those who opt to take the night shift like I do. We have an abundance of crime here in Blackstone. During the daylight hours, the hospital morgue is buzzing with activity: supervisors, technicians, coroners, medical examiners, and administrative staff. But during the night, it's mostly just me and the night janitor, Vincent, or the occasional detective who can't possibly wait for me to type up a report before hounding me for answers. It's part of the reason why I like it so much. It's peaceful.

I'm trusted to work alone, and sure, that's not usually how this is supposed to go, but I'm excellent at what I do. I have impeccable reports and rarely make mistakes. All of my work is checked by the senior forensic pathologist come morning, but they simply can't keep up with the workload during the day. Having me run autopsies and keep on top of reports through the night makes our team work.

Bodies roll through this basement morgue like a revolving door, and when they really start piling up, I'll ask for one of the pathology assistants to help me out. But for the most part, I prefer to work alone.

I like my peace. I like to be left the hell alone and kept away from other people's drama, but that doesn't mean I can go a whole day without running my mouth. I need that outlet, so I talk to my corpses. Though maybe *corpse* isn't the right term for them. Patient, perhaps? Customer? My opportunity to play Operation in real life? Who knows?

All that matters is that I'm not entirely going crazy while locked in the morgue, and while these bodies that wind up on my table can't exactly offer me an intelligent or engaging conversation, at least I have an outlet to keep me from losing my mind. Though if you asked my mother, she would assure you that I'm already well on my way to insanity, because what kind of smart woman gets so far through her medical training only to specialize in forensic pathology? According to her, I'm nothing but a disappointment. I could have been a world-class surgeon, someone for her to brag about to all of her friends. But instead, I play with dead people.

Mothers, right? Always our harshest critics.

There's not a single thing about me that she approves of. The way I wear my hair. The small apartment I chose to live in, despite my ability to rent something larger. My style of clothing. My tattoos. But most of all, my job.

If Mom had her way, I wouldn't have pursued a career at all. I'd be married to a millionaire and doing brunch with the girlies at the country club. I'd be wearing designer outfits with red-bottom heels while clutching my pearls at the audacity of the younger generation. To me, that's the perfect setting for a horror film. My sweet depraved soul prefers independence and I sure as shit don't need to be some rich man's pretty little wifey in order to have a fulfilled life. I'm doing more than okay on my own. You know, apart from the talking-to-dead-people thing.

My phone chimes from its spot on my desk, and a grin pulls at my lips, knowing there's only one person who'd be texting me at this time of night—Laith Mitchell, aka the only man with a one-way ticket straight to my vagina. He's one of the few people in my life who's never pushed for more than what I've been willing to offer, and I appreciate that more than he will ever know.

I wouldn't exactly consider him one of my best friends. We're not braiding each other's hair and spilling all of our secrets, but he's definitely someone who makes my days a little bit brighter. Life wouldn't be the same without him.

Glancing over the body on my table—a forty-six-year-old father of three who was suspiciously killed in his office building yesterday—I finish up my autopsy and make sure I have all my samples prepared to be sent over to the lab. If I'm right—and I usually am—this man ingested a lethal dose of cyanide along with his turkey sub.

The only question is, how the hell did it get there?

My guess: the wife. It's always the wife, and nine out of ten times, I'm on her side. You'd think men would learn their lesson about crossing a woman. If history has taught us anything, it's that a woman scorned is a woman you should fear.

After closing up the body and doing my best to make it appear as though this man didn't just have his chest cracked open, I zip up the body bag before rolling his corpse into the refrigeration unit.

The moment I can, I peel off my black gloves and toss them straight into the trash. Despite having my skin protected and untouched during my examination, I can't resist making my way over to the sink to scrub my hands until they're raw. While I love my job, there are more than just a few downfalls to it, but I wouldn't change it for anything.

Once the mark of death has been scrubbed from my hands, I drop into my chair before searching for my phone. I could have sworn it was over here somewhere. I move a stack of reports around, shuffle my keyboard aside, and when I feel a strange vibration right under my ass, I finally find it lodged somewhere beneath my scrubs and my crack.

Typical. I'm always leaving my phone in stupid places, and I'm not ashamed to say it's not the first time I've almost cracked the screen under my ass. Probably won't be the last either.

After retrieving my phone, I swipe my thumb across the screen, and a stupid grin rips across my face. Just as I expected, there's a new text from the one and only Laith Mitchell.

Opening the text, I find exactly what I was hoping for. And just like every time I open a text from Laith, I can't help but laugh at the name I saved him under the very first night we met.

Big & Long Schlong #2.

And no, I'm not exaggerating. Laith has always been overly proud of his large appendage. But I won't lie, the whole number-two thing is a bit of a sore point. I've always had a very healthy sex life, and before Laith, there was a string of men I could always count on, including Big and Long Schlong number one. But the day Laith came striding in with his smug attitude and his dick swinging around like an elephant's trunk, the others seemed to fade into the dark abyss of past lovers.

We've been playing the casual game for three years, and when it comes to sex, we're more than compatible. As far as I'm concerned, it works because neither of us has ever wanted more, and while there's certainly a real attraction and a potential for something in the future, it's not what either of us wants right now.

Big & Long Schlong #2: Working tonight?
Harper-Rayn: Aren't I always? I get off at 2.

My phone rings immediately, and an amused scoff rumbles through the back of my throat. "Yes?" I say, answering the call and wedging the phone between my ear and shoulder. Then as I wait for his response, I turn to my computer screen and madly click the mouse to get it out of sleep mode.

"You need me to bring anything? I was going to stop for a burger."

My gaze floats toward the clock on the wall. It's only ten. There are still four hours before my shift ends, and I doubt I'll be able to hold off eating for that long. I have one hell of an appetite, and the moment I get a break, I guarantee I'll be scarfing down whatever the hospital has on offer for its employees.

"Nah, I'll have eaten by then. But if you wanted to grab something, could you pick up a mask? Balaclava? Something along those lines?"

"A mask?" Laith asks, his tone hitching with excitement. "What's going on in that pretty little head of yours? Feeling a little kinky?"

"Ha! No," I laugh. "It's so I can pull it over your head and imagine it's literally anybody else fucking me. Hell, we don't even need the mask. Your to-go bag from McDonald's will do!"

The laugh that comes through the line is deep and seductive, and for a fleeting moment, I wonder what life would look like as his girl, but the thought is gone before it gets a chance to take root. It's not as though Laith and I haven't gotten a little kinky before. It's one of my favorite pastimes, but for the most part, we stick to what gets the job done the quickest.

"Oooh, shit. You've got jokes," he murmurs, the deep, playful tone making something lurch in my chest, making me wish that we could have just taken the dive and made it work. It would have been so easy between us, but the feelings simply aren't there. "Retract the claws, tiger."

I lower my tone to a seductive whisper. "Only if you get on your knees and beg."

Laith groans, and the sound does something wicked to me. "Do you like that? When I spread those pretty thighs and fuck your sweet cunt with my tongue? Is that what you want, tiger? You want me to taste you on my knees?"

Well, shit.

How am I going to get through the next four hours of work now?

"No, Laith. I don't want you to just taste me," I purr. "I want you to fucking worship me."

"Ahh fuck," Laith mutters. "Now I'm hard. You just had to go and take it to a whole other level with that fucking hypnotic tone of yours. Don't you know what you do to me? How the fuck am I supposed to wait until the end of your shift to get you on your back and watch you squirm? I'm going to be in a permanent state of hardness. Do you have any idea how fucking uncomfortable this is going to be?"

A shit-eating grin tears across my face as my chest fills with pride. "You could always take care of it in the shower."

"Fuck no. I'm not about to spoil my appetite, Harper-Rayn. Best believe I'm coming for you tonight. You better be ready for me. I'm hungry for your sweet little pussy, and you know just as well as I do that nothing else could possibly come close to satisfying me."

Heat rises in my cheeks, and my gaze flicks back to the clock, realizing that barely three minutes have passed. It's going to be one hell of a long shift. "I'll be ready," I promise. "I should be home by two thirty at the latest."

"I'll be waiting."

A stupid smile settles on my lips as the line goes dead, and as I lower the phone from my ear, I lean back in my chair, needing a moment for the heat to leave my body. Laith has a way of getting me worked up, and he generally doesn't care who or what needs to bear witness to me in those moments. He doesn't care if my legs are on either side of my gynecologist's ears with her speculum spreading me apart, or if I'm in the middle of Great-Aunt Pearl's ninetieth birthday luncheon. If he needs to get that elephant trunk wet, he'll be sure to let me know in the loudest way possible.

After taking a minute to cool down, I get started on the report from tonight's autopsy while doing what I can to slowly work my way through my large bottle of ice water. I always do what I can to keep on top of my health. I eat a balanced diet and work out as much as I can, but managing to keep myself hydrated has always been a struggle. Why is it so hard to remember to lift a bottle of water to my mouth every now and then?

First-world problems, right?

I get immersed in my work when a strange tingle sails across my body, making me uneasy. This isn't like the kind of feels that Laith had given me earlier—the hypnotic flutter in the pit of my stomach or the heavy, insistent pulse deep in my core.

No, this is different. So very different.

This is eerie.

My skin crawls, and I try to shake it off, but the feeling grows stronger. I swivel in my desk chair, my gaze sweeping around the room, and as my heart begins to race, I get to my feet. The door is locked, and apart from the overwhelming number of corpses in the refrigeration unit, there's not a body in sight.

I'm alone. I think.

Swallowing over the growing lump in my throat, I wander around the morgue. It's big and has many places to hide. Only to get in here, somebody would need an access card and would have to walk straight through the main door, which is directly to the left of my desk.

There's no way I would have missed someone coming in. I'm well and truly alone. I have to be, and yet goose bumps are still rising across my skin. I've been here since six, and the door hasn't opened once. But that doesn't mean that somebody couldn't have snuck in during the day. It would have been busy then. People coming and going as they please. I've suffered through more than enough day shifts to know that the door opens so frequently that there becomes a point when you stop glancing up. You stop caring who's striding through the room because you're there to do a job, and for the most part, so is everybody else.

Who would have known if somebody walked in and never walked out?

Well, fuck. That's not comforting at all.

My gaze continues surveying the morgue, and I slowly make my way around. Every step has the hairs rising higher on the back of my neck, and despite not having a single scrap of evidence, I know it deep in my gut—somebody is watching me, and I don't fucking like it.

CHAPTER 2

HARPER-RAYN

The giant bottle of water I'd consumed while working on my report suddenly makes itself known, and the overwhelming need to pee hits me like a freight train as I stand terrified in the middle of the morgue.

My heart booms like a bass drum, and I take the desperate urge to pee as a blessing in disguise, using it as my excuse to escape the one place that usually brings me peace. My feet pound against the linoleum, and within seconds, I'm flying through the door and making sure I hear the click of the automated lock behind me.

It's all in my head. It has to be.

There isn't a psychopath in the morgue waiting to turn me into chopped liver. Perhaps all the late nights and corpses are finally getting to me. I can only imagine what my mother would say, assuming I ever told her about it.

After hightailing it to the bathroom, I take my time, waiting for the eeriness to fade from my bones, but at this point, it would take a miracle for that to happen.

I'm well aware that what I do for work isn't considered a normal profession. Most people would say it's fucked up—most people being my mother, of course—and not to mention, the type of things I see aren't for the faint of heart. I usually counterbalance the horror with music, playing it throughout the morgue as I work and sing along to keep my mind off the heaviness of what's on my table, but tonight while I tried to piece together the mystery of the poisoned turkey sub, not a beat of music was played. I got carried away with my report, and perhaps that allowed the weirdness to creep in. That's all that happened tonight . . . right?

I'm not exactly thrilled with the lackluster excuses I'm telling myself, but they're better than the alarm bells ringing at the back of my mind, warning me that something isn't right. That somebody was in there, watching me like a stalker. But that's crazy.

This stuff only happens in movies, and I'm no Detective Olivia Benson. I wouldn't have the slightest idea how to get myself out of that kind of situation. I'd fumble at the first sign of trouble. I'm the girl in the movie who trips over her feet and all but offers herself up as a screaming sacrifice to the ax-wielding murderer.

Ahhh, crap.

I'm definitely overthinking this.

After wasting too much time in the bathroom, I wash my hands and splash water over my face, not caring that I was a cheapskate and dropped the ball when it came to purchasing a good waterproof mascara.

Black lines streak down my cheeks, and I grab some paper towels to clean myself up. But what does it matter? It's not like I see anyone down in my little refrigerated dungeon, and if there is someone lurking in the morgue, I'm never going to see the light of day again anyway. So who cares if I look like a drowned rat? Though I suppose someone I know will stumble upon my body come morning, and after all the tears, they'll get straight back to work and diligently scrub every speck of makeup from my body. I guess that means they're also going to see me naked, and if I'd known that earlier, I would have worn nicer underwear.

Just my fucking luck.

Feeling only a fraction better about my impending doom, I wander back down to the morgue with shaking hands. I clutch my access card between my fingers just to give me something to hold on to. Then as I hover in front of the big double doors of the morgue, I begin to fret, terrified of what I'm about to walk into.

This is ridiculous. I'm twenty-eight, for fuck's sake. I haven't been scared of the dark since I was a little girl. I don't get jumpy when watching scary movies, and I sure as fuck don't let silly shit get the best of me.

I'm going to walk back in there. I'll find my portable speaker and pump some music, so I can put this shit behind me. There are now only two or so hours left of my shift. I'll be fine. Then tonight, I can go home, meet up with Laith, and forget all about the weird tingles that sailed down my spine while he rails me with that big and long schlong—number two.

Finding new confidence, I hold my head high and swipe my access card before pushing my way through the heavy doors. I'm not a scared little bitch. I'm a badass forensic pathologist . . . almost. Shit like this shouldn't get to me. I'm a woman of science, and I don't let a strange little shiver down my spine send me running for the hills; I'm better than that. Besides, if my mind wants to play games on me, then I can play right back. I don't exactly know how I'm supposed to do that, but there's nothing I love more than petty games.

The door closes behind me with a loud *thud*, and the sound of the automatic lock clicking into place goes a long way to reassure me that I'm not going crazy. I just had a moment of weakness, but now that it has passed, I can get back to work being the boss bitch I've always intended to be.

Striding through the chilled morgue, I approach my desk while trying to remember where the hell I left my speaker, when something from the corner of my eye catches my attention. My brows furrow, and I turn while slowing my pace to an abrupt standstill.

My heart lurches into a fierce race as I stare across the massive room at the single black rose that lies in the center of my autopsy table.

What in the ever-loving fuck? This isn't possible.

The door was locked. Nobody was in here. I checked it before I peed. There's no way that rose could have found its way onto that table.

Unless . . . I was wrong.

This isn't just some bullshit my head has conjured because of a lack of music while writing up reports. I'm not going insane. The chills down my spine were real. The gut feeling was real. The fear was all fucking real.

There was somebody watching me, somebody inside the morgue with me.

The black rose stares back at me like a wretched taunt, and as a million thoughts and fears spiral through my mind like a wild tornado, I realize that gifting me a black rose is going to be the last thing that some fucked-up stalker is going to want with me.

I've seen this game play out a million times before. I've seen the women who wind up on my table. I've seen the sick way they're preyed upon. That can't be me. I won't allow it. Then, without a moment of hesitation, I nope the fuck out of there, running faster than my feet can possibly take me.

What if this person never left? What if they're still here, watching and waiting to put my cold, dead body on this very autopsy table?

Hell fucking no. That won't be me.

My feet pound one after another, only just reaching my bag in the nick of time. My timing is impeccable as I scoop it up, not bothering to check if everything is packed inside. If I leave something behind, then I wish it all the best in its future endeavors, but it'll be a cold day in hell when I stop and go back for something as trivial as my water bottle or the pack of gum that usually resides at the bottom of my bag.

With my belongings intact, I bolt for the door, the panic surging inside me like a torrential storm. My hand automatically reaches for my access card on my hip, frantically trying to swipe it to get the fuck out of here as my terrified gaze risks a glance behind me, desperately searching the wide-open space but coming up empty.

My movements are too shaky, and I have to swipe my access card three more times before the little red light turns green and I hear the familiar sound of the automatic door unlocking. Certain that somebody is about to come after me at any given second, I yank the door open and fly through it, clipping my shoulder on the metal edge in the process.

"Ahh, fuck!"

Pain surges through my shoulder, but I push through it. I'm sure that's going to hurt come morning, but right now, I couldn't care less. All that matters is getting the hell out of here.

My feet are thunderous in the empty hallways, but I push myself faster, desperate to get out of the basement. Then as I reach the elevator, my chest constricts with fear. Do I stand here like a fucking idiot, waiting for this mystery rose gifter to catch up to me as I twiddle my thumbs, waiting for the elevator to *ding* with its arrival, or do I take an even bigger risk and enclose myself in the stairs? I'd only have to sprint up three flights. How long could it possibly take?

Fuck. Stairs it is.

I know it's stupid, but I can't just stand here waiting. I have to keep moving.

My stomach knots with unease, and I take the leap, darting toward the stairwell before wrenching open the access door. It's creepy as fuck, but I forge ahead, not allowing myself a moment to linger on the fear.

The faster I run, the quicker I'll be out.

My feet slam against the old stairs, and the sound of my heavy breaths is almost deafening as I fly past the first flight. I try to listen for any other noises while keeping my gaze locked on my path, terrified of taking a misstep and falling.

The second flight of stairs passes in a blur, but the third feels like a whole fucking lifetime passes before I finally reach the floor I'm searching for. Then as I emerge onto the main floor of the deserted hospital, a sense of ease pounds through my veins.

There are a few people wandering around: night nurses and doctors. It's long after visiting hours, and the emergency department is in a different wing of the hospital. It's always busy over there, no matter what time of the day or night it is. But this little section of the hospital generally offers peace. Only right now, that peace couldn't be further away.

Despite feeling somewhat at ease, I don't slow my pace as I race through the hospital. The few people wandering around glance my way, but not one of them stops to ask me what's going on. Truth be told, I probably wouldn't have entertained their questions in the first place. Seeing random people in scrubs running through the hallways of a hospital isn't entirely an odd occurrence. Most of the time, you shuffle aside and let them pass while minding your own business.

I break out into the unusually cool September night, but the adrenaline keeps me from dwelling on it as I hurry toward the parking garage. When I arrived earlier in the evening, it was almost impossible to find a space, but now, after midnight, my little Honda Civic is one of a few cars in the lot.

As I hurry toward it, I dive into my bag, feeling around for my keys. Only as I get closer, I realize the internal lights are on, and for the second time tonight, I come to a dead stop.

No. No fucking way.

This is not happening.

I back away from the car as my every nightmare becomes a startling realization. There are a million reasons why the lights could be on. I could have simply not locked up properly or forgotten to turn them off when I checked my reflection in the visor mirror. Yet despite that, I'm not willing to take the risk.

I'm not becoming a statistic tonight.

Instead, I bolt around to the other side of the hospital, keeping to the busier pathways, each of them brightly lit with streetlights, until I finally reach the emergency room. People are everywhere—patients feeling sorry for themselves, doctors, nurses, irritated family members who would rather be anywhere but here in the middle of the night.

The rush of people offers me an out, and I collapse into one of the many chairs of the waiting room as the sounds of sick and injured patients fill the air. Coughs and groans would usually send me running for the hills, but tonight, I find it comforting.

After convincing myself to abandon my Civic for the night and have security check it out tomorrow, I book an Uber and wait. Tonight hasn't exactly gone as planned, but now that I'm out of there, I can try to regain some semblance of control.

I'm annoyed that I didn't get a chance to finish my report. I make a habit of being punctual with my work. I don't like getting behind or letting work pile up, especially when those reports could potentially help put a murderer behind bars. Letting down the team isn't my forte, but I'm sure they'll understand.

My Uber arrives only a few minutes later, and I rush into the car the moment I can. The driver steps on the gas, and I sink into the leather seat, knowing I won't completely feel at ease until I get home to my small apartment.

Shit. *Home.* Laith is supposed to be coming over.

I cringe and bring up his information on my phone, not even able to smile at his contact name. I hit call and lift the phone to my ear before hearing Laith's deep tone sailing through the little speaker. "Shit, tiger. Couldn't wait till the end of your shift? Are you that desperate for me?"

Damn. Why does he have to make this so hard?

"Hey," I say slowly, knowing he can immediately sense that something is off. "I'm sorry. It's been a weird night at work. Rain check?"

"What are you talking about? What happened?"

My lips press into a hard line, twitching and stretching as I try to figure out what the hell to say. But as I sit in the back of the Uber with the driver more than capable of listening to my conversation, I feel like now isn't exactly the best time to get into the details. "It's just—"

"One of your cases?"

"Umm . . . yeah," I say slowly, hating that I'm lying to him. "Look, I'm really sorry, but I'm not feeling it right now. I just need to go home, crash, and try to forget."

"Fuck that, tiger. You can't get rid of me that easily. Besides, what else am I supposed to do with this mask?"

"Laith—"

"Try and fucking stop me, Harper. I'm getting in the car now."

"Lai—"

The line goes dead, and I let out a sigh. Fucking men. Why do they always have to be so goddamn stubborn?

CHAPTER 3

HARPER-RAYN

Instant coffee sloshes in my *save a hero, fuck villains instead* mug as I trudge through my small apartment and collapse into a miserable heap on my couch.

Today sucks, and it's all my fault.

Actually, fuck that. It's not my fault, it's Laith's fault.

Laith and his stupid monster, elephant trunk of a cock.

After insisting that he was still going to come and rock my world despite my request for a rain check, the bastard never showed up. And though it was my intention to spend my night trying to forget about the weird black rose left on my autopsy table and how my skin crawled with unease, I had started to like the idea of him coming over.

Okay sure, his refusal to let me have my way made me want to throat-punch him, but the more I thought about it, the more I realized that being alone probably wasn't in my best interest. If I were going to forget about what happened in the morgue, then Laith was the quickest and easiest solution.

But noooooo. Apparently he didn't feel that showing up on my doorstep was necessary, and what's worse, he didn't even have the decency to text. I waited up for him for over an hour, and at that point, I realized how pathetic I was. An hour is way too long to spend waiting for a man. Though when it comes to Laith Mitchell, a dick appointment is a guaranteed good time.

He better have a mighty fine reason for bailing on me. From when I spoke to him in the Uber, it should have only been ten, maybe fifteen minutes before he was pounding on my door. Instead, I was left to fend for myself, wondering if the sound of the breeze on my bedroom window was something more, or if the dark shadows in the corner of my room were more than just a pile of laundry.

Had Laith been there, he would have eased my mind and the fears that took root within me, even if all he did was come over and crash in my bed. He has a calming nature, and last night, I could have used that more than I'll ever admit.

I've never been the girl who's afraid of the dark. To volunteer for the night shift at a morgue, you've got to have thick skin, but that doesn't mean that shit doesn't get to me every now and then. There have been cases that have rattled me to the bone. I've seen bodies appear on my table mutilated beyond comprehension. I know what kind of evil exists in the world. I know just how dark it truly gets, and though there was nothing more than just a feeling and a simple black rose, I was rattled.

Sure, seeing Laith wouldn't have diminished what I felt, but it would have gone a long way in making it just a little easier to shake.

Shit. I hope he's okay.

It's not like Laith to bail without a word.

I texted him a few times last night and again this morning, but so far, I've gotten crickets.

To be fair, there's a high possibility he simply fell asleep and is enjoying a sleep-in. It's way too early to send out a search party. He works long hours as a criminal lawyer, so I don't blame him. When he's working a case, shit can sometimes get heavy. Nobody gets that more than me. But one thing's for sure, if I'm wrong and he shows up on my table after being in a car wreck because he was coming to console me, it will shred me to pieces.

Damn it.

This whole situation is beyond fucked up. Not to mention, I'm hyperfixated on Laith bailing instead of focusing on the real matter at hand—the person who was in the morgue. My gut is screaming *stalker*, but the second I admit that, it becomes real. I'd prefer to be living in delusion and pretend it was all in my head. Forget about it and convince myself that it was a onetime thing, that it's not something I'll ever have to worry about again. But that could be a dangerous game.

My skin crawls with the thought, and as I start to feel uneasy about returning to work tomorrow night, a knock sounds at my door. My head swivels toward the sound, and my brows pinch as I try to figure out who the hell it could be. There are a few options. Laith coming over to grovel for forgiveness, or my best friend, Izzy, though I have no idea why she'd be here. She usually texts before she shows up, just to make sure I'm home first. And option number three: the black-rose gifter.

Unease trickles through my body, and I hesitate for just a moment, not wanting to answer the door. I don't really feel like being sliced and diced today. I have my mother's wedding anniversary dinner tonight with her new husband, and I can guarantee that there will be more than enough slicing and dicing going on there.

On the other hand, if I were to be brutally murdered, then I'd have a pretty good excuse to skip out on dinner. However, I'm sure my mother would still find something to complain about. Even in death, I'll never be good enough.

Another knock sounds through my apartment, and my best friend's voice comes booming after it. "Don't you dare leave me out in this hallway, you cum-guzzling thunder slut. I know your bitch ass is in there."

I let out a relieved breath, feeling the shakiness fade from my body as I get to my feet and put my villain mug down on my coffee table. I wasn't expecting just how uneasy that unexpected knock made me.

"There has been zero cum guzzling," I call out, shuffling toward the door before glancing through my peephole to confirm it's really her. Though had Laith actually shown his stupidly gorgeous face, I can assure you, the cum guzzling would certainly not be at an all-time low. I'd have a whole daycare in the pit of my stomach.

I find Izzy standing on the other side, her arms loaded up with bags of clothes while a to-go coffee cup balances on top, and judging by the way she's intently watching that cup, there's a good chance it's about to decorate my hallway.

Hurrying to unlock my door, I grab the handle and yank it open before diving for the coffee just in the nick of time. "Woah," I say, both of our eyes going wide.

"Holy fuck," she mutters, pushing past me into my home and dumping the bags of clothes on the ground at our feet. She looks down at the red marks the bags left on her hands and arms. "Who would have known bags of clothes would be so heavy?"

A scoff pulls from the back of my chest. "I think the bigger question is, why the hell are there three massive bags of clothes on my floor in the first place?" I ask with amusement as Izzy takes the to-go cup out of my hand.

I start glancing over the bags, wanting to peek inside, when Izzy starts her explanation. "You've got that anniversary dinner for your mom tonight, right?" she asks. "I came to make sure you didn't go looking like a drowned rat like you did last year."

I place a hand to my chest. "Oh, how very thoughtful of you. But unfortunately, your expertise on the matter is not required. I'm quite fond of looking like a swamp turd when I visit my mother. Her disapproval is such a reward. How will I possibly loathe myself without it?"

Izzy laughs and shoves the door with her ass, letting it swing closed. The second I hear the soft *thud*, I reach back, flick the lock, and slide the bolt into place. "I don't care how much you enjoy getting on your mother's nerves, you're going to look like a fucking goddess tonight, and there's not a damn thing you can do about it."

"Iz—"

"Don't even try to argue with me," she says, kicking the bags deeper into my apartment. "Besides, she expects you to turn up in your black ripped jeans and grungy cropped shirt. Imagine the shock on her face when you prove her wrong. Ohhh, and just think about her embarrassment when she has to face all her little country club friends after she's spent the past year telling them what a disappointment you are."

Damn. She used the magic words.

"Fine," I say with a heavy sigh. "But you're not about to get me into some pink frilly piece of shit. Give me something sleek and sexy, and if it isn't black, don't waste my time."

Izzy smirks and drops down to the bags, quickly unzipping the top and letting piles of black outfits spill out onto the floor. "Girl, this ain't my first rodeo," she says before fixing me with an exasperated stare, suggesting that I know better than to doubt her madness. And honestly, I should.

Izzy is a fashion designer and a damn good one at that. We met back in the early days of college and have been inseparable ever since. She specializes in women's fashion, leaning more into evening wear and business casual. However, every year, she dazzles the world with the most gorgeous line of prom gowns I've ever seen. She's a master at her craft, so if anybody is going to dress me for my mother's ridiculous anniversary dinner, it'll be Iz.

She pulls out one outfit at a time and lays them across my couch, mixing and matching heels to skirts and then trying the arrangements with different styles of tops. There's no doubting her skills. Every outfit she puts together is gorgeous, and despite not being my usual, I would wear every single one of them.

Izzy narrows it down to three different looks and stands back, surveying her work. "Hmmmm," she muses, glancing at the outfits before looking back at me. "I can't choose. All three would work for you. What do you think?"

Oh hell no. She should know better than to ask my opinion on this. I'm far too casual to know anything about what occasions require which outfits. If I had it my way, I'd be leaving my apartment in a pair of jeans, my Nirvana tee, and my hair thrown up into a messy bun. Maybe I would have gone the extra mile and left my hair down for a change, but it's not likely.

A sudden wave of nerves settles over me, and I gaze at the three outfits, trying to see if any of them scream out at me. The first is a plain black jumpsuit with a plunging neckline, dressed up with heels and an abundance of dainty gold necklaces. Next up is a sleeveless, fitted crop top with cutouts at the hem and a matching high-waisted, wide-leg pant that gives sexy-CEO vibes, and then finally, a black silk cami paired with a high-waisted leather pencil skirt that snatches the waist.

"Honestly, I'm leaning toward option two or three," I tell her. "Sexy CEO or flirty receptionist."

Izzy glances back at the outfits before she snorts out a laugh. "Oh shit. You're right," she mumbles before glancing back at me. "How were you planning on doing your hair?"

I shrug. "I don't know. Maybe a slicked-back ponytail."

"Yes!" she gasps. "In that case, you have to go with sexy CEO. That long black hair up in a high pony, along with siren eyes, will have everyone eating out of the palm of your hand. Not to mention, your mother won't know what hit her. The second she even tries to claim you're a disappointment, people will laugh her away."

Fuck yes. I've been waiting twenty-eight years to render my mother speechless.

"Alright," Iz continues. "Let's get you ready, and while you wash that bird's nest on top of your head, you can tell me why the hell you're still in your pajamas at four in the afternoon."

Ahhhh. Fuck.

Ten minutes later, I'm lathering shampoo into my hair while Izzy sits across my bathroom, slouched on the closed toilet with her feet propped up on the vanity. It doesn't look comfortable in the slightest, but Izzy has a gift for finding comfort in the weirdest places.

She's on her phone scrolling through social media as I rattle off the details of my night—or lack thereof. I tell her how Laith was supposed to come over but bailed after I left work early. When her face scrunches, I realize my mistake.

"Wait. Wait. Wait," Izzy cuts in, sitting up straighter and dropping her feet off the vanity. "What do you mean you left work early? You haven't left work early . . . ever. Were you sick? Dying? A bad case of the runs?"

Crap.

My face scrunches, and she sure as fuck doesn't miss it. "Spill it, Harper's Bazaar. What aren't you telling me?"

"Shit. Okay. Ummm," I start, unable to keep the cringe off my face as I try to figure out just how many details I'm going to tell her about my brand-new black-rose gifter. "You're going to think I'm insane."

She scoffs. "I already think you're insane."

"I know, but now you'll *really* think I'm insane."

Izzy's brows furrow, and she leans forward, bracing her elbows on her knees as she focuses intently on my face. "What the hell is going on?"

I cringe again. "Okay, so it was just me at work last night. I'd finished my autopsy and was writing up the report when I got this gut feeling that I was being watched. Like, it was full-on. I'm talking my blood ran cold, and I had goose bumps all over my skin. I was freaked out, and as you know, it takes a lot to rattle me. I looked around and couldn't see anything, but I couldn't shake the feeling."

Izzy gapes at me. "You realize you work in a morgue, right? You're constantly surrounded by dead bodies, messing with their corpses and cracking open their chests. It was only a matter of time before you pissed off the spirit world."

"Ghosts? Really? You're trying to tell me I was being haunted by a ghost?"

"No. Not a ghost. A spirit."

A smirk pulls across my lips. "Look who's insane now," I tell her as I make the conscious decision not to tell her about the rose I found on the autopsy table. She'll think it's all in my head anyway. I don't need her worrying about my sanity, at least for now. If something else happens, something significant, then sure, I'll let her know then.

Izzy rolls her eyes. "Alright then, Dr. Genius. If it wasn't a ghost or a spirit, which is clearly the obvious answer, then who or what the hell was it?"

"I—" I pull myself up short because honestly, I have no fucking idea. "That's a very good question."

"I'm telling ya," she says, getting comfortable on the toilet again. "You pissed off the spirit world."

I turn around in the shower and tip my head back under the water to rinse the shampoo out of my hair while secretly hoping she's right. Kind of. Being haunted by an angry ghost is better than the alternative of being brutally murdered by some psychotic stalker, right? But something tells me that a ghost isn't capable of leaving a black rose in the middle of my autopsy table.

Fucking hell. Am I seriously entertaining the idea of it being a ghost . . . or spirit? I'm a woman of science, for fuck's sake. There's no such thing as the spirit world. What happened last night, that was real. I felt it in the way the hairs stood up on the back of my neck and the way my gut sank with unease. That shit doesn't happen for nothing. While I may not believe in ghosts, I certainly believe in a woman's intuition, and last night, it was screaming at me.

After finishing in the shower, I grab my towel and dry off. Then as soon as I step out onto my fuzzy bath mat, the bathroom turns into a whole production line. Makeup and hair products spill off the counter while Izzy dives through my underwear drawer, figuring out which pieces would work best with my new sexy CEO outfit for the night.

"So, what are the chances your mom's been screwing around on Daddy Slater?" Iz calls from my bedroom, still digging through my underwear drawer.

My face immediately scrunches with distaste. From the moment my mother started dating her current husband—Elias Slater, aka my stepfather—Izzy has been obsessed, and she hasn't been shy in letting me know.

Izzy is all for the sugar-baby lifestyle—not that she needs it—and Elias offers just that. He's tall and mysterious with the whole salt-and-pepper thing going for him. There's no denying that he's attractive, and while he certainly gives very serious *don't fuck with me* vibes, he's always been nice to me. But when I look at him, all I see are the bags of money my mother is sucking dick for. She's fooling herself if she thinks she's going to get her grubby hands on it. Elias would have that money locked up tighter than the facelift she got last year.

His brother, on the other hand . . .

"You're grossing me out," I call back.

Iz strides back to the bathroom, propping her shoulder against the doorframe while holding my black lace thong. "God, I would be such a cum dumpster for that man."

Ughhhhhh. "Excuse me while I throw up."

Izzy laughs and pushes off the doorframe, striding into the bathroom and shoving my underwear at me. "What's the problem? You don't approve of your bestie being a semen demon for your daddy dearest?"

"I—what?" I mutter gaping at Izzy. "Semen demon? What the actual fuck is wrong with you?"

"Just keeping it real, baby," she says, fishing for my hairbrush in my bathroom drawer. "But in the spirit of keeping it real, what do you think he's like in the sack? I bet he's a beast. Don't you think? With a body like that and those eyes. Good lord. The things I'd let that man do to me."

"You have real issues. You realize that, right?"

Iz laughs. "What are the chances of you bringing a plus-one to this thing tonight?"

"Don't even think about it," I warn her. "Mom is still salty about the time you offered to give him a handy under the table at the Christmas party. Trust me, you showing up tonight isn't going to do me any favors."

"It's not you I'm looking to do favors for," she tells me, a wide smirk cutting across her lips.

"I don't know if I've told you this lately, but you're gross. I need to bathe in a sea of bleach after hanging out with you."

"Says the bitch who spends her nights talking to dead people and playing with intestines," she laughs.

I go to argue back, but the words get caught in my throat. She's got one hell of a point, and there's not a damn thing I can say to defend myself right now. I do speak to dead people, and I have been known to spend hours at a time playing with intestines. However, my idea of *playing* most certainly differs from Izzy's.

All I can do is grin back at her, and not a moment later, we dive back into getting ready. Izzy works on brushing my hair while I prep my skin for makeup. Then soon enough, I'm standing back in front of my full-length mirror, gazing at the woman staring back at me.

I'm not the type to fawn over myself, but fuck. I look hot.

I like what I see, and more than that, I look successful. I look like a woman who's been looked over and disregarded too many times, and now she's ready to grab the world by the balls and make it her bitch.

CHAPTER 4

HARPER-RAYN

Okay, so leaving my car at work when I have to trek out to my mother's fancy gated community probably wasn't my brightest idea. But in my defense, running away from it like a madwoman was a necessity at the time. Right now, though, I'm definitely starting to regret it.

Mom lives with Elias in their big, shiny mansion thirty minutes from the city. They've spent the last eighteen months renovating, and the amount of money Elias dumped into this place to make Mom happy is absurd. I suppose when you have that kind of disposable income, a home renovation is a blip on the radar, and how can you put a price tag on keeping your new wife happy?

My Uber pulls up at the main entrance of the gated community, and I lean out the back window to enter my code. The little light flashes green and the gates slowly begin to peel open as I laugh to myself. I'd almost expected the code not to work.

The Uber driver hits the gas, and we sail through the main entrance of the gated community, and I find myself staring out the window. This area never ceases to amaze me. Don't get me wrong, just because I'm not frothing at the mouth at my mother's conquests doesn't mean I'm unfazed by it all.

All of these properties are incredible, and I rarely get to see them at night. During the day, they're just massive homes, hidden behind manicured hedges and elaborate gates, but at night, they're lit up like the Fourth of July. Lighting is built into the landscaping and architecture, and it's absolutely flawless. It takes my breath away, and while I'll never be the girl who strives to own something like this, I will always appreciate its beauty.

My driver pulls up at my mother's home, and as he parks against the curb, dread settles heavily in the pit of my stomach. I would prefer to cover myself in peanut butter and wander into the woods with the bears than to set foot inside this property, but the consequences of not showing my face far outweigh the consequences of being mauled by a hungry bear.

On second thought, maybe not. Either way, I'll still be mauled by a rabid animal.

After thanking my driver, I step out onto the sidewalk and grimace as I stare up at my mother's elaborate property. There's no denying it's incredible. It's just like all the others within this community. The only difference between this home and the others is that behind the beautiful double doors is a monster wearing Manolo Blahnik heels and a venomous smile. She's poised and ready to strike the moment I enter. In fact, I can't remember a time when she hasn't belittled me, looked down on me, or spoken to me as if my accomplishments were trivial.

Here's hoping that my outfit tonight might temporarily disarm her.

Ha! What a joke.

Approaching the gate at the bottom of their long driveway, I'm momentarily surprised to see they have security marking off names. I hadn't expected them to go to such extremes for something as trivial as a dinner party for their wedding anniversary. It's not as though they've invited royalty, just their snobby elitist friends, colleagues, and then of course, family as an afterthought.

A man in a black suit steps forward, holding a tablet. "Name," he murmurs, looking bored.

"Harper-Rayn Madden."

He nods in acknowledgment before dropping his gaze to the tablet, and I watch in astonishment as his finger scrolls through a long list. Any moment, he'll find my name and give me the go-ahead, but as the seconds tick by, I start to wonder if my mother even remembered to add my name to the guest list.

A few more seconds pass, and I'm starting to get offended at this point. I mean, shit. How far down the list did she put me?

"Ahh, here you are," the security guard says a moment later. "Go on through, Miss Madden."

"Gee, thanks," I murmur.

Slapping on a fake smile while mentally preparing my body armor, I put one foot in front of the other and head up the long driveway. I feel as though I've run a marathon by the time I reach the front door, only as I go to knock, I find myself hesitating. I could still make a break for it.

A swan dive into a forward roll across the lawn, which would turn into a commando crawl beneath the prickly hedges. That certainly sounds better than walking through this door. But would it really be worth the hell I'd pay for not showing up?

Not even close.

Nerves capture me in a choke hold before I finally lift my hand and knock against the stained wood, ignoring the fancy ornate knocker that looks freshly installed. I blow out a breath, but before I can even take another, the huge door swings open to reveal my mom's beaming billionaire husband.

Elias Slater.

He stares back at me, offering me a forced smile that quickly turns into a moment of awkward silence between us. The two of us have never meshed well. I don't have anything against him, I just don't know him. Nor has he gone out of his way to get to know me either, but I prefer it this way. After all, what's the point? In a few years, my mother will find someone impossibly richer and Elias will be an afterthought.

Come to think of it, I wonder how tight that prenup was. I'd love to get my hands on a copy of that, if only for a few seconds.

"Harper," Elias booms, his forced smile morphing into something a little more genuine. "How lovely to see you again."

"Uhh, thanks," I say, feeling just as awkward as his greeting.

The words have barely left my mouth before my mother steps into Elias's side, her face already scrunched with irritation. She doesn't say a word, just stares at me, her gaze starting at my face before dropping to my body and scanning over every inch of me. "Oh," she says, sounding off guard. "You're, uhhh . . . It's nice to see you actually put a little bit of care into your appearance for a change."

"Good to see you too, Mom."

"Would it kill you to at least pretend to be happy to see me?" she murmurs, stepping in closer and keeping her tone low. "Everybody is here. Do not cause a scene."

"Wouldn't dream of it."

Her lips press into a hard line, and she drops her gaze down my body again, the judgment in her eyes stinging like a bee. And with that, she lets out a huff of disapproval, plasters a fake smile across her face, and turns on her heel to return to her many guests.

I'm left hovering in the open doorway with Elias, and he attempts another welcoming smile. "Don't take it to heart," he says almost like a coo. "Your mother loves you. She's just nervous about the party. She's put so much effort into making tonight perfect."

"Right."

"Why don't you come on in? Make yourself at home and mingle. Your brother is here somewhere," he tells me. "I'm sure he'll be happy to see you again. How long has it been? Two? Three years?"

Jonah is here?

It was nice of him to call and let me know he was coming. I could have bought something for the kids, maybe arranged some time to catch up after the bullshit parade Mom insists on putting on.

"Three," I confirm with a cringe.

Jonah and I have a strange relationship. We've never had a falling-out, but we've never gone out of our way to build a healthy relationship either. Jonah was always the kid who could do no wrong. He was the perfect big brother who set the bar so impossibly high that I didn't stand a chance of trying to reach it. Next to him, I was always pathetic.

He was the favorite. He was coddled and swooned over, celebrated and loved. While I was nothing but a disappointment—the stain on Mom's shimmering reputation. I've always resented Jonah because of it, and that resentment forced a huge wedge between us.

I do what I can to avoid him because the reminder of how

inferior I am stings too much. At the same time, Jonah goes out of his way to avoid Mom because the pressure of always having to be perfect is suffocating.

He lives out of state with his wife and twin daughters, raising them in a way that is nothing at all like how we were raised. He's a great father, the kind I always wished we had growing up, and his wife, Emily, is simply beautiful. Inside and out.

His avoidance of Mom is partially why I haven't seen him in three years, but I can't pretend it's all on him. We're just shitty siblings. There's nothing more to it.

I give Elias an awkward smile before stepping through the open doorway. People are everywhere, and despite bringing my A game, I still feel severely underdressed. The women around me look ready for the Met Gala, and all I can do is roll my eyes. They're aware this is just a dinner party, right?

I try to find amusement in it as I walk deeper into the lavish mansion, passing through the grand foyer and into the open living and dining area. As I gaze around, looking past the people and to the actual home, I pull myself up, my brow arching as I take it all in.

I have to give it to Mom, she certainly has the best interior decorators money could buy. This house is incredible on any given day of the week, but the team she hired to dress the table and decorate has blown it out of the water.

The long rectangular table is huge, seating at least sixty, and is set to perfection with gold and silver finishes. Tall candle arrangements have been woven in and out of low floral sets with picturesque vases and fine china. The low-hanging chandeliers above the table reflect against the fancy glassware, and honestly, this table is fit for royalty. It's simply flawless.

"Well, shit," a familiar voice says from beside me, sounding just as bored as I pretend to be. "Almost didn't recognize you without your usual sweatpants."

A stupid smile pulls at the corner of my lips as I glance over to find the one and only Jonah Madden. "Speak for yourself," I tell my brother. "I almost didn't recognize you without your head shoved up Mom's ass."

"Wow. Going in hard, huh? Not even a smile or a hug for your big brother."

Despite knowing he's just trying to be a smartass, it still puts me on edge. "I don't see you offering the same," I say, immediately feeling as though I need to be on defense.

Jonah smiles and shakes his head before throwing his arm around my shoulder and pulling me into his side. "We grew up together. You'd think we'd know how to act like normal fucking people around each other."

"Never gonna happen."

Jonah laughs and releases me before stepping up to the table and yanking out a chair, putting a single flaw in Mom's perfectly set table, which is oddly satisfying. "Come on," he says. "There's a lot to catch up on. Sit down and fill me in on everything that's happened in the world of Harper-Rayn Madden over the past two years."

"Two years?" I laugh, taking my seat. "Where the fuck have you been? I haven't seen you in three years."

"Three?" he says, as he becomes deep in thought. "No, that's not possible. It's only two. I saw you at that disastrous New Year's Eve party at their old place."

I nod, a smirk pulling at my lips. "Yeah," I agree. "Three years ago."

Confusion flashes in his eyes before understanding begins to dawn, and then he simply looks horrified. "Three fucking years, huh? Aren't I a piece of shit?"

I scoff. "Couldn't agree more, but if you're a piece of shit, then I'm right there with you."

Jonah laughs, but the sound is cut off by my mother's shrill tone coming from the other room, sending a chill down my spine. Judging by the cringe on Jonah's face, he's feeling it too. "If I'm going to make it through this dinner, I'm going to need a stiff drink."

"Make it two," I tell him, both of us getting straight back to our feet. "And don't even think about giving me some bullshit chick drink. I want the good stuff."

"Just as well, I found Elias's private stash earlier."

"Now you're talking."

An hour later, Jonah and I are sitting at the grand dining table, surrounded by Mom's closest friends. We cackle like a couple of high school cheerleaders, to my mother's dismay, which only makes it better. I've really needed this time with my brother.

I ask him all about the twins and how they're settling into preschool, and after covering the basics of his wife's new job, he dives into the ins and outs of my life.

Elegantly dressed servers have descended upon the table with trays of dinner plates just as Elias stands at the head of the table. He opens his arms wide, and just when I think he's about to give some long, drawn-out speech about how wonderful it is to be married to my mother, he turns his attention to the entrance of the dining room.

"Better late than never," he booms as a smirk cuts across his face.

All eyes turn toward the newcomer, and my breath catches in my throat when I find Elias's younger brother, Knight Slater.

Fuck me! Am I drooling? If he weren't my step-uncle, I'd climb him like a goddamn tree.

He's fucking gorgeous. At least six foot four with a body that could send any woman to an early grave. It's clear he takes care of himself, and even through his black shirt, I can see the defined ridges of his abs and pecs. But all of that has got nothing on his face. His eyes are dark gray, and there's something about them that draws me in. He holds my attention in a way no other man ever has. It's dangerous.

Now, Laith is good in bed. Great actually. He knows how to get the job done, and apart from last night, he's never let me down. But a man like Knight Slater? He doesn't just get a pass mark. He carries himself with an air of dominance that makes me think he would tear a woman to shreds and not stop until she's gasping for air on the floor. He seems like the type of man to throw a woman around, slam her up against the shower wall, and rail her until she comes apart.

The question is, how the hell is he still single?

A shit-eating grin pulls across his lips, lighting up his whole face, and while he's the most attractive man I have ever laid eyes on, I can't give myself even a moment to appreciate his smile. I'm too distracted by the way his tight black shirt fits around his strong body, the fabric straining over his bulging tattooed biceps. Fuck, what I wouldn't give to sink my teeth into those.

I'm drooling in seconds. Perhaps taking shots with Jonah wasn't a good idea after all. There's no doubt about it: I'm going to make an ass of myself tonight. It's one thing to laugh with Jonah about Mom's flood of scathing stares, but to try and keep my cool around a man like Knight? I'm well and truly fucked.

Knight is a SWAT officer, and judging by the black tactical pants, boots, and lack of tie, I'd dare say he just got off work. I can only imagine the scowl on Mom's face at his attire, but I can't seem to tear my eyes off him to check.

"Brother," he says, striding straight up to Elias and clapping him on the back before looking down the table and noticing how the food is just being served. "Looks like I arrived just in the nick of time."

"Doesn't sound like a coincidence at all," Elias teases before nodding toward me. "There's a space down beside Harper. Make yourself comfortable."

My eyes widen in horror before my whole damn head swivels like a bobblehead doll to stare at the space beside me, and what would you know, the only available seat at the table is right here next to me.

Fuck. There's no avoiding him now.

Knight makes his way along the table, stopping to greet my mother, and judging by the hostility in both of their eyes, there's still no love there. Knight continues down the table, pausing by my brother. "How ya been, Jonah? Long time."

"Yeah, good," Jonah responds, twisting in his seat to shake Knight's hand. The rest of the guests have turned their attention back to the servers, and every last person is completely oblivious to the way my palms have started to sweat.

Knight doesn't skip a stride, moving farther along before stopping right behind my chair. His hands fall onto the backrest of my seat, and next thing I know, he's leaning down, his warm lips pressing against my cheek.

"Morticia," he rumbles, using the nickname he gave me the day he realized I spend most of my nights working in a morgue, and honestly, I love it.

"Morticia Addams" fits me perfectly. Well, kind of. I have long jet-black hair and might enjoy playing with dead people. Not to mention the majority of my wardrobe is pitch-black. But it's not as though I own a gothic castle and drive a hearse. I get it, though, and there's no denying it, when that name comes out of Knight's mouth, something always clenches deep inside me.

Personally, I think I'm more of a Wednesday, but once the name was given, it stuck.

Knight's lips linger on my skin just a moment longer than necessary, and I'm sure he has absolutely no fucking idea how my skin blazes under his touch. If he does, he doesn't let it show.

Shivers shoot down my spine, spreading across my skin, and I suck in a breath, trying to act as though his very presence doesn't send me spiraling. Only in doing that, I inhale the scent of his delicious cologne, rendering me momentarily speechless.

Knight folds his large frame into the seat beside me, and it doesn't go unnoticed how his hand remains on the back of my seat. I do what I can not to look, because the second my eyes land on that warm, tattooed, olive skin and take in his sharp stubble-covered jaw, I'll melt right here in my seat.

We don't see each other often. As far as I'm aware, he works a lot. He takes his job very seriously, while also doing everything in his power to avoid these events just as I do. Apart from the fact that he's a SWAT officer, I really don't know that much about him, nor do I want to.

Well, okay. That's a lie, but if I allow myself to get closer to him, I know without a single doubt that I'm going to dig myself a hole that I'll never be able to get out of.

He's my step-uncle, for fuck's sake. Nothing can ever happen here, but that doesn't mean I can't fantasize about it. He might be my step-uncle now, but will he be when I'm all alone in my bed tonight, thinking about the way those strong arms could throw me around? Fuck no.

"Knight," I respond, holding his gaze as he makes himself comfortable.

He grins back at me, his gaze eating me up as I take a sip of water, trying to control the heat rising in my cheeks. "Well, don't you look like a snack."

I blanch, water sputtering from my mouth and across the table setting in front of me. I do what I can to feign a cough, but it's too late, I already have my mother's undivided attention, and the scowl across her face is one of her best.

"Excuse me," I say, picking up my napkin and dabbing at my lips while Knight chuckles under his breath beside me. "Wrong hole."

Mom narrows her stare, and I swear, the woman looks as though she's about to murder me. I look away, not allowing her to continue her silent scathing. Instead, I turn my attention back to the beast beside me.

"I wasn't expecting you to show your face tonight," I comment. "You're usually the first one to pull out some ridiculous excuse about why you can't come. What happened? No damsels currently in distress?"

Knight laughs and I can practically see the jokes about pulling out and not coming on the tip of his tongue. "I tried, but Elias was there when I received the notification of my shift change. Couldn't get out of it even if I tried."

"I know the feeling all too well."

"Tell me about it," he says, just as a server sets a plate of food in front of him, and honestly, I don't have a clue what it is. I want to call it chicken, but my God, it doesn't smell like chicken. "This right here is why I avoid these things. No offense, but your mother wouldn't know what a good meal is if it smacked her in the face."

"Oh, I know," I laugh. "She tried to serve us bull's balls last Christmas. I had to stop for a burger on the way home."

Knight takes his fork and starts moving food around his plate while I reach to take another sip of water, only I'm distracted by the soft buzz of my phone in my lap. I scoop it up and find a new text from Laith.

My lips press into a hard line as I swipe my finger across the screen, opening his message. I'm still pissed about last night, but sitting next to Knight right now with his arm resting on the back of my seat, I can't seem to care about being stood up.

Big & Long Schlong #2: Sorry, tiger. Something came up. I'll make it up to you.

I roll my eyes, and for a moment, I consider not responding at all, but truth be told, if roles were reversed, he wouldn't get moody with me. He'd simply demand that next time, I make it up to him tenfold.

Harper-Rayn: You better! I had to resort to using my friends in my bedside drawer, and you know how they never quite keep me satisfied for long.

Big & Long Schlong #2: Promise. I'll swing by tonight and throw you around like a rag doll until we're both spent.

Harper-Rayn: Wish I could. Busy tonight. I'll let you know when I'm free.

Big & Long Schlong #2: xx

A soft touch on my shoulder has me glancing up, and I find Knight's dark gaze locked on my skin. "Something happen?" he asks with deep concern in his tone. "This looks sore."

My gaze drops to my shoulder, and I find the bruise I'd gotten after bolting out of the morgue last night. "Oh yeah," I say. "It's fine. I had a slight run-in with a door at work. I can confirm, the door won."

"Yeah, no shit," he says. "You need to ice that."

"I'll get right on it," I laugh, though he and I both know that's not going to happen. I've not always been the best when it comes to taking direction, especially when it comes to caring for myself.

"So, Harper," comes Elias's voice a moment later, dragging my attention away from his dazzling brother. "How's work going? Still working down in that morgue?"

He says the word *morgue* like it's dirty, and as his voice sails through the room, I notice the other guests quiet down and look at me, patiently waiting for a response as though it's any of their business. "Uhhh . . . yeah," I say, feeling awkward. "I'm still working on my residency in forensic pathology."

My mother's sigh is almost comical, and sure, I'd have probably laughed if it weren't for the other sixty or so guests listening in to her disapproval. "Oh, honey. I'm just not sure this is the right job for you. You're dealing with dead people all day. Putting your hands—ugh. No. I really must insist, it's not too late to take another path. You could still be a surgeon. A . . . A heart doctor perhaps."

"A cardiothoracic surgeon?" I ask.

"Yes, darling. Exactly that. I want better for you. Something you can really excel at. Something where you can be recognized for your work."

I shove my chair back as I abruptly stand, balling my hands into fists, trying to convince myself not to launch across the table and show her just how good I am at my job. "No, Mom. You don't want better for me. You never have. You just want me to have a job that you can boast about to all your fancy little friends. You're embarrassed by my career, and that's on you, not me. But guess what? You're not the only one embarrassed here. The way you carry on with these ridiculous dinner parties and act like you belong in this world is humiliating. You're a broke bitch from Queens."

I resist the urge to shrink as her guests gasp and whisper, and my mother places a hand on her chest as though she's offended. "How could you?" she sobs, pulling out the waterworks and dabbing her eyes. "After everything I've sacrificed for you."

"The only thing you've ever sacrificed is your knees when you spent three years sucking dick for a ring. Well, congratulations. I guess all your hard work paid off." I reach for the table and scoop up my glass of champagne before holding it up toward the happy couple. "Here's to you and your ability to deep-throat. And to you,

Elias, I hope she doesn't blow all your money in one go. I'd keep a sharp eye on that one if I were you."

Lifting the rim of the glass to my lips, I throw back every last drop before slamming the glass right back down. "As always, Mother, it's been a pleasure." And with that, I drop a kiss to Jonah's cheek before walking my ass right out of the hellhole otherwise known as my mother's home.

CHAPTER 5

KNIGHT

If there's one thing a dinner party with my brother and his bitch of a wife can guarantee, that's a shitty meal and one hell of a good show. And just as I expected, tonight was no different.

I stare after Harper as she bails, itching to go after her, but it wouldn't be appropriate. I shouldn't be running after my sister-in-law's daughter. She's my step-niece, for fuck's sake. Not to mention, she's only in her late twenties. Twenty-seven? Twenty-eight? I don't fucking know, but what I do know is that she's way too young for me. No matter how desperately I want to bend her over my kitchen counter and fuck her raw.

Elias would murder me. I can't go there.

I've had more than my fair share of inappropriate relationships to last me a lifetime, nor do I care what Elias thinks, but to taste Harper-Rayn? That hits a little too close to home. With her, there'd be no going back. I'd destroy her.

I've always found her intriguing. When her mom started dating Elias, Harper was barely twenty years old, and eight years later, that desire to have her has only intensified. So I do what I can to stay away.

She's the forbidden fruit, dangling before me, daring me to take a bite, and I'm the fucking viper in the garden, ready to burn it all to hell.

Call me a fucking egotistical, cocky bastard, but I know she's just as intrigued as I am. I see it in her eyes every time she looks at me, the way her bright green stare eats me up. I see it in the way her cheeks blaze when I call her Morticia, and the way her skin prickles with goose bumps at my touch.

Fuck, that sweet little vixen wants me.

I wonder if she thinks about me? If she thinks about the way I'd feel inside her. How full she'd be. How I'd taste hitting the back of her throat. Because fuck, I think about it all the goddamn time. I've imagined it night after night. There's no denying it, if she weren't my brother's stepdaughter, I would have already had her.

"Everything is okay," Elias says, getting to his feet and speaking to all of his guests, trying to get back on track. "Nothing to be concerned about. Just a little family squabble."

The guests murmur and nod, and despite appeasing them, my brother can't help himself as he goes on. "Women, right?" he chuckles, being the sexist pig he's always been. "Now, please, get back to your meal and enjoy the company. Fill your glasses and your stomachs."

Elias takes his seat, placing a hand on Mae's back. "It'll be alright, my love. She's weak, so she acts out. She's jealous of the life you have built with me and too stubborn to admit when she's wrong. She'll come around one day. She just needs time."

Mae shakes her head, really putting on the waterworks now. "I just don't understand what I ever did to deserve a daughter like that. She's so ungrateful for everything I've done for her. Can't she see I've only ever wanted what was best for her?"

What a load of steaming bullshit.

There was a time long before Mae when I thought my brother was the smartest man I knew. He built an empire from the ground up, made his first billion within ten years, but then in walked Mae, and that pedestal I had him on quickly chipped away. Now he plays the role of the perfect doormat for a woman who would bleed him dry given the chance. If only Mae actually knew what kind of man she was actually married to.

Though one thing is for sure, Harper must have been on to something. Her mother must suck cock as though she's digging for gold.

The longer I watch Mae put on her pity party, the harder it becomes to sit here, and as the irritation becomes too much, I go to get up, but Jonah beats me to it. He pushes back from the table and gets to his feet. "I uhh . . . I should go check on Harper. Make sure she's not trying to drive her ass home."

I all but fly to my feet. "No, no," I say, desperate to get out of this room. "Stay. Eat. I'll go."

Jonah's face scrunches; he's looking at me as though I've lost my mind, and maybe I have, but anything is better than staying here and listening to Mae's pathetic sob-fest. "Huh? Why?"

Good fucking question.

My gaze flicks toward his mother and not a moment later, understanding flashes in his eyes. "Right. Gotcha," he says. "But fair warning, if Harper's going down, she's going down swinging. She'll have something to say, and if you don't give her your full, undivided attention and let her rant, you better watch your back."

A smirk pulls at my lips. A fiery Harper-Rayn? Yes please. I'm getting hard just thinking about it. "Noted," I say, before nodding to Elias and attempting a smile for Mae to be polite, but honestly, it comes out as more of a grimace.

I don't wait around, spinning on my heel and hightailing it out of this ridiculous mansion. I reach the grand front door in seconds, and the moment I pull it open, I hear someone manically pacing at the end of the long driveway, muttering to herself under her breath.

Pulling the door closed behind me, I make the trek down the driveway, watching Harper-Rayn attempt to wear a hole in the pavement. I go out of my way to walk with heavy steps so she knows I'm here, but she's so lost in thought that she doesn't notice me until I'm barely a foot away.

"Shit," she gasps, momentarily pausing before getting straight back to pacing. She shakes her head, clearly still haunted by her own thoughts, and I simply wait, knowing the onslaught is coming. "She just . . . She makes me so angry."

"So she should. The woman is a narcissistic bitch."

Harper pauses, and I can't help but notice the way her long hair falls over her creamy shoulder. She usually has it up in a messy bun, but like this, I can't stop picturing how easy it'd be to wrap it around my wrist and pull her head back until she arched that sweet back of hers.

"Wait," she says, her brows pinched together. "You agree with me?"

I nod. "Vehemently."

Her brows fly up in surprise, and she nods right back at me, her lips pursed. "Good to know," she says before taking a breath and meeting my stare again. "Did I take it too far? I bet she's in there putting on a show about how horrible her ungrateful daughter is."

"Oh, she's definitely eating up every bit of attention she can get," I tell her, not bothering to sugarcoat it. "The waterworks are a bit overkill, though."

"Shit. She's crying?"

"Oh yeah."

"I'm going to have hell to pay."

I shrug. "Probably, but she deserved it. Dismissing everything you've achieved in front of a room full of people was uncalled for. Personally, I would have gone in harder, but the broke bitch from Queens and the three years on her knees sucking dick for a ring really were crowd-pleasers. You should be proud of yourself."

A grin cuts across her lips, and the way her eyes sparkle lets me know she's going to be just fine. "I am. I've been waiting years for that moment."

"Good. Now, why the hell are you hovering out here? Where's your car, Morticia?"

Her cheeks flush at the stupid name, and I fucking love it. "I'm not driving," she tells me. "I'm waiting for an Uber, which is really screwing with my whole storming-off thing. I could have timed that better."

An Uber? Not on my fucking watch.

I shake my head and indicate for her to follow me. "Come on. I'll drive you."

I start walking toward my truck when her voice flutters behind me. "That's okay. You don't need to do that."

"I'm not telling you again, Morticia," I say, not bothering to halt my step or even look back at her. "Get in my fucking truck."

"I—shit."

The sound of her heels against the pavement cuts through the night, and I do what I can to keep the smirk off my face as she hurries after me. I unlock my truck and climb in, and within seconds, the passenger-side door is flying open. Harper climbs in with a huff before fixing me with a hard stare, and I make a point not to look at her as I start the engine and let the truck roar to life.

"You know, you really don't need to do this. I would have been fine in my Uber."

"You've been drinking, you're upset, and after your little outburst in there, you can't exactly be trusted to make good decisions. So I'm driving your ass home whether you like it or not."

Her stare on the side of my face is laser sharp, and I let out a sigh. "Something you need?" I ask, bracing my hand against the headrest of her seat as I reverse out of my spot.

"I never realized how bossy you are."

I glance toward her, meeting her curious stare, and as those bright green eyes lock onto mine, I can't help but notice the way her thighs press together. "You haven't seen anything yet, Morticia. Keep huffing and puffing like that, and you'll find out just how bossy I can be."

She zips her lips, and I watch her swallow hard before finally turning my attention back to the road. I hit the gas and waste no time sailing out of this fucked-up gated community and back onto the highway.

"So," she starts. "Still responsible for the oversupply of bodies that wind up in my morgue?"

A grin cuts across my face, and I scoff. She knows damn well that my SWAT team doesn't put bodies in the morgue. We're the best team in the state. The best this country has to offer. We get in, get the job done, and get the fuck out of there without casualties. But that doesn't mean I won't play along.

"Of course," I tell her. "I wouldn't want to put you out of business."

Harper laughs and fiddles with my music when I glance over at her. "Tell me what really happened with that bruise on your shoulder," I tell her. "And this time, cut the shit."

She cringes, and her hand falls away from my dashboard. "I technically wasn't lying," she tells me, shoving her hands under her thighs as though that could somehow keep me from getting to the bottom of this. "I was coming out of the morgue, misjudged my stride, and slammed my shoulder straight into the metal edge of the door. Hurt like a bitch."

I narrow my stare on her. "You're still lying to me, Harper-Rayn. We've got a long drive ahead of us, so I suggest you start talking. Otherwise, I can guarantee that this is not going to be a comfortable ride for you."

Harper glances away, and the guilt flashing in her eyes is more than enough to tell me that I'm heading down the right track. The only question is, why does she feel the need to lie about this? What's she keeping from me?

"It's . . . It's really nothing," she finally says, the shift in her tone like a silent plea for me to drop it. "And you're going to think I'm insane."

I shake my head. "I'll be the judge of that."

She lets out a shaky breath, and I give her a moment to string her thoughts together. The seconds turn into minutes, and just when I'm about to demand answers, she shifts in her seat and glances toward me. "Do you still work as an active SWAT officer? Like being called out to scenes every day?"

I nod and glance down at the black tactical pants and boots I'm still wearing from my shift. "What gave it away?"

She rolls her eyes and huffs again. "Are you going to be an ass the whole way home? Or are you going to chill the fuck out at some point?"

"Well, damn, Morticia. Tell me how you really feel."

"Just answer the question."

"Yes," I respond with a sigh. "I'm still an active SWAT officer. Team leader to be exact. I'm in the field every day. But I don't understand how that has anything to do with your shoulder ending up black and blue."

Harper ignores me and continues with her line of questioning. "How common would you say stalkers are? And I don't just mean someone sending threatening letters with newspaper cutouts like in the movies. I mean, how often are women getting slaughtered by crazed, sick men?"

Slaughtered?

My head whips toward her, and I bring my truck to a screeching stop in the middle of the empty highway. "The fuck are you talking about? Is someone stalking you?"

Her eyes go wide, and she looks around in a panic. "What the hell, Knight? You can't just stop in the middle of the road. Someone will run into us."

"I'll stop wherever the fuck I want. Now answer the goddamn question. What the fuck is going on? Is someone stalking you?"

"No—I . . . I don't know," she finally says, her tone filled with an odd mix of fear and exasperation. "It's just something kinda weird happened at work last night. It's the first time anything like it has happened, and to be completely honest, I don't know if it was real or if I just made it all up in my head, but it freaked me out."

"Start talking, Harper. I'm not fucking around this time. Give it to me straight."

"Can you at least pull over to the side of the road? I don't feel like becoming roadkill tonight."

I groan and hit the gas, moving over just enough to satisfy her before fixing her with a demanding stare and completely cutting the engine to make a point. "The fuck is going on?"

"Okay, so last night—"

"In the morgue?"

"Yes. I was working on a report—"

"Alone?"

"Jesus. Yes. Are you going to interrupt every sentence that comes out of my mouth?"

"Only if you don't hurry up and give me the information I'm looking for."

Harper scowls at me. "You're impossible. You know that right? You'd think as a trained officer, you'd have a little more patience with shit like this."

I grip the steering wheel, white-knuckling it as I try to find my composure. "For the love of all that's holy, Morticia. Tell me what the fuck happened in that morgue."

Her eyes blaze with fire, and I have no doubt that she's itching to argue, but she thankfully gets on with it, sensing that I'm reaching my boiling point. "Okay, so I was writing up a report when I got this strange feeling that I was being watched. I had shivers going down my spine and goose bumps everywhere. It freaked me out, so I looked around but couldn't see anyone, and my desk is right by the door. Nobody could have come in or out without me knowing, but I couldn't shake the feeling."

"Okay," I say, trying to calm myself. "Then what happened?"

"I figured it was all in my head, so I went to the bathroom and splashed water on my face, but when I came back, there was a black rose just lying in the middle of the autopsy table."

My back stiffens, and I stare at her.

"A black rose?" I ask, my mind instantly reeling, going through all the stalking cases I've ever worked on and trying to see if anything rings a bell, but there's not enough to go on. I've never had a case where the suspect has left a rose before, particularly a black one.

"It was messed up, and I didn't want to hang around to find out how it got there, so I ran. Which is how I caught my shoulder on the door, by the way. I wasn't lying about that."

"Fuck. Give me your phone."

Her brows furrow, but she hands it over, and I immediately put my number into her contact list, not even bothering to check if it's already there. "I'll check it out," I tell her. "But if anything like that happens again or if you feel unsafe, even if it's just a feeling, you call me. Understood? I'm turning your location on and sharing it with me, so I'll know where to find you if I have to."

"You don't need to do all of that," she tells me. "It was probably all in my head. Working alone in a morgue was bound to get to me at some point."

"I'm not just offering you a ride home to be a good guy, Harper," I say, handing her phone back. "This could potentially be your life. Don't fuck with that. If there's some guy out there, and your life is at risk, I need to know about it."

She nods, and I push her on it, certain that she's going to shrug my warning off, just as I've seen so many young women do in the past. "Promise me, Harper. Tell me you'll call."

"I'll call," Harper vows.

I hold her stare for a moment longer, and seeing a strange uncertainty within her eyes, I turn and focus on the road ahead, giving her a moment to breathe.

The thought of someone stalking this girl makes me feel sick, but realizing that there's not a damn thing I can do to help her right now, I let out a breath and start the engine before pulling back out onto the deserted highway.

We drive in silence, and the heaviness sinks around me. I itch to reach out to her, to tell her it will be okay, but how the hell can I possibly promise that? I don't know if it's going to be okay. I don't even know if any of this is real. I've never wanted someone to be delusional more than I do right now, and up until she told me about the black rose, I could have almost believed that it was all in her head.

Time passes quickly in our weighted silence, and before I know it, I'm pulling up to the curb outside her apartment complex, not a word exchanged between us since the highway.

"Umm . . . thanks," Harper says, glancing toward me, only to look away as fast as humanly possible, an awkwardness settling between us. "I—wait. How did you know where to go? I never told you where I live."

Ahh fuck.

I was too caught up in my thoughts that I forgot to pretend that I had no idea where she lives. I didn't even attempt to ask her for directions. "Uhh. Elias pointed it out to me a few years back. Guess it just stuck," I lie, knowing damn well I searched her information the second I realized she'd rented an apartment and had no one else looking out for her. I've kept an eye on her for years, checking in from afar just to make sure she was doing all right. Not that I would ever tell her that.

"Oh, okay. Well, umm . . . yeah," she mutters, grabbing her purse and double-checking she has all of her things before swinging the door open.

She starts climbing out when I call after her. "Are you going to be okay? Do you need me to do a sweep of your apartment?"

The fuck was that? A sweep of her apartment? What the hell is wrong with me? Are these the kinds of lows I'd sink to just to get inside her home? What's going to happen then? I'll accidentally trip and fall straight into her tight little cunt?

I'm such a piece of shit.

"No, but thanks," she says, climbing out of my truck. "I'm a big girl. I can handle myself. Besides, I felt fine at home last night. It's just work that messed me up."

"Okay," I say, nodding toward her phone in her hand. "Don't forget. Call me if you need me. And in the meantime, try not to get slaughtered by a crazed lunatic."

"Ha. It's not a crazed lunatic I need to watch my back around," she says as a wide grin stretches across her face. "It's my mom. After humiliating her in front of all of her bitch friends, I'm going to have to sleep with one eye open."

"Well, if I happen to get a call in the middle of the night for a hostage situation, at least I know who it'll be for."

Harper laughs. "Very true, but promise, if it comes down to having to take her out, do me a solid and let me take the shot."

"Well, shit, Harper. That got dark fast."

"I work night shift in a morgue, spending most of my time with my hands inside rotting corpses. Not to mention, I may or may not have a stalker. That wasn't dark. It barely scratched the surface of the gray area," she says, stepping back from my truck and closing the door between us. And with that, she offers me a small smile before walking around the back of my truck and heading straight up the stairs to the main entrance of her apartment complex.

I wait just a moment, making sure she gets in alright. Then after entering her access code, she pushes the door open before pausing and glancing back. Another small smile crosses her face, and after her fingers flutter in a soft wave, Harper disappears inside, leaving me more fucked up than ever before.

CHAPTER 6

HARPER-RAYN

My hands grip the last door of the morgue refrigeration unit, and I tear it open before grabbing the empty stretcher tray and rolling it out. I all but shove my head inside the unit and peer around, checking every last corner before finally determining that there's nobody hidden inside. Well, at least no *live* bodies.

I've checked every possible space, right down to the small areas inside the old filing cabinets. There's not a single doubt in my mind, I'm alone as can be. Well, mostly. I came in an hour before my shift to do all of my checks. My supervisor is still here and a bunch of the admin staff, but they'll be gone soon and when they are, I need to know that I'm well and truly alone.

I've already peed and made sure my water bottle is filled, so there'll be no excuses for me to leave the morgue unattended tonight. Meaning absolutely no chances for some creep to sneak in and leave me unwanted gifts.

I've been watching the door. I know exactly who is inside the morgue and am taking note of the moment they leave. Nothing is getting by me tonight.

"Are you about done taking stock of my morgue, Madden?" my supervisor, Dr. McKullan, asks as he skillfully dissects a pair of lungs, his whole attention locked on what he's doing.

"I am indeed," I respond, striding over to my desk and unpacking my bag to get ready for my shift. "Is there anything you want me to do? I can scrub in if you'd like."

"Your shift doesn't start for another forty minutes."

"That's alright. I don't mind starting early," I tell him, always down for a chance to learn from the master. Dr. McKullan is at the top of his field, one of the highest-regarded forensic pathologists in the country. Residents would kill to learn from him, so any chance I get, I take with both hands.

"Alright then," he says, not bothering to look up. When he's zoned in, he's zoned in. There's no distracting this man. "Why don't you finish this autopsy? I want to look over your techniques, make sure you haven't been getting sloppy during your night shift."

I laugh. "Sloppy? Me? Never!"

Dr. McKullan chuckles to himself. "I'll be the judge of that," he says. "Now go scrub in, and you can take over."

I don't waste a second, hurrying across the morgue to get prepared, and before I know it, I'm back and ready to go. I settle in beside Dr. McKullan, and despite him already being well and truly into the autopsy, he has me start from scratch, meticulously looking over my skills while silently nodding in approval.

"Were you planning on explaining why you felt the need to come in an hour before your shift and search every crevice of my morgue?"

"Oh, umm . . . I was just making sure it was safe," I say as I begin carefully removing the organs, but I realize too late that I forgot to filter the words falling out of my mouth.

"Safe?" he asks. "Have you been feeling unsafe? Has something happened?"

"No, no," I rush out, lifting my gaze from the heart cradled in my hands. "Nothing happened. I just like to make sure everything is as it should be. You know, a girl can never be too cautious, especially when working the night shift."

He narrows his gaze on me, and as his thick, graying brows furrow, I realize he's more than aware that I'm lying to him, but he thankfully doesn't push me on it like Knight did.

"Concentrate, Dr. Madden," he murmurs, indicating downward to the heart in my hands. "Never take your eyes off your work, especially when you have a heart in your hands. The slightest distraction could cause you to miss integral information."

Fuck. I more than know better.

"Sorry," I say, restarting my examination.

"Now, tell me what you see."

Two and a half hours later, Dr. McKullan is just starting to pack up his things. He stayed almost an extra two hours after the end of his shift just to work with me, and I've never been so grateful. "You're doing good work, Harper," he tells me. "You're going to go far in your career. Now, when you're ready, close up and get started on the report. The detectives have been hounding me for this one for two days."

"Will do," I say with a nod.

Dr. McKullan offers me a slight nod, and a moment later, he swipes his access card against the card reader and a soft beep sounds through the morgue. The moment he's gone, I call out to Siri to play Paramore and to crank the volume.

I get lost in my work, closing up the body before jumping straight into the report, and just as always, my work consumes me. I'm just finishing up the report when my phone chimes from my desk, stealing my attention away.

My gaze drops to the screen and a stupid smile pulls at my lips finding a new text from Big & Long Schlong #2, and an earlier one from Izzy.

Izzy: Harper's Bazaar!! You never told me how your night went. Did Daddy Elias finally see the light and leave your mom? You know I'm going to be your new stepmom one day.

She's so fucking gross. But I'll call her later and give her all the sordid details, which will probably turn into a three-hour conversation that will end with me needing to pour bleach into my ear holes.

For now, Big & Long Schlong #2 is requiring the rest of my attention.

Big & Long Schlong #2: I think we need to implement a loyalty card program. Every time you get dicked down, we'll punch a hole.

Harper-Rayn: What's in it for me?

Big & Long Schlong #2: Every tenth visit comes with a free gift.

Harper-Rayn: Now you're talking!

Harper-Rayn: Hold up. What kind of gift can one expect from the dick-me-down loyalty card program? Because if it's some shit like one free spank, then I don't know. If I'm going to the effort to remember to get my hole punched ten times, then the reward better be worth it.

Big & Long Schlong #2: Fair call.

Big & Long Schlong #2: How about every tenth visit, I eat your pussy till you scream?

Harper-Rayn: I get that anyway. Go hard or go home, right? I'm thinking more along the lines of a threesome. I've always wanted to get fucked by two dudes at the same time. I'll ride you while someone else takes my ass.

I put my phone down as I wait for Laith's response. He's always been a little weird about sharing. It's not the first time I've brought up wanting to explore a threesome, but he's never really gotten on board with the idea. I don't mind, though.

When it comes to me and Laith, it's only ever been about convenience. We get in, get the job done, and then we're on our way. Adding a third . . . That's where things could get complicated. Neither of us has the time to filter through our contacts to find someone we think would not only be down but make it worthwhile.

Laith's text doesn't come for a few minutes, but when it does, surprise pulses through my veins.

Big & Long Schlong #2: Fuck . . .

Big & Long Schlong #2: Does it have to be two dudes? Not two chicks?

My brow arches. I expected him to either umm and ahh over it or completely shut the idea down, but the fact that he seems to be considering it has hope surging through me. Is there a chance I might actually get this?

Harper-Rayn: Hey! This is my loyalty card program. Not yours. I'm the one reaping the benefits here. If you want two chicks, then you better let me punch your hole ten times.

Big & Long Schlong #2: Wait. Are we talking about the same thing here? Or are you wanting to peg me? Because you know damn well that my ass is off limits.

A booming laugh tears through me, and I swing back in my desk chair as I prop my feet up on the lip of the bottom drawer of my desk. A million responses filter through my brain, and while I could console his fears and let him know that I respect his boundaries, I can't resist the urge to tease.

Harper-Rayn: Start prepping that ass, Laith! I've got a monster cock hidden in my bedside drawer with your name on it. You're going to love it. I mean, the first nine inches will burn, but after that, it'll be a breeze!

His response comes a minute later with two simple words that have me cracking up even more.

Big & Long Schlong #2: Fuck you.
Harper-Rayn: You know you can't resist me.
Big & Long Schlong #2: I'll think about the threesome . . .
Harper-Rayn: Thank youuuuu.

Giddiness bubbles through me, and when it gets too hard to concentrate on my work, I push my phone away and try to focus. I can think about threesomes tomorrow. Right now, I have a body that deserves a thorough report.

A soft beep sounds through the morgue, and my back instantly stiffens as my gaze snaps toward the door. I knew my last shift left me shaken, but after talking with Knight about it, I felt somewhat more at ease. I had started to convince myself that maybe it was just some sick joke played by bored kids wanting to screw with me. But up until this very moment, I hadn't realized just how much of a choke hold it has on me.

The door begins to open, and my hand curls around the pen on my desk, expecting the worst. I'm not a cold-blooded killer by any means, but if it came down to it, I would know exactly where to stab the pen to cause the most damage. I'd be the one walking away from this, and while that snippet of information goes a long way to comfort me, that doesn't mean that I'm not terrified right now.

The door begins to open, and I suck in a breath, preparing to scream if need be, and as I mentally war with the fear pulsing through my body, I watch as the night janitor, Vincent, strolls in without a single care in the world.

My body sags and I stare at Vincent, needing just a few seconds for my brain to comprehend that I'm not currently in mortal danger.

God. I'm an idiot.

Vincent drags his cleaning cart behind him before settling it in its usual position by the door as my fingers relax and I release my death grip on the pen.

"Oh, Miss Harper," Vincent says, his eyes going wide as he takes me in. "Are you okay? You look like you've seen a ghost."

"I, ummm . . . Yeah," I say, swallowing hard as though that can possibly ease the way my hands tremble beneath the table. "All good. How are you? Busy night?"

"Oh, you can say that," he says, chuffed to be having a conversation. Vincent often tells me that I'm the only person who'll speak to him during his shift. It's heartbreaking, but I'm not surprised. The night crew at the hospital isn't always the most welcoming. I've had more than my fair share of run-ins with people who want nothing to do with me. But despite how I like to work in peace, if someone were to walk into the morgue, you bet I'm going to go out of my way to make them feel comfortable.

"How's Lila?" I ask. "Still struggling with kindergarten?"

Vincent lets out a breath as he scoops up the antiseptic spray from his cart. "Yeah, unfortunately, kindergarten is really kicking our ass," he tells me as he steps up to the autopsy table and starts to clean it, despite me already having done it barely two hours ago. "I think her teacher reminds Lila of her mother. It hasn't been that long since she passed, but they have similar features."

My heart grows heavy. Vincent's wife passed a little over a year ago, leaving him as a struggling single father of three little girls. He's barely been getting by. He works an office job during the day, then has his janitorial shift during the night while his girls are watched by his mother. It breaks my heart. He's doing everything he can to support his children and ensure they have a good life, all while grieving the loss of his wife.

"Damn. That must be hard," I say, unable to imagine the hell he must be going through. Not to mention, the hell his daughter would be going through as well. Starting kindergarten is a huge adjustment for any kid, but to show up every day and see your dead mother in the eyes of your teacher must be so confusing.

Vincent gives me a small smile. "It is, but we're getting there," he says fondly before diving into all the highlights of Lila starting school. He chats away for almost an hour, and after finishing the ins and outs of kindergarten, he tells me all about the milestones of his other daughters, talking like the proudest father in the world.

For a fleeting moment, I'm jealous. I had an absent father growing up. He couldn't even remember to call on my birthday, and then one day, he just stopped calling altogether. I don't even know where he lives anymore. I don't even know if he's still alive, but it doesn't matter to me anymore. If he doesn't care to know about me, then I won't waste my time being hurt by him. Besides, it was a long time ago. I've more than gotten over it.

Vincent, though? He's what I picture a real father to look like. As for what I think a real man is . . . shit.

Knight fucking Slater.

I've always known he was a delicious bowl of bossy snacks, but he surprised me last night. I wasn't prepared. I know it's wrong to think about him like this. To picture how wildly our bodies would fit together. To think about the way I'd lick the sweat off his defined chest while he fucked me raw, but damn. That man.

He's my step-uncle, and that's as far as it should go. I shouldn't want him to bend me into a pretzel, and I sure as fuck shouldn't want to know how effortlessly he could pick me up and throw me across the room. With him, the idea of a threesome wouldn't even cross my mind because if I had all of that, if I was the woman who got to say he was mine, I wouldn't dare share.

But it's just a stupid fantasy, and up until now, I've been pretty good at keeping it hidden, but now that I'm older and know exactly what I like, the hunger within me is almost impossible to ignore.

Knight Slater is dangerously sexy with one hell of a filthy mouth. He's not the clean-cut billionaire businessman like his brother who lures women in with his money. He's rugged and oozes sex appeal, and after the way his dark stare seemed to rake up and down my body . . . I'm a fucking goner.

Knowing I won't get anything done while Knight circles my brain, I wrap up what's left of my report and print it up for Dr. McKullan to review and send off first thing in the morning. As Vincent does his thing, I start working out which autopsies need to be prioritized for the rest of my shift.

There are six bodies awaiting autopsies. Four men and two women, and out of all of them, we have four murders and two assumed natural deaths. The natural deaths will more than likely be covered by Dr. Sanders during tomorrow's day shift. She loves her job, but she's a sweet soul, and sometimes these darker murder cases can be too much for her. On the other hand, I thrive on the darkness.

Out of the four murders, one is particularly brutal, and I instinctively reach for that file. What can I say? I have a depraved little soul that needs to be fed.

I flip through the notes and familiarize myself with the case just as another soft beep sounds through the morgue. My head snaps up, and with Vincent wrapping up for the night, I don't get the same vicious fear pulsing through my veins as I had when I was alone.

The door is opened wide, and the familiar sound of a gurney rolling on the linoleum tells me that I have another incoming body. I let out a sigh. We're already stockpiling bodies, and at this rate, we'll never get through it all.

"Jesus," I mutter, watching Detective Gray stride in with the coroner, both of them wearing grim expressions, telling me this isn't just another natural death. This is another murder, and a horrifying one at that. "What is going on with the crime in this city? There's more murder than there is natural death."

Detective Gray lets out a heavy sigh as he signs off for delivery of the body. I do the same as the coroner lines the body up with my autopsy table, and after initialing for delivery, I take the end of the body bag and help transport the body over.

"I'm sorry to ask," Detective Gray says, sounding as though it's been one hell of a long night. "I know you're slammed, but this case . . . It has left a lot of us rattled. If there's any way we could get this report as a matter of urgency, I'd really appreciate it."

"Oh, sure," I say, already scooping up the other case file and dropping it back on top of my ever-growing pile of work.

"Thanks, Dr. Madden."

"Of course," I say, giving him an awkward smile. I've worked alongside him for what feels like years, and apart from him stopping by to demand reports, I don't really know a damn thing about him. "I'll get it done through the night, and I'm sure Dr. McKullan will be in touch come morning."

Detective Gray smiles tightly and nods before hastily getting out of here with the coroner tight on his heels, not even bothering to give me any details on the case. What's up with that? The two of them have probably been at the crime scene for hours, and I can guarantee the coroner already has a fair idea of the cause of death, yet they share nothing.

Frustration trickles in as I scoop the file off the top of the body before flipping through the details. Without any more small talk, Vincent scurries to pack up. He's not super fond of dead bodies. In fact, he makes it a point not to come in here while I'm working. We learned that the hard way in the form of vomit splattered from one end of the morgue to the other. Since then, we go out of our way to ensure he doesn't accidentally see human brains cut open on the table.

Vincent rushes out a hasty goodbye, and I offer him a quick wave, my attention already focused on the work in front of me. The files are barren, and it pisses me off. Twenty-two-year-old male. That's it. No other details to go on. Considering Detective Gray's urgency to get the final report, I assumed he'd have given me more to start with.

No location listed, no rundown on weapons or substances found at the scene, and nothing about why the hell they both looked so grim. It's unprofessional and screams that the job was rushed. Were they so desperate for answers that they didn't take the time to write down literally anything? Shit. If they want to catch this guy's killer and make a charge stick, then making sure everything is done correctly is an absolute priority. Detective Gray knows better than this.

My gaze turns toward the body bag on the table, and I let out a sigh. "Well," I say to the body. "If nobody else is going to do right by you, then let me be the one to offer you the respect you deserve."

And with that, I reach for the zipper at the top of the body bag and drag it down.

CHAPTER 7

HARPER-RAYN

"What in the ever-loving fuck is this?"

Horror pulses through my veins as I take in the corpse before me, completely mutilated by some kind of blade. I've never seen anything like it. I have documented more than my fair share of stab wounds, but this is different. There are slices cut from the man's skin, on his arms, face, neck, and thighs—all of this before I've even had a chance to cut him out of his clothes.

Bile rises in my throat, but I swallow it down and get on with my job. I wasn't hired to be the bitch who runs away screaming . . . the other night excluded. I'm a professional, and while this is one of the most horrendous things I've ever seen, I can take it. I'm sure there will be a day when I see worse, but for now, I need to do the job I was trained to do.

Putting aside the unease, I look closer at the wounds covering his body before grabbing my camera to properly document every single marking on his skin. I get the rest of my tools prepared and quickly get used to the idea that tonight's shift is going to run long. This isn't the kind of autopsy that will be over in the standard four hours. This one will keep me here well into the morning.

"Okay," I tell the body, taking a DNA sample of his saliva and locking it into a jar. "Let's see if we can figure out what the hell happened to you."

I start cutting through his shirt when it becomes clear that the blade markings left on his chest are spelling something out and my movements become quicker, needing to know what it says. After reaching the bottom of his shirt, I carefully move the fabric aside. Then as I take in his bare chest, I suck in a disturbed gasp.

SMILE FOR THE CAMERA, KITTEN

"What the actual fuck?" I murmur, reaching for my camera again. "'Smile for the camera'? Who the hell did this to you?"

I shake my head as I try to comprehend the type of bastard who would leave a message like this on somebody's skin, and for what purpose? Who is this kitten and why does it have to smile for the camera? Is there something much deeper to all of this?

A shiver sails down my spine, and I can tell the motive behind all of this is going to be despicable. We're not dealing with the usual run-of-the-mill opportunistic killer. This guy was precise. He planned all of this. All of these markings on the victim were done postmortem, and while I'm glad the victim didn't have to suffer through that kind of torture, I can't help but wonder how fucked up one must be to mutilate a dead body to send a message.

I draw my gaze away from the deeply etched words on his skin and begin removing the rest of his clothes. I fold everything neatly and slide it all into separate evidence bags, along with his shoes, wallet, and jewelry—confirming this was definitely not a mugging gone wrong. Every article has to be meticulously photographed and documented, and once all of the nitty-gritty is out of the way, I can focus on the body.

I start from the head and work my way down, documenting every last gash on his body. I measure the length and depth of each one, and as I reach his chest and start documenting the letters etched into his skin, my stomach clenches.

This is fucked up.

I've been working for almost an hour when I finally make my way down his left arm. I'm barely even halfway through my external examination, and there's not even a hint about how this man was murdered. Usually, by this point in my external examination of a murder victim, there would be a clue, some kind of glaring marker to give me a good idea of what happened, but on this man, there's nothing, and I don't like it.

Continuing down his arm, I reach the top of his hand and notice similar carvings on his fingers below each knuckle.

My brows furrow, and I lean in closer, trying to decipher the markings only to realize they're letters, just like the ones on his chest. This is another message from the killer.

Grabbing a piece of paper, I write down each letter, and after thoroughly checking the left hand, I move onto the right, finding five more. By the time I'm done, I have ten odd letters, but as I look at them, I can't quite decipher what they mean.

NYARREPRAH

Whatever happened to a simple gunshot to the chest? Why do people have to do shit like this? It's fucked up, and then some poor doctor has to spend hours examining some killer's handiwork. Who the hell put this system into place? Surely, it had to be a man, right?

I try to move on from the carvings on the fingers, but my gaze keeps bringing me back to the ten little letters scrawled on the paper. There's something about them, something familiar, but I can't quite figure it out.

My stare shifts from the paper back to the letters on the left hand.

"What if I've been reading it wrong?" I muse to my victim. People generally read from left to right, but if the killer was standing over the victim, the letters would have been written from his point of view. It's flipped.

I need to be reading this from right to left.

My brows furrow as I hastily grab my pen and start reversing the letters.

HARPE—

My brain works faster than I can move the pen, and I only get halfway through before it becomes abundantly clear what the letters spell out, and I can't physically keep going.

Harper-Rayn.

My hands start to shake, and I drop the pen so quickly, it clatters to the autopsy table before rolling and falling to the ground. Is this . . . Is this supposed to be a message for me?

"No. No. No. No. No," I begin to chant, unease pounding through my chest like poison. I had foolishly begun to convince myself that the bullshit that happened during my last shift was a one-off, that maybe I'd imagined the whole thing. But this? Fuck.

Whoever this guy is, he's escalated quickly. It's one thing to stalk a woman at work and leave her a black rose on the autopsy table, but to kill a man just to send a message? This is too much. I didn't sign up to be involved in this guy's bullshit.

My chest heaves, and I do what I can to calm myself. I'm here alone. It's just a message. There are no shivers sailing down my spine, so as long as I'm safe here in this building, then there's no reason to panic. I need to finish my job, scrape every ounce of potential DNA off the body, and have it personally delivered to the lab.

Detective Gray needs to catch this guy, and if I don't follow through on my part, then locking up this bastard is only going to take longer.

There's no time for me to freak out. I need to keep my cool.

With shaking hands and a new resolve to finish what I started, I grab my ruler and pick up where I left off, checking over every last carving left on the body and documenting them with perfect precision.

Only as I work, my attention is drawn back to the message left on this man's chest.

SMILE FOR THE CAMERA, KITTEN

Holy fucking shit.

Am I the fragile little kitten? Is this message for me, too? Am I being watched?

Dread sinks heavily into the pit of my stomach, and as my back stiffens, I can't help but look around the morgue. There are cameras everywhere, exactly the same as the surveillance cameras throughout the rest of the hospital. But the one in the far back that has a view of every last inch of the morgue flashes with a blue light, and I know deep in my gut that's the one.

He's been watching me. All this time.

The overwhelming need to throw up surges through my body, but I hold it back, determined to see this through. I'm no longer just afraid of this guy, I'm fucking determined. Not to mention, I'm nobody's fragile little kitten.

Turning my back on the camera, I focus on my work, being extra thorough as I document everything. Once the front is done, I turn him over, and the cause of death becomes a little clearer. There's a massive cut on the left side of his torso, right below his ribs, that's currently being held together by medical-grade staples.

"What the fuck did this asshole do to you?" I ask my corpse as I look over the wound and take note of the horrific bruising surrounding it, telling me that this injury happened while he was still alive.

I let out a heavy breath and get busy, and just like his front side, it takes me almost another two hours to document every last gash in his skin. When I finally get to the internal part of the autopsy, I've never been so relieved. Only, there's a stark curiosity booming through my chest from the massive wound on the victim's back.

Why is it there, and why does it feel so important?

With shaky hands that piss me off, I take my scalpel and make my Y incision, cutting deeply from both shoulders and down through the center of the chest, distorting the message left there. I go right down to the pelvis, and the moment I fold back the skin, I realize that something isn't right.

All of the internal organs have been shifted around, each one of them showing visible signs of trauma, but on top of that, there's also a foreign object here. Something long, partially hidden within the rib cage, but it's covered in blood, making it impossible to decipher.

My brows furrow, that wicked unease growing by the second.

What the hell is this?

After documenting the foreign object and taking multiple photographs from different angles, I reach back into the body cavity, and as my hand slips up into the rib cage, I immediately notice that the lungs are displaced. A shiver dances down my spine, and I try to ignore it as I focus on the object.

Curling my hand around it, I carefully remove it, but there's something so familiar about how it feels in my hand. Is this a—fuck.

A rose.

My chest heaves, fear doubling down, and as I release the object onto the autopsy table, it becomes as clear as day. It's a black rose, just like the one that was left here the other night on this very autopsy table.

Tears well in my eyes as I come to the realization that this man was murdered simply for the sick need to send me some fucked-up message, and he wasn't just killed in a humane way. He was slaughtered. Sliced open while still alive only to have to feel his organs being cut out. At least the good news is that he would have quickly bled out and wouldn't have had to deal with the pain for long.

I can't even imagine the type of agony this man has suffered through.

"I'm so sorry," I tell him as the tears roll down my cheeks. "I'm so sorry."

Wanting to give him the respect he deserves, I swallow over the lump growing in my throat and continue with my work, vowing to do whatever I need to catch this asshole.

Carefully removing each organ, I examine them thoroughly, weighing and measuring before taking detailed notes on any irregular markings. I find his lungs smashed down into his abdomen, and they mostly look okay. This man was fit and clearly took care of himself. He wasn't a smoker, and his lungs generally appear healthy. However, that doesn't change the fact that they were disturbed within the body.

What kind of sick fuck plays around with someone's organs? Was killing him not enough of a thrill? At least it seems like the victim was already deceased by the time the killer got around to playing surgeon on the lungs.

I work on autopilot, mentally trying to distance myself from the work in front of me, but the moment my hand gently curls around the heart, unease settles deep in my gut. Hearts usually have a smooth texture, but I can feel the deep gouges under my fingers.

My brows furrow and I slowly pull the heart out of the chest cavity, and the moment I place it down on the examination table, horror rocks through me.

More carvings stare back at me, and despite how unsettling the first ones were on the skin, this takes it to a whole new level.

I swallow over the growing lump in my throat, and as my hands shake, I lean in closer and do what I can to decipher the words.

TAG, YOU'RE IT

CHAPTER 8

KNIGHT

Tossing my keys on my entryway table, I stride through my door before kicking it closed behind me. It's been one hell of a long day, and an even longer night. I haven't had a break in over twenty-four hours. But that's what you get as the leader of the best SWAT team in the country.

I was called in to deal with a hostage situation a few hours after dropping Harper at her apartment. I didn't even get a chance to look into her stalker situation, and it's been eating at me ever since. I arrived at the scene a little after eleven p.m. and spent the next twelve hours having to play by someone else's rules, all while the bastard gunman terrorized a family.

I'm not a patient man, nor do I enjoy falling in line under someone else's command. Especially when that person has no business calling the shots. There's only so much bullshit I can handle, and after sitting around, twiddling my fucking thumbs for twelve hours, I devised my own plan with my team.

We had that family safe and the gunman down within three minutes.

That should have been it, but my supervisor doesn't like having his judgment questioned. My team then spent another twelve hours having our asses handed to us, but to be honest, I think my supervisor just likes the sound of his own voice. I don't regret it, though. Never have. It's not the first time I've crossed a line to save a life, and it won't be the last.

The thud of my closing door has barely faded from my entryway when my phone comes alive in my pocket, and I groan, hoping like fuck I'm not being called in again. I need to eat, and as soon as that's done, I'm going to crash for the next week. I'm fucking wrecked.

Dread begins to fill me as I slip my hand into my pocket and pull my phone out. It's a little before two in the morning, and if it's not some woman calling to see if I want to fuck, then it's work. It's always fucking work, and honestly, I'm not down for either right now.

A number I don't recognize flashes on my phone, and for just a moment, I consider rejecting it. As it continues to ring, my stomach knots, and my thumb instinctively swipes across the screen.

"Hello," I say, my back stiffening.

A sniffle comes through the phone before I hear a tone that I'd recognize anywhere. "Knight?"

"Harper? What's wrong?" I ask, my fingers closing around my keys, more than ready to take off and find her. There's only one reason why Harper-Rayn would be calling me, and it has everything to do with the bullshit she told me in my truck last night.

"I . . . I'm sorry," she cries, sounding more than rattled. "I've been at work, and . . . I didn't know what to do. I didn't want to call you, but you said I had to call and—"

My blood runs cold as I make my way out to my truck, realizing that in the past thirty seconds it's started to rain. "Where are you? I'm coming to get you."

"No. No, no," she rushes out, taking a shaky breath as I hear the familiar sound of her windshield wipers in the background. "I'm in my car. I'm just . . . Something really messed-up happened at work. I don't . . . I don't know if I can be alone."

I pause in my driveway, my hand hovering in front of the truck door, rain immediately beginning to soak through my clothes. "Is this the same shit you were telling me about last night?"

"Yeah," she says in a small voice.

"Are you safe?"

There's a short pause, and I can almost imagine her checking her rearview mirrors and making sure she's not being followed. "I'm not sure. I think so."

"I've just gotten home from work. Come to me. You can stay here and then we can figure out what the fuck is going on."

"Are you sure?" Harper says. "I don't want to impose."

"You're never an imposition, Morticia," I tell her, my voice softening at the idea of getting to see her. "You can stay here as long as you need. Do you know where I live?"

"Uhhhh . . . yeah. I think so," she says. "I'll be there in ten."

"Okay. Drive safe, and keep an eye on your mirrors. I'll be waiting for you."

The line goes dead, and I find myself waiting outside my home, leaning against the pillar of my entryway that offers just a bit of shelter from the rain, all while keeping my eye on the road, anxious for Harper to get here.

The minutes tick by slowly, and I resist the urge to get in my truck and start searching for her. If she hadn't said that she was safe in her car, then I'd already be flying toward her.

I put the front porch lights on so she knows which home is mine, and barely a minute later, her headlights crest over the hill in the distance, the light distorted by the rain. Then despite her still being a good distance down the road, I push off the pillar and step out into the downpour.

Her speed slows as she approaches my driveway, and the moment I can make out her face through the windshield of her old Honda Civic, something eases in my chest. She pulls up to the curb and cuts the engine as I make my way down the driveway toward her car.

The rain is heavy against the windows, making it too hard to make out the more subtle features of her face, but I see her clearly enough to know her eyes are on me. I can *feel* it.

Striding up to the driver's door, I open it for her, and the way her gaze lifts to meet mine through the darkness—those big green trusting eyes—is crippling. She's looking at me as though I'm her fucking savior, and as much as I want to swoop in and save the day, I can't be that for her.

It's too dangerous. I can't allow myself to get too close, but that doesn't mean I'm just going to leave her to fend for herself. As soon as I figure out who the fuck has been tormenting her at work and put a fucking stop to it, I'll have no choice but to force distance between us again.

She's off limits. My step-niece. I shouldn't crave her like this.

Her gaze wavers, and when she lets out a shaky breath, I realize that whatever happened at work still has her rattled. "Come on, Morticia," I say, offering her my hand. "Come inside and tell me what the fuck is going on."

Harper visibly swallows before gently placing her small hand in mine and allowing me to help her out of the car. Her skin is blazing against mine, sending shock waves through my body, and for a fleeting second, I panic that she can sense the kind of effect she has over me, but she's far too shaken to see what's right in front of her face.

I do what I can not to hold her hand for too long, and after she clambers out of her car, I take her bag, close the door behind her, and then watch as she rushes through the rain.

"Fuck. It's cold," she mutters, darting through the puddles pooling on my driveway.

It's a short dash to my front door, and by the time she reaches it, she looks like a cold drowned rat with her arms crossed over her chest, silently shivering. Goose bumps spread across her skin, and my selfish stare lingers way too long, knowing just how quickly I could warm her up.

Goddamn it. What I wouldn't give to fuck the goose bumps out of her system.

Harper doesn't barge into my house, just simply waits for me to open the door and welcome her in. I don't know why I expected—*hoped*—for anything different. I want her to be comfortable enough to stride through the door like she owns the place, but in reality, she's never been here before. She shouldn't feel comfortable, and I shouldn't want her to.

Off. Fucking. Limits.

After opening the door, I wave her through, and as she hurries past me, her perfume hits my senses. I breathe her in, immediately intoxicated by her scent.

My hands ball into fists at my sides, and I call on every ounce of self-control not to slam this door for the sole purpose of throwing her up against it and claiming every single fucking inch of her. Instead, I close the door like a normal fucking human being and follow her into my home.

"Take a seat. Make yourself comfortable," I murmur, indicating toward my couch as I stride past her. "I'll grab you a towel to dry off."

"Thanks," Harper says in a small voice as water drips off both of us.

I make my way down my hall to the linen closet and grab a towel before turning on my heel and heading straight back to her. Only she's not sitting down. She's hovering in the corner and carefully toeing off her shoes as though terrified of traipsing water through my home.

I resist the urge to smile as I hand her the towel, and she awkwardly thanks me again before drying her face and arms. I reach for my tactical belt and unclip it, and as I feel her stare on me, I glance up to see the way her eyes are locked on my movements, sailing over my body and lingering on the way my wet black shirt sticks to my skin.

I clear my throat, and Harper's gaze snaps back to mine. "Take a seat, Morticia. Tell me what the fuck is going on."

"Right."

Harper blows out a shaky breath and makes her way over to my couch as I drop my tactical belt on the hallway table. She sits down, and as I cut through my living room to join her, those big green eyes track my every step.

Her hands visibly shake. "This is messed up."

I nod. "You spend your days cutting open corpses. If whatever this is has you so worked up, then I can only assume it's messed up."

"Okay," she continues, taking a deep breath and blowing it out slowly. "So a new body came in. You know Detective Gray? The hot one?"

"Gray?"

"Yeah. It was a brutal murder, so he wanted it prioritized as a matter of urgency, so I started right away, and this body . . . I've never seen anything so—"

She lets out another breath, not being able to find the words, but I nod, understanding where she's coming from. I've seen more than enough bodies to know how she feels. There are some that rattle you to your core, and years later, you'll still be thinking about it. And this, I get the feeling this is that for her.

Harper shoves her shaking hands under her thighs as if to settle herself before going on. "There were cuts all over his body. There must have been hundreds of them, and as I was documenting them, I realized the ones over his chest weren't so random. The carvings were words. It was a message."

I pull back, staring at her more intently, not liking where this is going. "What? A message for who?"

She shakes her head. "It read *Smile for the camera, kitten.*"

"What the hell?"

"My thoughts exactly," she mutters, sounding sick to her stomach. "But I kept going, and when I reached his hands, I found more carvings on each of his knuckles. Ten fucked-up little jagged letters. And shit, Knight. It spelled out my name. *Harper-Rayn* across his knuckles."

I fly to my feet, my eyes wide as I gape at the beautiful woman sitting in horror on my couch. "Your fucking name?" My stomach knots with unease, and I quickly realize this is more than just another bad case. This is related to the bullshit that went down during her last shift. Her stalker.

Harper nods. "That's not even the worst part."

"How the fuck is that not the worst part?" I demand, beginning to pace my living room, desperate to get to the bottom of this. The idea of some asshole targeting her like this makes me want to break.

"When I started the internal portion of the autopsy, I found a black rose," she tells me on autopilot, trying to distance herself from the horror of it all. "Just like the one that was left on the table the other night. It had been shoved up in the rib cage. All the organs had been disturbed, and the heart—"

Harper whimpers and cuts herself off, and I drop down on the couch beside her, taking her delicate hand in mine. "Tell me, Harper. You're safe now."

She clutches my hand like it's her only lifeline, and I don't dare pull away. "There was something off about the heart. It had been disturbed in a different manner, and when I started to inspect it, I found more carvings."

"What did it say?"

Harper visibly swallows. "*Tag, you're it.*"

"The fuck?"

"Yeah," she mutters. "I didn't hang around much longer. I closed up as quickly as I could and came straight here. I've never had to deal with anything like this before. I just—I don't know what to do. The other night they were just watching me and leaving a black rose, but this . . . Whoever this is has escalated, and now some poor guy was brutally murdered just for the sole purpose of this asshole sending me a message. I can't be responsible for that. I never asked for this."

"I know," I say, pulling her closer to me. "It'll be okay. You haven't done anything wrong, and you're sure as hell not responsible for this. We'll figure this out, and I'll find this asshole. I swear, Harper, I'm not going to let him hurt you. You're safe with me."

"You can't promise me that," she says, her big eyes filling with tears. She hastily pulls away from me and wipes her eyes on the back of her hand before getting to her feet. "I'm sorry. I'm just—I'm all kinds of fucked up right now."

I stand and take both of her hands, demanding her full attention, and it doesn't go unnoticed how her body immediately calms at my touch. "We're going to get to the bottom of this," I vow, holding her stare until she understands how deeply I mean each word that comes from my mouth. "I will not let you get hurt."

Harper holds my stare. "I'm not cut out for this *having a stalker* bullshit."

"No one ever is," I tell her, reluctantly releasing her hands. "Have you spoken to anyone about this? Detective Gray?"

She shakes her head. "No. I wasn't sure if I should. I want to, but what if all I do is aggravate this guy and make it worse? I don't know the procedure here."

I nod, understanding her worries, and if she were anyone else, the first thing I would do is go straight to my team, but the idea of aggravating this asshole only to have him escalate even more doesn't sit well with me.

"Look, leave it with me. I'll swing by the morgue tomorrow and check it out. Gray should have some leads by now. I'll see what they know. In the meantime, I think you should stay here tonight. You're in no condition to drive."

She shakes her head, and I see the refusal on her lips. "I—"

"Don't even think about arguing with me, Harper-Rayn. You're staying in my spare room whether you like it or not."

She cringes. "Are you sure that's really a good idea?" she asks, guilt flashing in her eyes, and suddenly I don't think it's her current situation she's referring to. It's the intense sexual tension she feels between us. The same one I've felt since the moment I met her. And she's fucking right. Having her sleeping under my roof isn't a good idea, but I'm not about to turn her away.

"What seems to be the problem, Morticia?" I ask her, my lips quirking into a wicked grin. "Don't think you can keep your greedy little hands off me?"

Harper sputters in shock, her eyes widening with surprise. "I, ummm . . ." She scoffs, clearly not having expected me to voice the one thing we've both shamelessly ignored for years. "I'm glad you think so highly of yourself, but that's not going to be a problem for me."

"Right," I say, stepping past her. I make my way toward the hallway while calling over my shoulder. "I'll grab you some dry clothes. There's food in the fridge if you're hungry."

"Wait. Knight," she rushes out, hurrying a few steps after me.

I pause at the opening of the hallway and turn back, meeting her haunted stare through the darkened room. "What's up?"

"When you speak to Detective Gray tomorrow . . ." She cringes and lets her words fall away.

"Don't worry," I murmur, eating up her innocence and knowing that with one touch I could shatter that innocence like glass. "I'll keep your name out of it."

Harper nods, and her eyes fill with gratitude. "Thank you."

"Get some sleep," I tell her.

And with that, I make my way down the hallway, wondering how the fuck I'm supposed to go all night without putting my hands on this girl and fucking her out of my system. One thing's for sure, it's going to be the hardest night of my life.

CHAPTER 9

HARPER-RAYN

What the hell was I thinking coming here? I should never have called him, but what choice did I have? What happened last night . . . I can't just allow this shit to go on. I need to get to the bottom of it, and having someone like Knight Slater in my corner could only be good.

I hope.

I've spent all night sleeping in his spare bedroom. Scrap that. I didn't actually sleep. I tried, but the very knowledge that he was in the next room kept me wide awake. I bet he couldn't sleep either. His body was probably burning the same way mine was, fire pulsing through his veins, daring him to come to my door and take what he's always wanted.

My body was buzzing all night, and the need to go in there and take everything I've craved for so long was killing me. I could smell him all around me, my skin burning from the feel of his shirt wrapped around my body. It was too much. Just the thought of what he could do to me . . . fuck.

I'm in trouble, and I don't mean the kind of trouble I could find myself in with my new stalker. I mean the *definitely going to fuck my step-uncle and see a whole new version of family drama* kind of trouble.

What the hell is wrong with me?

Step-uncle. Step-uncle. Step-uncle. He's my fucking step-uncle!

Why is that so hard to get through my head? Probably because the man is an Adonis, and even in the middle of my freak-out last night, he had the audacity to ask me if I have the ability to keep my greedy hands to myself.

Holy hell.

There's no doubt about it. Knight Slater knows exactly what he does to me. The question is, does he ever plan on doing anything about it?

It's a little after nine in the morning, and I've spent way too many hours tossing and turning in Knight's spare bed. Though I think it's clear that I would have preferred to spend my night tossing and turning for a whole other reason, but that's neither here nor there, and if anybody asks, I would deny it with everything I have.

I need to get out of here, preferably before Knight gets up. I'd love to avoid facing him over an awkward breakfast.

Throwing the blankets back, I get out of bed and grab my things before quietly tiptoeing across the room. I open the door and peek out into the hallway. Knight's bedroom door is wide open, but I can hear the shower running, and I let out a sigh of relief before traipsing down the hallway to the main bathroom.

I quickly pee before splashing water over my face, and for just a moment, I consider taking his shirt off and putting my rain-soaked clothes back on. After a moment of reflection, I decide that if he wants it back, he's going to have to peel it off my body. Preferably extra slow with those dark eyes locked on mine and a promise to turn me into his sweet little cream pie.

After finding a new toothbrush in the drawer, I get myself ready for the day. At some point, I'm going to have to take a quick power nap before returning to work tonight. Not that it's really in my best interest to keep working through all of this, but I'm not about to neglect my career for this asshole stalker.

I brush my long hair with my fingers before pulling it up into a messy bun. I can deal with it properly when I get home. It's a hot mess, and after being hit with the rain last night, the flyaway hairs have become a real problem.

The little makeup I put on before work last night is mostly smeared across the pillow in the spare bedroom, but what managed to survive the night still looks acceptable, and with that in mind, I make my break for it.

Taking all of my shit with me, I creep back out into the hallway, and still hearing the running shower, I smile to myself. He's not catching me out today. After the night I've had, along with the lack of sleep, I can't be trusted to make good decisions.

I'm going to have to schedule a meeting with Laith ASAP and start punching that loyalty card hardcore.

Making my way down the hall, I hold my breath, trying to be as quiet as a mouse, when a deep, delicious groan sounds through the house.

"Ahhhh, fuck."

Whaaaaaat?

I come to a dead stop in the center of the hallway, my breath catching in my throat as my heart leaps into action, madly pounding. Is he . . . ? No. There's no fucking way.

"Mmmm."

Sweet baby Jesus. He is.

Knight Slater is jerking off in the shower. Good lord, have all my Christmases arrived at once? What the hell have I done to deserve such a heavenly gift sent directly from the big man upstairs?

Maybe Knight thought I'd already snuck out. Or perhaps that ego of his is simply so big that he doesn't give a shit what I overhear. He's putting on a show, and if that's the case, it would be rude not to appreciate a performance.

Nerves pulse through my veins, threatening to pull me under, but I haven't had a coffee yet, and I can't be held accountable for the stupid things I do.

Turning on my heel, I creep back up the hallway, pausing in front of Knight's open bedroom door.

My bottom lip catches between my teeth, and as I let out a shaky breath, I finally step inside. My nerves take on a life of their own. They're electrifying, and as I put one foot in front of the other, another soft groan fills the room.

A heavy pulse thrums between my thighs, and my breath comes in faster. Just a few more steps, and I'll be there. Steam flows out the open en suite door, and I find myself hovering in the doorway, my shoulder propped against the frame.

This is the boldest thing I've ever done in my whole life, and yet I can't bring myself to turn around and leave.

My gaze shifts toward the shower, and I thank the Michael B. Jordan gods that his shower is entirely glass. Knight is completely naked, and the water rushing off his sculpted body makes my mouth water. Every delicious, tattooed inch of him is perfect. So fucking tall with those broad shoulders and his wide chest. The deep ridges of his abs trail down to the most breathtaking V, and then finally, that massive, thick, veiny cock in the palm of his hand.

I suck in a gasp.

His muscles bulge and flex with his movements, and his eyes are closed as he works his fist up and down his impressive length. Soft grunts and groans fill the small bathroom, and I've never wanted anything more.

Knight rolls his head back as his tight fist works up to his tip and the thick column of his throat bobs as the pleasure works through his body. His eyes open just a fraction, meeting mine through the steam-filled bathroom, and for a moment, I panic.

My heart comes to a dead stop, but as he keeps working that thick cock, I realize he's not about to stop just because he has an audience.

"I, uhh . . . Just came to tell you that I was leaving." My hungry stare rolls up and down his body, completely infatuated by the thick veins leading to the tip of his impressive cock.

"Oh yeah?" he rumbles, his Adam's apple bobbing up and down.

A stupid smirk pulls at the corner of my lips, and I push off the edge of the doorframe, holding his wicked stare. "You look a little . . . caught up. I'll see myself out."

My smile widens, and without another word, I turn on my heel and stalk out of his bedroom—despite the way my body so frantically craves his touch.

"Where the fuck do you think you're going?" Knight's possessive tone rips through the room behind me, bringing me to an immediate standstill.

I turn on my heel to find him standing right where I'd been only a moment ago, his cock still braced in his big hand as the water drips off him, making my mouth water. He's fucking glorious.

"Home," I say, knowing damn well that my cheeks are flushed.

"Get on your knees, Morticia."

Well, shit.

His tone is a stark demand, no room for argument and as my brow arches, and as his fist continues working his thick cock, I find myself dropping to the carpet, my knees spread like the perfect little submissive whore I want to be for him.

Knight holds my stare from across the room, his intention crystal clear in his stormy gray gaze, and as he slowly strides toward me, I realize that even if he doesn't touch me, I'll be ruined for the rest of my life.

My chest heaves with anticipation, burning inside me, coiling like a spring ready to explode. He inches closer, and I feel myself begin to crumble. Anything he wants, I'll give it to him without question.

Knight moves in front of me and reaches out, grasping my chin as his thumb dances across my jaw, and I have the sudden realization that I would happily spend every night of the rest of my life on my knees for this man.

His eyes shudder as he continues working himself, and I can't tear my eyes away, that dazzling cock just inches from my face. Beads of water linger on his skin, glistening in the soft morning light streaming through his bedroom window, and my tongue itches to lap up every last drop.

"Mmmmm," he groans, that tone full of the sweetest seduction. "Such a pretty girl."

Butterflies swarm through my stomach, and I can't respond, so I just hold his gaze as he works himself right to the edge. When he releases his grasp on my chin, I suck in a deep breath, desperately needing his touch on my body.

His hand moves around the back of my head, and when he grips my hair and pulls my head back, the anticipation becomes too much to bear.

"Open."

His voice is thick with need, and I oblige within seconds, opening my mouth as wide as it'll go, inviting him in. Knight doesn't hesitate, pushing himself right to the back of my throat, filling my mouth to the brim, and I close my lips around him, letting my tongue explore as I keep my eyes locked on his.

He's right on the edge, and I quickly work him, sucking hard as he pushes past my gag reflexes. His hold tightens in my hair, and I reach up to curl my fingers around the base of his cock, squeezing tight.

My other hand curls around the back of his strong thigh, digging my nails into his warm skin.

"That's my good little whore. Show me how much you want it."

I work and work, pushing myself to my limits as my cunt pulses with desperation. I need him to fuck me, to shred me to pieces, and claim every inch of me.

Knight groans, and as my head bobs up and down over his cock, he pulls me in tighter. "Fuuuuck, Harper. I knew you'd be a greedy little vixen."

Pride swells in my chest as a grin pulls at my lips, but I fight against it, determined not to mess with my flow, but when his eyes flutter again, I know I've got him. Hook. Line. Sinker.

His grip tightens in my hair as his other hand returns to my chin, grasping tight, and with those dark, wicked eyes locked on mine, he comes hard, shooting his hot load right down the back of my throat.

"Swallow it," he demands, but the request is not necessary. I wouldn't waste it even if I could.

I greedily swallow him down, taking every last drop he has to offer as his chest heaves with frantic breaths. He stares at me in astonishment as though he can barely believe what the fuck just happened here, and honestly, neither can I.

Knight slowly inches out of my mouth, and I make a show of

licking my lips. "*Now* you may go," he growls in that deep, thick tone that drives me wild. His lips quirk up into the filthiest grin, and with that, he turns on his heel and stalks back to his bathroom, leaving me writhing on the floor, untouched and desperate for more.

CHAPTER 10

HARPER-RAYN

Men are fucking assholes.

That was the longest drive home of my life. My thighs are cramping from continuously trying to squeeze them together. I've never experienced this kind of raw desperation before. I almost lost control and flicked the bean at a red light. If it weren't for the guy in the lifted RAM beside me with a perfect view into the driver's seat of my car, I probably would have done it too.

I come to a stop in the underground parking garage beneath my apartment complex, and as I get out of my Honda and hightail it to the elevator, I mentally list which of the battery-operated friends in my bedside drawer are going to get the job done best.

There's no denying it, despite how capable they are of getting me where I need to go, nothing could possibly satisfy the raw need within me. Not now that I know exactly how Knight Slater tastes on my tongue.

How could he just leave me panting on his bedroom floor like that, completely unhinged and desperate? It's like this is a game to him. I know they say it's always best to leave them wanting more, but he didn't need to take it quite so literally. I didn't even get a butt slap, let alone a finger or two. At this rate, I could have used his whole damn fist.

Shit.

I really am a desperate whore for him.

His fist? What the hell is wrong with me? I know I'm not always the classiest woman and don't fit into the high-society world my mother is in, but surely I'm not that bad. I sound like a rabid animal in heat.

Taking the elevator up to my floor, I replay this morning for the millionth time in a row, and just like every other time, I'm left wondering what the fuck it means. I had my step-uncle's dick in my mouth. And what a magnificent dick it was.

That doesn't make it any less wrong. Surely this is somehow illegal, right? It's not as though he's my actual uncle. That would be completely fucked up, but because he's married into the family, I suppose it's only partially fucked up. So, in theory, it's not really *that* bad.

Either way, I'm a whore for my uncle's cock.

On the plus side, I always knew he wanted me. For years I've tried to convince myself that I've imagined it all, that this intense sexual tension is nothing but a schoolgirl fantasy that I've completely made up. But this morning, he proved that it's as real as it gets. He's wanted me all these years, just as badly as I've wanted him. The only question is where do we go from here? Was it a one-time thing, or are we going to be sneaking into the linen closet to fuck at every family function from now until the end of time? I'm not exactly opposed to that idea.

The elevator *dings* its arrival on my floor, and I slink out of it, dragging my feet as I contemplate the ins and outs of how a secret relationship with my step-uncle is supposed to play out. And honestly, since I've been so consumed by Knight Slater, I haven't even thought about the carvings or the black roses that have tormented my brain for the past forty-eight hours.

It's as though Knight Slater's cock is some kind of magic pill, and as long as it continues to make everything else fade away, then I'll become its biggest champion, its most selfish addict.

"What the fuck are you wearing?" A familiar voice comes from down the hall, breaking me out of my Knight-Slater's-cock-induced fog.

Izzy stares at me from the end of the hallway, her brow perfectly arched as she takes me in wearing nothing but Knight's massive T-shirt and holding my damp clothes scrunched in my hand.

"Uuuuuhhhhh."

"I know a walk of shame when I see one," Izzy announces to my whole apartment complex. "And considering Laith is deathly allergic to sleepovers, you better start talking."

Goddamn it.

I hurry the rest of the way down the hallway and furiously shush my best friend. "Would you shut up? I don't need the whole building knowing that I spent my night—"

"Getting railed?" she finishes for me.

"Jesus Christ," I spit. "I didn't get railed. No railing was going down. Just—"

"The fuck? You're half naked, wearing some man's shirt, and you're trying to tell me that you didn't get fucked within an inch of your life? I swear, Harper's Bazaar, I have never been more disappointed in you than I am right now."

I roll my eyes and frantically unlock my door before ushering her into my apartment so that my neighbors aren't subjected to this conversation. "Get your ass inside before I have to beat it," I warn her.

"Oh. I have spicy Harper today. Yes please," she declares, strutting through the open door and leaving me in her wake. "And for the record, I'd love a good beating, but only if it's followed by a good praise session."

"You're going to make someone a very happy man one day."

"Don't I know it," she says as I kick the door shut behind me, finally giving us just a fraction of privacy for me to dive into the details of my night. Though considering the walls are paper thin, I don't really know just how much privacy we're going to get. "Spill the beans, you filthy little freak. I want to hear all about it."

"Okay," I say, all but skipping across my apartment to delve into the details. "But it's a little . . . controversial."

Her face scrunches with confusion, and the way she watches me is as though she's trying to pluck the details straight out of my brain. There's a long silence before her eyes suddenly widen, and she sucks in a loud gasp. "Holy fucking shit. It's Daddy Elias. I knew it! Tell me all about it. I want every fucked-up detail."

I scoff in disgust. "It's not Elias, and for the billionth time, can you please stop calling him Daddy? It makes my skin crawl."

"But he's so delicious. I bet he fucks like a lion."

I give Izzy a blank stare, and she lets out a huff. "Fine," she says. "I'll stop imagining riding your stepfather like a cowgirl, but I draw the line at not calling him Daddy. That's never going to change, so you might as well get used to it."

"You know you're a pest, right?"

"Of course I do. Now tell me all about it. Who's this mystery guy?"

I cringe, not sure how this is going to go down. "It's Knight," I tell her. "The forbidden step-uncle, but I swear, it's not what you think."

"Wh-huh? Knight? Since when . . . Wait. How did you even end up at his place? He doesn't live with your mom, does he?"

I shake my head. "No, he's got his own place. I just . . . " I let my words fall away, realizing I don't have a good explanation for this. At least, not one that doesn't include being honest about what happened at the morgue last night, and I'm not about to go into the details with her. After all, the last conversation about it didn't go particularly well. "It wasn't anything too exciting. I got a flat after work and knew he lived close, so I called him and he helped. But then we were both drenched from the rain and because his place was closer, we just went there, and he insisted I stay. You know, because driving in the rain is dangerous and all."

She narrows her stare, not believing me for a second, and honestly, she shouldn't, I'm a terrible liar. Everybody knows it. "And then what?"

"And then nothing. He lent me a shirt because my clothes were wet, and then I slept in the spare bedroom."

"You slept in the spare bedroom? What the fuck is wrong with you? You had a golden opportunity, and you let it slip right through your fingers."

I shrug. "I mean, not entirely."

Izzy sits up straighter on the couch, grabbing the cushion from behind her back and hugging it to her chest as she pulls her legs up beneath her, getting extra comfortable. "Don't even think about holding back on the details."

I laugh, and a stupid grin cuts across my face. "Okay, so this morning, I could hear him in the shower, and I didn't want all those awkward goodbyes, so I was going to sneak out, but then I heard him—"

"Heard him what?" she rushes out, her eyes widening as if knowing the juicy part is coming.

"He was getting off. He was groaning and grunting, and those moans. Holy fuck. I've never heard anything so hot, and so—"

"Oh please, God, for all that's holy, tell me you went in there."

I grin, and she throws herself to her feet, her hands pumping the air. "YES! I fucking knew you were a filthy little slut. Hell yes! I take back anything bad I've ever said about you. You're officially my new queen."

I laugh as I roll my eyes. "Cool your titties," I tell her. "It's not like I stripped down and fucked him stupid."

"Then what the hell happened?" she demands, dropping back to the couch, her mood quickly plummeting, and for a moment, I fear for the metaphorical crown she just placed on my head. Despite not completely rocking his world, I still feel as though I deserve the title of being her new queen.

"Okay, so I went into his room and stood in the doorway of his en suite, just long enough to get his attention, and just when he thought he had me, I turned and left. Only, he wasn't about to let me go."

"Holy shit. What did he do?"

"He followed me out of the bathroom, buck naked with his cock in his hand, and demanded I stop. Then when I turned around—"

"Oh God. Don't stop there. WHAT HAPPENED?"

"He said, '*Get on your knees*,' in this deep, seductive tone, and fuck, Izzy. I've never dropped to my knees so fast in my life. I was a goner. I was like the perfect little Anastasia Steele, waiting for my master to fuck me into oblivion."

"Damn. That's hot," Izzy breathes. "I need to find a man like that."

I nod, never agreeing more.

"Tell me he fucked your mouth and called you a dirty little slut?"

I grin. "Would a man like Knight Slater do anything different?"

"Oh God!" Izzy falls back against the couch, crushing the cushion to her chest, lost to the fantasy of finding herself a wild, dominant man like Knight. "Tell me the rest. I know damn well it didn't stop there. Give it to me hard."

I laugh and cringe at the same time. "That's just the thing. That asshole fucked my mouth like it's never been fucked in its life, and just when I was about to demand the favor be returned, he walked away. He didn't lay a single hand on me, and now I've got the worst case of clam jam in my life. It's blue balls on crack."

Izzy howls with laughter, clutching her stomach. "Holy shit. If that were me, I'd be pissed, but because it's you and Knight, it's hilarious. I guess that's what you get for attempting to fool around with someone who should be on the permanent 'Don't suck cock' list."

"So not funny."

Izzy smirks before launching into a rundown of her night with the male model who was on set of the photo shoot for her winter line. Personally, I'm not a fan of mixing business with pleasure, but Iz has never had the same reservations. Though I suppose after sucking my step-uncle's cock on his bedroom floor, my standards and morals aren't as high as I'd always assumed.

Can you really blame a girl? Knight Slater has some pristine dick. It would have been a crime against womanhood to deny it. In theory, I was doing myself a favor. After all, curiosity killed the cat and all that shit. If I never took the plunge and found out, I would have always wondered, and now that I know, I am forever ruined for any other dick.

Mom must be on to something. There's something addictive about Slater dick.

Getting up from the couch, I start sorting through my wet clothes. "What are your plans for the day?" I ask as Izzy kicks her feet up onto my coffee table and makes herself at home.

"I've got a Pilates class at eleven, and then I was going to work on my designs for next fall."

My brows shoot up, and I whip around to gape at my best friend. "Next fall? We only just started this fall."

Izzy smirks. "I can't help that I like to be prepared. The designs have been bouncing around in my head for weeks, and I need to get them out. Though I'm sure between now and next fall, I'll change them a million times. Not to mention, nailing down a fabric is going to be a nightmare. Every time I think I've found what I want, something better appears."

I chuckle to myself. "I'd hate to be your assistant."

Izzy laughs, knowing just how right I am, and as she goes to respond, her words are cut off by the sound of my phone screeching to life on the couch. Iz leans over to where I was just sitting and scoops it up before checking the screen, her face twisting with unease. "Ugh. It's your mom."

"Ugh. No thanks. Let it go to voicemail. I don't need to spend the next hour getting berated for how deeply I offended and embarrassed her at her sham of a dinner party."

"Are you sure?" Iz asks, a teasing smirk pulling at her full lips. "I could just swipe my thumb across the screen. Really, it'd be no hassle at all."

My eyes widen with horror. Despite knowing she's teasing, I have no doubt that she'll actually do it. "Don't even think about it, Izabelle Grace Davenport."

Her grin widens, and I watch as her thumb gets closer to the screen. "What's in it for me?"

"You—" The call goes dead, and I let out a heavy sigh, my heart hammering in my chest. "I don't need that kind of trauma so early in the morning."

"Early?" she asks, her gaze dropping back to my phone. "It's—oh no. It's ten thirty. I'm going to be late for Pilates."

Izzy flies to her feet, scrambling for her things. "I'll call you later," she tells me. "But just so you know, I wanna go out on Saturday night. I need to let loose and shake my ass. And by letting loose and shaking my ass, what I really mean is that I need to get wicked drunk and be railed in a filthy club bathroom by some sweaty stranger with a huge cock."

I nod. Some things never change.

"You got it," I tell her, not really down for a messy weekend, but if I don't go, then she'll end up going by herself, and I can't let her do that. After all, she needs someone to make sure her bad decisions aren't going to come back and bite her on the ass.

"Yes!" she cheers, racing through my door. She doesn't bother with a goodbye, and I move across my apartment behind her, closing the door and making sure every last lock and bolt are firmly in place.

As soon as I turn back around, my phone chimes with a new voicemail notification, and I laugh to myself, because honestly, if I don't, I'll probably cry. I can only imagine what kind of message my mother has just left for me, but just because it's there doesn't mean I have to check it. I can save that disappointment for another time.

For now, I have a scheduled appointment with a blue bean and every last battery-operated toy in my bedroom drawer, and I don't plan on leaving until the job is well and truly done.

CHAPTER 11

HARPER-RAYN

Nerves pound through my veins as I walk into work for the night. Dr. McKullan would have spent the day going over my notes from last night, and he's bound to have some questions.

He's the best at what he does, and while the black rose has been entered into evidence, there's no way he would miss the carvings on the victim's chest, fingers, and heart and not be capable of figuring out the message.

He'll know, and he'll ask all the questions that I won't be able to answer, and once he realizes that I'm not exactly safe working here alone at night, he'll revoke my night shift privileges. I'll have no choice but to go back to working the day shift with everyone else, and while it's not particularly the end of the world, it doesn't work with my preferred lifestyle.

Making my way to the door, I swipe my access card and head inside the morgue to find the day shift workers packing up. They mind their business, going about whatever they're doing, not sparing me a second glance.

My brows furrow, and I turn my attention to Dr. McKullan as he strides across the morgue collecting his things. "Ahhh, Dr. Madden, ready for a busy night?"

Uhhhh . . . What? That's not quite what I was expecting. Where's the lecture or the refusal to allow me to work without security? What about being reprimanded for bailing halfway through my shift last night? Hell, the last two shifts I've bailed early and haven't completed the work laid out for me. Why isn't he handing my ass to me for that? And why the hell isn't he asking me why my name was spelled out on the knuckles of a victim who's currently chilling out in our refrigeration unit?

"Yes, Dr. McKullan," I say, my fingers nervously twitching at my side, waiting for the other shoe to drop. "Anything new come in today?"

"It's Blackstone. There's always something new," he chuckles.

"Indeed, there is."

"Okay, I'm heading home. I'll be on my cell if you need anything, though you rarely do."

I give him an awkward smile, trying to take the compliment, but I'm far too confused to take it for what it is. "Sure thing."

Dr. McKullan gets back to gathering his things, and within the space of three seconds, the room empties out, and once again, I'm left alone in the eerie morgue. A few days ago, I would have bragged about how much I love being alone in the morgue, but after my past few shifts, it doesn't quite hold the same allure.

Trying to shake it off, I settle in for the night and dump my bag on my desk before going over the few files that have been left out. After determining what needs to be prioritized, I wander over to the refrigeration unit and find who's up first.

My fingers curl around the handle, preparing to open the locker, when my gaze shifts across the unit to the locker that holds the unlucky bastard who became a pawn in my stalker's sick game. A shiver rips across my skin as my stomach clenches with unease.

All I need is one shift where I don't have to run out of here absolutely terrified. What I really need is to find a shred of self-preservation and not show up to work. I might as well paint a target on my back at this point, but I never claimed I was smart. I enjoy my work, and I'm not about to let this bullshit keep me from doing what I love. However, there's no denying that before getting into my car and driving here tonight, I wondered if it's even worth it.

Is risking my life for my career really the act of a woman whose sanity is fully intact? I hardly think so. But I also never claimed that I wasn't insane. I guess the question is: Who's more fucked up—me or my mystery black-rose stalker? Don't get me wrong, my stalker spends his nights sending me messages via decomposing organs, but I voluntarily work night shift in a morgue, slicing and dicing corpses, and there's a special place in every asylum reserved for women like that.

Trying to ignore the offending locker, I keep my attention focused on the job at hand and just as I twist the handle, the familiar beep of someone entering the morgue sounds through the silence.

My back stiffens, and I whip around, my gaze locked on the door as my heart starts to race. My shift has only just begun. I figured I'd at least have a few hours to get some work done before the chaos started. I mean, shit. If this asshole is going to keep fucking with my work, then he should do the decent thing and wait until the end of my shift. There's only so much slacking Dr. McKullan will tolerate before he loses his shit, and I pride myself on being someone who constantly completes my work.

As the door opens, I shuffle toward my autopsy table, discreetly reaching for the scalpel and hiding it beneath the table. I won't be caught unaware like last night's victim. If anybody is getting cut into a million little pieces tonight, it sure as fuck won't be me.

Time seems to slow when one of the night nurses from the emergency department steps through the open door. "Here we are," she says, offering a beaming smile to whoever stands outside the door. "Just let me know if there's anything at all I can help you with."

"Thanks, love, but I've got it from here," a familiar voice says, making my unease shift into pure confusion.

Is that . . . ?

Knight Slater strides through the door of Blackstone's only morgue, and I stare at him, gaping as my brain tries to comprehend what the hell is going on. Somewhere deep in the very back of my brain, I know he's here to figure out what the fuck is going on with the victim from last night, and yet all I can think about is the way he stood before me, dripping from the shower, and demanded I get on my knees.

Fuck, I was such a whore for this man.

Surely it was a moment of weakness. He's my step-uncle, and therefore it will never happen again.

Who the hell am I kidding? If he told me to offer up my ass on a silver platter right here in the middle of the morgue, he and I both know that I wouldn't hesitate for even a second. Perhaps my stalker might get a show for a change.

"Uhhhhhhhhh . . ."

"Calm down, Morticia," Knight rumbles in that deep, thick tone that's quickly becoming the only thing that circles my brain. "I haven't come to test just how quickly I can get you on your knees. I need to see that body."

My jaw drops, and all I can do is stare at him. The audacity of this man.

I fucking love it.

"You got me on my knees once, Slater. Good luck making it happen again," I tell him, casually placing the scalpel back on the table as though I weren't about to slice him from tit to dick. Turning on my heel, I stalk over to the locker that houses the body he's come to see.

Knight follows my every step, and the closer he gets, the harder it becomes to breathe. Why the hell can't I get this morning out of my head? I need to get my shit together, especially considering that I'm about to unlock the unit that houses a nightmare that's bound to send me into a tailspin.

I need to concentrate.

Blowing out a breath, I step up in front of the locker, and as I reach for the handle, Knight moves in right behind me, his wide chest pressed against my back.

Every thought drains from my brain as my body launches into overdrive, his sheer proximity leaving me breathless. I become frozen to the spot, not trusting my body to move even an inch, and when he leans into me, the uncontrollable need to become his is all I can focus on.

"Let's make one thing clear, Morticia. I don't need luck," he murmurs in that thick, addictive tone. His lips are so close to my ear that his breath brushes across my skin and his chest vibrates against my back.

Goose bumps rise over my skin, wreaking havoc on my body, and when his big hand falls to my waist and squeezes, my knees sway beneath me. "When I want you on your knees, I'll fucking have you on your knees, Harper. You won't deny me. You'll drop to the ground like my perfect little whore and love every second of it. Pleasing me is what you crave. I saw it in your eyes this morning. You were greedy for my cock, and no amount of attitude is going to change that."

Wet. Why am I suddenly so wet?

I clear my throat, acting as though his words haven't completely ruined me, before glancing over my shoulder and meeting his heated stare. "We'll see about that," I challenge, before making a point of waving him away. "Now, if you don't mind. I take my work very seriously, and I don't recall dealing with overly emotional horny SWAT men being in my job description."

Knight smirks, and the way his dark eyes shimmer with silent laughter tells me that he knows I'm full of shit. He has me right where he wants me. All he's got to do is say the word, and I'll give him anything he asks for.

We're playing one hell of a dangerous game, and he doesn't seem to care about the risks.

As if playing along, Knight steps around me, positioning himself on the other side of the drawer, his stare holding mine hostage. "Open the locker, Morticia."

Ha. Dick.

I was going to do it anyway, but now when I do, it looks as though I'm only doing it because his grumpy ass demanded it.

Rolling my eyes, I tighten my hold on the handle and give it a quick twist before opening the small door and grabbing the roller table. I slowly pull it all the way out, and as the bagged body stares back at me, the same unease I felt last night comes back tenfold.

My face scrunches, and I feel Knight's gaze locked on my face, but I do what I can to swallow the fear before finally reaching for the zipper at the top of the black body bag. "You ready for this?" I ask him, suddenly not feeling so playful. "It's messed up. Not like the bodies you're used to seeing."

"I can handle it, doll."

My cheeks flush at the way he calls me *doll*, but I push it aside and let out a breath. Just because he seems to be ready to see hell in human form doesn't mean I'm ready to see it again. "Okay," I whisper, clutching the zipper and slowly pulling it down.

Knight's gaze drops to the body, and as I reluctantly pull it open, my brows crease with confusion. "Wait," I mutter, hurrying to unzip it the rest of the way before grabbing the sides of the bag and yanking it open. "This isn't it. This isn't the body from last night."

I shake my head as Knight's gaze comes back to mine. "It's cool. Maybe you got the wrong unit."

Unease pounds through my veins, and I grab the side of the body bag, checking over the identification number. "No. I don't get things wrong. Not at work," I tell him, knowing damn well this is the very bag I placed the victim into last night. It has my handwriting, the same rushed letters and numbers from where my hands were shaking. "It's the right bag, but . . . someone has moved the body."

"Moved the body?" he asks. "Is that normal?"

"No," I breathe, already knowing that something sinister is at work here. I push the drawer back in, giving myself some space to walk by it before grabbing the next unit and quickly unlocking it. I drag the next drawer out, unzipping the body bag and peeking at the body inside before pushing it back and checking the next. "Never. We can't risk cross-contamination. It's a cardinal rule. Nobody in this morgue would ever make such a critical mistake. This was . . . shit."

One by one, I continue checking, getting frantic in my movements before pointing toward the other end of the refrigeration unit. "Start checking those ones."

Knight doesn't hesitate, moving down the other end of the long unit and swiftly opening each locker. He pulls out each drawer, mimicking my movements and carefully pulling down the zipper to check who lies beneath. "What did the victim look like?"

"Dark hair. Olive skin. Five o'clock shadow. He was tall. You'll be able to identify him by the carvings on his chest. You won't miss it."

Knight nods and keeps checking, and I watch with a sinking stomach as each drawer he checks is swiftly pushed back in and relocked. "Nothing down here," he tells me a minute later.

We meet in the middle, and as I close the final door, I glance up at Knight. The look in his eyes tells me he already knows what I'm about to say. "It's gone."

"How is that possible?"

I shake my head again, my heart pounding violently inside my chest. "It's not possible. Nobody would have touched it. They wouldn't risk messing with the chain of custody. The only person—"

My words fall away, fearing what we both already know.

"This asshole came back."

A terrified whimper escapes from my lips, and when Knight steps into me and pulls me into his strong arms, I fall into them as though that's exactly where I belong. "This situation is becoming too dangerous for you, Harper. Perhaps you need to—"

"No," I rush out, pushing back and meeting his haunted stare as panic pulses through my veins. "I know what you're going to say, but stepping back from my work is not an option. This is my career, and I've worked too hard to risk losing it now. Taking time off or messing with my schedule isn't an option. We just need to find this guy and lock his ass up."

"Finding him isn't going to happen overnight, Harper. This shit takes time, and now that the body has mysteriously vanished. I . . . I don't fucking know."

I press my hands to my temples and start pacing the length of the refrigeration unit. "What am I supposed to do?" I ask, unsure if he even has the answers I desperately need. "This is messing with my head. I've never felt fear the way I have the last couple of nights."

"I don't know what to tell you," he murmurs. "Common sense would tell you not to work night shift in a morgue until the threat is gone. But if stepping back from your work for a little while isn't an option, then you need to speak to your boss and let him know what's going on. You know you can always call me if you need anything, but you need to see if hospital security could have someone watching out for you."

I nod, knowing he's right, but I don't like my options.

The moment I tell Dr. McKullan, I can wave goodbye to my night shifts. As for asking hospital security to keep an eye out, that's not entirely a bad idea. I can't fault that. I'm going to have to talk to them anyway. It's one thing to not tell Dr. McKullan the finer details of last night's case, but now that a body has gone missing, a report needs to be filed, and an investigation will be opened.

Knight watches me for a moment, and there's no denying that he has something to say, only as he reaches for me and goes to open his mouth, a notification comes through on his phone. "Shit," he mutters, checking his messages. "I'm being called out to a scene. I've got to run, but I'm going to talk to Detective Gray and see what he knows."

"Okay," I say, nervously crossing my arms over my chest. I was brave before, but now that Knight is leaving me alone here for the night, that courage is slipping away. "Let me know if he has any leads."

Knight nods, and with that, he turns and stalks out the door, leaving me alone in the morgue with nothing but my own determination and sheer idiocy to keep me safe.

CHAPTER 12

HARPER-RAYN

Water spurts out of my mouth like a violent, messy fountain as I read Laith's latest text.

Big & Long Schlong #2: Fuck, tiger. I'm gonna turn that tight little meat pocket into a pretty glazed donut.

If there's one thing I will always appreciate about Laith Mitchell, it's that he knows how to keep me on my toes. I never know what I'm going to get with him, and I love that about him. There's nothing quite like a man who can keep a woman interested.

The only problem is, no matter how enticing his words are or just how well I know he's going to put it down, I don't think I could let him touch me, not without picturing my step-uncle in his place.

What the fuck is wrong with me? One taste of Knight Slater, and I'm ruined. But is it really that bad? Laith probably wouldn't care if I was thinking about another man while he was fucking me into oblivion. Knowing him, he'd probably get off on the idea and treat it like a challenge.

It's not as though we have a moral high ground that we fuck by. There's no contract stating I can't be interested in someone else, and we're sure as fuck not exclusive. We're free to do and please whoever we want. We just have mutual respect for one another and a good moral compass. You know, apart from when I'm daring him to disrespect me in the filthiest ways.

After putting my water bottle down and grabbing a few tissues from the holder on my desk, I quickly mop up my spilled water and hope like hell that I haven't ruined any of the notes I took on the two autopsies I've meticulously worked through tonight.

Once my desk is back in order, I grab my phone again as a stupid smile pulls across my lips, and I prepare myself to rip this fucker from limb to limb.

Harper-Rayn: Ever refer to my pussy as a meat pocket again, and the only meat pocket you'll be turning into a glazed donut is some crusty, old fleshlight that's been handed down from father to son for the past seventeen generations.

Big & Long Schlong #2: I just threw up in my mouth.

Harper-Rayn: I love that for you. But just remember, when you dig your crusty fleshlight out from under your bed, don't forget to peel off that old solidified jizz your granddaddy left behind. Oh, and while you're busy picking away at it, just know, it was your sweet old granny he was thinking about while he fucked that thing raw. I really hope he didn't throw out his back in the process.

Big & Long Schlong #2: I hate you.

Harper-Rayn: Meat pocket.

Big & Long Schlong #2: Okay. You've made your point. I'm a cunt.

Harper-Rayn: A big, loosey-goosey, floppy cunt who knows damn well that the only time you get to disrespect me is when you're putting it down.

Big & Long Schlong #2: How ever shall I make it up to you?

Harper-Rayn: I'm not totally against the idea of being turned into a glazed donut.

I hit send before slowly typing out another message, yet with every new letter, I feel dread sinking deep into my stomach. I don't understand it, and while my finger hovers over the send button, I can't bring myself to pull back.

I don't owe Knight anything. We're not together and we're sure as hell not about to become anything more than a random, crazy morning blow job. He's my step-uncle, for fuck's sake. I should be pushing this thing with Laith, not fantasizing about the way Knight's veins felt against my tongue.

I hit send.

Harper-Rayn: Tonight?

Fuck. Fuck. Fuck.

Why do I suddenly feel so sick?

This was a mistake.

Harper-Rayn: No. Shit. My bad. I'm sorry. I shouldn't be trying to lead you on right now. I know we always said we'd be honest about our situationships and there might be something with this other guy. It's probably nothing but—

I get halfway through typing out my rambled response when Laith's response finally comes through, and before I've even finished reading through his message, I quickly delete my text before I accidentally hit send.

Big & Long Schlong #2: Sorry, tiger. I've got court in the morning. You've got no fucking idea how badly I wish I could, especially after leaving you hanging the other night. I owe you big time.

Harper-Rayn: I'm heartbroken. My tears are rolling down my thighs as we speak.

Big & Long Schlong #2: Fuck. You're going to be the death of me.

Harper-Rayn: Looking forward to it ;)

Laughing to myself, I put my phone away and try to focus on the report in front of me, but my little freak-out over potentially seeing Laith tonight is screwing with my head.

Bottom line: There shouldn't have been a problem. There shouldn't have even been a second of hesitation on my part. Yeah, okay. Knight Slater is every kind of delicious I always knew he would be, but Laith is realistic. He's safe. He gives me more than what I need and knows where my boundaries are—most of the time. It's easy with him.

Knight would be nothing but chaos—but a sexy chaos. The kind of chaos that would leave my mother in tatters, and there's no denying the allure that brings.

What am I even doing weighing the options as though either one of them actually exists? A relationship with Knight isn't even something that's on the table. It was a onetime thing. He doesn't strike me as the kind of man who's about to get possessive. Though there's no denying how damn hot that would be. As for Laith, we set our boundaries in cement a long time ago. Neither of us wants anything more than just a casual hookup, so what the hell does it even matter?

Neither of these men poses any kind of threat to my immediate single status, and that's the way I want to keep it. I don't want to be tied down . . . Well, at least not metaphorically. I certainly wouldn't argue if Knight wanted to strap me to his bed and have me in every possible way.

Damn. Now there really are tears rolling down my thighs.

I need to get a grip—or another vibrator.

Standing from my file-covered desk, I stretch out my body and take three quick laps around the empty autopsy table, desperately needing to get my head in the zone. I can't be thinking about this shit while I'm working. It's unprofessional and not to mention disrespectful to the victims I'm trying to report on. If they knew the filthy thoughts that were rolling through my head while I was trying to work on their cases, they'd be rolling in their graves. Well, when they eventually get one, of course. I suppose they'd be rolling in their body bags instead. Though that doesn't have the same ring to it.

I shake out my hands and mentally bitch-slap myself before grabbing the back of my desk chair and preparing to sit back down. Only as I start to lower my body, I hear the familiar sound of an access card being denied on the other side of the morgue door.

My back stiffens as my heart lurches in my chest, and I find myself standing impossibly still. I've been on shift for close to seven hours. It's the longest I've lasted over my past few shifts, and after Laith's texts and my mental flip-flopping over a certain step-uncle's megacock, I had almost forgotten to be wary. Yet with one slight noise, I'm back to being the terrified train wreck who raced out of here just last night.

I'm an idiot. I got too comfortable.

The sound comes again and my stomach sinks. My hands immediately start to shake, and without a single doubt, I know it's *him*. The door handle rattles, and an almost silent yelp tears from the back of my throat.

Holy fucking shit.

My gaze darts around the room, trying to figure out a game plan, and when the door rattles even harder, I lose all train of thought. All I know is that I need to get away.

Fat tears spring from my eyes, and when the soft beep of the access card being denied again sounds through the morgue, I bound across the room. Shivers race down my spine, turning my blood to ice, and my stomach knots in agony.

My hands shake uncontrollably as I try to figure out a plan, but I'm at a loss. There's only one way in and one way out. I'm trapped.

As the person on the other side of the door shakes the handle again, I find myself backing up against the refrigeration unit, and without another thought, I whip around, finding the only possible solution. I grip the handle, and with shaky hands, I unlock each unit, trying to find an empty bay, and the moment I do, relief floods my veins.

Fear grasps me in a choke hold as I frantically scramble inside the refrigeration unit, pulling the door closed behind me. I can't lock it from the inside, but it's my only chance of survival. If this asshole makes it in here, my only hope is that he'll look around just long enough to assume I'm not here and leave. But that's ridiculous, right? My computer is still on, my notes spread across my desk, my phone and water bottle left behind. He'll know. A man so capable of dissecting a body and removing each organ for his own sick pleasure isn't a man who overlooks the small things. He'll know I'm here. The only question is, what will he do once he finds me?

Tears well in my eyes, pooling before falling over the side of my face, and I hastily blink them away before swiping at my wet cheeks.

The door outside the morgue continues to rattle, continues to beep with every denied swipe of the access card, and for a fleeting moment, I think that I might just get out of this unscathed. My chest heaves, the sound of my heavy, terrified breaths taunting me that I'll give myself away.

Why me? What does he want?

I'm just a normal girl trying to make it in the world. I'm nothing special, nobody to obsess over and watch through hacked cameras. There's nothing interesting about me, nothing to capture someone's attention. I'm just Harper-Rayn Madden, a nobody who's terrified of commitment.

The horrid smell of death lingers thick in the air, and I do what I can to drown it out: closing my eyes and focusing solely on the noises coming from outside as the beeping and rattling finally come to a stop. My back stiffens, and I listen closer, trying to track the sound of footsteps going up and down the hall, but I can't figure it out.

Is he gone? Am I safe?

Seconds turn into minutes, and just when I think that everything is going to be okay, the footsteps return, coming closer and closer until they're right outside the morgue door again.

"No. No. No. No. No."

My heart lurches for the tenth time in as many minutes, and I grip the edges of the steel roller table, my knuckles turning white. This can't be happening.

The chill of the refrigeration unit bites into my bones, and as I close my eyes and will my racing heart to calm, a soft beep sounds through the morgue. My stomach sinks with dread and not a moment later, the automatic lock releases and the door pushes open.

I hold my breath, terrified to make a single noise, and as tears roll freely down the side of my face into my hair, I listen as someone welcomes themselves into the morgue, leaving the door open behind them. The seconds seem to drag on, every footstep killing something deep within.

The steps are too heavy to be a woman, too purposeful to be the janitor, Vincent. It has to be the sick bastard who's been fucking with me night after night. I mean, shit. He's made a streak. Why fuck with that now? Three for three, right?

I should have listened to Knight. I should have spoken to Dr. McKullan and been moved off the night shift. But all that would achieve is having one of the other girls put straight into this position, and if anything happened to any of them because of my mystery black-rose stalker, I'd never forgive myself.

It has to be me. This shit started with me, and it's sure as fuck going to end with me. Knight is going to figure this out. He's going to find this asshole and put him away for the rest of his goddamn life, and if he happens to receive just a smidge of bodily harm in the process, I won't be mad about it.

I listen as the man makes his way around the morgue, moving from one side to the other, lingering at my desk, and I can't help but wonder what he's doing over there. Making a copy of my apartment keys? Giving a rim job to the mouthpiece of my water bottle like a sick fuck?

This isn't helping to keep me calm.

The cold starts to ache, and my body violently shivers as the footsteps move again, and just when I think it's over, just when I think he's about to make his way out of the morgue and leave me the hell alone, the footsteps grow closer.

I hear something dragging across the front of the refrigeration unit, inching closer and closer until it's right outside my locker. My heart pounds frantically, and I clench my eyes closed and hold my breath, trying to be as quiet as possible.

This is it. This is how I die.

I'm not ready. There's so much I haven't done, so much of the world I haven't seen. I haven't even had a chance to tell my mother to go screw herself. Well, I kind of did, but I only stabbed the knife through her back. I haven't had the chance to twist it. And as for Jonah, I know our relationship has been strained for all these years, but it would kill him if something were to happen to me. I need a chance to mend that relationship before life is brutally stolen from me.

The tears flow faster as I continue holding my breath, having to awkwardly let it go before trying to hold it again in my effort to remain quiet.

The handle of my locker rattles for just a second, and I curse myself for being so foolish. He has access to the morgue cameras, of course he knows exactly where I'm hiding. How could I be so stupid?

A whimper fights its way free, and just when I think it's all over, the familiar sound of the handle twisting into place fills the inside of the refrigeration unit. My back stiffens on the cold table, realizing I've been locked inside. My chest heaves with terror-filled gasps. I've never been someone who suffers from claustrophobia, but right now, I'm almost convinced that I do. It's one thing hiding in here and hoping he goes away, but it's a whole new fear realizing I've been locked inside for him to come back and play with anytime he sees fit.

Another whimper escapes from my lips, and I clamp my freezing fingers over my mouth as my body violently shakes from the cold. I have to get out of here, but with this monster still lurking just outside, I don't stand a chance.

Time slows, and I try to calm myself, saving every ounce of energy I possess, having no idea when I might need to call on it. I simply listen, biding my time as he continues to move around the morgue, and then finally everything goes quiet.

The cold, steel door slams, and the only noise I hear is the manic thumping of my pulse in my ears.

I slowly sit up, my body dangerously stiff from the cold. There's only so long somebody can survive in here. Don't get me wrong, there are ways someone could survive, but I don't intend to feast on the bodies around me. At least they're already dead, so if it came to it, I won't have to kill anyone just to eat. Silver linings, right?

The rest of my team would be due to come in for the day shift in just a few hours, so it's not exactly the end of the world. I can make it until then, but the truth of the matter is, I don't want to. I want to get the fuck out of here and run as far as I can. I was an idiot to stay here tonight. I should have listened to Knight, though I'll never tell him he was right. That just seems too easy.

He'd never get himself locked in the morgue refrigeration unit with a bunch of dead bodies. God, how little he'll think of me when he finds out this is how I spent my night. I suppose I don't have to tell him about this, but what benefit would that do for me? If I want this asshole caught and dealt with, then it's in my best interest to be as forthcoming as possible, even if it means certain humiliation.

I go to start checking the door when the table creaks under my movements and I come to a screeching halt. I know I heard the door shut, but that doesn't mean he was on the opposite side of it. Is he gone or is he waiting me out?

No. No. No. No.

Why is this happening to me?

I listen intently to the sounds from outside of the refrigeration unit, and after what I assume is ten long minutes of nothing but pure silence, I decide it's time to take the risk.

Crawling to the end of the table, I shove against the locked door and cringe at the feel of the freezing metal against my cold fingers. Trying to rattle it free is agonizing, and there's no use. It's not going to budge.

"Fuck," I mutter as more tears form in my eyes.

One by one, I move across the inside of the refrigeration unit, carefully climbing over sealed body bags and hoping like fuck I'm not disturbing the bodies inside. I try each door, cursing myself for being so meticulous in making sure the doors were locked.

I reach the locker on the very end—the one at the very top that we rarely use because of the lock that always gets jammed—and straddle the empty rolling table facing the inside of the door. If I were going to have any chance of breaking one of these locks to get out, this would be my best bet.

I pump my fingers to get the blood flowing before realizing I'm going to need something to jimmy the lock open. I feel the pocket of my scrub shirt for my trusty pen and instantly hate myself, finding my pocket empty. I took it out earlier while writing my notes and never put it back.

Fucking rookie error.

Feeling my pants pockets, I find the little metal piece off the top of my soda can, and while it isn't exactly ideal, it's better than nothing. Immediately getting to work, I pinch the little piece of aluminum between freezing fingers and do what I can to release the jammed lock from the inside.

I slip a few times, cutting my thumb and leaving a small pool of blood on the table between my thighs, but my desperation to get out of here doesn't hold me back. I keep prying the old lock, bending the soda tab in the process, but as the lock finally begins to give way, my relief keeps me going.

I don't dare stop, pushing my fingers past their limits, even when they're cut up and bruised. I clench my jaw, giving it everything I've got. Finally, the latch is freed, and I can shove the door open from within. I immediately stick my head out, breathing in the fresh air as tears streak down my face.

My gaze snaps around the room, and realizing that I was right, that the prick is actually gone, has me sagging with relief, and I'm free to take my time as I crouch down and roll the table out of the top locker.

My hands shake, and my teeth chatter from the cold, but the moment I can, I inch off the edge of the high table and drop straight to the floor. My feet ache from the impact of the linoleum beneath me, and my cold knees instantly give out, but I don't care. All that matters is that I'm free.

For now.

Then, not skipping my chance at freedom, I hastily close the locker behind me before hightailing it out of there, grabbing my shit on the way and not daring to look back.

CHAPTER 13

KNIGHT

Metal lockers clang through the room as the boys grab their shit so we can finally get out of here. It was a quick call out that we had under control in no time, but it was a rough one. It's always fucking rough when kids are involved, and while everyone came out alive and unharmed, it was a close one.

My team drove back to the station in silence, and once their heads finally hit their pillows, I have no doubt they'll remember the terror-filled screams of the children we just saved.

I blow out a heavy breath and grab my wallet, keys, and phone from my locker before quickly closing it up. Most of the guys will hang back and shower before leaving, especially those who just ended up working a double, but I prefer to shower in peace at home.

"I'm out," I tell the boys, closing my locker. "You guys good here?"

"Yeah, boss," Diesel says from beside me, eyeing Ace with venom as he walks by.

"Ease up on him," I warn Diesel. "It's not his fault you morons have the same taste in pussy."

Diesel clenches his jaw, and I have to laugh. Diesel, Ace, and I have been in this together since the beginning. We were all rookies together, been through the worst you could imagine, and because of it, they're my closest friends. They have always had my back, just as I've always had theirs. The only time we ever clash is when there's a woman involved.

These two assholes are permanently single. They like no-strings fucking, but where it all goes wrong is when it comes down to who they're going to take home. If they're out at a bar and there's a room full of women, they'll both want the same one. It's been an ongoing issue. Honestly, it would be easier if they buried the hatchet and just shared.

Diesel mutters to himself, and I can only imagine the insults flying from his lips, but I'm too fucking tired to care. Instead, I keep it moving, watching Ace with a close eye, knowing it wouldn't take much to set him off, and considering whatever bullshit that's going on between them seems fresh, I wouldn't put it past him to create a Diesel-shaped hole in the wall.

Ace takes his ass into the bathroom, and I let out a sigh of relief before leaving, knowing I won't have to worry about those assholes tonight. If they didn't break just then after the night we've had, then they'll be alright to keep their fists to themselves. But come tomorrow, there'll be one hell of a nasty sparring session.

My bets are on Diesel, though. He can be a rough motherfucker when he snaps. He's the silent brooding type, but fuck, when he lets go he really fucking lets go.

I make my way down to the parking garage, and just as I reach my truck, I see Detective Gray pulling in. After throwing my shit into the back of my truck, I wander down to Gray, waiting for him to park his car and get ready for his shift.

"Yo, Gray," I call out, approaching him as he's heading toward the station.

"Slater," he mutters, giving me a hard stare. "Still an asshole?"

"Try me and find out," I tell him, all too aware of the many times we've butted heads over the years. He's a pretentious prick, and I don't have time for that shit. Naturally, we've never gotten along, but when it comes to working a case, we've always been able to put our differences aside.

Gray rolls his eyes. "What can I do for you?"

"I just have a question about the homicide you picked up last night? John Doe. Stab wounds. You dropped him at the morgue."

Gray pulls away, his brows furrowed as he looks back at me, his head already shaking. "I picked up a case, but it wasn't a homicide.

I attended the scene of a house fire. An old Korean couple suffered from smoke inhalation. The husband passed at the scene, but I didn't accompany the body to the morgue."

"No shit," I murmur, wondering if in Harper's panic, she named the wrong detective. "Do you know anything about the John Doe?"

He shakes his head again. "Not sure. It's been a busy few days. I haven't heard anything," he tells me. "Let me get in, and I'll ask around."

"Thanks, man. Appreciate it."

He simply nods and takes off, ready to start his shift, and I make my way back to my truck, feeling as though I just took a massive step back. It's been killing me that I don't know anything about the asshole who's been tormenting Harper at work and leaving disfigured bodies in the form of fucked-up little messages. She doesn't deserve that shit, and soon enough, it's going to escalate, and when it does, I need to be there to make sure she doesn't fall. However, there's no denying how much easier it would be if she weren't such a stubborn little vixen and told her boss that she can't work the night shift anymore, but I understand her reasoning. That doesn't mean I agree with it.

After getting in my truck and backing out of my space, I hit the gas and start heading home, more than ready to call it a night. It's a little after four in the morning, and I'm fucking wrecked, but what's new? That's the risk you take when you work as a SWAT officer. It's just part of the package deal.

I get halfway home when I'm hit with an alert from my home security app, and I pull out my phone to check my cameras. Glancing between my phone and the road, I see a familiar car pulling up on the curb outside my home.

"What the fuck?" I mutter to myself, watching as Harper-Rayn bails out of her little Honda Civic, crossing her arms tightly over her chest, and rushes to my front door. She knocks furiously and hits the doorbell a few times, despite me clearly not being home.

"Fuck," I hear her say through the cameras.

She begins pacing in front of my door, and I press the gas harder, knowing she wouldn't show up out of the blue unless something happened. Keeping my eye on the road, I exit out of my security feed before opening the phone app, and within seconds, Harper's voice is coming through the Bluetooth in my truck.

"Knight, I—"

"What's wrong, Morticia? Are you okay?"

"Wait. How did you know I was—cameras. Right."

"Answer the question, Harper. What are you doing hovering outside my door looking like you just saw a fucking ghost? And why are you shivering like that? It's not even cold."

"I . . . I can't help it," she rushes out, her teeth chattering. "I can't get warm. I got locked in the refrigeration unit and—"

"The fuck?"

"This again?" she demands. "Are you ever going to let me finish a whole sentence before interrupting me? I mean, fuck. You're the one asking the questions, and still you won't let me get a word in."

"Harper," I warn.

"FUCK!" Harper lets out a breath, and the frustration in her tone is crystal clear, but despite the way she rants at me, it's clear I'm not the reason for her frustration.

"Start from the beginning, Morticia," I say in a soothing tone, knowing she'll give me exactly what I need. "I'm only a few minutes away."

Harper sniffles, and I listen as she takes a calming breath, but the chattering of her teeth doesn't dare stop. "Okay, so I was just doing my thing at work when I heard someone trying to get into the morgue. The access card wasn't working, and he must have tried at least twenty times, but the automatic lock was denying him entry. He was grabbing the handle and rattling the door. It freaked me out, and with no other way out of the morgue, I had no choice but to climb into the refrigeration unit."

"Shit, Morticia."

"You're telling me," she mutters. "I thought that was it, but then he came back with a new access card, and this one let him in. At first, he was just wandering around, and I kept thinking to be as quiet as possible so he wouldn't know where to find me, but then he walked straight over to the refrigeration unit, and as if knowing exactly which one I was in, he twisted the lock and trapped me there."

"He has been watching you through the cameras."

"My thoughts exactly," she says. "It's almost as though he was locking me in there so he could come back later and—well, I don't know what he wants with me."

I drag my hand down my face. I've been asking myself the same fucking question ever since she first told me about this asshole. "How'd you get out? Did someone come get you?"

"I wish. My phone was still on my desk, so I couldn't call for anyone, but I found one of those little aluminum soda tabs in my pocket so I could jimmy one of the locks free. It wasn't easy, though. My fingers were freezing by that point, and now I can't seem to get warm. And I know I could have just gone home, but—shit. I'm sorry. Maybe I shouldn't have come."

"Don't be stupid, Morticia. You know you're always welcome. I'll get you a key so you don't have to wait outside next time."

"That's not—thanks."

I turn the corner to my street, and as I see her Honda up ahead, a strange calm pulses through my veins. "I'm just pulling up," I tell her before ending the call.

I pull into my driveway a second later, and as I do, Harper lifts her head, locking her gaze on mine through my windshield. She looks fucking terrified, something that clearly didn't come through on my surveillance cameras.

After cutting the engine, I all but bail out of my truck and race across the pavement to get to her. She remains seated on the step leading up to my front porch, and as I get closer, she lifts her chin, following my every movement.

Harper presses her lips into a worrying line. "I'm sorr—"

I reach down and grip her arms, pulling her off the step and straight into my arms, holding her within my warmth. "If the next word out of your mouth is *sorry*, I'm going to bend you over my fucking knee and turn your ass red," I growl, unable to keep from noticing just how cold her skin is. She must be freezing. "Don't ever apologize for coming here. You understand me?"

Harper nods against my chest, and I can't help but breathe her in, but I regret it almost instantly. "Goddamn, Morticia. You smell like death."

"What did you expect? I spent almost an hour climbing over corpses currently decomposing and experiencing different stages of rigor mortis."

"That's . . . fucking disgusting."

Harper scoffs in agreement, and while I'd love to stand here until the sun rises and hold her in my arms, I need to get her inside.

Reluctantly releasing her, I step around her and unlock the door before leading the way inside. "Are you hungry?"

Harper shakes her head. "Just cold."

I nod. I could wrap her in a million blankets and tuck her into bed, but this chill seems bone deep, and the fastest way to conquer that is to shove her into a hot shower and have warm soup or hot chocolate waiting for her afterward.

"Come on," I say.

Harper follows me into my home, and I hastily lock up behind her before leading her into my bedroom and straight through to my en suite. I could have easily taken her to the main bathroom, but having her in my space like this just seems better. Plus, the main bathroom only has a bar of soap and maybe a spare toothbrush. I rarely have visitors, and when I do, they know if they want to shower, they're going to have to cater for themselves.

Okay, that makes me sound like a dick, but it is what it is. I don't like my home being too comfortable for others. I prefer my visitors to come for a good time, not a long time. Harper, though, she could stay here every day of forever, and I don't think I'd care one fucking bit.

As we enter the bathroom, I don't hesitate to reach into the shower and turn on the hot water. She stands awkwardly shivering in her scrubs, not knowing how this is going to play out. With her so cold, I don't care for the usual formalities. I simply grab the hem of her shirt and lift it over her head.

"Pants," I say.

Her lips press into a tight line and she begins to toe off her shoes, and as she does that, I lean back into the shower and make sure the water temperature is just right. When I turn back, she's standing before me in nothing but a black bra and matching thong, and while I'd give the whole fucking world to have her, I resist the animalistic needs pounding through me. But there's no denying it, she's fucking stunning. Agonizingly breathtaking, and it kills me that I can't have her as my own.

Harper moves to reach around herself to unhook her bra, and I start to make my escape, knowing damn well that if she were to even look at me right now, I'd be in that shower with her, claiming every inch of her creamy skin.

"There are clean towels on the shelf," I tell her, pointing them out as I stride back toward the door. "Everything else you'll need should already be in the shower."

"Thanks."

Stepping out of the en suite, I close the door behind me, giving her all the privacy she needs. Then as she showers, I make my way into the main bathroom and have a shower of my own before taking off to the kitchen and making her hot cocoa.

Once back in my room, I grab one of my shirts for Harper to wear to bed, knowing damn well that I'll probably never see it again—considering the last shirt I let her borrow is nowhere to be seen, but I don't care. I actually kind of like it.

Then, the moment I can, I shut off the light and climb into bed.

Harper showers for almost forty-five minutes, and my chest aches for her, realizing she's probably just standing under the hot stream of water, waiting for the chill to leave her bones. I stare at the darkened ceiling, convincing myself that she doesn't need me to stride in there like some misguided hero and check on her, when I hear the sound of the water shutting off.

I've never been more awake in my life.

There's silence from the bathroom, but the movements I do hear are done with intent and haste, telling me she's no longer a fucking ice cube. And when she opens the en suite door and steps out in nothing but a towel with the bathroom light shining behind her, she looks like a fucking angel.

Harper leans against the doorframe, staring at me in the dark, and I can't help but notice that she's a completely different person than the one who walked in there almost an hour ago.

"What do you need, Morticia?" I ask, my tone deepening as I see the hunger building in her eyes, my cock flinching to life beneath the sheets.

A soft smile pulls at the corner of her lips, and she pushes off the doorframe before striding right to the end of my bed, every step done with explicit intention, and when she steps right up onto the mattress, I almost come in my fucking pants.

Harper doesn't take her eyes off me as she continues toward me, walking across the mattress with the kind of confidence I love in a woman. "You think you can have me on my knees and just walk away?" she asks, her tone shining brighter than any star in the fucking sky. "I don't think so."

My brow arches, and I sit up a little straighter, my back against the headboard as she steps over my legs, placing a foot on either side of my thighs. "Is that so?"

"Damn straight," she tells me. "I don't do favors for grouchy men without expecting something in return, and unfortunately for you, I've come to collect."

"Baby, there ain't nothing unfortunate about that."

She steps even closer, her feet now on either side of my hips and her body so close I can smell her. "That's where you're wrong," she smirks. "There's no happy ending for you. Only me. If I had to suffer all day with the worst case of blue balls known to man, then so do you."

Harper pauses, her tongue rolling over her bottom lip. "Hear me, Knight Slater. You will not come. Nod if you understand me."

I don't fucking hesitate, nodding my head like an obedient little yes-man.

Morticia grins, and it blows me the fuck away. "Good boy," she purrs.

Fuck me. This woman is going to kill me.

"Then what are you waiting for? Take it," she demands. "Give me what I want."

I dive in like it's Christmas fucking morning, reaching up and gripping the towel before ripping it off her slender body. Her tits are perfect, full, and perky, and when the slightest gleam of light sparkles beside her nipple, I realize it's a piercing.

I lean forward, desperate to get those sweet nipples in my mouth, to tease and torment her with my tongue and watch her squirm beneath my touch, but that's going to have to wait. Right now, I need to taste her.

Gripping her thigh, I lift it over my shoulder and she has no choice but to knot her fingers into my hair to maintain her balance, and as I lock my hand around her back and take a firm hold of her ass, I lean in further and inhale her sweet scent.

"Oh God," she groans, but before the words are even out of her mouth, I close my lips over her waiting cunt.

She's fucking soaking for me, and I don't doubt that she's been thinking about this since the moment she got into the shower. Maybe this right here is exactly why she took so long, desperately trying to work up the courage to come out here and demand what she wants.

I lap her up as though I'll never get to taste her again, and the moment my tongue flicks over her clit, her knees threaten to give out. I hold her up, my free hand working up her toned waist before cupping her breast. She groans and presses her hand over mine, silently asking for more, and I don't hesitate, squeezing firmer before curling my thumb over her pebbled nipple.

My tongue works her cunt, circling her greedy clit as her hips rock against my face, and as I nip and suck, I release my hold on her ass and bring my fingers to her entrance. I slowly push them inside, and as she tightens her hold in my hair and sucks in an audible gasp, I keep going, splitting my fingers deep within her and working the walls of her tight pussy.

She's fucking delicious.

"Fuck, Knight!" she cries out when my fingers curve inside her. "Yes. Right there!"

I grin against her sweet cunt and give her exactly what she needs, rolling my fingers over her G-spot until her legs shake.

Harper throws her head back, and her long, wet hair cascades down her spine, and fuck, what I wouldn't give to wrap it around my wrist and fuck her blind. But I'm nothing if not a gentleman, and after letting me fuck her sweet mouth, she's deserving of everything I've got, even if it means spending what little is left of my night with agonizing blue balls.

I don't let up, eating her pussy like a fucking buffet. Nipping. Sucking. Squeezing. Licking. And as I learn her body and just how she likes it, I give her even more.

She starts to pant, pulling my hair as though she physically can't keep herself up. "God, I'm gonna come," she cries out, her panting getting heavier as I pinch her nipple, making her body tremble. "Fuck!"

My fingers work her deeper, massaging her walls as she clenches around me, on the fucking edge. My tongue circles her clit, and when she cries out one last time, she comes for me like the good little vixen she is.

Her pussy shatters, wildly convulsing around my fingers as her body spasms. "Yes. Knight," she groans, barely able to keep upright as my cock painfully flinches, so fucking desperate for a release, but I don't dare. I'm playing by Harper's rules tonight, and if she demands that I go to bed with blue balls, then that's exactly what I'll do.

I grip her waist, holding her still as I keep working her body, draining every last ounce of pleasure out of her and claiming it as my own. My tongue never stops flicking her clit, never stops circling as my fingers continue massaging her walls, tormenting her G-spot, and the more intense her orgasm becomes, the more her body becomes a slave to my touch. Her hips jolt as her body spasms, and fuck, she's so damn delicious.

She reaches her high, but I don't stop until her knees physically give out. She collapses into an exhausted heap on my lap with her leg still hooked over my shoulder. Harper leans back on her palm, desperately trying to catch her breath as those wild, satiated eyes remain locked on mine.

I make a show of licking my lips before simply waiting. The ball is in her court tonight. This was her game, she's calling the shots. But come morning, my debt will officially be paid, and her little rules will no longer matter.

She relaxes for just a moment before dropping her gaze to her hand and noticing a few stray strands of my hair on her palm. I almost laugh. She really pulled my hair tight enough to pull some of it out, but fuck, I'd let this woman scalp me for just the chance at doing that all over again.

Harper smirks before collecting the stray hairs off and casually handing them back to me while making a point of shifting around on my lap, feeling the hardness of my cock beneath her firm ass. "These belong to you."

I nod before watching as she casually scootches to the end of my bed and gets to her feet as though her legs aren't still trembling. Then without another word, she collects my shirt off the end of my bed, shrugs it on, and then sashays her ass right out the door.

"Oh, Knight?" she says, pausing at the door and glancing back.

I arch a brow, knowing damn well that whatever's about to come out of her mouth is about to destroy me. "Even think about stroking that mouthwatering cock tonight, and I'll make it my personal mission to make sure you never get to taste my sweet little cunt ever again."

I groan. Just the thought of my lips between those thighs makes my cock ache with need. "You're killing me, doll."

Harper's gaze darkens with a lethal desire before hitting me with the most dazzling smile I've ever seen. "Sweet dreams, *Uncle Knight*," she coos before breaking into a wicked laugh and sailing her perfect ass down the hall to my spare bedroom. All while leaving me a fucking mess. My cock is harder than it's ever been with no way of relieving the ache, and my head is spinning from the torturous way she called me Uncle.

There's no fucking doubt about it. Harper-Rayn Madden dominated this round. But come tomorrow, the ball is back in my court, and I have every fucking intention of making it count.

CHAPTER 14

HARPER-RAYN

My thighs shake at just the memory of Knight's tongue circling my clit, and as I stand at his breakfast bar, sipping my coffee, I can't believe I actually did that. I can be more than bold when asking for what I want, but walking across his bed and demanding he eat my pussy while ignoring the raging hard-on in his pants was insane.

I fucking loved it.

It was incredible, and even now, hours later, my eyes are still rolling in the back of my head, and yet I can't help but feel embarrassed about it. It was too much. I was too forward, too bold, and now my step-uncle knows exactly how I taste, how I sound when I come, just how desperate I am when I'm on the edge. But do I regret it? Not for one damn second.

His mouth on my body was intoxicating, so much more than I thought it was going to be, and damn it, I need more. I will never not need more from that man, but damn it. I shouldn't want him. It's profoundly wrong.

Off. Limits.

I need Izzy to tattoo the words across my forehead, and maybe then I'll remember not to let cocky, broody SWAT officers take advantage of me. Though truth be told, I'm the one who took advantage of him last night, but I'm not sure he'd see it the same way. He was far too eager to even consider the idea that I was taking advantage. He was hungry for it. Starved. And the look in his eyes when he closed his mouth over my pussy and tasted me for the first time . . . Fuck me.

I will never recover from this. Not in a million years.

I continue sipping my coffee when I hear Knight step out of his bedroom and make his way up the hall. My cheeks instantly blaze, and as I lean against the breakfast bar, I tip my head forward, letting my hair cascade over my shoulder and cover my face.

Shit. Shit. Shit.

I had originally planned to grab my things and make a break for it, but a split-second decision had me waiting around for him, and now that he's only a few steps away, I've never wanted to run so fast in my life.

This is humiliating. Is he going to bring up last night? Put me in my place for calling him a good boy and having my wicked way with him?

What was I thinking?

The tattooed beast of a man strides down the hallway, and I risk lifting my head and glancing at him. He's shirtless, wearing nothing but a pair of tactical pants. The fly is done up, but the button is popped at the top. And goddamn. I've never seen anything so delicious in my whole twenty-eight years.

Every inch of his tattooed body is flawless, and the evident bulge in the front of his black pants tells me he's out for revenge.

A grin pulls at the corner of my lips, and I studiously stare at the countertop as though it's suddenly the most interesting thing in the room. Knowing that he's most likely spent the night thinking about fucking me has pride swelling in my chest, and I make a show of sipping my coffee, acting as though his very presence isn't sending me spiraling with the filthiest hunger.

"Morticia," he rumbles, stepping right in behind me, his big body instantly crowding me.

"Knight," I respond, closing my eyes and breathing him in as I slide the second coffee mug aside, letting him know that it's his if he wants it.

He leans into me, his big, muscled arm curling around me as he reaches for the mug, only he bypasses it and goes straight for mine, picking it up and drinking every last drop before placing it back on the counter, far away from my reach.

I swallow over the nervous lump forming in my throat and remain silent, having no clue how this is about to play out, but when he drops his hands to the counter on either side of my waist, caging me in, I can't help myself. "Is there something you need?" I purr, refusing to meet his stare.

Knight scoffs before dipping his head and trailing his nose up the length of my neck, inhaling my scent as he presses his large body against mine. "Your game is over, Morticia. Favor repaid," he says, his tone so thick with desire it's almost hard to make out the words past the rapid thrumming of my pulse in my ears. "And now you think you get to walk around my house in my shirt, wearing no fucking panties and not have me fuck you?"

I suck in a breath.

I can practically hear the smirk in his tone. "You don't get to leave me craving your sweet little cunt all night and not expect me to give you exactly what you've really been wanting all these years."

I scoff, playing it up, despite knowing how right he really is. "Really now?" I murmur, glancing back over my shoulder and meeting his darkened stare, his eyes penetrating right through to my greedy soul. "You sure about that?"

His stare seems to smolder, and within the blink of an eye, his hands drop from the counter and take my waist before lifting me up onto the barstool and placing me on my knees, putting me at the perfect height, lining my cunt up with that thick, beautiful cock of his.

I suck in a gasp, and as he pushes me forward, making me lean onto the breakfast bar, he lifts my shirt up over my naked ass, exposing me in the most erotic way. I don't dare stop him, and when he reaches down between us and his fingers suddenly swipe through my wetness, a shiver sails down my spine, quickly spreading through my body.

"Oh, I'm sure. You're soaked for me, pretty girl. You've been thinking about this all fucking night," he murmurs, that rich confidence speaking right to my soul. "Tell me, just how hard did you have to fuck yourself with your fingers last night just to curb the hunger?"

Only three times, but I'm sure as hell not about to tell him that. "You wish."

Knight laughs as his fingers return to my cunt, slowly pushing inside me, curving just right and rolling over my G-spot, making my body tremble. "I heard you, Morticia. Heard the way you caught your breath when you were close, heard the subtle groans of frustration knowing it would never be as good as it is with me." His lips brush over my skin, sending a furious wave of goose bumps scattering across my sensitive skin. "Do you know how fucking hard it was not to burst in there and take you, to resist the allure of your sweet little cunt, to not even fuck my hand?"

My hips rock back and forth, grinding over his hand as his fingers torment me in the most consuming way. "How hard?"

"It was fucking torture."

"You should have thought about that when you left me on my knees, desperate for you."

Knight laughs. "Oh no, doll. This isn't my problem. This one is all yours, because unlike you, I don't mind spending my night rock hard, listening to the way you fuck yourself, because all it does is work me up, and at some point, all that pent-up frustration needs to be released."

"And let me guess," I purr. "You're going to release it on me?"

"Every last bit of it."

I groan, anticipating what he has in store for me, and as his fingers split inside me, my knees almost give out on the barstool. His gaze burns over my skin like lasers as he grabs my ass and spreads me open.

"Mmmm, so fucking beautiful," he rumbles, trailing his fingers through my pussy and inching higher. "Has anybody ever claimed your ass?"

I nod. "Mm-hmm, but no one as big as you," I tell him. "You'll tear me in half. Destroy me."

"Do you like it?" His thumb skims the area in question, offering a little pressure.

"Most of the time," I tell him, grinding against his hand.

"Good girl," he says as I hear the distinct sound of his zipper releasing. "You're off the hook for today, but don't think I'll forget, doll. I *will* claim your ass, but when I do, you'll be begging for it."

I press back against his thumb, loving the pressure as his fingers massage the walls of my pussy. "Mmmm, so bossy today."

Knight scoffs before gently removing his fingers from deep within me, making me yearn for more, instantly feeling the loss. "Next time you want to play the role of dom, you better make sure you're truly ready to play," he tells me before lifting his glistening fingers to my lips. "Suck them clean, Morticia. Taste how fucking sweet you are."

Oh God. This man.

My mouth falls open without hesitation, and as he pushes his thick fingers inside, I roll my tongue over them, sucking them clean. "Just like that," he purrs as I feel him release his thick cock from the confines of his pants behind me. "Condom?"

"God, no. Don't ruin a good thing," I breathe. "I'm on birth control."

Knight groans, and while I don't exactly know him intimately or know how many sexual partners he's had, I trust him implicitly. Without a doubt, he would never touch me if there was even a chance he wasn't clean.

He grunts behind me, and I hear the soft sounds of his fist pumping up and down his cock, and fuck, I've never been so jealous. I want every ounce of his pleasure.

"Take me, Knight."

In one swift move, Knight fists my hair, wraps it around his wrist, and yanks my head back, forcing my spine to curve and my hips to thrust toward him. I'm silently begging for him to have his wicked way with me, and he understands precisely what I want.

"So fucking beautiful," he growls as my pussy clenches. I'm absolutely drenched for him. He closes the small gap between us, and when I feel his bulbous tip against my clit, slowly dragging through my wetness, my body trembles.

"Don't make me wait."

"Patience, Morticia. I'll give you what you need, but I intend to take my fucking time as I devour every goddamn inch of you."

Fuck yes.

His cock flinches against my clit, and my eyes roll as he slowly drags back toward my entrance. My body shakes with anticipation as it all becomes too much. He keeps me on the edge, teasing and tormenting me with a silent promise of just how thoroughly he's about to fuck me, and when I finally feel his tip at my entrance, a sharp gasp escapes my lips.

"Inch by fucking inch, Morticia," he tells me, slowly pushing inside, taking me one inch at a time.

"More," I pant, desperately trying to push back against him, to impale myself on that thick cock, but he holds me too tight, having complete control to destroy me at his leisurely pleasure.

"Ready for two?"

"Please."

He inches in more, taking me slightly deeper, and though he's barely inside me, I already feel myself beginning to stretch around him. My body trembles, and I realize if he takes it any slower, I'm bound to break. "God, Knight. Now."

His palm cracks against my ass, and I suck in a loud gasp, my pussy tingling as wave after wave of undiluted pleasure rocks through my body. "What did I tell you about being patient?"

Holy hell. I've never felt so alive in my life, but when he gives me a third inch my pussy spasms around him, stretching to accommodate his sheer size. "Fuck!" I cry, and when he gives me a fourth and then a fifth, my thighs begin to shake.

Knight groans. "How much more can you take?"

"All of it," I breathe.

"Six?"

"Yes."

He inches deeper, and when his cock flinches inside me, it fucking destroys me. My chest heaves against the counter of his breakfast bar, and I reach forward, gripping the edge and white-knuckling it as he gives me a seventh inch.

"Oh God," I groan.

He rocks back a little bit, giving me just a moment of respite before he pushes back in, giving me eight and then nine, his fingers tightening on my ass. "Fuck, baby. You take me so well," he murmurs. "Do you have any idea how fucking good you look taking my cock?"

My only response is to clench my walls around him and his soft gasp is more than enough for me.

"Give it all to me," I beg, knowing he hasn't bottomed out yet, but I'm not about to hold back, not from this beast of a man. I want it all. I want to feel how far he can stretch me, how deep he can take me.

"You sure?"

"Please."

Knight groans and pulls back on my hair, and as my pussy quakes around him, he finally relents, slamming the rest of the way inside me, and fuck, he must have a good ten inches on him. "Yes," I groan, feeling as he bottoms out, offering up everything he's got as my walls work to stretch around him. "I need you to move."

His hand shifts from my ass to my hip, gripping tightly. The sharp sting of his fingers biting into my skin is the only sign of his desperation. "I . . . fuck, Morticia. You're going to ruin me."

"Not before you ruin me. Now move."

His hand comes down in another sharp spank on my ass, a warning for my impatience, and if this is what I get for being a little impatient, I can't wait to see what's in store for me when he realizes I also have an attitude.

Knight doesn't wait to reprimand me, just simply drags his hips back, letting that thick, veiny cock slide right out and hover at my entrance. As I release the edge of the counter and slip my hand down between my thighs, slowly rolling circles over my needy clit, he slams back inside me.

"Oh, fuck!" I cry.

He sucks in a sharp breath through his clenched teeth, panting just as heavily as I am. My walls shatter around him, and just when I think I can't take it, he enters beast mode and really starts to fuck me. His hips roll, taking me at every angle as I work my clit, my lazy, slow circles morphing into tight, frantic rubbing.

It's incredible, and it doesn't take long before I feel that familiar coil tightening deep inside me, threatening to explode. With every delicious thrust, my body comes alive, taking me right to the edge and driving me wild. He pushes me to my limits, and as his body rolls, his hips thrust, and his fingers dig into my hip, my world crumbles.

I've never felt anything more thrilling, more intense.

I need it. Need everything he has.

He fills me to the brim, claiming me, ruining me, and as my fingers roll over my sensitive clit, I can't hold on to it any longer. I come hard, my hand gripping his at my hip as my body shatters like glass, imploding into a million ruined pieces.

"Just like that," he tells me, as if coaxing every bit of my orgasm out of me. "Show me how tight that little cunt can squeeze me."

And damn it, I do.

My pussy contracts, wildly spasming around his thick cock as he keeps thrusting, taking me higher than I've ever been before and putting last night's fiery orgasm to instant shame. Knight groans, his fingers so tight on my hip as my eyelids flutter. My orgasm crashes through my body like a tsunami, pulsing through my veins, the intensity too much to bear.

My fingers ball into tight fists as I cry out, the smell of raw, undiluted pleasure thick in the air, and just like that, it's not oxygen I need to breathe, it's him. Only him.

"Fuck, Knight," I curse, gritting my teeth as the intensity builds inside my core.

"Hold on to it, baby," he grunts, his jaw clenched tight.

"Fuck. Fuck. Fuck."

It's too much as I finally hit my high and start crashing down the other side. He lifts me off the barstool and whips me around, planting my ass on the edge of the counter before slamming back into me.

Knight lifts my thighs, spreading them as far as they'll go while refusing to skip a beat. His precise thrusts take me even deeper, but the animalistic need in his dark eyes and the way his body rolls with each powerful thrust instantly has that coil tightening once again.

I lean back, balancing myself on one palm as my other hand grips his massive shoulder, my nails digging into his warm skin.

He pants, looking down between us at the way he slams into my pussy, his thick cock glistening with my wetness, and damn it, I look down too. We're perfect together, and when he grabs my hips and inches me right to the edge of the counter, he takes me at a whole new angle, thrusting impossibly deeper.

I gasp as his cock massages me from within, and when he drops his thumb to my clit, I throw my head back, the instant pleasure blowing me the fuck away. "Oh God," I groan, my chest heaving as our bodies grow sweaty.

Knight grips my chin with his other hand, lifting it until those dark eyes are locked on mine, and as he leans in, his lips only a breath away, the tension between us grows to an all-time high, the intensity in his eyes holding me captive.

"Harper," he moans, and just the sound of my name on his lips sends me spiraling.

"Knight, I—"

"Let go," he murmurs, a deep ache in his tone. He needs me to come with him, and fuck, there'll be no argument from me.

His thumb circles my clit, the pressure better than I could have ever achieved on my own, and as those wicked hips roll and thrust deep into me one more time, the coil springs, and my orgasm tears through me, my walls wildly convulsing around him.

He lets out a pained groan, his fingers tightening on my jaw, and not a moment later, he releases, reaching his explosive climax and emptying himself, hot spurts of cum shooting deep inside me and making me feel like a fucking goddess.

"Holy shit," I breathe as we both come down from our high, the tension still so thick between us.

He drops his lips to my forehead in a gentle kiss as his fingers fall away from my chin and clit, giving me just a moment to find myself. He doesn't pull out of me, leaving himself buried inside me as he braces his hands on the counter beside my thighs, caging me in.

My legs relax, locking around his hips and holding him there as I lift my gaze to meet his heavy stare. "Where the hell did that come from?"

Knight laughs. "That's what a night of blue balls will do to a man."

A stupid smirk stretches across my lips when he reaches for the front of my shirt and slowly pulls it up over my head, revealing my naked body beneath. We remain in silence, and when his fingers drop to my body, I let him explore, trailing them across my skin and watching as a wave of goose bumps begins to rise.

My eyes flutter, enjoying his touch more than I should. "Mmmm . . . This is dangerous," I murmur as those fingers brush over the curve of my breast before circling my nipple and trailing over the small piercing. "We can't keep doing this."

The corners of his lips pull into a wicked grin, and as his gaze collides with mine, I realize I'm in deep. "Do you want me to stop?"

I groan. He knows damn well I don't want him to stop. His touch is like the oxygen I need to breathe, pumping life right into my veins. "Don't you dare."

Knight laughs before a seriousness washes over him, but he thankfully doesn't stop touching me. "I know what you're saying," he tells me as his other hand falls to my center, his fingers lazily circling my clit. "As you so kindly reminded me last night, I'm your uncle."

"Step-uncle."

He grins again. "We've crossed a line, Morticia. Something we can't ever go back from. I'm never not going to know how fucking sweet you taste or how well you take me." Then as if to prove a point, his cock flinches inside me, and I groan, tipping my head back as the pleasure swells inside me. "I'm not going back. I'm never going to walk into a room where you are and not have you."

"It's wrong," I tell him. "We're family. My mother is going to murder me when she finds out, and your brother—"

"Let me worry about Elias," he says. "And as for your mother. What she doesn't know can't hurt her."

"So you're saying?"

"That I don't fucking care what society tells me is right and wrong, and considering how easily you let me bend you over my fucking counter, I doubt that you care either," he tells me. "I'm not looking to put a ring on your finger, Harper, but I will fuck you every chance I get."

"No strings attached?" I confirm. "I don't do boyfriends or exclusivity. Men are too overly emotional for that shit."

"Speak for yourself," he mutters. "But are you looking to fuck someone else?"

An image of Laith flashes in my mind, but as his fingers slowly work over my clit, the image fades away as though it were never there to begin with. "Is that going to be a problem? You're not the jealous type, are you?"

Knight scoffs. "Not in the slightest, but it'll be a fucking problem if I'm balls deep and you scream out some other man's name."

I laugh. "Interesting. What are you gonna do? Spank me again? Or do you have a few more tricks in your arsenal? Because you should know that I don't shy away when things get rough. It excites me."

Knight groans and presses just a little harder against my clit before gently pinching. "Calm down, pretty girl. I'm calling the shots here."

"We'll see about that," I tell him, tightening my leg around him and pulling him closer. "Truth be told, there is someone else. Laith Mitchell. It's nothing serious, we just . . . fuck when the need strikes. He's not interested in me as anything more than a friend, and that feeling is mutual. You have nothing to worry about. But as for you and me, this can never be anything more than sex. It's too . . . muddy. Lines have already been crossed. We can't make it any worse."

Knight nods, and I bite my lip. "What is it, Morticia?"

"I mean, this is going to sound pretty shitty of me, and while I appreciate that you're not a jealous person and don't care, I can't really say the same about me. I am a jealous person. I'm a downright jealous bitch, so if there is another woman, I can try to be okay with it, but you should know that every time you're not buried inside me, I will automatically assume that you're buried in her. That's my problem, though. I don't want exclusivity, so I'll deal with it if I have to."

He laughs. "And here you are trying to tell me that men are the ones who are overly emotional."

"Shut up."

Knight grins and slowly pulls out of me before dropping straight to his knees between my thighs, his tongue slowly rolling over my clit and making me groan. He stops and looks up at me. "For the record, there is nobody else. I don't plan on that changing, but if it does, I'll be sure to let you know."

His mouth closes over my clit, and I can't physically respond. All I can do is close my eyes and enjoy the ride as his tongue draws lazy circles over the most sensitive part of my body. I tip my head back as the pleasure pulses through my veins.

I'm just about to come for the third time this morning when his phone rings and as he works my clit, he digs into his pocket and pulls out his phone, hitting accept and holding it to his ear. "What?" he mutters, pulling back just an inch to speak before diving right back in.

He doesn't stop tormenting me with his skilled tongue as he listens to whoever's on the other end before pulling back again. "Fuck. Be there in ten minutes."

He ends the call, and just when I think he's about to bail on me, he tosses his phone on the counter, scoops his arms under my thighs, and drags me even closer before diving right in. "You've got thirty seconds," he warns me.

I grin. "Challenge accepted."

CHAPTER 15

KNIGHT

As I scoop Harper off the counter, her legs lock around my waist, and I carry her down my hallway as my tongue rolls over my bottom lip, savoring her taste. Her body slumps against mine, and I hold her up, keeping her safe in my arms.

She's fucking wrecked after coming three times on my kitchen counter, and despite barely being able to hold herself together, I feel an overwhelming sense of pride booming through my chest. Watching her come apart for me, learning her body, and feeling the way she squirmed under my fingers was incredible, and now I'm fucking pissed that I'm being called in to work.

If I could stay here and make her come all day, I would, but instead, I have to deal with a hostage situation at the mall. But the moment I can, I'll be right back here, buried inside her again.

Was it a little premature to declare that I have no intention of walking away from this? Probably, but I can't fathom the idea of never touching her again, never tasting her, never feeling the way she takes me inch by fucking inch. That doesn't mean I'm ready to settle down, put a ring on her finger, and shoot a few babies into her guts. Harper has made it more than clear that's not what she wants, and considering she's my step-niece, I think that's a good call.

There was a firm line drawn, but after the past few days, I can see the line fading away in the distance. We bounded right over it and gave it the middle finger on the way past. Harper's not wrong, though; this is a slippery slope. One wrong move could have this crumbling around us, and yet I can't seem to care.

I've held back for years out of respect for her mother and my brother's marriage, but I suddenly don't give a shit. Elias will have more than enough to say about it when the other shoe finally drops, but until then, I have every intention of fucking this girl into oblivion. Though one thing is for sure, the moment I can, I'll be figuring out who the other asshole is she's fucking and running a background check. I know she's not my girl, and it's not my place to put my nose where it doesn't belong, but after the shit that's been going down at the morgue, I can't be too careful.

Reaching my room, I toss Harper down onto my bed, and she immediately grabs a pillow and squishes it to her face. She inhales deeply and groans with pure bliss. "Hmmmmm, smells just like you."

A stupid-as-fuck grin pulls across my face, breaking my carefully placed façade, and I turn my back before stepping into my closet and searching for clothes. She'll never know how fucking happy it makes me to see her naked and comfortable in my bed, breathing me in as though she already misses me.

What the hell is wrong with me? Keeping this strictly about sex is going to be a challenge when I want nothing more than to make her fall in love with me—to make her mine. "What else were you expecting?" I mutter, clearing my throat and trying to remember that I'm a fucking SWAT officer at the top of my game, not some lovesick puppy desperately fawning all over a woman who only wants him for his cock.

Harper scoffs and shakes her head as I find a black shirt and pull it on. "What a shame," she says with a teasing sigh. "I like you better naked."

"You'll like me any fucking way I give me to you."

"Ooof, and the bossy asshat makes a return."

I roll my eyes and continue getting ready, all too aware of the clock I'm on. I have all of eight minutes to get my ass out the door and to the station. I'll be cutting it close, but I'll still make it with a minute to spare. "What's the deal with those nipple piercings?" I ask, finding my tactical belt and clipping it into position as her gaze rakes over me with desire, making it damn clear that she doesn't only prefer me naked. She likes a man in uniform, and right now, she's practically frothing at the mouth.

"Ahhh, what about them?" she responds, an edge to her tone as she watches me through a narrowed gaze.

"Aren't you worried that you're going to need a defib machine one day and end up frying your nipples off?"

Her jaw drops, momentarily stuck for words. "I, uhhh . . . I thought you were going to say that you weren't into them."

"Oh, baby," I groan, glancing at her on my bed again, her tits more than on display. "I've never been more into anything in my life. Won't lie, it was a nice surprise. I assumed a lot of things about you, but not that. I like it."

She bites down on her bottom lip, her cheeks flushing with the sweetest shade of red. "Good, because I don't have any intention of getting rid of them anytime soon. But it makes me wonder, would it really fry my nipples if I got zapped?"

A laugh tears from the back of my throat. "No, if the pads are placed correctly, there won't be an issue. Your nipples will remain intact and unfried."

"And if they're not placed properly?"

I shrug. "Why don't I go get my defib machine so we can find out?"

The spare pillow on my bed comes hurtling toward me. "You're an asshole."

I can't help but laugh as I effortlessly dodge the flying pillow, though it's not hard. Her aim is fucking terrible. "Metal is an electric conductor. If the pad is placed incorrectly, you run the risk of the shock taking a shortcut through your piercing instead of being delivered to the heart as intended, but fear not. While you might not be revived, your nipples will be safe."

Harper stares at me. "That's comforting."

"Thought it might be," I murmur, checking that I have everything I need. "Are you heading into work tonight?"

She shakes her head. "I'm not on the schedule, but I'm thinking about heading in for a few hours during the day to catch up on the things I couldn't get done while I was too busy running out of there."

I let out a breath, realizing how sick I am over the idea of her going back into that morgue alone. "Okay, good," I say, striding up to her on my bed. I lean down and curl my hand around her throat, gently squeezing as she tips her head to meet my stare. "I have to go. You're welcome to stay here as long as you want, but I'll be working tonight. Won't be home until sometime tomorrow."

"Okay. I might stay and hack your computer to figure out what kind of weird kinky porn you watch, and then I'll probably head off."

I laugh. "Good luck with your search," I tell her. "Make sure you lock up behind you."

With that, I drop a kiss to her temple before walking out, feeling a pang of regret deep in my gut at having to walk away from her, especially while she's naked in my bed. What kind of red-blooded man walks away from that?

As I turn out of my bedroom, I glance back for just a moment, watching as she stares after me with a dreamy haze in her soft green eyes. She pulls my pillow tight to her chest, and fuck me, I could wake up to that every day of the rest of my life and never get bored.

This woman is going to ruin me, and I think I might just let her.

I arrive at the station just in time, and after a quick debrief, my team is locked and loaded, roaring toward the mall. There's an active hostage situation, and from what little information we've been able to gather, it started as a domestic dispute between a young couple, which quickly escalated when the store clerk got involved.

Our understanding is that the store has been closed, the roller doors pulled down with multiple shoppers trapped inside. The rest of the mall should have been successfully evacuated by now, leaving us the space we need to get in and get the job done.

Depending on the scene when we get there and any new information that may arise, the plan is to split into three teams. Diesel, Ace, and I are heading Teams A, B, and C. My team will be responsible for infiltrating the store, most likely through the ventilation system in the ceiling above the store, dropping in through the changing rooms, and then taking out the suspect.

Diesel's team will be responsible for freeing hostages, and after Ace pulled the short straw after pissing off Diesel yesterday, his team will be acting as backup for Teams A and B. His team will also be in charge of any immediate medical requirements and surveillance.

While in transit, the entire convoy discusses the plan of attack by radio, making sure we're all on the same page. Then, after arriving at the scene and being briefed on all updates, we're given the mall blueprints from security and the on-scene officers.

Feeling ready to take this bastard down, my team moves with precision, each one of them knowing their role and exactly what's expected. They've never let me down and are constantly exceeding those high expectations. Their training is like no other, pushing the boundaries of what should be possible.

They're fucking machines and nothing less than my brothers and sisters. Each one of them has saved my ass at some point or another, just as I've done the same for them, but that's how a well-oiled team is supposed to operate, especially in SWAT. There's no room for mistakes.

My team rushes forward in a single-file line, a hand on the shoulder of the officer in front, heading straight for our position as Team B veers to the left, moving toward the front of the store. Team C follows behind, ready to create a perimeter and jump in where needed.

Reaching our position, Anders and Hunter create a brace, and I waste no time stepping up onto their forearms. They lift me toward the ceiling of the mall, and I remove the large ceiling plate that conceals the ventilation system, sliding it aside before gripping the ledge and hauling myself up.

One by one, my team follows until the five of us are situated in the ceiling, crawling through the dusty cavity until we have a bird's-eye view into the store below, getting a look at our suspect and the well-being of the hostages for the first time.

A young man, maybe in his early twenties, paces the store, and it's clear by the new addition of Diesel's team hovering on the other side of the doors that he's suddenly not feeling so brave. He's clutching a blade in his hand, and while I can't make out any other weapons, I'm not able to rule them out.

From my vantage point above, I can make out at least seven hostages. All women, two minors, but there could be more in the dressing room or hidden behind the counter. Until I get down on the ground and survey the store properly, I won't truly know the extent of this situation.

"BACK OFF," the suspect screams through the store, his words directed at my men outside, and judging by his jerky movements, erratic behavior, and too-wide stare, I have to assume he's high on either coke or meth.

"I just want to talk, man," Diesel says in a calming tone. In this situation, he's the voice of reason, but truth be told, there's nothing Diesel would want to do less than to talk it out. He's a broody motherfucker who would prefer to race in, guns blazing, and save the hostages. Unfortunately for him, hostage negotiations are part of the job, and he's actually pretty fucking great at it. He could sweet-talk anyone into believing that life in maximum security prison is nothing but a summer vacation.

The suspect shakes his head, looking frantic, and in a rush of panic, he reaches for the closest hostage. He violently yanks a young woman into him, locking his arm around her body and holding his blade to the base of her throat. She whimpers in fear as another woman on the ground screams in horror. "I SAID BACK OFF," the man screams, his voice cracking and making it clear he's got no fucking idea what he's doing. He's desperate, and that makes him dangerous.

A cool, calm, and collected suspect generally knows what they want and can be reasoned with, but men like this have no idea what their endgame is. They're motivated by emotion and will act out the moment they feel just the slightest pressure.

With the situation heating up, I hold my hand up by my face and turn back to the rest of my team before indicating for them to keep going. I'm not about to lose anybody on my watch, and certainly not because of this asshole.

Quickly making our way through the ventilation system, we come to the store's changing rooms, and I get straight to work removing the large ceiling tile and silently sliding it aside. Someone gasps from down below, and I peer through the hole, finding three more hostages, each of them cowering in fear, hidden well in the changing stalls.

They appear to be a group of friends, older teens if I had to guess, and I hold my finger to my lips, willing them to remain silent as I grip the edge of the ceiling cavity and begin lowering myself into the store.

I drop the rest of the way, landing without a sound before promptly moving to the entrance of the changing rooms and getting a view of the store beyond. One by one, my men fall into formation behind me, and as Diesel continues his hostage negotiations like the fucking pro that he is, my team swiftly moves onto the main floor of the store, not a single one of us making a sound.

We move with stealth and precision, the type of flow that can only come with years of intense, crucial training. Even now after being at the top of my game for the past decade, I won't dare skip out on my training. We're always bettering ourselves, always finding new ways to excel as a team.

We fan out under the radar, covering every corner of the room until we have him surrounded.

"What's your name, man?" Diesel asks in that too-calm tone that could convince me to jump straight into an active volcano as he holds the suspect's attention.

The suspect narrows his gaze as though trying to figure out Diesel's angle, but coming up with nothing, he gives in. "Ry—Rykin."

"Rykin, I'm Diesel," he says. "I bet this isn't how you intended your day to turn out, huh?"

Rykin scoffs as I survey the situation with a keen eye, watching his response to each of Diesel's questions. "That's an understatement."

"Listen, I'm here to help you. You don't want to be here. You seem like a good kid. How about we find a solution that gets everyone out of here without anybody getting hurt?"

Rykin stares at Diesel before glancing back at the hostages, only his gaze lingers on the young woman cowering in front of him, tears streaking down her cheeks. "No," he says, a manic desperation flashing in his eyes. "No. It's too late for that."

"Why's it too late, Rykin? Talk to me. I'm right here. All you have to do is let these people go, open the door, and then we can talk it through, figure out how to get what you need."

"No," he says more firmly, his grip tightening on the hostage in his arms, and he presses the blade to her neck so tightly that she whimpers. "NO. SHUT UP. I KNOW WHAT YOU'RE DOING. YOU'RE TRYING TO GET IN MY HEAD, BUT IT WON'T WORK. IT'S TOO LATE."

His hands tremble, and the hostage becomes frantic, her eyes darting around the store, trying to figure out her own game plan.

"Fuck," I mutter under my breath as my team discreetly inches closer, more than ready to take action as it becomes increasingly clear that Rykin isn't going to entertain negotiations.

"Why don't you let me in?" Diesel prompts, stepping closer toward the locked door and making a show of releasing his weapon, trying to appear as an ally. "You don't want to hurt these people."

Rykin's breathing becomes labored and erratic, and his gaze darts around the room, trying to figure out an escape, but I've seen that look a million times before. If he's going down, he's taking as many hostages with him as possible, but I won't let that happen on my watch.

The woman locked in his hold is going to be an issue, though. She's too worked up, too scared, and just as I make a slight movement, trying to catch her eye to let her know we have the situation under control, she makes her move, slamming her elbow back into Rykin's gut with one hell of a battle cry.

The people around her gasp in horror as Rykin lets out a pained scream, his eyes snapping to the woman almost as if in slow motion. She shoves him away, his bladed hand inching away just enough for her to throw herself forward.

She crashes to the floor and immediately tries to scramble away, but Rykin is too close to the fucking edge, and without hesitation, he throws himself after the woman, the blade coming down in a shallow arc.

BANG!

My weapon rings out with a direct kill shot right between Rykin's eyes. His body goes limp before he's even hit the floor, and all I can do is shake my head, all too aware of the paperwork that's going to follow.

CHAPTER 16

KNIGHT

My team all but broke through the door of the locker room after we arrived back at the station. That wasn't exactly the outcome we were hoping for in the store, but once I saw the desperation in Rykin's eyes, I knew that was how it would end, and there's no denying it, we feel every loss. Even the ones who deserved it.

It's sad really. Not many of our hostage situations leave me guessing. The majority of the time, it comes down to pure stupidity mixed with an unfortunate amount of desperation, and nine out of ten times, it's a deadly mix.

As I unload everything from my tactical belt with a heavy heart, my phone buzzes from within my locker with the familiar alert of my home security app. I quickly grab it and swipe my thumb across the screen just in time to see Harper striding out of my home, still wearing my old T-shirt.

A stupid smile pulls at the corner of my lips. There's something about this woman in my clothes that does something wicked to me. Harper pauses on my front porch and turns around looking directly at the camera, and a deep curiosity pulses through me, wondering if maybe she forgot something. Only the curiosity disappears the moment she grips the hem of her shirt and raises it up, quickly flashing the camera with those perfect, pierced tits.

"Fuck me," I mutter, unable to take my eyes off her.

Harper laughs to herself on my porch before pointing directly at the camera and then to herself, only to then mime sucking the world's biggest cock. She laughs again, but when she turns and walks away, she grabs the shirt again, flashing that perfect ass. And fuck, for a man who trains to have composure in the most volatile situations, I'm bursting at the seams.

"Well, shit," Ace says, getting the drop on me as he peers over my shoulder and glances at my phone. "Whose ass is that?"

I toss my phone back into my locker before grabbing Ace and slamming him up against it, my hand braced around his throat. "Even think about jerking off to that ass and I'll hack off your little shrimp dick with a rusty nail and feed it to you. Understood?"

Ace grins. "How the mighty have fallen. You went and got yourself a girl."

"Damn it," I hear Diesel say from across the locker room.

"I did not go and find myself a girl," I tell him, knowing damn well Diesel is listening too. "All I'm saying is this one is off limits. I'm not with her, we're just . . . I don't fucking know what this is. It's new. Very fucking new, and until I figure it out, you don't get to comment on her ass, and if I hear you even mention it, I will have no problem singeing the memory right out of your brain."

"Fuck, Knight," Diesel says, suddenly a lot closer before smacking the back of my head. "You've got it bad."

"I don't got nothing bad."

"So who is she?" Ace asks as I release him from my hold.

"She's no one that you need to be concerning yourself with," I say, desperately needing to get the spotlight off me. After all, I'm not quite ready to tell them I spent the morning buried inside my step-niece. "You two have enough girl problems of your own to be worried about mine."

Diesel scoffs, his gaze shifting to Ace. There's still hostility there, but I gotta give it to the assholes, they're good at keeping a lid on it while we're out in the field. But now that we're back at the station, all bets are off. "Thanks for the reminder."

"Come on, man. You know she wanted a piece of this right from the start," Ace taunts. "They all do. Nobody can resist all of this."

"Amy Cartwright. Grade nine biology," Diesel says, starting to list off all the women who have shamelessly rejected Ace. "Trina

Kent. Sarah McLoud. Bar Jessica. Insurance Jessica. And don't forget my fucking cousin Jessica. There's Maggie from—"

"Okay, okay," Ace cuts in, knowing this list is bound to get long. "Maybe not every last living soul on earth wants to get on their knees for me, but no matter how many rejections I've had, they don't mean anything because, at the end of the day, I've had your sister, and that will always be more than enough."

Diesel's face drops and Ace launches into a sprint, knowing damn well he's about to have his ass handed to him. "I'm going to fucking kill him," Diesel roars, taking off after Ace toward the station gym.

I let out a heavy sigh.

Ace would never cross that line with Diesel, but that doesn't mean he wouldn't taunt the fucker about it, and with the two of them already bickering like an old married couple, this isn't going to go down well.

There's an hour until our actual shift starts, and Diesel isn't going to waste a second of that time teaching Ace a lesson, and honestly, he deserves it. Ace knows that Diesel's sister is a sore point for him, but there's also a good chance Ace baited him on purpose. He hates when they fight, despite how he goes out of his way to make it worse, and though it's entertaining, things are just better when they're getting along.

I head toward the station gym, striding through the door to find Ace already flat on his ass on the sparring mat. "Is that all you got?" he taunts Diesel as I shake my head, hoping like fuck Diesel doesn't break him. After all, I'm going to need both of them sharp and focused during our shift. They need to get this shit out of their system, but they also need to remember they have careers to think about. So if they can't manage their shit, I have no problem heading over there and putting both of them in their place.

I take a seat on the bench by the sparring mats to supervise the children when I notice Detective Gray pass by the door. He glances in, and seeing me sitting here, he pivots and strides into the gym. "Slater," he says with a slight rise of his chin.

I get to my feet and meet him in the middle, hoping like fuck he's got some good news for me. "Were you able to figure out who's running up that case?"

He shakes his head, instantly putting me on edge. "That's just the thing. I've been looking into it since you mentioned it, and I can't find anything that matches the description you gave me from that night. I've asked around, and no one knows what I'm talking about."

My gaze narrows on him, suspicion rattling me. "You sure?"

Gray shrugs. "Don't know what to tell you. I'm positive. There's nothing in the system. No homicides were logged for that night. Maybe you got the details wrong."

Unease begins to plague me as I remember the look in Harper's eyes when she came to my place after that shift. She was terrified; even her hands were shaking. Nobody can feign that type of terror. There was a body and a message. Now that the body is no longer in the morgue, there is suddenly no information logged in our system, and the detective who dropped the body off wants to claim he knows nothing about it. I can only assume the worst.

"Right," I say slowly, my suspicions making me feel sick. "I must have my wires crossed."

Could Gray be the asshole responsible for all of this? The one who's been watching her, the one who's been sending sick messages in the form of mutilated human hearts? Or is he just a pawn in somebody else's sick game?

I need to get to the bottom of this.

Heading back to the sparring mat, I pull out my phone and bring up a number for someone I haven't thought about in a long time. After I hit call and hold it to my ear, the phone rings three times before a feminine voice answers.

"Knight?" Carly asks in a hesitant tone. Not that I blame her. The last time we spoke, she was confessing her undying love after we'd slept together once. I ran the first chance I got. I don't even know why I still have her number in my phone, but I've never been so glad that I do now.

"Hey, Carly. How have you been?"

"I, ahhhh . . . I'm confused. Why are you calling me?"

"Do you still work in security at Blackstone Hospital?"

There's a short silence, and I can only imagine the millions of questions floundering through her brain. "Yes," she finally says.

"Listen, I really need to get some footage—"

Carly cuts me off with a scoff. "Oh hell no. I'm not putting my ass on the line for you," she tells me. "You know damn well there's a process to gain hospital security footage. Go through the proper channels. I can't help you."

"Please, Carly," I say, lowering my tone. "I wouldn't ask if this weren't important. Going through the proper channels . . . fuck. It might be too late by then, and this is personal. I need that footage."

There's another beat of silence before she finally lets out a subtle sigh. "What do you need?"

"The footage for the past few nights in the morgue. There's been some weird shit going on down there, and I need to get to the bottom of it before someone gets hurt."

"By someone, I'm assuming you're talking about a girl," Carly mutters, an edge to her tone, telling me she's still a little pissed about the way I bailed on her, but what did she expect? It was a one-night stand gone wrong.

"Yes, she's a girl, but this one is different. She's . . . family. My niece."

Bile rises in my throat when referring to Harper as my niece, and while I know it's mostly true, I'm working double time to try and put that little snippet of information aside. Right now, I need to play all the cards I have, and if Carly is still sour about what happened between us all those years ago, then I need to play it smart, and mentioning who Harper really is to me isn't going to cut it.

Carly pauses for a moment as if deep in thought. "I can maybe get you the last twenty-four hours without raising alarm bells, but I can't do anything more than that. I'll need higher security clearance for that."

"The last twenty-four hours will be great," I say with a sigh, knowing that while that may not give me Gray delivering the body, it'll sure as fuck give me the stalker locking her in the refrigeration unit. If it is Gray, we'll be able to identify him, and then all of this shit can be put to rest. Harper will be safe, and Gray will be well on his way to spending the rest of his life behind bars.

"Okay. Is there anything in particular you want me looking for? A certain time frame, perhaps?"

"Uhhhhh. Probably anywhere from two in the morning through till four. Somebody was able to gain access to the morgue while my niece was working. She hid in the refrigeration unit only to be locked in, so we just want to rule out any foul play," I tell her, trying to downplay it so as to not cause alarm, not knowing just how far this thing might go.

"Oh shit," Carly says. "Give me an hour to review the footage. I'll send you anything I find."

"Thanks, Carly."

"Hey, ummm . . . are you still an asshole?"

A stupid smile pulls across my lips. "Yeah, Carly. I am," I say, glancing up at the boys to find Ace in a headlock with his legs flailing around on the sparring mat while his face turns an unnatural shade of red.

"Damn. That's what I was worried about."

"You can do much better than me. Go find someone who'll treat you like a queen."

She lets out a broken sigh before ending the call, and as I put my phone away, I get to my feet and call out to Diesel. "Knock it off. You're gonna kill him, and then I'm going to have to explain it. That's a lot of paperwork I'm not down for."

Diesel sighs and releases his hold on Ace, and as he remains sprawled on the sparring mat, trying to regain consciousness, I step in his place and give Diesel a fight that he'll actually have to work for.

Thirty-eight minutes later, my phone chimes with an incoming email, and I pull back from Diesel before stepping over Ace, who's now asleep on the fucking mat. I sit right back down where I had been earlier and don't hesitate opening the email. I don't bother scanning over the message Carly sent before bringing up the surveillance footage from the morgue last night.

The footage starts a little after two in the morning. There's a clear view of the whole morgue. Harper is situated at her desk, and from the look of it, she's immersed in her work, though there's no denying she's clearly distracted by her phone, and I can't help but wonder if this is the other guy she was telling me about. Laith Mitchell. I think that was his name, which also reminds me that on a completely unrelated note, I need to run a background check today.

I scroll through the footage, waiting for something to happen, when Harper's head snaps up. Her attention is locked on the door, and even though the footage is slightly grainy, the fear in her eyes is crystal clear. She rises, hesitates by her desk, then moves, and in a split-second decision, she races across the morgue and climbs straight into the refrigeration unit.

My heart hammers, desperate to see what actually went down last night, and I fast-forward through it again, waiting for more movement. When the door finally opens, I bring my phone closer to my face.

A man walks into the morgue, dragging a cart behind him, only he leaves the cart in the doorway to brace the door open. When he pulls cleaning products from the cart, I let out a sigh. It's just the janitor.

I scroll through the footage, watching him make his way around the room, wiping everything down before briefly mopping the floors. Then when he trails by the refrigeration unit, I watch the very second he realizes one of the doors was left unlocked and casually flips it, having no fucking clue that Harper was hidden within. The whole thing was nothing more than Harper's fear playing on her mind because of the bullshit that had happened during her other shifts, and I hate that for her.

Quickly checking the time and seeing that I have a few minutes before my shift, I find Harper's number and hit call before holding the phone to my ear and casually striding away from Diesel and Ace.

It rings twice before Harper's sweet voice comes through the line. "Is there something you need?"

"I'm gonna need my shirt back."

"Ha. Good luck with that," she murmurs. "You're going to have to peel it off my body with your teeth."

"That won't be a problem," I tell her. "But while I'd love to stand here and do this all day, I've got more pressing things to discuss."

"Oh, and what's that? You need a list of all my favorite vibrators ranked in order of just how quickly they get the job done? Because that won't take me long. I've already got it written up in my notes."

My mouth opens as I go to respond, but the words fall flat, and for the first time, I'm fucking speechless. "We're gonna discuss that list in great detail," I tell her. "But this is about last night. I was able to get the security footage from the morgue."

She sucks in a gasp, and I cringe, hearing the immediate change in her mood, even over the phone. "You got it?"

"Sorry, doll. I should have eased you into that, but yeah. I know someone in security and was able to get those few hours from last night, but if we want anything from the previous nights, we'll have to submit an application, and it could take weeks."

"Fuck," she mutters. "Did you find anything?"

"Yeah, I uhhhh . . . It was just the janitor in there last night."

I can practically hear her shaking her head through the phone, and I pull my phone away for just a second to forward her the email. "No," she says, sounding out of breath. "It couldn't have been. I could sense him there."

"I don't know what to tell you, Harper. I've reviewed the footage, and it's clear. I've just forwarded it to you so you can see for yourself, but despite it being the janitor, you did the right thing. You were scared and you hid, and because of that, you safe. Had that not been the janitor and if you had just stayed at your desk, the night could have ended very differently."

Harper sighs. "Your email just came through."

Knowing she's opening the footage just as quickly as I had, my lips press into a hard line, and despite my shift starting, I wait with her, letting her go through the motion. "Shit. It really is the janitor," she murmurs with a pained groan. "I'm so embarrassed. Who locks themself in a refrigeration unit because they're scared of the janitor?"

"Don't be embarrassed," I tell her. "Like I said, considering everything that's happened, you did the right thing. But at least you can sleep easy knowing it wasn't some crazed murderer. Besides, it was worth it to watch you come out of that shower and demand I eat your tight little cunt while laying down the rules."

"Knight," she groans.

"Listen, I wanted to ask you, the night the body came in, you said that it was Gray, right?"

"Yeah," she says, confirming what I thought. "He came in with that weird coroner and said this one needed to be prioritized, so I got started straightaway."

"Right, okay."

There is a slight pause. "Why?" she finally asks, an edge to her tone.

"It's nothing. Just wanted to confirm."

"Knight," she demands, that edge hitching higher and taking no prisoners, making it clear she won't stop until she's satisfied we're on the same page.

I groan. "I spoke to Gray yesterday, and he mentioned that he didn't pick up a case that night. He was on scene at a house fire. An older man died from smoke inhalation, but he's adamant he didn't set foot in the morgue that night."

"No, that's not right. A different body came in that matches that description, but Gray was definitely there with the coroner. I saw him with my own eyes."

"Yeah, I believe you, doll. I just don't understand why Gray would lie about it," I muse; none of this makes sense. "I spoke to him about it again, and now he claims that there's nothing in our system about a homicide that night matching the victim's description. He's insisting that I've got the details wrong."

"What the fuck? Is he saying I made it up?"

"I don't know what he's trying to say, but it seems suspicious to me. I don't like it," I tell her. "I don't know Gray that well, but I've never liked him. Either way, I'm going to keep looking into it."

"Okay," she says nervously. "Do you think it might be him?"

"Honestly, I'm not sure. He doesn't strike me as the stalker type, and from what I know of him, he doesn't have the extensive medical experience one would need to pull off the shit that was done to the victim. He knows something, but he could be a pawn in a much bigger game."

"Fuck."

"My thoughts exactly," I tell her. "But listen, I have to run, okay? My shift started, but if you decide to go into work, just keep your eyes open, yeah?"

"I will."

"Alright, Morticia. I'll see you later."

And with that, I end the call, more determined than ever to get to the bottom of this shit and figure out who the fuck has been messing with my girl.

CHAPTER 17

HARPER-RAYN

Embarrassment plagues me as I watch the footage of me climbing into the refrigeration unit for the millionth time. How could I have been so stupid? I was crying in a freezer, terrified for my life, all while Vincent made his way around the morgue, minding his business as he mopped the floors and straightened up my desk.

I should be stronger than that, but this stalker has turned me into a mess, and Knight probably had to call in a favor to get the footage of the biggest false alarm known to humankind. I'm humiliated. Not to mention, he had to deal with me showing up on his doorstep in a shambles for no reason.

I'm sure that when he looks at me now, all he sees is a scared little girl, lost in her own paranoia. He's a freaking SWAT officer at the top of his game, and I'm a joke. I need to be cared for because a janitor at work unknowingly sent me into a panic.

This asshole stalker has turned me into a laughingstock.

I suppose my time with Knight was fun while it lasted. There's no way he's going to touch me now. I don't exactly know what type of women he goes after, but I know he doesn't deal with other people's drama. And right now, I have an abundance of it.

Oh no. He probably thinks I'm my mother reborn.

The very thought sends a stabbing pain shooting through my stomach. With one hand cupped over my mouth, I jump out of bed and scramble to my bathroom. Just as my knees hit the ground in front of the toilet, I proceed to throw up every last scrap of food in the pit of my stomach.

A sheer layer of sweat coats my forehead, and I roll my ass straight into the shower, needing to somehow pull myself together, but with all the bullshit currently going on and the new addition of Detective Gray suddenly appearing suspicious, I don't know if I have what it takes.

I sit shivering in the bottom of the shower as the water takes far too long to warm up, but once it does, it's fucking scalding. I spring to my feet, frantically adjusting the temperature as my ass takes the brunt of the hot water.

Today is not my day—apart from the mind-blowing sex I had on Knight's kitchen counter this morning. That was pretty freaking amazing, but everything since that has been nothing but a downward spiral.

After leaving Knight a spicy message on his home security camera, I took my ass home, got ready for work, and just as I was about to get in my car, Knight's call came in. After that, I did what I could to hold my head high and head to work with the intention of catching up on work, but Dr. McKullan was quick to reprimand me for slacking in the first place.

I promptly fell apart in the bathroom, and I don't just mean a handful of tears here and there; I'm talking snot running down my face. It was mortifying. My face was blotchy and red, and my eyes were puffy and sore, but there's no denying that I deserved it.

By the time I pulled myself together and walked back into the morgue, I looked like a natural disaster had aimed every ounce of its destruction at me. I was a mess. Hell, I looked like a group of men had run a train on me. Only, it wasn't a domestic train taking me from city to city, this was a long-haul, international-type train.

I'm not typically someone who cries. I despise tears. They make me feel weak, and yet these past few days have turned me into a complete wreck. I don't recognize myself right now. I don't feel as though anything is right. I like my independence. I like feeling as though I have my shit together. I've prided myself on how I've built a life and a career without anybody's help, and day by day, I'm crumbling.

I stay in the shower until the water runs cold, and honestly, it's not that long. My apartment has the worst water heater known to humankind. It makes taking long, dragged-out showers impossible—unlike at Knight's place, where I could stand under the hot water for what seemed like a century. It was incredible.

After I wrap a towel around myself and head to get dressed, my phone rings from somewhere on my bed, and I hurry across the room to answer it, hoping it might be Knight, Izzy, or even Laith. When I pick it up and see my mother's name across the screen, disappointment pounds through my veins.

I immediately silence the call before tightening my towel around my chest, not having the energy or the will to find something comfortable to wear to bed. That is future Harper's problem—as is dealing with my mother. I've already had a rough day. I don't need to make it worse.

After swiping away the notification, I go to flop down onto my bed, but something across the room catches my eye. My head whips up to my dresser, and there, sitting among the mess of makeup, cheap jewelry, and skin care is the bloodied black rose I'd pulled out of the victim's chest cavity.

I suck in a petrified gasp, my eyes widening in fear, and just as my body starts to violently shake, movement in my full-length mirror steals my attention. My gaze snaps across the room to the mirror, and fear cripples me as I take in the masked man hovering right behind me.

A wretched scream rips out of me, terror pounding through my veins as I go to run, but he's too quick. He steps into my back and braces one hand over my mouth, muting the sound of my cries as he pulls me in hard against his chest.

He's massive. Must be at least six-foot-four. Maybe six-five. And the strength radiating from his body is like nothing I've ever experienced. Trying to break out of his grasp is a waste of time. He's a fucking machine, built of pure muscle and malice.

Tears roll down my cheek as he holds me still, and his other hand reaches for the towel as I feel his laser-sharp stare on me through my full-length mirror. My chest heaves, panic infecting me as I watch him closely.

He's wearing all black: tactical pants, boots, a shirt that accentuates his muscular build. His shoulders and chest are broad, and I can only wonder what's hidden beneath that terrifying mask. It's somewhat of a gothic skull, but its jaw is wide open with sharp, talonlike fangs.

I've never seen anything like it.

The man leans in even closer, his lips just a breath from my ear as I try to focus on anything but the intoxicating scent coming off him. He smells like my darkest desires, and it fucks with my head. I shouldn't want to feel how his hands feel on my body. Shouldn't want him to have his wicked way with me, and yet, despite my overwhelming fear, if that's what he wants, I'll give it to him in a heartbeat.

"We're going to play a game, kitten."

His voice is like velvet, addictive and mesmerizing, every syllable sending shivers across my skin. He releases the knot in my towel, letting it fall to the ground until I'm standing naked in his arms. While I know I should run, or scream, or put up a fight, I can't help but want to please him—even if I have no idea what his endgame is.

His big, calloused hand finds my waist and trails over my skin. "If you scream, you fail. If you run, you die. But, kitten, you will hide, and I will find you."

I swallow over the lump in my throat, keeping my eyes on him through my mirror, watching his hand skim up to my tits, firmly cupping them and squeezing tight before trailing down past my ribs and over my hip. What does he want from me? Just to play some twisted game of hide-and-seek? I don't fucking know.

I go to speak, and he eases his hold over my mouth, dropping the hand to my body, satisfied that I'm not about to scream.

"What happens after you find me?"

His eyes seem to penetrate right through to my soul through the mirror. A rumbling groan vibrates through his chest. "You become mine."

Holy fuck.

You become mine. What does that even mean? Will I become his in a sexual sense, or does he mean he'll claim my whole entire existence?

My chest heaves frantically, knowing exactly where his hand is aiming, yet I don't try to stop him. I don't cry out. I don't scream. I don't even try to push him away. Instead, I wait on bated breath, knowing just how dangerous this man can be.

Is he really going to kill me like he did the last victim? Or will he let me off the hook if I can play his game?

His fingers dip low between my thighs, and as they skim over my clit, my hips jolt with involuntary excitement. He rolls them over the sensitive bud again as if learning how responsive my body can be. I suck in a breath, and as his fingers continue exploring, they dip lower to my entrance.

My legs shake with nervousness, and as the heel of his palm rubs against my clit, he slowly drags his fingers through my wetness. "That's a good kitten," he rumbles, his breath brushing my shoulder. "Always ready."

Sweet baby Jesus.

My pussy clenches, and then finally he pushes his fingers deep inside me, making my knees weaken beneath me. His other arm locks around my waist, keeping me upright, the same way Knight had to the other night, and I can't help but wonder if this terrifying man behind me is the same one who was buried deep inside me on his kitchen counter.

Physically, they match. Height. Build. Everything is ticking boxes.

Knight is covered in tattoos, though, and this guy is covered in clothes, making it hard to tell, but that very thought has me relaxing just a little. I don't think it's Knight. I don't think he would go to the lengths of stalking me at work and murdering a man in cold blood just to send me a message, but if it were him, I don't think he'd hurt me. I don't know if he'd have it in him.

His fingers work me deep, rolling inside me, splitting and

massaging as the heel of his palm works my clit. My body is worked to the edge, the strange mix of fear and pleasure confusing my system as my nails dig into his muscled forearm.

As his fingers curl inside me, massaging that mystical place that only a few have ever found and worshipped, my eyes begin to roll in the back of my head.

Everything tightens, and I clench my jaw, the rapid intensity building in a way I wasn't prepared for. "Oh, fuck. Knight."

His body stiffens behind me, and suddenly his big hand is at my throat, squeezing as his fingers keep working me. His gaze locks on mine through the mirror, and I see nothing but evil staring back at me, turning my blood cold. "Call me by another man's name, and this game will only be fun for one of us. Understood?"

Okay. It's not Knight.

I swallow over the fear and hastily nod, and as his fingers tighten on my throat, it becomes harder to suck in a breath, but as he does that, his fingers buried in my cunt pick up speed.

He pushes me to my limits, and as I gasp for air, my world explodes. My orgasm tears out of me like a burst of wild lightning. Hot pulses of raw pleasure rock through my veins as my pussy shatters, my walls erratically convulsing around his skilled fingers.

He doesn't stop working my body, grinding his palm against my sensitive clit as his fingers roll inside me, intensifying every second of my pleasure until I finally start coming down from my high.

When he finally eases up on my throat, I take a hasty breath, desperate for sweet oxygen as he slowly pulls his fingers out of me. My knees weaken, and he releases his hold on me, leaving me scrambling to stay upright as he steps around me, making his way to my bedroom door.

Then just when I think he's going to disappear, he turns back, locking those deadly eyes on mine. "Ready or not, kitten. I'm coming for you."

And with that, he's gone, leaving me gasping for air.

I fall to my knees, grabbing my discarded towel and pulling it over me as though that could somehow protect me from whatever the hell just went down in here. And as the black rose stares at me from my dresser, I finally understand what this is.

He's playing a twisted game of hide-and-seek, and when he finds me, he'll have me anyway he wants. And if I deny him, if I run or scream . . . it's game over.

CHAPTER 18

HARPER-RAYN

Ice clinks in my glass as Izzy and I hit the pre-drinks as hard as possible, preparing for one hell of a good night at whatever bar or club she decides to drag me to. Honestly, she's told me the name of it three times already, and I still haven't got the slightest idea where we are going.

"Have you ever tried waxing your own cooch?" she muses as she leans in toward my bathroom mirror to apply a second coat of mascara as I struggle to dress myself.

"Uhhh . . . What?"

"Well, have you?" she pushes. "I was reading this book, and on the very first page, the girl was talking about how she tried waxing and tore her whole lip off, and then her brother had to drive her to the emergency room while she was spread-eagle with wax, hair, and half her lip hanging off. It was traumatic, and I just feel you need to be careful with this shit."

"What kind of pussy-traumatizing books are you reading?"

Iz scoffs and laughs. "Hey, that's tame. The book I read last week had the girl accidentally use a Taser on her vag, thinking she'd picked up one of those little vibrators. Now *that* was traumatizing. I had to check through my bottom drawer to make sure I didn't accidentally put a Taser in there. I don't want that shit happening to me."

"Do you even own a Taser?"

"No," she laughs. "But a girl can never be too careful."

"Cheers to that," I say, lifting my glass and taking a healthy sip, welcoming the burn of vodka sailing down my throat. Taking the drink with me, I head into my closet for a pair of shoes, but I hesitate over the first pair and grab another. "Which shoes am I supposed to wear with this?"

"Show me," Iz calls back.

Taking my shoes for a stroll across my small apartment, I hover in the bathroom doorway, holding them up and waiting for Izzy's approval, because let's face it, when Izabelle Grace Davenport is around, she must have final approval of every materialistic portion of my life. I won't have it any other way.

Izzy glances toward the options, her face twisting in disgust. "Are you serious?" she scolds. "You bring me an old pair of sandals that are falling to pieces over a pair of sexy knee-high boots. There is no option. Throw those rank sandals out."

"Hey. They're my favorite," I say, realizing I left my drink in my closet.

"You're such a liar. There's a layer of dust caked on them. The last time you wore them, your mom was still pregnant with you." Iz laughs at herself, and honestly, I'm right there with her. Where the hell does she get this shit from? "Don't think for one moment that I haven't noticed you didn't answer my question."

My mind goes blank, and I try to figure out what the hell she's talking about. "What question?" I demand, tossing the sandals over my shoulder and backing up to drop my ass on my couch to put my boots on, only I miss and end up on the floor. Maybe I've gone a little too hard on the pre-drinks.

"Waxing your own coochie? Don't tell me you do that."

I scoff. "No, this coochie has been lasered to silky smooth perfection," I tell her, certain she already knew that. "In my younger years, I've been known to give the good old Brazilian wax a try, and let me tell you, it was a horrendous disaster every single time. Zero out of five stars. I do not recommend."

Izzy howls with laughter from the bathroom. "Was it a leg-propped-up-on-the-bathtub kind of situation, or a towel on the floor and a mirror staring right at your bush?"

My cheeks flush, heating with embarrassment, but when it comes to me and Iz, nothing is off-limits. "I'm ashamed to say all three."

"Three?" she laughs, sticking her head out of the bathroom and gaping at me. "I only said two. What's the third option?"

My phone rings from somewhere in the kitchen, and I drag my ass off the floor, one boot off and one boot on. "Saved by the bell," I laugh, hurrying to find my phone and cursing myself for not leaving it on the counter like a normal fucking person.

"What? No! What's the third option?"

I ignore Iz as I dig through drawers and check the pantry before finally looking in the freezer and finding my chilled phone hanging out by the Oreo ice cream. *Big & Long Schlong #2* appears on my screen, and I swipe my thumb across the screen, accepting the call.

"Oh, heyyyyy," I drawl, holding the phone away from my face as I search the screen for the little FaceTime button.

"What . . . What the hell are you doing?"

"Turn your camera on, Mr. Big and Long Schlong Number Two."

Laith groans. "You know damn well I'm not number two," he says as his dazzling smile appears on my screen. "Don't you think it's about time I get prime position at the top?"

"Ooooh, can't help you," I tease, taking Laith along with me into the bathroom so Izzy can say hi as she continues working on her makeup. "I'm actually thinking of demoting you to number three. Actually, potentially number four. The jury's still out on that one."

His jaw drops, and as Izzy's brows furrow, I realize I've said too much. She knows all about my thrilling few days with the alluring Knight Slater, but I haven't said a word about the man who appeared in my bedroom, demanding I play a twisted game of hide-and-seek that ended with me coming hard on his thick fingers.

"Four?" Laith sputters. "How the—just how many dicks have you been riding? I know it's been a little while since I blew your mind last, but shit, tiger. I think my feelings are hurt."

"Your feelings?" Izzy mutters beside me. "As far as I was aware, there's only one new dick bouncing around Harper's face, and here I am finding out there could be two."

"Oh, shut up," I laugh. "There is only one new dick in the picture. I just meant that it's so fantastically massive that it would be criminal for it not to take out both first and second place."

"I . . . I'm still offended," Laith mutters. "In the very least, I should be holding on to third. You haven't even thought about Big and Long Schlong Number One in years. I think he should be the one demoted. Not me. After all, I'm the one putting in all the work."

Izzy scoffs. "From what I've heard, you're going to have to up your game. You've been slacking, and while your new loyalty card remains unpunched, someone else has been taking our girl to poundtown."

"Let him," Laith scoffs. "She always comes running back when she realizes nobody does it better than me."

Forgetting I'm on camera, I scrunch up my face, knowing that while Laith is certainly a high achiever, he could never compare to how it was with Knight. Even how it was with my stalker in my bedroom. It was certainly strange, but there's no denying just how intense it was.

"What the hell was that look for?" Laith demands, a hint of panic surging through his stare. "Don't tell me this new guy puts it down better than I do."

I cringe again, and Laith looks horrified. "No. That's not possible. Nobody gives it to you like I do." Laith pauses a moment, shaking his head as though he can't possibly believe what he's hearing. "I need to sit down."

"You'll always be my . . . second favorite."

"What was that pause?" he demands. "Why'd you pause like that? What's there to think about? Is there . . . Is there another favorite above me and this new guy?"

"No. Not above the new guy," I clarify.

"Oh, sure," he scoffs. "So just potentially above me, then?"

A laugh bubbles up my throat, and I watch as Laith strides through his apartment, taking me into the kitchen where he helps himself to a drink, all while shaking his head.

"You're buzzed, aren't you?" he says, and that playful tone in his voice shifts to something a little more serious, prompting me to walk back out to the living room where we can have just a scrap of privacy.

"Sure am," I tell him, more than feeling myself right now.

"This new guy," he says, a slight edge to his tone, but something I can't quite place. Jealousy maybe? "Is it anything serious? Do we need to pump the brakes for a minute? I don't want to overstep if you're starting something good."

A soft smile pulls at my lips, loving the way he cares about what's best for me. "I love you, Laith. You know that, right?" I tell him. "But to be honest, with this new guy, it's complicated. If anything, it's probably just fun. It can't progress into anything more than that, even if there might be real feelings there. I just—" I cut myself off and let out a heavy sigh. "We still good?"

"Always good, tiger," he murmurs. "Let me know when you figure it out. I'd hate to lose you in that way, but I want everything for you."

"Right back at ya," I say as a dorky smile pulls across my lips.

Laith messes around with something off camera, and a moment later, I see a little card appear on the screen. "I suppose getting this printed was pointless," he says as I lean in a little closer to make out what's on the card, only to find the words *Dick-Me-Down Loyalty Card* at the top, and ten perfect squares below.

"You didn't?" I gasp, laughing.

"Of course I did."

A howling laugh tears out of me, and I shake my head, more than impressed with his dedication to the cause. "Don't get rid of that too soon," I tell him. "Who knows how long it'll be before I'm knocking on your door again."

Laith grins. "Oh, I know you'll be back," he says, making a show of putting the loyalty card right back into his wallet to keep safe.

"But listen, tiger. If a heart needs to be broken, make sure it's not yours."

"My heart's not capable of breaking. You know that."

He rolls his eyes. "I'll let you go. Don't be a stranger. And don't write yourself off tonight. Be safe."

"Hey," I rush out before he goes. "Have you ever thought that maybe you and I, one day in the future—"

"Might end up together?" he finishes for me. I nod, and he muses his response before finally giving it to me. "I've wondered about it before, but I also think that if something were going to develop between us, it would have happened by now. I love you, tiger. We have amazing chemistry, both physically and emotionally, but we're friends. I think that's where we shine."

"I think so too," I tell him. "But if we get to fifty years old and we're still playing this game, put me out of my misery and just marry me so I don't die all alone."

Laith laughs. "You've got yourself a deal."

I smile and meet his stare through the phone. "I love you too, you big dork."

"Yeah. Yeah." He winks, and with that, my screen goes black. There's no denying the small ache in my chest, but I appreciate him. Hell, sometimes I think he knows me better than I know myself.

My phone immediately rings again, and I laugh to myself, swiping my thumb across the screen to answer Laith's call as I make my way into my closet to find wherever the hell I put my drink. "Forget something?" I chime.

"Excuse me?" My mother's voice comes through the line.

"Huh?" I grunt, pulling my phone away and staring at the screen, wondering how the hell we ended up here, only for me to realize that in my assumption of Laith calling back, I didn't bother to check the screen. "Stupid. Stupid. Stupid."

"What did you just call me, young lady?"

"Not you, but—wait. Young lady? I'm twenty-eight. I'm hardly a child for you to reprimand."

"And yet you still act like one."

I roll my eyes and walk back into the bathroom before putting my call on speakerphone, allowing Izzy to overhear whatever bullshit my mother is about to spout at me. "Is there something you need, Mother?"

Izzy's eyes go wide through the mirror, and she points at my phone in shock. *Is that your mom?* she mouths, unable to wipe the surprise off her face, but that surprise is quickly joined by the sheer excitement of the fresh bullshit she knows she's about to get ringside seats for.

"You haven't returned any of my calls, and I dare say you had no intention of actually answering this one. After the way you humiliated me and your father at our anni—"

"WOAH! Hold the fuck up, Mom. What have you been smoking? *My father?*" I scoff; the absurdity of her referring to him as that leaves me more than ready to go another round with her. "Elias is not my father. Not even close. He's your billionaire of the week, just some sorry bastard for you to sink your claws into and bankrupt."

"Don't you dare speak about my husband in that tone, you ungrateful child. Do you have any idea how good he's been to us?"

"To us? That man hasn't done shit for me except keep you off my back. But that's only because you've been too busy on yours."

Izzy's eyes all but burst out of her skull as she silently whoops and starts fist-pumping the air. *Go off, girl,* she mouths again. *Get the bitch.*

"You . . . You . . . wretched child."

I sigh. "Do you actually need something, or are you just calling to reprimand me for something to do? Because if so, I'm going to hang up. I have plans tonight, and you're keeping me from them."

"Who's on the phone?" we hear from a deeper tone, further in the distance.

"Only my ungrateful daughter," Mom responds before pulling out the waterworks and putting on a show for her husband. "I really don't know what I've done to deserve such disdain from her. I raised her the best I could. Gave her everything I had, and she treats me like a monster."

Gag.

"Ease up on her, Mae," Elias says, his voice a little louder, probably getting closer, and now that I've spent more time with Knight,

I can't help but notice slight similarities between their tones. "She's just trying to find her way, and it doesn't help that she felt attacked the other night. Allow her time to lick her wounds. She'll come around when she's ready."

Izzy's jaw drops, and her hand presses to her heart, her eyes going wide. "Is that . . . Is that Daddy Elias?" she whispers while my mom is distracted.

Again, I reiterate the importance of a gag.

I roll my eyes and nod as Izzy puts on a show of falling against the bathroom wall, needing to fan herself while Mom goes straight for the defense. "Attack? Who attacked her? I simply gave my opinion on her career, and as her mother, I have every right to give my input. It's not my fault she can't accept someone who has a different opinion."

Mom and Elias go back and forth as I keep my eye on Iz, watching as she drops to her knees and mimics pulling Elias's fly down and physically taking his dick out of his pants. My face scrunches with disgust, but when she mimes needing two hands just to hold his dick, I can't help but laugh.

My best friend goes to town, giving Elias the best imaginary blowjob he'll ever receive. She gives an award-winning performance, pretending to gag before fondling his imaginary balls.

"Mom?" I say, wanting to get this over with while Izzy scrambles across my bathroom floor and starts digging through my cupboards before finding some props to go along with her performance. "Mom? I need to go."

Mom lets out an irritated sigh before finally getting to the point of her call. "There will be a full family dinner at our home next weekend. Attendance is mandatory. No negotiations."

"You're kidding if you think I'm going to another dinner at your place."

Izzy jumps straight back into her performance, gripping Elias' two-hander cock and getting back to work, somehow gagging on that thing.

"As I said, Harper-Rayn, it is nonnegotiable. You will be there whether you like it or not," she says as Izzy adds sound effects.

"Elias has invited his brother, and Jonah has agreed to bring the family. You will not ruin this for me."

Hmmm. Knight is going to be there? Suddenly this doesn't seem so bad. "Fine, I'll be there," I say, eyeing my best friend with curiosity. "But I'm bringing Izzy."

Mom groans. "Why do you have to be difficult about everything?"

Izzy reaches the climax of her performance, still kneeling on the shower floor, and squirts cum, otherwise known as my good body wash, all over her tits. She reaches up and grips my showerhead before holding it by her pussy and turning it on, letting water shoot across the shower, mimicking that her favorite Slater brother left her gushing like a waterfall, and all I can do is give her a round of applause.

"I'll see you there with Izzy, or I won't see you at all," I tell Mom. "Now if you don't mind, I need to go."

Mom groans again, and before I can get another word in, she ends the call, leaving me grinning at my best friend.

"Ten-out-of-ten performance," I tell her, holding up every last finger I've got just to get my point across. "The props really put you on the map, but if you knew the things I've done with that showerhead, you wouldn't be so comfortable with it."

Izzy gapes at me, getting to her feet and putting the showerhead back in its holder. "You're such a little skank," she tells me, which is rich coming from the woman who just gave an award-winning air blowjob to my stepfather. "I think I'm going to need a shower."

"To clean the cum off your tits or to cool off?"

"Both," Izzy laughs, and after peeling her clothes off, she adjusts the water temperature. "Wait. Did I hear you right? Did you just force an invitation to your mom's family dinner on me?"

"You bet your cum-covered tits I did."

She lets out a sigh. "Okay, but you should fully expect that I'm going to try and rail your stepdaddy," she tells me. "If you accidentally walk into a room to see a repeat performance of what you just saw, mind your business."

"Noted," I say, and with that, Izzy steps under the water, starting the whole getting-ready process right from the beginning.

CHAPTER 19

HARPER-RAYN

The music vibrates right through to my soul as Izzy and I waste our night away dancing on the sticky nightclub dance floor. It must be . . . shit. I can't even begin to guess what the time is. We didn't end up leaving my apartment until after ten, and since then, I've allowed the alcohol and music to take control.

My body sways as I do everything in my power to forget the guilt that's been coursing through my veins since the moment I decided not to clue Knight in on the bullshit that went down in my bedroom with my stalker.

As far as I'm concerned, Knight thinks my home is safe, and if he knew that my stalker showed himself and physically touched me, I can guarantee he would have me wrapped in bubble wrap and handcuffed to the headboard of his bed. Though on second thought, that might not be the worst thing in the world.

On some level, I know I need to tell Knight what happened, but how can I tell him that I allowed a stranger to touch me, and not only did I like it, he made me come?

I have to keep this to myself, at least for now.

Tonight, though, all I need to worry about is having a good time.

The overhead strobe lights flash as Izzy and I let loose, our bodies rolling as we sip on our drinks and have the night of our lives. Men have come and gone, but for the last hour, I've had two all over me, and while I'm not about to drop to my knees and take them both at once, I'm more than happy to let them grind against me and make me feel like the most desirable woman they've ever laid eyes on.

The loud music makes it almost impossible to hear a word either of them says, but truth be told, I don't care what they have to say. Tonight is about being free, being desired, and getting wildly drunk. Izzy and I laugh as another man approaches her, and the sultry look she gives him is all the approval he needs to move in behind her and let her grind her ass all over him.

I can't help but laugh as she blows this man's tiny mind, barely laying a finger on him, and honestly, it makes me wish that Knight were here, grinding up against me, but that's never going to happen. We can't be anything to each other, and if I were smart, I wouldn't have said a thing to Laith. I would have continued to allow him to rock my world, and hopefully he would have rocked it so well that I worked Knight right out of my system. Assuming that's even possible, of course.

Working Knight out of my system? Shit. That's a tall order.

Is it even possible to work someone out of your system when you haven't even had nearly enough of them yet? But despite how he thinks I'm about to become his little needy whore, I can't. We have to force a divide between us. I have to stop running to him every time something fucked up happens at work. I can't rely on somebody I can't have because, sooner or later, I'll become attached, and when that happens, I'm up shit creek without a paddle.

The music makes me feel alive, and the more I drink, the more I forget about the bullshit of this week and just allow myself to have fun. My body moves, and as the random men dancing with me take my waist and put their hands all over me, I can't help but picture the way Knight would dance, the way he would touch me, the way his hips would grind against my ass. And damn it, I've never needed anything more.

As I fantasize about the one man I shouldn't want, the music shifts, and the alcohol starts to make my brain feel fuzzy. A strange shiver tingles my spine, making the hairs stand up on the back of my neck.

My body goes stiff, and I whip around, my eyes wide as I search the faces of the people around me.

He's here.

My stalker is here, and his eyes are locked on me.

Fear rockets through my chest, and as my body comes to a stop, one of the men leans in with his hand still on my waist. "You good, baby? You look as though you've seen a ghost?"

I swallow over the fear, trying to remember the rules of his deadly game of hide-and-seek as I search for him in the crowded club, but it's useless. I don't know who I'm looking for, don't know the lines of his face, the color of his eyes. I'm looking for a needle in a haystack.

My heart hammers. What the hell does he want with me?

If I scream, I fail. If I run, I die.

He's here to play.

The man's hand tightens on my waist, and I realize he's still waiting for a response, and I plaster on a fake smile. "Oh yeah . . . I . . . just need another drink."

He nods, and a stupid grin lifts the corner of his lips, probably thinking he'll have a better chance at fucking me in the men's room if I'm wasted. "Stay here. Dance. I'll get it."

I smile and nod, and as his hands drop away from my body, I make a mental note not to drink a sip of whatever fresh bullshit he brings me. I'm usually pretty trusting overall, but not when it comes to strange men in a club offering me drinks.

His friend immediately moves in, stepping behind me and taking my waist as he rolls his hips against my ass. His hands skim across my waist, and I've got to give it to him, he knows what he's doing. For just a fleeting second, he almost makes me forget about the shivers down my spine.

My body loosens up again, and as I dance with this man, my gaze continues scanning the club. I search every single face, bypassing Izzy's as she locks lips with the perfect stranger she's dancing with, and despite my current predicament, I take a moment to cheer her on. She works so hard. She deserves a night to let her hair down and get crazy. I just hope this guy can keep up with her. She has high standards for the men she takes to bed, or in this case, the men she screws on the end of the bar.

Something pulls my gaze across the room, and as the bodies move and sway to the music, a dark figure steps out of the shadows. The familiar gothic skull mask stares back at me, and I falter, my body falling back against the man's chest behind me. He takes it as an invitation to hold me tighter, his cock pressed up against my ass.

Not good.

I can't tear my eyes off him as his penetrating stare leaves me breathless, yet as my body moves to the music, I can't help but feel as though he enjoys it. If I play his game, give him what he wants, then what do I have to lose? It's better than the alternative of running for my life and ending up in a body bag, waiting for Dr. McKullan to perform my autopsy.

I have to play his game. I have no other choice. And with that, I decide to put on a show.

I use the man behind me as my prop, moving my body against his as I keep my eyes locked on the captivating stranger across the room. I tease him with my moves, arching my back and giving him exactly what he wants, making sure he gets the perfect view of my body.

The man behind me gets into it, sensing the change in me and assuming it has everything to do with him. His hands become bolder on my body, grazing over my tits before dipping low between my thighs and cupping my pussy. I grind against his hand as the hypnotic stare from across the club leaves me desperate for round two.

The way he brought my body to the edge in my bedroom was everything, and though I know the risks involved, I can't help but want more. I want to drop to my knees for this man. I want to make him lose control the way he did for me.

The man behind me leans in, his lips brushing my ear intimately. "You wanna get out of here?"

I shake my head, still keeping my eyes on my stalker. "I'm not ready to leave," I tell him.

"We don't need to leave," he says. "But I need to fuck you, you little tease. You wanna take a ride on my cock?"

Ugh.

I shake my head. "I just wanna dance."

His grip tightens on my waist, and while the idea of being fucked into oblivion is doing wicked things to me, it's not him or his friend I want touching me. Plus, the idea of being gang-raped in the alleyway behind the club isn't as appealing to me as I'm sure it is to him.

He groans in my ear. "Come on. I know you're down for it. Promise, you'll love it."

I turn in his arms, realizing I'm going to have to get rid of this guy somehow, and seeing as though he's thinking with his dick, there's probably only one way to do this. "Okay, but I'm not leaving with you," I finally tell him, beaming up at him as I continue moving my body against his, pressing my tits into his hands. "Why don't you go to the bathroom, and I'll meet you there in a second?"

His lips twist with excitement, an uneasy pride shining in his eyes, and he looks at me as though he's just gotten away with something. "Okay, tease. Don't keep me waiting long."

"I won't."

His hands fall away from my body, and he slinks away to the men's room. The moment he's out of sight, I slip away into the crowd, grazing past Izzy to let her know I'm still alive. But with her lips still more than occupied, I doubt she even realizes it was me who just touched her.

I make a mental note to keep my eye on her, and as the alcohol begins to make me wobbly on my feet, I find my stalker across the room. I can't help but gravitate toward him, my pussy throbbing with a wild need that only he could possibly satisfy right now.

Nerves spike in my chest, but with his dark gaze locked on mine, nothing is holding me back. I beeline toward him, and the closer I get, the more secluded we become from the rest of the club. My tongue rolls over my lips, my chest heaving with the same mix of fear and desire I felt in my bedroom, and damn it, I need to feel his hands on my body.

My knees shake with every step, but as I move right into his personal space, I turn on my heel, plastering my back against his chest in the same way we stood in my bedroom. His hand immediately locks around my waist, claiming me as though I've always belonged to him.

"I guess you found me," I tell him, playing into his game.

He doesn't say a word, but his approval is right there in the way his hips begin to roll with mine, our bodies moving together as we inch deeper into the shadows. I feel his cock up against my ass, and I press back against it, teasing him with everything I have.

I reach up behind me, locking my hand around the back of his neck as I tip my head back, the music claiming my soul and intoxicating me with its beat.

His hand moves down my body, and when it slips beneath the hem of my skirt, I welcome his touch. His fingers pull aside the delicate fabric of my thong, and then just like in my room, he pushes his skilled fingers deep inside me.

I groan, my body falling against his as he holds me up, and I reach down between my thighs, gripping his hand and holding it there. Our bodies continue moving to the music as the palm of his hand grinds against my clit, sending me into a world of bliss.

My hips jolt as the pleasure rocks through me, and when his fingers split inside me, I lose my fucking mind. His fingers massage my walls as I completely lose myself, not caring about the hundreds of bodies crammed into the club or the fact that any single one of them could look this way and see.

We're hardly being discreet, and yet all that matters is feeling the same intense high that I know he's capable of giving me.

He continues grinding his cock against my ass, and I throw my head back against his chest. His other arm locks around my body, touching me everywhere and bringing me to life. It's intoxicating.

I need more.

His fingers take me higher as his palm works my clit, and when his fingers curve inside me, reaching my G-spot, my world explodes. I shatter like glass, my orgasm creeping up on me with a fierce intensity and knocking the breath right out of my lungs.

I cry out, my nails digging into his skin, and as he keeps working me, I ride out the wave, still frantically trying to catch my breath. "That's a good little kitten," he murmurs in my ear with that exhilarating deep tone, the vibrations against my back making my eyes roll in my head.

As I come down from my high, his hold relaxes on my body, and when he pulls his fingers free, he brings them to my lips. "Open," he demands.

I don't hesitate, sucking his fingers clean as I feel his laser-sharp stare on my face. When his fingers fall away, I find myself lost, not knowing where it goes from here. I've played his game and given him exactly what he came for, but what now? Does he walk away like he did the other night, or now that I've been a compliant good girl, will he finish it?

My heart starts to race, and when he goes to step around me, I find myself reaching for his hand. I know I should fear him. I should slip into the crowd and hide, or at the very least call Knight and have him take me home, but instead, I pull him back, shaking my head.

"Where the hell do you think you're going?" I press my hand to his chest as he stares at me through that horrifying mask. "You got to play your little game, and now it's my turn."

Taking his hand, I lead him through the club to one of the many private booths. It's covered in darkness, and despite the hundreds of people around us, not one of them is paying attention to us. We're just as alone as we would be had he broken into my apartment again.

He doesn't say a word, just allows me to take the lead as my heart pounds with devilish excitement. I push him down into the booth; he leans back in the cushioned chair, his knees slightly spread, and I step right between them before gripping his shoulders and leaning down toward him. "Are you ready to see just how wild this little kitten can be?"

He takes my waist, his fingers digging into my skin, and before he gets a chance to respond, I drop down between his thighs. Reaching for his belt, I slowly release it while keeping my hungry stare locked on his. A thrill pulses through me, my pussy throbbing with need, and as I undo his pants and reach inside, the excitement only gets better.

He's huge, just like Knight, and fuck, I can't help that voice in the back of my mind telling me this could be him. He's ready for me, rock hard with protruding veins leading up to his tip, and damn, it looks angry. Just the way I like it.

My tongue rolls over my lips as I grasp the base of his impressive cock, holding firm as my fist works up and down. He reaches for me, and I just know he's wanting to take control, to dictate how this is going to go, but I smack his hand away and shake my head. "My turn," I tell him. "You'll sit back and take it anyway I'm willing to give it."

I can practically feel the groan vibrating through his chest, and I resist calling him a good boy, wanting to save that only for Knight.

My fist works right to his tip, and sensing that he's already on the edge, I lean forward and close my mouth around him. My tongue works over his tip, and as my fist works back down to his base, my mouth follows, taking him right to the back of my throat.

I give him everything I've got, not daring to take my eyes off his, and the more I work him, the quicker he starts to lose control. His hands ball into fists at his sides as I push right past my gag reflex. Tears well in my eyes, but I don't stop, determined to bring him to his knees.

His hips jolt beneath me, and just when I think he's about to blow, he reaches for me, whipping me around until I'm straddled backward over him. "Fuck me, kitten," he growls in my ear. "Show me how you ride me."

Yes, sir.

He reaches beneath my skirt, finding my thong and tearing the fabric clean off my body before gripping my hip and guiding me down over his massive cock. He fills me to the brim, and I immediately throw my head back as my walls stretch around him. It's not like with Knight who allowed me a chance to adjust to his size. No, he just takes me, and fuck, I love it.

I cry out, groaning with undeniable pleasure as I grip his knees for balance. He reaches around me, his skilled fingers coming down over my clit, and as he rolls tight little circles, I start to ride him, rocking my hips as I work right to his delicious tip and dropping straight back down again.

"Oh, fuck," I moan, my body responding to his touch so damn fast as that familiar coil already begins to tighten. I bounce on his cock, being his perfect little whore, taking him deep as my walls fall to pieces around him. My hips jolt with a fierce pleasure, and when his fingers capture my clit and gently pinch, hot bursts of electricity rip through my body.

I come apart, my pussy violently spasming around his thick cock, and as the intensity overwhelms me, he takes my hip to keep me moving, not allowing me to give up just yet. I ride out every second of it, and as his fingers keep tormenting my clit with his wicked pleasure, my high intensifies, pulsing through me.

I clench my eyes as I lose control of my body, every last inch of me either spasming or convulsing, my pussy gripping his cock as though it will never let go. "Squeeze me, kitten. Fucking squeeze me."

His tone is raw and desperate, and as I keep rocking my hips, grinding and bouncing over him, he finally falls apart, coming hard as he grips my hips and shoots hot spurts of cum deep inside my greedy cunt.

His hips thrust beneath me, taking me deeper as he empties himself, and as I come down from my high, my body goes limp, barely able to hold myself up against his knees.

He pulls me against him, leaning me back against his massive chest as I take a moment to catch my breath, and as I do, his fingers lazily roll over my sensitive clit. "What a hungry little devil you are," he murmurs in my ear. "You love riding my cock, don't you?"

His words send shivers sailing down my spine as I bite down on my bottom lip. Did I love riding his cock? Every fucking second of it. So what the hell is wrong with me?

I nod, not really knowing how to respond to this man in a way that doesn't somehow break the rules of his deadly, twisted game, and I hear his soft laugh in my ear. "I'll be coming back for more, my sweet kitten. Now that I know how tight your cunt can squeeze me, I won't be letting you out of my sight."

And with that, he lifts me off him and places me down in the booth beside him before getting to his feet. He turns to face me, that penetrating stare holding mine as he fixes his pants, and the way he watches me is almost like a challenge, daring me to try and make a break for it, but I won't dare break the rules.

If I run, I die. And to be honest, I'm not sure I'm done playing his wicked little game either. He's only just getting started, and I can't wait to see what he has in store for me next.

The music pumps around us, people laughing and squealing as they have the time of their lives, completely unaware of the world-shattering orgasm I just had in this booth.

He holds my stare just a moment longer when I hear Izzy rushing in. "Harper's Bazaar!" she squeals, stealing my attention away. "Here you are. I've been looking for you everywhere."

Izzy crashes down beside me, barely taking notice of the terrifying man she just pushed past, and when I flick my gaze back up to meet his, he's gone, not even a shadow of him left behind.

CHAPTER 20

KNIGHT

Elias gazes at me with an uneasy stare as he lifts his glass of whiskey to his lips, sitting back in his ridiculous armchair, fitting right into the billionaire lifestyle. It suits him. Well, at first when he was still grateful for his achievements and success. Now he's just arrogant, but he puts on one hell of a show being the powerful businessman by day and doting husband by night.

Truth be told, he's a piece of shit, and it took me a really long time to figure it out, but now that I see it, it's impossible to ignore. It's mostly the reason why I keep my distance. That and his gold-digging wife. Fuck, she's a punishment. I get why he keeps her around. She's not bad on the eyes. She looks just like an older, pearl-clutching version of Harper, but . . . so much less. Plus, from what Elias says, she goes off in the sheets, not that I particularly want to know about that.

He's a good twelve years older than me and was raised by our father to be cold and callous, just as he was. On the other hand, I was an accident that my father had no interest in. I was seen as weak and not worthy of his time. After all, he was too busy turning Elias into his clone. But I preferred it that way. I was raised in the same household, but I only had my mother's affection. She was sweet and loving, and she only ever thought about what was best for me.

The day my father came home and blindsided Mom with a divorce and his new nineteen-year-old fiancée was nothing short of a blessing. Mom and I took off and started our own life together while Elias was stuck under his thumb. The only time I ever saw my father after that day was at his funeral, and the only reason I went was to make sure the old bastard was actually dead. And now Elias is a carbon copy of our old man.

He's forty-eight and on his third marriage, each of which fell apart because he was cheating with younger women, and when I say younger, I mean barely legal. Which is also why I don't care to get to know Mae.

Sooner or later, she'll be kicked aside and left begging for scraps because of the ironclad prenup Elias shoved down her throat. Though I'm sure Mae thinks she can get herself knocked up and give him an heir to his throne in order to claim a chunk of his billions for herself. It won't work, though. Elias has the best lawyers money can buy. Whatever he says goes, and if he wants Mae to scrounge for pennies the rest of her life, then that's exactly what she'll get. It's in her best interest to play his game, and she better hope that he doesn't tire of her. Though I have to give credit where it's due. Considering they've already been married five years, she must be doing something right. But sooner or later, something is bound to break.

Elias finishes what's left of his whiskey, and as he stands from his armchair and strides across the room for a refill, he looks back at me. "You free next weekend?" he asks. "Mae wants to organize a family dinner."

I scoff. "Right. Because the last one went so well."

Elias rolls his eyes, probably just as irritated by Mae's pathetic performance as Harper was, though there's no denying that he does a much better job at hiding his disdain. "This will be family only. I think it's Mae's attempt to smooth things over with her daughter."

My brow arches. "And she thinks having dinner is the way to do that?"

I shake my head. It's crystal fucking clear that Mae doesn't know shit about her daughter. If she wanted to smooth it over, she would apologize and leave her the fuck alone.

Elias refills his whiskey and immediately lifts the glass to his lips, having another long drink. "Apparently," he says with a scoff, his well-structured façade beginning to slip. "If I had it my way, I'd be down there knocking on Harper's door and teaching that girl a lesson myself."

The fuck?

I keep quiet, watching him, waiting for whatever comes out of his mouth next. "Making a scene like that in front of my guests. Some of them were colleagues worth billions, and that girl had the audacity to act like a teenage brat."

I lift my glass to my lips to hide the scoff that tears from the back of my throat. After all, teenage brats are his favorite. "You don't think things would have gone differently had Mae not provoked her?"

"Please," he mutters, shaking his head. "Mae can be a daft bitch at times, but it's not as though she said anything Harper hadn't heard before. Besides, what's a little criticism between family? If her mother can't give an honest opinion, then who the fuck can?"

Me. That's who. And in my opinion, Harper should have burned the fucking place down on her way out. "Right," I say slowly, not agreeing in the least.

"She needs that bad attitude fucked out of her."

I choke on my whiskey. "Excuse me?"

"Oh, come on, Knight," Elias murmurs, making his way back to his pretentious armchair and dropping down, being careful not to spill his whiskey on his designer suit. "Get off your fucking high horse. You can't sit here as a red-blooded man and tell me you haven't noticed how fuckable that girl is. She's stunning, and there's no denying how much she wants me. I see it when she looks at me. She can barely hold back."

I stare at my brother in disgust. I always knew he was a piece of shit, but I never realized just how deep that ran. "You mean your stepdaughter?" I ask, making sure he's got his head screwed on straight and it's just the whiskey talking. But fuck, there's no denying how sick he's making me feel.

He scoffs again. "That doesn't mean shit. I've had stepdaughters before. Didn't stop me then, and it's not going to stop me now. I just gotta wait for the right time to let her pounce." He pauses to take another long drink, throwing back what's left of the glass. It's his third tumbler of whiskey in less than ten minutes. "I bet she'd go off. What do you think? I reckon she'd be a little whore like her momma, thirsty for my cock and calling me Daddy until I hand her my black card."

I place my glass down on the side table before getting to my feet. "Brother, I can guarantee that girl doesn't even notice you, let alone tolerate you," I tell him before dropping my hand to his shoulder and leaning in, letting him feel the threat behind my stare. "You lay a hand on Harper without her consent, and I'll burn your whole fucking empire to the ground."

He holds my stare, his gaze narrowing. "Ahh, it seems the apple doesn't fall far from the tree. You fucking want her too, don't you, little brother? Have you been fantasizing about taking that sweet cunt just as much as I have?"

I let out a breath, needing a moment to find just a fraction of composure before I beat the shit out of him in his damn armchair. "You're drunk, Elias. Sleep it off before you say something you can't take back."

Elias laughs as I stride out of the room, heading straight for the door. "You'll see, Knight. It's only a matter of time before she's mine."

If only he knew that I already know exactly how she tastes, how she pants when she's getting close, how her nails dig into my skin as she comes. But he'll never fucking know because he'll never fucking touch her. Not if I have anything to do with it.

I shake my head, gritting my teeth in an attempt not to turn around and show him precisely what I think of him. It wouldn't even be hard. He's a sloppy drunk and spends more time in boardrooms than in a gym. Sure, we're the same height, and we have more similarities than I care to admit, but when it comes to muscle mass, he's got nothing on me. Not to mention the years of vigorous training I've been through to ensure I'm in peak physical condition. I'd snap him like a fucking twig, and what's more, after those comments about Harper, I'd enjoy it.

I'm just getting into my truck when my phone lights up with an incoming call from Ace, and considering my current mood, I almost let it ring out, but something has me answering his call.

"What's up, man?"

"Diesel and I are only just getting off. We're gonna head out to that new bar on 2nd. You down?"

My face scrunches. I don't particularly want to head out, especially after the fresh bullshit I just discovered in my brother's private bar. However, if I were to go home, I have no doubt that I'll spend the rest of my night picturing Elias and Harper together, and it's not a pretty sight. He will do whatever he can to hold his money over her and force her into compliance, but he'll be barking up the wrong tree. Harper isn't anything like her mother. She's not a gold digger, and she's certainly not frothing at the mouth to be with the man her mother is screwing.

Letting out a heavy breath, I glance at the time. It's a little after two in the morning, and while I know I should go home, a drink with the boys will do me a world of good. "Yeah, alright. I'll be there in thirty minutes."

After ending the call, I turn on my truck and feel it rumble to life beneath me. Without skipping a beat, I hit the gas and get the fuck out of this hellhole.

With no traffic on the road, it takes a little over fifteen minutes to reach the bar. After parking and heading inside, I find Diesel and Ace sitting at a table, already halfway through their first drink.

"Aye," Ace calls over the loud music and the sound of the mechanical bull competition happening deeper in the bar. "I thought for sure you were gonna bail."

I scoff and take the beer out of Diesel's outstretched hand, appreciating it more than they could know. "Not tonight," I say, knowing they have more than enough experience with me bailing on nights just like this for his assumption to have merit. "I need this."

"Ahh yeah," Diesel murmurs. "You had that thing with your brother."

Ace scoffs, knowing my disdain for my brother. "How'd that go?"

"As expected," I mutter, lifting the rim to my lips and taking a long drink. "He talked. I listened. Then I left before I beat the shit out of him."

Diesel smirks. "So standard, then?"

"Pretty much."

The boys and I relax and talk shit, and soon enough, a few of the other guys on the team are showing up and letting loose. They tell me about their shift. It was quiet, which no doubt means our next shift is going to be more chaotic than any of us are prepared for, but if anyone can handle it, it's my team.

I sit back and listen to the mayhem around me, letting my mind wander, and just as I go to lift the glass of my second beer to my lips, a howling laugh comes tearing through the bar from the back of the room.

My back stiffens, hearing the familiar tone as all eyes turn toward the mechanical bull competition, and there, riding the bull like a fucking cowgirl, is Harper-Rayn Madden, her short skirt flying up and flashing every one of my boys.

"Well, fuck," Ace says beside me. "I'd recognize that ass anywhere."

I grab him by the front of the shirt and pull him in. "What did I tell you about her ass?" I say. "Don't make me wrap this glass around your head." He laughs, knowing damn well how to get a rise out of me, and as I make my way toward Harper, I can't help but notice Ace trailing along. Ace isn't the type to just sit back and allow shit to happen without stirring the pot, so I turn and meet his stare. "Sit your ass down before I break your legs and make you sit down."

He laughs again, his gaze shifting over my shoulder to Harper, and there's no denying the attraction there. "You screw it up with that one and I'll be right there to take your place."

I roll my eyes but am thankful when he retreats to the table and drops down with the guys. He says something to Diesel, and when both of the fuckers glance my way, grinning like the morons they are, I can only shake my head.

By the time I reach Harper, the whole team will be watching, and I don't doubt they'll have scorecards ready to produce for every move I make. Every glance in her direction. Every fucking touch.

Letting out a heavy breath, I stride through the bar, wishing I hadn't left my drink behind, but judging by the way Harper swings around and laughs on that bull, I can only assume she's wasted. As I get closer, I notice she has a friend with her, cheering her on, but considering she can barely stand, I have to assume she's just as drunk as Harper.

I step right up to the side of the ring, crossing my arms over my chest as Harper holds on to the bull with one hand, swinging the other in the air as though she were whipping a lasso. She rocks back and forth, her body being thrown from side to side, and I have no fucking idea how she isn't throwing up by now. There's no denying it, though, she's killing this competition.

As she whips back and forth, her gaze locks onto mine, and she lets out an excited squeal, her face splitting with the biggest smile I've ever seen. I won't lie, it warms something in my cold heart.

"New number one," she whoops.

Her friend sucks in a breath, moving far too close to the mechanical bull to be considered safe. "New number one?" she squeals with excitement, and it takes me a minute to place her. Izabella maybe? Izabelle? I think I met her at Mae and Elias's wedding. "Holy SHIIIIII—"

The mechanical bull takes her out, slamming into her ass and sending her hurtling face-first into the padded wall of the small arena. She lands with an *oomph*, holding her glass up high, somehow not spilling a drop, and just as I go to help her, Harper leaps to her feet and bounds toward me.

She drops to the floor, her legs up in the air and her skirt flying up to reveal everything she has to offer. She looks up at me with those big innocent eyes, and I fucking melt. "Harper," I scold, leaning down and reaching for the front of her skirt and quickly pulling it down before holding out my hand to help her up. Her friend howls with laughter. "Where are your panties?"

Harper laughs and allows me to help her to her feet before gripping my arms as she climbs out of the small arena. A beaming smile rips across her face followed by a quick hiccup. "I lost them," she laughs. "Poof. They just disappeared. Ripped right off me."

I gape at her. "They just disappeared, huh?" I resist the urge to look around, assuming that her lack of panties has everything to do with this other asshole she's been with, the very reason she didn't want to be exclusive—not that exclusivity was on the table in the first place.

She nods and holds up her hand, making fireworks with her fingers. "Poof."

"Dare I ask how they just magically vanished into thin air? Are you here with someone?"

She nods before grabbing her friend and almost knocking her off her feet. She hooks her arm over her shoulder before declaring. "I'm here with Izzy. The Iz-meister. The one and only Izabelle Grace Davenport. Sounds fancy, right? Just rolls off the tongue. Izabelle Grace Davenport. She's a fashion designer, you know. She'll be killing it at New York Fashion Week before we know it."

I nod, and a part of me is pleased that she's not here with another man, but that doesn't shed any light on the whereabouts of her underwear. "Hi, Izabelle. Good to see you again."

Izabelle grins at me. "Well, hi to you too, Mr. Get On Your Knees. You may call me Izzy."

I arch a brow and glance at Harper, surprised to find that she shared that snippet of information with her friend, and she has the audacity to laugh about it. "What? Was I not supposed to go blabbing about the guy who took me in during my hour of need and then had his wicked way with me on his bedroom floor in the form of trying to bruise the little dangly thing in the back of my throat with his enormous cock? Oh, I'm sorry. I had no idea, Your Majesty."

She hiccups again, and it quickly turns into an awkward burp that makes me uneasy. "Whoops."

"Harper," I say, holding her attention. "Just how much have you drunk?"

Both of the girls hold up their hands, trying to count as they rattle off the details of their many trips to the bar. "Ummmm . . . I think seven . . . teen." She grins, and then the grin slips away. "My tummy feels ooshy."

"Ooshy?"

She nods. "Ooshy gooshy."

Ahh fuck.

"Come on. I'm taking you home."

Her eyes widen with excitement. "Are you going to hit me with that bossy dom shit again? Because I won't lie, I enjoyed that. Though between you and me, I think I'm bossier."

"Harper," I warn.

"You know, I'm quite the cowgirl," she says, deep in thought. "I've recently been in practice of my reverse cowgirl techniques, and I'm proud to announce that I'm a top-tier screw with a deliciously delectable derrière."

"Indeed," I agree, putting my hand on each of the girls' backs and leading them out of the bar. "You have a very delectable derrière. Nobody is arguing there," I tell her. "But no. I'm taking you straight home, putting you to bed, and that's it. Don't even try it."

Both of the girls laugh, and just as I get them out to my truck and manage to get Izzy into the back seat, Harper leans against my door, propping out her hip and smirking at me as though she knows something I should know. "The joke's up, Knight. You followed me here, didn't you?" she says, narrowing her gaze as though she's trying to catch me out. "I'm not mad about it."

Something twists in my gut, and an uneasiness floods through my veins. "The fuck are you talking about?"

"In the club. That was you, right?"

I shake my head. "Do I look like the type of man who spends his Saturday night in a club?"

Her brows furrow, and she almost looks sad. "So it wasn't you?" she asks, her shoulders slumping. "I could have sworn. He's tall just like you. Bossy too."

My stare narrows, and I step into her, gripping her chin and forcing her stare on mine, not liking where this is going. "What the fuck are you talking about, Harper? Who's bossy? Is this your stalker you're talking about? Was he there tonight? He talked to you?"

She presses her lips into a hard line and nods, guilt flashing in her eyes. "You're mad."

I clench my jaw and try to put my frustration aside, knowing now isn't the time to get into it, especially when she's barely able to string a proper sentence together. "Why would I be mad at you, Morticia?"

She grins and glances away. "Because I let him do naughty things to me again."

My face falls as my heart hammers right out of my fucking chest. "You did what?" I ask. "Wait. Again? The fuck is that supposed to mean? You've seen him twice and let him touch you?"

She giggles, but the giggles quickly turn into hiccups. "He likes to play dirty little games and say naughty things in my ear. I thought—"

"Fuck me," I breathe, stepping back and pushing my hands through my hair. I pace in front of her, not understanding how she could let this happen, but more than that, how could she not tell me? This happened twice and she hasn't said a single thing. How the fuck am I supposed to protect her from this asshole if she's letting him have his way with her? Fucking hell.

"You let him touch you?" I clarify, already burning with questions that are going to have to wait until she's not intoxicated.

She bites down on her lip and looks at me with such guilt it's almost heartbreaking. "I thought it might have been you."

"For fuck's sake, Harper. Are you trying to get yourself killed?" I demand, suddenly understanding what the fuck happened to her underwear.

Her bottom lip quivers, and I immediately feel like an ass. "You wouldn't hurt me."

"No, I wouldn't," I tell her. "But I'm not this guy. I'm not him, and he sure as fuck will hurt you, Harper. You can't let this happen. Do you have any idea how many times I've seen this? It never ends well."

She rolls her tongue over her bottom lip and glances away, her tone lowering to almost a whisper. "But I liked it."

I blow out a breath, having no fucking idea how I'm supposed to navigate this. All I know is that this situation is escalating, and sooner or later, he'll get what he wants from her, assuming he hasn't already had enough, but when he does, he'll end her life.

"Come on," I say, "get in the truck. I'm taking you back to my place where I can keep an eye on you, and in the morning, we're going to talk about this."

Harper groans and lets out a heavy sigh, but thankfully she wanders her ass around to the other side of my truck and climbs in. I reluctantly get in as well, and the moment I turn on the truck, Izzy falls asleep in the back seat, her soft snores filling the cab.

Just fucking great.

It's a short drive back to my place, and yet the unbearable silence makes every passing second feel as though it's dragging on. Harper doesn't say a word the whole drive, and I keep my mouth shut, trying not to rip into her about allowing this asshole to put his hands on her.

There's got to be more to this story. Harper-Rayn is a smart girl. I don't believe that she'd just willingly let this happen, no matter how good she thinks it's going to be. Not even if she truly thought it was me.

By the time we reach my home, there's no waking Izzy, and I have no choice but to haul her over my shoulder. As Harper gets to her feet and tries to walk, it's clear that this isn't going to be as easy as I'd hoped.

Harper squeals as I toss her over my other shoulder and stride into my home. If I'm lucky, my neighbors aren't watching me bring two intoxicated women into my home. I can only imagine how this looks.

Taking them down to my spare room, I put the girls on the bed, and Harper immediately crawls across the sheets, helping take off Izzy's shoes. Once she has the blanket pulled up to her chin, Harper gets to her feet and wobbles across the room, disappearing into the bathroom. She emerges a few minutes later with her hair down and most of her makeup scrubbed off.

Her outfit smells like a bar, and I get her yet another shirt before leaving her to it and getting myself ready for bed. I go to the bathroom and wash my face before standing at the sink, bracing my hands against the cool porcelain and wondering what the fuck I'm supposed to do.

I can't help somebody who doesn't want to be helped. I don't need to protect her from her stalker, I need to protect her from herself.

Finishing up in the bathroom, I peel my shirt off and make my way to bed, but when I tug the blankets back, Harper is already curled up inside them. I stand and watch her for just a moment, hating how much I like her there. Knowing this will complicate things for me so much more, I climb in behind her and pull her straight into my arms, letting her curl up on my chest, and hoping like fuck I don't fall in love with this girl.

CHAPTER 21

HARPER-RAYN

Stupid. Stupid. Stupid.

It's my first night shift of the week, and so far, I've done everything in my power to avoid Knight Slater like the plague. Yesterday morning, I woke up in his bed with his arms locked around me, and for just a moment, I never wanted to leave, but then the memories of Saturday night rushed back, as did all the words I said to him outside his truck.

Like I said, stupid.

I just had to go and open my big mouth, but I was so certain that it was him, despite the whole *don't call me by another man's name* shit that the stalker decided to almost suffocate me over. So I suppose maybe it isn't Knight after all.

There are too many coincidences. The night the body showed up in the morgue, I drove like a maniac to Knight's place, but he had only just gotten home. If it were him, he could have absolutely beaten me back to his place. Not to mention the night I was locked in the refrigeration unit. I went straight to his place, and again, he was only just getting home. Both times he was out. Though I know we technically cleared up the whole refrigeration unit mishap, and it wasn't the stalker at all, but if it were, Knight absolutely could have been a suspect.

But in that club and in my room, I could have sworn it was Knight. The way he plays, the bossiness, and the filthy demands. Just the way he works my cunt. It has to be Knight. Nothing else makes sense to me. He's the same height as well. He ticks all the Knight-shaped boxes. How could it not be him? But then, I don't believe Knight is a killer, and I sure as fuck don't believe that he'd ever wrap his hand around my throat and squeeze until I almost pass out. Don't get me wrong, I think Knight would absolutely experiment with that, especially if I asked nicely, but he wouldn't take it as far as the stalker did.

I'm in trouble.

After opening my big mouth on Saturday night, I had no doubt that Knight would have a shitload of things to say, and if it weren't for Izzy not being a morning person, I would have hauled her ass out of there in an Uber. But that woman sleeps like the living dead, and I had no choice but to face Knight. At least, I thought I was going to face him, but he woke up to a work call and had to take off. He reminded me on his way out that our conversation wasn't over.

Joke's on him, though, because I had no intention of waiting around to talk. I didn't even risk leaving a message on his home security system on my way out. I just bailed with Izzy and have held my breath ever since.

I feel my time is running out, though. He's not going to let things fester after I drop a bomb like that. He'll be barging through my door the moment he can, and when he does, he'll have more than enough to say.

Mondays are always chaotic in the morgue. Blackstone's crime rate is absurd, and as a result, bodies tend to pile up. Though I have it on good authority, after spending a good hour locked in the refrigeration unit last week, that we have more than enough space to house all the bodies that the Blackstone criminals want to throw our way. You'll never see me complain about it, though. After all, it's wonderful to have such great job security.

I sit at my desk, trying to get through my latest report, and I'm proud to say that with my mind so heavily focused on Knight's disapproval, I haven't been jumping at every little sound in the morgue. Or maybe that's because I've finally got a handle on this stalker's game.

It's twisted, but it's all just a game, and when you know the rules, it's easy to play along. Hell, it's not only easy to play along, it can be extremely rewarding. Though I have to admit, my thighs have been burning ever since my spontaneous reverse cowgirl performance in the middle of the club. Or perhaps it's from the mechanical bull. It's hard to tell.

The words flow on the report, and I'm just about done when the familiar sound of the door opening has my head whipping up. My breath catches in my chest, almost expecting to see Knight or a satanic mask walking through the door, but when I see the janitor's familiar cleaning cart, I let out a relieved sigh.

"Hey, Vincent," I call out, turning my attention back to my computer screen.

"Who the fuck is Vincent?"

My head snaps back up to see a new janitor, this one much younger than Vincent, and judging by his scowl, he doesn't seem pleased to see me. The feeling is mutual.

"Just the usual night janitor," I mutter, turning back to the report as he moves around the morgue. "What happened to him? He never misses a shift."

"Do I look like I know what happened to some loser janitor?"

I don't bother to point out that he just managed to insult himself, so I just offer him an awkward smile instead. "Sorry, just trying to figure out if this is going to be a permanent change. I like to know who I can expect coming in and out."

The new janitor scoffs, and I immediately miss Vincent. "My schedule ain't none of your business, bitch."

Well, shit.

Knowing I don't have a good poker face, I turn back to the computer again and get back to work before he's able to see the deep scowl pulling at my lips. I don't like this guy even a little bit, but assuming he just wants to get in and get his job done, then I'm more than happy to keep my mouth shut and ignore him.

He grabs the antiseptic spray and some old dirty rags and gets to work, moving around the morgue and putting in the absolute bare minimum, spreading more germs than actually cleaning them.

I clench my jaw to keep from saying anything, but the moment this asshole is out of my morgue, I'm going to have no choice but to reclean everything he's touched. I just hope someone in another department who doesn't run the risk of being alone in a room with him has the good sense to report him.

I need Vincent back stat. I hope this is only a temporary situation.

The longer he's here, the more he seems to give me the creeps, though not in the same way my stalker does. This is different. The new janitor seems like the kind of guy who would rob you and then spit on you when he was done. My stalker is more of the . . . Well, I think it's clear what type of man my stalker is.

God. That club was fun. It shouldn't have been, but it was.

Am I sick for wanting to do it again?

The janitor seems to linger longer than necessary, and every time he wanders close to me, I grip my trusty pen, more than ready to plunge it deep into the side of his neck if need be. His eyes on my back are unsettling, and I'm pissed off that I can't focus on my work at all.

Now I know I've done some questionable things over the past few days, but dropping to my knees for a man like this? Absolutely not. He's got another thing coming if he thinks he's about to get something out of me.

My computer screen goes into sleep mode, the dark screen allowing me to see everything behind me like a mirror, and just as the janitor sweeps back around toward me, the soft beep of the morgue doors sounds through the room.

I let out a shaky breath and relax my hold on my pen as the big doors open. The coroner walks in with two gurneys being pushed by hospital staff, two police officers, and one of the newer detectives I haven't had a chance to get to know.

"Double homicide," the coroner says as the bodies are delivered onto the autopsy tables.

I give him a tight smile, still feeling awkward with the janitor loitering, but I put it aside, certain I don't need to be concerned now that there's a room full of people, three of those being cops.

I move in beside the first body as the detective hands over a file and launches into an explanation of the murders, and just as expected, he follows up his summary with the typical declaration of just how quickly I need to prioritize these autopsies.

I nod and give false promises just like always, but honestly, there's something that seems exciting about these cases. I glance at the clock on the wall as the cops and the hospital staff file back out of the room, and seeing that I have just enough time to get both of these autopsies done and will have time to write up their reports before the end of my shift, I reach for a pair of gloves.

The coroner is just walking out as I reach for the zipper at the top of the body bag. The janitor pauses in the middle of the room, gaping at me in disgust. "The fuck? You're not going to do that shit while I'm here."

Having had enough of this asshole, I pull the zip right down to expose the body. "You're in a morgue. This is what we do," I tell him, not even bothering to look up as I reach for a scalpel, despite not even being close to needing it yet, but he doesn't need to know that. "If you can't handle it, there's the door."

I glance up to find his face scrunched and pure evil reflected in his eyes as he grips the handle of his mop like a weapon, and so I simply open the body bag wider, watching as his face turns an uncomfortable shade of green.

"If you don't mind," I say, bringing the tip of the scalpel to the victim's chest, despite him still being fully clothed. "I need to get started."

The asshole gags, and I roll my eyes as he bails on whatever fresh bullshit he was about to throw my way. He races out of the morgue with his cart dragging behind him and his tail tucked between his legs in shame.

I scoff. What a loser. I just hope that Vincent will be back tomorrow.

Having a little peace and quiet, I put the scalpel down and get to work properly, removing the body from the bag, and as I take in the victim's face, I pause, my back going stiff.

"No," I breathe, my eyes widening in horror, seeing the face of the man I was dancing with in the club the other night, still wearing the same clothes that rubbed up against my body, the same clothes I spilled my cocktail on.

Horror blasts through me, and I quickly search the body for any signs of trauma, trying to figure out what the hell happened to him. When I saw him last, he was perfectly fine. He was going to the men's room with the idea that he was about to get lucky.

How the hell did this happen?

My stomach sinks at the realization that my DNA will be all over his body, and there's no doubt that, sooner or later, the detective will come knocking at my door to ask questions. I don't know what the hell I'm going to tell them. The last time I saw him, he was perfectly fine.

I get started, documenting everything as I go and making sure not to miss a thing. I remove his clothes, placing each article in its own evidence bag before setting it aside and getting started on any jewelry or foreign objects attached to his person.

Heaviness pulses through my chest, recognizing the familiar cuts across his skin. They're not quite as vicious as the ones I saw on the previous body, but there's no denying they were created by the same weapon and delivered by the same hand.

This was the work of my stalker.

Bile rises in my throat, but I keep going, certain that there will be a message left behind, but where? I try to put my personal feelings aside, being professional with every second of this autopsy, yet there's a sharp pang of guilt resting in my chest. This man is dead simply for dancing with me in a club.

Tears form in my eyes, but I blink them away, trying to be strong. I won't fall apart. I can do that when I get home. Right now, I have a job to do.

I get to work, documenting every wound on his skin, measuring the length, depth, and width of each one, and as I work my way down the front of his arms, I see strange burn marks on his palms.

My brows furrow, and I lift the victim's hand to get a better look, and I find the palm of his hand completely singed. "What the fuck?" I breathe, taking it in with unease, not able to make sense of any of it.

My gaze continues over his arm, and as I look further down his wrist, I notice that the cuts are deeper, more purposeful, and I can't help but flip the victim over to get a better idea of what's going on here. As I look over him, I start making out little letters in the vicious carvings, and my stomach knots with dread. Writing down each letter at a time, first down his left arm and then the right, I come up with two lines of words.

PAY THE FINE
IF YOU TOUCH WHAT'S MINE

His hands were burned to a crisp simply for having his hands on me as we danced. It's my fault. I knew he was there watching, and I used this man to tease him. I let him touch me, let him grind against me as I tried to gain a reaction out of my stalker.

This man lost his life because of me.

I can't hold back a second longer, and the tears finally fall when I remember the second body that was just delivered. The coroner mentioned it was a double homicide, and that snippet of information makes my stomach jolt. A double homicide could only mean . . . fuck.

I move across the room, positioning myself beside the second body as I hastily grab the zipper and pull it down, desperate to reveal the face hidden beneath, and just as I thought, horror blasts through my veins, making me sick.

The second man I was dancing with stares back at me, his cold, lifeless body covered in the same vicious cuts, and I know without a doubt that somewhere hidden beneath his clothes is another foul message that I don't have the strength to look for just yet.

"No. No, no, no," I cry, the weight of their lives resting heavily on my shoulders. I didn't use this man in the same way that I used the other, but apparently that doesn't matter. He danced with me, so that must mean his life should be taken from him.

Big, fat tears fall down my cheeks, and I drop to my knees, wondering how the fuck I got here. I knew my stalker was capable of this. Of course I did. I saw the body with my own eyes, but a part of me hoped that if I played his game and followed his rules, nobody else would get hurt. But I'm playing a game of checkers while he's playing chess. There are rules I didn't even know to look out for, and now two more men have lost their lives.

A thick lump forms in my throat, making it hard to breathe, and I realize how foolish I was to assume that Knight had anything to do with this. This isn't the act of a highly respected SWAT officer at the top of his game. It's the act of a cruel, callous man who's sick in the head.

The thought of Knight has me scrambling to my feet, and I move across the morgue on autopilot, tears still welling in my eyes as I reach for my phone. I find his number and immediately put the phone to my ear, not even taking off my latex gloves first.

The call rings once before Knight's deep tone comes through the line. "Oh, now you suddenly want to talk to me," he mutters, a slight hint of amusement in his tone. "Don't act as though I haven't noticed you've been avoiding me, Morticia. We still need to talk."

I suck in a breath, the sound coming out as a whimper, and there's no masking the fear in that little noise.

"What's wrong?" he rushes out. I can hear his keys jingling in the background, and I know he's already on his way to me.

"I need you to come to the morgue," I say, turning around to take in the bodies. "You need to see them before he takes them away."

"Sit tight, doll. I'll be there soon."

CHAPTER 22

HARPER-RAYN

The second Knight walks through the door, my panic begins to ease. Then before I can even tell him what's going on, he steps right into me, pulling me into his warm arms and holding me tight, his hand drawing soothing circles on my back.

"You're okay now," he murmurs, that deep tone calming me in a way he will never truly know. "Everything is okay now. You're safe."

I suck in a shaky breath, wishing I could stay right here in his arms for the rest of my life, despite knowing how upset he is with me right now. I was so wrong. Knight can't be the stalker. There's no way that a man who can offer me this type of safety and comfort could be the man responsible for the two bodies on my table.

"What's going on?" he asks, slowly releasing me, his gaze locked and loaded on mine, waiting for any sign I'm about to break.

Taking a step back, I try to pull myself together, hating how weak all of this is making me feel. "Two bodies just came in," I tell him, indicating toward the autopsy tables and watching his brows furrow, wondering where the hell this is going. "They're dead because of me."

He steps a little closer to the bodies, his gaze sweeping over them before coming back to mine. "You're going to have to fill in the blanks, Morticia. How are they dead because of you?"

"Saturday night," I start. "When Izzy and I were at the club, I was dancing with both of these men. I knew the stalker was there, and I used them to tease him. Their hands were all over me. This one," I say, pointing out the body that's mostly still in the body bag. "He went to the bar to get me another drink, but then just never came back, but I didn't think anything of it. And this guy," I say, adjusting my stare to the other body. "He was getting really handsy and wanted me to go home with him, but I wasn't down. So just to get rid of him, I told him I'd meet him in the bathroom and he left, but he never came looking for me when I didn't show up. Both of them just . . . ceased to exist."

Knight looks back at the bodies, looking over them with a skilled gaze. "These . . . these are the guys you were dancing with?" he asks, uncertainty flashing in his eyes, and honestly, the bite in his tone is throwing me off. Is he jealous? No, that couldn't be it. Knight doesn't strike me as the jealous type. But there's definitely something running through his mind. I just wish I knew him well enough to be able to decipher it.

I nod and he looks even more confused.

"And you said the stalker saw you with both of these men?"

"Yes. Both of them. It had to be the stalker, right? He did this because of me."

Knight glances at me, and the hint of pity in his eyes almost tears me to shreds, but I push it away, before hurrying forward to show him the carvings across their bodies, the burned palms, and the message left on the skin of the first victim. I still haven't gotten around to searching for whatever foul message has been left on the second body, but part of me doesn't want to. I've been reluctant to look further, and honestly, I'm starting to go with the theory of what I don't know can't hurt me. Ignorance sounds peaceful.

"Here, look," I say, stepping right up to the first body, and waiting just a moment for Knight to join me. "See these markings on his arms? They're identical to the ones left on the first victim that came in last week, and in my professional opinion, they were created using the same weapon."

Knight leans in, looking over the vicious markings on the man's arm as if trying to make sense of them.

"Do you see the letters?"

"Letters?" he asks, his gaze snapping back to mine, his brows furrowed with a deep confusion before shaking his head. "What letters?"

"In the carvings," I say, pointing them out. "They're hard to make out of the skin, but once you see it, there's no denying they are there, plain as day. Down both arms. It reads *Pay the fine if you touch what's mine*."

He looks closer, trying to see what I'm seeing, then shakes his head. "I'm sorry, doll. I'm not seeing it."

My jaw almost drops. How can he not? It's crystal clear on the victim's skin. "Here," I say, showing him again and using my fingers to point out the jagged lines of each letter, but as his brows continue to inch, I know he's not seeing what I can so clearly see, and honestly, I've never been so disappointed.

He pulls on a set of gloves from my desk and looks over the rest of the body, taking a special interest in the man's burned hands. "These injuries aren't fatal, though," he muses. "How were they killed?"

I shake my head. "I haven't worked that out yet. Apart from the hands and the carvings, there are no other visible markings on their bodies. I'm hoping there might be some clues when I start the internal part of the autopsy, but so far, I've got nothing."

Knight straightens to his full height and takes a breath, clearly still deep in thought. He rips off his gloves and tosses them into the trash, and without another word, he strides across the room to an empty table, grips the side, and hangs his head. My heart breaks for him. I hate that he's involved in this. After dumping my own gloves into the trash, I creep up behind him and slip my hand up the back of his black shirt, letting my fingers skim over his warm skin.

He shakes his head. "I don't know how to help you, Harper," he murmurs. "Not when you don't seem to want to help yourself."

Something shatters inside me, and I've never felt more like a child being reprimanded by an angry parent. "I'm sorry," I whisper, the sound getting caught in my throat.

He lifts his head and turns toward me before gripping my hips and lifting me right onto the empty table. His hands come down on either side of my thighs, caging me in. "I don't know what's going on here. Before the club, there wasn't even a whisper of having seen this man in person, but then you tell me that you've seen him twice. What the fuck is going on? What aren't you telling me?"

Guilt swarms through my chest, and I see the very moment he sees it reflected in my eyes.

"Harper," he murmurs. "Please."

I swallow hard and nod, knowing I have to tell him this. I have to be an open book, and as much as I think I can handle my stalker by playing his wicked games, the truth is, I have no idea what I'm doing.

"On Friday night, I'd just gotten out of the shower, and when I walked into my room, he was in there waiting for me."

"Fuck, Morticia. In your home? That bastard was in your home and you didn't tell me?" Knight groans, pulling away from me as he pushes his hands back through his hair, his strong arms bulging with each movement. He lets out a breath, his cheeks blowing out. "Did he . . . Did he rape you?"

I shake my head, feeling the overwhelming need to burst into tears, but I hold myself together. "No. But he touched me. I was naked. I had a towel wrapped around me, and he pulled it off. He stood behind me with one hand clamped over my mouth while his other hand . . ." I cringe, letting the sentence fall flat. Knight is a smart man. He can work out exactly what he was doing with his hand.

Knight returns to me, his hands now lingering on my thighs. "You wanted him to?" he asks, his tone flat, not accusatory or prying, and I appreciate that more than he'll ever know.

I nod, wanting to be as honest as I can. "I didn't push him away if that's what you're asking. I was scared at first. I didn't know what he wanted or how far it would go, but once he started, there was this overwhelming rush. I knew I shouldn't have wanted it, but I did. Then as his fingers, you know, he explained the rules of his twisted little game."

"Game?"

I cringe again. "Hide-and-seek. He said, *If you scream, you fail. If you run, you die. But kitten, you will hide, and I will find you.* They're the rules he's playing by, and so I figured that if I stuck to that and gave him exactly what he was after, then I'd be okay. I didn't try to get away or call for help. I just let him, and I . . . I hate that I liked it."

"It's okay, doll," he murmurs, his hands squeezing my thighs, and it's clear from his tone that he's struggling with this just as much as I am. "You're okay. I'm not judging you. I just need to understand. I can't—fuck. I can't make this go away if I don't know what he wants."

"Me," I say blatantly. "He just . . . wants me."

Knight is silent for a minute, simply trying to make sense of everything and remain calm, doing everything in his power not to turn this into an interrogation. "What happened after?"

"Nothing," I say. "The second I . . . finished, he let go of me and left. But he stopped at the door and said, *Ready or not, kitten. I'm coming for you*, which reiterates that this is nothing more than a twisted game to him."

"Okay," he says with a nod, clearly deep in thought. "This is good news. Games have rules, and he's set out his rules for you, which means he likes structure. He's probably playing by a set of his own rules, and that means he'll be predictable."

"Killing those two men for touching me in the club sure as fuck wasn't predictable."

"Wasn't it? He's killed before to send you a message. He clearly didn't appreciate having other men all over you, and so he felt the need to send another message. It's a pattern."

Shit.

"Tell me what happened in the club."

Double shit.

I cringe, and I know he sees the guilt in my eyes.

"He touched you again?"

I nod and my cringe deepens, the guilt radiating out of me, daring him to question me.

"He fucked you?"

"More like I fucked him."

His brow arches, and I clarify. "You saw me. I was drunk. Really fucking drunk, and when I saw him there, I had this moment of fear, but then he didn't hurt me the night before, and I figured, if I played his little game, he'd get what he wanted and leave. I'd also gotten in my head that he might have been you. He's tall and built, and I was thinking that if it were you, you would never hurt me. So I went up to him, and just like in my room, he made me come, and it was so good, but then he went to leave and I—"

"What did you do, Harper?"

"I pulled him back and said something about him having his fun and now it was my turn, and I took him over to one of those private booth things, and I just . . . did it all. I went down on him and just when he was about to finish, he grabbed me and straddled me over his lap, and I just went for it."

"Fuck, Harper. You stole control of the game. You changed his rules."

I drag my hands down my face and Knight pulls me into his arms, my face crushing against his strong chest. "What am I going to do?" I groan, my words muffled by his shirt.

"Well, for starters, let's try not fucking the serial killer."

"I'm so stupid."

"Yeah," he agrees. "Probably wasn't your finest moment."

I resist giving him a hard stare. Most men in his position would just agree with me to make things better, but not Knight. He doesn't bother to hold back. He calls it as he sees it, and honestly, I like that in a man.

A heaviness settles over me like a torrential storm when Knight pulls back and wraps his big hand around the base of my throat, using his thumb to force my chin up, meeting his heavy stare. "I just have one question," he murmurs, his tone dropping low as he holds me captive with those dark, tantalizing eyes.

"And what's that?"

His thumb brushes along my jaw, and his touch makes me forget about everything else. "Did he make your legs shake the way I do?" he murmurs. "Does he fill you and make you scream the way I can? Does your tight little cunt squeeze him like you do to me?"

A grin pulls across my lips, and I lean in closer, desperately wishing he would close the gap between us. "That was three questions."

"Answer," he demands in that bossy tone that somehow always turns me on.

My thighs clench on the table, and I shake my head, my hand slipping up the front of his shirt, my fingers splaying across his warm skin. "Nobody feels like you do," I tell him in a breathy whisper. "Nobody can fill me like you. Nobody can take me as deep as you do. He's good, great even, but the way you make me come is unmatched. You destroy me, Knight. You shatter me like glass every time your hands are on my body."

He leans in, his lips barely a breath away as his hands tighten on my thighs. "I don't know what the fuck this is, doll. But you belong to me. Understand that. You will never be his, no matter how hard he fucks you, how many times he sneaks into your bedroom and makes you come on his fingers. You're mine."

I suck in a breath, his words capturing me in a choke hold. As his chest heaves with anticipation, he moves in closer until his lips brush past mine. Just as I go to melt into him, the startling realization of the surveillance cameras giving my stalker a bird's-eye view right into this moment terrifies me.

"No," I rush out, shoving him away.

Knight stares back at me, his brow arched. "No?"

"We can't do this here," I tell him, panic rising in my chest because it might already be too late. "The cameras. He's watching everything I do, and I won't put a target on your back like that. You said it's a pattern, and if that's right and he's watching you with your hands all over me . . . I can't have you show up in a body bag on my table."

Knight steps right back into me, gripping my hips and pulling me right to the edge. "You think I'm scared of some asshole playing a children's game?" he says. "I know what I want, Harper, and he's not about to keep me from taking it."

I swallow hard, desire pulsing through me like liquid gold. "I'm just trying to protect you."

His eyes soften, and his hand returns to my neck, his thumbs brushing across my jaw. "I appreciate that, but I don't need your protection. I'd rather you be vigilant in watching your own back. I can handle myself and you at the same time."

I shake my head. "It's a two-way street, Knight. I feel the same way. I've always been independent. I've never needed to rely on anybody. I don't like feeling like a pathetic damsel who needs her sexy SWAT officer to rescue her. It makes me feel weak."

"Are you asking me to back off when it comes to this guy? Because I can't do that."

"I know," I murmur. "But I just need you to understand where I'm coming from and why I sometimes find it hard to open up. Hell, even why I pushed so hard against exclusivity. I need that independence."

"Speaking of. If your relationships are a threat, you need to let this other guy know."

"I, uhhhh . . . sort of already did."

He pulls back, his gaze narrowed. "You told him about your stalker."

"Not exactly," I say. "But I told him about you. By accident. Kind of."

"I don't know what to make of that."

"All that you need to know is that Laith is a really nice guy, and while yes, we've had a sexual relationship for a while now, we're friends first. We're honest, so after you and I . . . you know. I let him know. I didn't think it was fair to keep him in the dark like that, so he took a back seat."

"A back seat?"

"Mm-hmm," I murmur. "He's always wanted what's best for me, and he and I . . . If something were going to happen between us, it would have happened a long time ago. So while you and I are doing whatever the hell this is, he doesn't want to be a factor that could potentially keep something from happening. He respectfully bowed out until I figure that out."

Knight moves in tighter, holding me as though he's never seen anything so precious in his life. "And what exactly do you think could potentially be happening here?"

I shake my head as a stupid smile pulls across my lips. "Don't ask questions that neither of us knows the answer to, let alone is even a little bit ready to hear."

He laughs, and the sound does something wild to me. "Fair point," he murmurs, his gaze shifting to the camera up on the wall behind me as his hand slowly trails higher on my thigh. Indecision flashes in his dark eyes, and I know exactly what he's thinking. Does he risk his life just to touch me, or does he burn it all to hell just for a moment of heaven?

His gaze comes back to mine, his hand shifting to the back of my neck. "Fuck it. Let him see that you belong to me." And not a second later, his lips crash down on mine. Hunger slams into me as I melt into his touch, his hand shifting to the side of my thigh, guiding it around his waist.

His tongue swoops into my mouth, and I groan as his cock grinds against my needy pussy, and before it even occurs to me where we are or what we're about to do, my hands are greedily pulling at his shirt, desperately trying to pull it over his head.

The moment it's gone, I dive for his body, my hands all over him, exploring and committing every sharp ridge of his muscled frame to memory, needing that touch more than I need my next breath. His lips are like a potent drug against mine, and as he reaches for my scrub shirt and pulls it over my head, the hunger becomes too much to bear.

"Knight," I pant.

"I've got you, doll," he murmurs against my lips, locking his arm around my waist and lifting me just enough to rip my pants down, taking my thong along with them. He settles me back on the table, and I scramble for the front of his pants as his lips work their way down to my neck, sending shivers soaring across my skin.

I free that massive cock from the confines of his pants and curl my hand around his base. My fingers hold firmly, pumping up and down, and before I can even make it to the top and roll my thumb over his tip, Knight's hands are at my hips, scootching me right to the edge of the table, and lining me up perfectly with his cock.

My legs lock around his waist as his big hand closes over mine on his cock and guides his tip right to my entrance. "Fuck," he groans as he slowly pushes inside me, my pussy already throbbing for more. "I've been dreaming about this sweet little cunt since the moment I tasted it."

A stupid grin pulls at my lips, and before I can even think about responding, Knight pushes deep, stretching me wide as my eyes roll.

My serial killer stalker is good, but he could never make me feel like this.

Knight pushes the rest of the way, bottoming out as a deep, guttural moan pulls from my chest. "Oh God, Knight," I pant, never feeling so full. My walls stretch around his impressive size, and with every slight flinch of his cock inside me, I fall to pieces.

"You feel that, doll?" he growls, his fingers digging into my hip as I clutch onto his arm, desperately needing to hold on. He inches back, making my body spasm before slamming back into me. "Nobody can fill you like I can."

"Nobody," I agree.

"And every time he takes this sweet little cunt," he growls, pulling his hips back again, "he will know that he'll never compare. Never make you come the way I can. Never take you this deep. Never make you shatter like I do."

"Never."

His lips return to my neck as his hips thrust deep, and I tip my head back, needing so much more. He gives me all of him, pushing me right to the edge, and when I reach down between us and roll my fingers over my clit, my hips jolt with raw, intense pleasure.

I grip his shoulder, my nails digging into his skin and leaving little crescent moons behind. "Knight," I pant.

"I know, doll," he grits through a clenched jaw. "I've got you."

He pushes me to my limits, his thick cock massaging me from within, stretching and filling me in a way he never has before. My eyelids flutter, and I cry out, that familiar coil tightening until there's nothing left to give.

"Oh God," I groan, my body already starting to spasm.

"Let it go, Harper."

His words destroy me, and the tight coil explodes as my orgasm takes over, ripping through my body and destroying everything in its path. I shatter like glass, just as he knew I would, and as my high rocks through my body, Knight reaches his climax, coming with me and shooting hot spurts of cum deep inside me.

"Yes," I gasp, clutching that strong, tattooed body like it's my only lifeline, and as we each come down from our high, he drops his forehead to mine, holding me as though he'll never let go.

"Fuck, Harper," he grits. "What is this?"

"If I knew . . . I probably still wouldn't tell you."

Knight laughs but remains seated within me, and honestly, I can't handle the idea of him pulling away from me just yet. "I won't lie," he murmurs, his hand gripping the back of my neck again. "Knowing you've had another man in your mouth makes me fucking jealous. I want to erase every memory of it from your beautiful mind and replace them with ones of our own."

I tip my head back, meeting his hauntingly gorgeous stare. "I thought you didn't get jealous."

"There's always a first time for everything."

I laugh, and he slowly pulls out of me, leaving me feeling empty. "He didn't come down my throat like you did," I remind him. "Nobody gets to do that to me. But I let you."

His brow arches, suspicion thick in his stare. "You don't let men come in your mouth."

I grin and jump down from the table before pushing up onto my tippy toes, despite still being a good foot apart in height. "Only my favoritest of uncles."

Knight groans, and with that, I find my scrubs and underwear before pulling them back on. "Now, if you don't mind, I need to sterilize this whole room and get back to work. Unless you're ready to go for round two? I could always shove my head in the refrigeration unit and call out for my big brave step-uncle to help me get unstuck."

Knight smirks, knowing damn well what I'm referring to. "You're trouble, Harper," he rumbles, stepping into me and clutching my waist, holding me there. "But when I take you next, it won't be some cheap remake of cheesy porn, it'll be hard and fast with you sitting on my fucking face."

My whole pussy clenches, and he smirks as if knowing damn well what just happened below the belt. "I have to run," he continues. "Try not to get yourself stuck in the refrigeration unit, because it might not be me coming to get you."

"Yes sir, bossy, sir," I tell him. "I suppose I'll see you at Mom's ridiculous dinner—assuming you're going, of course."

"I might be able to make time to watch you go for round two with your mother," he says before stepping away. A small smile pulls at my lips; I'm still wondering what the hell this is growing between us. "And Harper?" he says, pausing near the door.

I glance up, trying to hide the smile that's threatening to rip across my face.

"Don't be a stranger. If something happens, big or little, you call me. I'll be there."

I nod, and as my cheeks flush, Knight slips out of the morgue, leaving me to sterilize the room from top to bottom and get back to work, but first, I need to deal with the mess he left behind; the very thrilling mess that's dripping down my thighs.

CHAPTER 23

KNIGHT

The soft hues of the pinkish sky linger above as I make my way up the driveway toward Elias's front door, and while this is the last place I want to be, the idea of seeing Harper again keeps me moving.

It's Friday evening, and the last time I saw or even spoke to her was on Monday. And when she potentially has a serial killer stalker following her every move, one who also likes to get her off, it's nerve-racking. I was starting to wonder if she'd become another one of his victims lying in the morgue or if she wasn't calling because he already had her busy on her back.

There I go with the jealous bullshit again.

It doesn't sit well with me. I've never been the jealous type, and yet with Harper, I can't seem to help myself. Every thought of another man touching what I've touched has driven me wild with rage. But that's my problem, not hers. She told me from the start that she's not down with being exclusive, and while I was more than happy to agree at the time, I'm starting to wonder if maybe I'm wanting something more.

I can only imagine how that conversation will go down.

Striding up to the door, I find the very reason for my raging jealousy pacing back and forth, not even bothering to knock on the door.

"Thought you weren't going to be a stranger," I say, watching as she jumps right out of her skin. She didn't bother dressing up like she did for the last dinner party. She just kept it all Harper tonight with black jeans and a sexy crop top, all pulled together with a leather jacket. Her long black hair is thrown up into a messy bun with bits falling out to frame her petite face, and I can't help but stare.

"Holy fucking shit, Knight," she gasps, doubling over and bracing her hands on her knees, desperately trying to calm herself. "You scared the crap out of me. You should know better than to sneak up on a woman who's currently dealing with a killer stalker."

I arch my brow and step straight into her, locking my arm around her waist and pulling her in hard against my chest, knocking the breath right out of her lungs. "Where the hell have you been, doll? My bed's getting cold without you."

Her bright green eyes widen, and she shoves out of my arms before frantically looking around, making sure nobody overhead me, but we're the only ones out here. "Jesus Christ, Knight. Are you trying to get my ass handed to me? If my mother knew that we were . . . that we . . . you know, she'd have me committed to a psych ward and start throwing holy water at me from the door."

"Your mom has more to worry about than who her grown daughter is fucking," I tell her. "But I'm sorry. I will strive to be more . . . discreet. And I suppose I'm also sorry for scaring you earlier. That wasn't my intention, but you're the one hovering outside the door of a home that's expecting guests. So that one is on you."

She rolls her eyes, and I narrow mine. "Why are you so jumpy? Has something else happened?"

She shakes her head. "No, actually. Nothing. It's been a normal week, and every time I manage to make it through my shift without a body or someone watching me, I get more paranoid that it's about to happen. I've barely slept all week."

"So you haven't seen him all week?"

"Not even a little bit."

"Not even a random black rose?"

"Nope."

"Well, shit," I mutter. "You must have thrown it back so hard in the club last week that the bastard is still recovering."

Harper laughs and glances away, her cheeks brightening with the sweetest blush. "Or perhaps he's been licking his wounds because he saw me over the camera saying that he could never give it to me as good as you do."

"Yeah," I laugh. "I agree. It's definitely that."

Harper lets out a breath and glances up at me, those big green eyes filled with regret, and for just a moment, I wonder if it's me she regrets. "I've been out here for twenty minutes trying to convince myself to go in," she tells me. "I can hear my brother in there with the twins and his wife, and Mom is doting on them like she's never seen anything so perfect in her life, and I just . . . I don't want to be here."

"Nobody is forcing you to go inside," I tell her, pointing toward the retaining wall around the manicured hedges and watching as her bright eyes shift toward it with longing. "If you're not ready, we can just chill here."

She nods and wanders over, sitting her firm ass down and blowing out a heavy breath. "Been busy?" she asks.

"Don't give me that shit," I say, getting right into it. "Where the fuck have you been?"

"Me?" she argues, her eyes going wide. "It's a two-way street. I didn't see my phone ringing either, Mr. You Belong To Me Now. I mean, what am I supposed to do with that? You know this was supposed to be strictly sex only. You're my uncle, for fuck's sake. I can't want you like this."

"But you do want me," I murmur, ignoring the uncle jab as pride swells in my chest, realizing she's just as fucked up over me as I am for her.

Harper groans, and the sound does something wicked to me. "I swear, sometimes you only hear what you want to hear. We can't do this."

"Can't or shouldn't?" I challenge. "They're two very different things."

Harper's face lights up with a wide grin, and I don't doubt that she's forgotten all about why she shouldn't be walking through that door. "You're impossible. You know that, right?"

"I like to refer to it as determination."

She rolls her eyes and slumps against the retaining wall, keeping her stare locked on mine.

"Whatever happened to those two bodies?" I ask, inching closer, unable to keep my distance. "Ever figure out the cause of death?"

She shakes her head. "Not even a little. I stayed all night and searched every inch of those bodies but found nothing. There were obviously smaller injuries, but nothing that could determine how they died. It's been driving me insane all week, and to make matters worse, when I went in for my next shift, Dr. McKullan had done up his own reports, stating their injuries were consistent with a car wreck. He concluded the first guy died from blood loss and the other from swelling of the brain."

"The fuck?"

"That's what I said, and so I went to look over the bodies again, and surprise, surprise, the two bodies were of men who were actually involved in a car wreck."

"So the bodies from the club are gone?"

"Yup," she says, popping the *p* before letting out a frustrated sigh. "Poof. Just like my panties at the club. But I gotta give it to this guy, he sure loves consistency."

"That he does," I muse as Harper lets out a sigh and gets to her feet, suddenly feeling ready to face the fresh hell on the other side of the door. She steps up to the door, and I hold back, not wanting Elias or her mom to assume we showed up together.

She knocks, and as we wait for someone to answer the door, I find myself stuck on the two bodies that arrived for Harper in the morgue.

There's something off-putting about them. Something that's leaving me uneasy, and yet I can't put my finger on it. I didn't get a good look at their faces considering one was face down on an autopsy table and the other was still half inside a body bag, but they didn't strike me as the type of men Harper would find herself grinding against in a club. Though I suppose I don't really know her well enough to know what her standards are when she's been heavily drinking, but judging from the snippet I saw last weekend, she's a free spirit. All that mattered to her was having a good time.

I spent a good chunk of the week looking into the double homicide, and just like the first body, there wasn't a single detail about it in our system. No detectives to question, no leads, no evidence or suspects, and it's left me unsettled. Either this asshole is really fucking good, or he's got someone working with him, and right now, my suspicions keep coming back to Detective Gray.

As for the state of the bodies I saw in the morgue, they brought more questions than answers. The two men had clearly been injured, but the lack of an evident cause of death leaves me scratching my head. I've never seen anything like it. The carvings on their arms also brought more questions. I don't know if it's just my lack of imagination, but I couldn't make out the message that Harper could so clearly see. She even went as far as to point them all out, but I couldn't see a damn thing.

The carvings themselves were particularly brutal. They were deep and violent, and yet to me, they seemed a little more random. Almost like they were made from jagged bits of glass, not a blade, but Harper is the professional here. If she says the cuts were made with a blade, then I'm taking her word for it.

The door opens, and not a moment later, Harper's mother stares back at us with a forced smile. She takes in her daughter, and her smile falters, almost looking disappointed that she's here to disturb her peace.

Irritation burns through me. I don't understand how a mother could be so cold to her child, especially one as beautiful as Harper. I swear, if she just put her hostility aside and took a moment to get to know her daughter, she'd finally understand how fucking amazing she is. It's her loss, and if she doesn't want to take the time to mend bridges with Harper, then I'm more than happy to fill that time keeping her occupied.

Mae's stare shifts from her daughter to me, as she plasters a fake smile across her face. "Oh, Knight. How wonderful to see you again," she beams, completely ignoring her daughter's presence.

"Always a pleasure, Mae," I say, stepping in right behind Harper and discreetly giving her ass a firm squeeze, watching her jump and gasp before doing her best to cover it up.

"Mother," she says bluntly.

"Harper. I trust you are well."

"Yes."

"I see your friend Izabelle is not here."

"No, she so desperately wished she could attend, however, she came down with an unexpected case of explosive diarrhea. She sends her regards."

"Oh," Mae says, shrinking away from us as though she could somehow catch Izzy's germs just from being in the same vicinity as her daughter. "How . . . unsettling. Do wish her well for me. Shall I send her a gift basket?"

"No," Harper mutters, hiding a smirk as she attempts to shove my hand away from her ass, only enticing me to squeeze a little harder. "That won't be necessary."

"Very well," Mae says with a tight smile. "You might as well come in."

Mae turns on her heel and stalks away as Harper whips around and shoves me in the chest. My hand falls away from her perfect ass. "Keep it up and I'll make sure the only thing you ever sink into again will be a rusty meat grinder operated by a man named Butch," she whisper-yells, scolding me with the kind of tone that has my cock stiffening in my pants. "Tonight is already going to be a disaster. I don't need to be dodging your curveballs as well."

"Promise," I say with a grin. "I'll be on my best behavior."

Harper shakes her head and sighs, knowing damn well that I'm full of shit. But speaking of being full of shit . . . "Explosive diarrhea, huh?"

"Oh yeah," Harper says as we follow her mother through the house, our voices low. "It's a real issue. There's shit flying up the walls. Poor girl."

"It's always shits and giggles, until someone giggles and shits."

I can't help but laugh, which earns me a suspicious stare from Mae, glancing back at me over her shoulder, and the way she watches me next to Harper has me wondering if she knows something she shouldn't, but that's not possible.

"Hurry along, Harper," she scolds, turning back to watch where she's going. "I thought I told you to be here on time. Dinner is going to get cold."

Harper balls her hands into fists before pumping them in and out, visibly trying to calm herself. Or at the very least, doing everything in her power not to tackle her mother to the ground and turn this dinner into a smackdown.

"Me?" Harper scoffs. "Do you not notice the mountain of a man beside me who was also late? Why isn't he getting the famous Mae Slater scolding?"

"He is not my undependable daughter who likes to embarrass me at events."

Harper stops in the middle of the living room, letting out a frustrated sigh. "Is this seriously how tonight is going to play out, because if this is the bullshit I'm in for, then I might as well leave now."

Mae stops and looks back, and I subtly move in beside Harper, discreetly showing where my loyalties lie. Mae's gaze shifts to mine. "Do you mind, Knight? I need to have a private word with my daughter."

"Actually, I think I might just hang around. I wouldn't want to miss the main event of the night," I say, getting surprised glances from both of them. "Though between you and me, I'm feeling a little ravenous, and after you mentioned dinner getting cold, I think it's best we hurry along to the dining room and get this shit show started."

Mae gapes at me, and I smile at her daughter, waving her through the living room. "After you."

"Oh," Harper muses, feigning delight as she places a hand against her chest. "Who would have known that a brute could be such a distinguished gentleman?"

Her eyes flash with darkness, and I know for a fact that she's remembering the way I ate her pussy, knowing damn well that I am anything but a gentleman. Then not wanting to get caught alone with her mother, she hurries past me and makes her way into the dining room.

The whole family is here just as expected.

Elias sits at the head of the table and stands when Harper strides into the room, offering her a polite smile, which I know is really anything but. Then as she turns to greet her brother and his wife, Emily, I keep my gaze locked on Elias, watching the way his stare lingers on her body just a moment too long.

Sensing my stare, he glances back at me, and the smirk that pulls across his lips makes me think that he believes we're one and the same when it comes to Harper. But he'd be dead wrong, and if he were going to attempt to move on that bullshit, he'd have me to deal with.

Harper gives her brother a warm hug, and I can't help but notice that things seem to be getting better there. They usually just grunt at each other. She moves on to Emily before dropping straight down and pulling her twin nieces, Haylee and Taliah, straight into her arms.

She chats animatedly with them, loving every second of it, and as she beams at them, something swells in my chest. A strange image of Harper, pregnant and barefoot, smiling at me from our kitchen and wearing nothing but a thong and one of my shirts lingers in the forefront of my brain, and the second it made itself known, I realize that's going to have to be scrubbed from my memory with bleach.

I can't want a future like that. I can't even pretend to want that. Not without getting my ass kicked by Harper. If she knew, my balls would currently be tied around my throat like a bow tie.

I make my way over to Jonah, and he immediately holds out his hand in greeting. "Hey, Knight. How're you doing?"

"Yeah, good, man. You?" I say, gripping his hand and offering a firm shake.

He nods. "Nothing to complain about," he lies, because fuck, just being here in this room means he has plenty to complain about. His gaze shifts between me and Harper. "Did you, uhhh . . . did you guys come together?"

Have we come together? Indeed we have, but not in the context he's referring to. "Nah, just ran into her at the door," I say. "Pretty sure she was about to bail."

Jonah laughs. "Wonderful. It's gonna be one of *those* dinner parties."

Mae strides in, seeming to have recovered from whatever the fuck just went down in the living room. She stands at the opening of the dining room, her arms outstretched. "Dinner is ready," she announces. "Please find your seats."

I shake my head and find a seat, unable to figure out why Mae always wants to put on these elaborate dinner parties. Even when it's just family, she's always trying so hard to be something she's so clearly not.

The guests shift around the table to take their seats, and by the time Harper has finished with the girls and is looking for somewhere to park her ass, her eyes widen in horror, realizing the only seat available is right next to me.

I laugh to myself before reaching for the glass in front of me and the pitcher of ice water, doing what I can to mask my pleasure. I pour myself a drink before reaching for Harper's glass and filling hers too.

When a waiter slides a plate in front of me, I look down with disdain. I can't even tell what the fuck we're eating, but what I do know is that it tastes like stale cardboard. I don't even know how cardboard can taste stale, but leave it up to Mae to hire Blackstone's worst caterers.

Harper makes a face with every bite, and I don't doubt that the second she's out of here, she'll be stopping to grab a burger. Hell, I might even join her.

And then, just as expected, all hell breaks loose.

CHAPTER 24

KNIGHT

The sound of cutlery scraping against Mae's fine china fills the dining room when Harper shifts around in her seat, removing her jacket and twisting around to hook it over the back of her chair. And fuck me, she looks gorgeous in her black crop. It hugs her body just right, and I don't doubt that at some point tonight, I'll be tearing it off her slender body with my teeth.

As if she senses my gaze, her stare lifts to mine. Her brows furrow, and she pretends like she doesn't know exactly what she does to me. "What?" she says, pure innocence in her velvety tone.

I shake my head and look away, not wanting to draw attention, but as I focus on the table and the people around me, it becomes clear that I'm not the only one who's noticed just how fucking delicious Harper looks tonight.

Elias shamelessly stares at her, his gaze roaming over her tits and exposed waist, and as my grip tightens on my fork, bending the metal, Mae glances up. She looks at her husband, putting on the smile of a perfect doting wife, but it falters a moment later, realizing what—*or who*—has his undivided attention.

Her gaze flicks between Harper and Elias a few times, panic rising in her stare as Harper minds her own business, completely unaware of the tension growing around the table.

"Harper, sweetheart," Mae says in a fake, condescending tone. "It's getting quite breezy with the windows open. Why don't you pop your jacket back on? I wouldn't want you catching a cold."

Harper lifts her head and glances back at the windows as if just realizing they were open. "Oh, I'm fine," she says with a slight shrug. "I'm not cold."

"Harper," Mae says, her tone shifting and taking Harper by surprise. "Jacket. Now, please."

Harper gapes at her mother as silence falls around the table, eyes beginning to shift, waiting for some kind of showdown. "What's the big deal?" Harper says. "I'm not cold. I don't need a jacket, hence why I took it off."

"Look around you," Mae seethes while trying to keep the polite smile on her face at the same time she scolds her grown daughter like a delinquent child. "Your outfit is inappropriate. You are at a dinner party, and you come wearing nothing but a sports bra. You're making everybody uncomfortable."

Harper's gaze drops straight down to her top, her brows creasing with confusion, and honestly, same. There's not a damn thing wrong with her outfit. She looks fucking divine. "What are you talking about?" Harper asks, looking back at her mother's scolding glare. "This is a designer shirt. Part of the Izabelle Grace summer collection. I would hardly call it a sports bra. I thought you would actually like it."

Mae scoffs. "I have every piece of that collection, and I can assure you, such a profound, up-and-coming designer would never include such a trampy piece."

"Really?" Harper grunts, making it damn clear that Mae has no idea that the elusive Izabelle Grace is the one and only Izzy who is currently shitting up the walls of her apartment with explosive diarrhea.

"Yes, now please have just a little respect and put your jacket back on. This is a dinner party, for God's sake, and had you attempted to answer even one of my phone calls, you would have known that tonight's event was business casual."

"Business casual?" Harper scoffs. "It's dinner. With family. This isn't some fancy event that's going to end up photographed for some bullshit magazine. But if you insist on bitching people out for their choice of attire, then focus on G.I. freaking Joe beside me. He looks like he's about to go commando crawling across the fucking desert. All that's missing is the sniper rifle across his back."

"Hey," I cut in, gaping at the little she-devil beside me. "Don't bring me into this shit."

"Lower your voice," Mae spits. "Knight is dressed appropriately for someone on call. You are half naked at my dinner table. You're making the children uncomfortable."

"The children are fine," Harper scoffs.

With Elias's gaze still locked on Harper's tits, Mae lets out a frustrated sigh, slamming her cutlery down on the table. "I have had just about enough of this," she mutters, her sharp stare shooting straight across the table to Harper. "First you completely ruined my anniversary dinner, and now you're making a scene again. Do you have any idea how disrespectful you have been? Do you have no shame? No care for my feelings?"

"Ooooh," Harper laughs, gripping her fork way too tightly, sending a seething glare straight back at Mae. "You do not want to start with me, Mother. Not unless you care for being humiliated all over again—and in front of your grandchildren, no less."

"Now, now," Elias says, putting his hands out as if to calm the situation before it can go up in flames, but honestly, I think he's hoping for it. He enjoys dinner and a show more than anybody, but for appearances, he has no choice but to play the role of the perfect doting husband. I don't get it, though. He could treat Mae like dirt, and she'd still hang on to him like a leech. "There's no need for this to get out of hand. Harper, please just put your jacket on so we can move past this and have a nice dinner."

"You wretched child," Mae spits at her daughter, ignoring her husband. "I have only ever given you the best, and this is how you repay me."

"The best?" Harper demands, completely abandoning her meal, shoving her plate away, and tossing the fork down as well. She gets to her feet, taking a deep breath and bracing her hands against the table, and I prepare myself for whatever is about to come next.

"I have been nothing more than a hindrance to your existence. I was never good enough. Never pretty enough. Never smart enough," Harper starts, every one of her words breaking something deep inside me. "My grades weren't as good as Jonah's, so I was an embarrassment. I didn't excel in sports like Jonah did, so naturally that made me a failure. Not to mention the shame I brought upon you because I chose not to spend the rest of my life in debt and attended a normal, run-of-the-mill college and not some big Ivy League like Jonah did."

Mae scoffs as though the thought of which college Harper attended is still a sore point, and I've never wanted to fling a fork across a table so badly in my life.

"I have never been good enough in your eyes," Harper continues. "And sure, most of my life I have sat by and bitten my tongue, but I'm done, Mom. I have worked too damn hard to get where I am to allow you to continue shitting all over my successes and achievements. Yes, I work in a morgue. Yes, there are dead bodies. And yes, Mom. I perform autopsies as part of my daily routine, but I enjoy what I do. I fucking love it. I'm on track to become one of the best forensic pathologists in the state, and I can't for the life of me figure out how the hell you aren't proud of that."

Tears well in Harper's eyes, and I resist the urge to reach out to her.

"I don't know what I have done in my life to make you despise me so much, but I am done. I am done trying to win your approval, because at the end of the day, I will never be what you want me to be."

Mae just stares at her daughter, her eyes filled with an ugliness that tears me to shreds, and when she crosses her arms over her chest and arches a brow, I realize this shit has only just begun.

"And here we are, bringing everything back to you," Mae sputters. "What were you hoping for? That I would fall to my knees and beg your forgiveness for being the best mother I could be? You are ungrateful, Harper-Rayn. I brought you here so that you could see how shamefully you humiliated me during our anniversary dinner party, and allow you the chance to apologize. But instead, you want to spout all this nonsense at me and claim I was a poor mother. Shame on you."

Harper gapes at her mother, and it doesn't go unnoticed how the twins' heads bounce from left to right across the table, watching the showdown like a tennis match.

"Wow, Mom. You really are a piece of work," she says, shaking her head in wonder. "You want an apology? Well, here you go. I'm sorry that I don't want to be a damn thing like you. I'm sorry I have done everything in my power to not be your perfect little clone. I'm sorry that when forced to sit around this ridiculous table, I lashed out after you shamed my career and my achievements in front of a room full of strangers for entertainment. But most of all, I'm sorry that you have allowed yourself to become such a hateful and despicable human being."

With that, Harper shoves away from the table, but not before reaching for the neck of a full wine bottle and taking it with her. She storms away, and just when I go to follow her, Mae puts on the waterworks, reaching for a napkin and dabbing her dry eyes.

"Oh my," she wails as Elias hurries to her side, pulling her into his arms, his gaze locked on Harper's ass as she storms away. "I just don't understand how she can be so horrid. What have I ever done to deserve such treatment?"

Jonah groans from across the table, disgust in his eyes. "Knock it off, Mom. Don't you think this routine is getting old?"

Mae whips her stare to the golden boy. "What did you just say to me?"

"You heard me," he says, getting to his feet and indicating for his wife to rise as well. "Harper's right. You've treated her like shit since we were kids, and I was too distracted by everything I had going on to notice, but now as a father myself, I see it clear as day. You have diminished every accomplishment she has ever made, and she has every right to be hostile about it. I'm surprised she even still agrees to come to these bullshit dinners."

Emily reaches for her girls, their little hands in each of hers as Mae looks on in horror. "Where . . . where do you think you're going? Dinner has only just begun."

Jonah lets out a heavy breath. "We're leaving," he says. "I was reluctant to bring Emily and the girls. I knew this might happen, but you swore to me that it would be different this time, and I trusted you. But the second Harper walked through the door, you made your intentions clear. You wanted my family and Knight here in the hopes of humiliating her. Well, congratulations. Mission accomplished."

"No. No, you can't leave," Mae says, throwing herself to her feet, her fake tears all but abandoned.

"I'm not hanging around for my children to witness their grandmother's narcissistic attempt to crush their aunt," Jonah says. "Your act is getting old, Mom. Harper is an incredible young woman with one hell of an amazing career ahead of her, and you are missing out. You should be using this time to get to know her, not tear her down at every opportunity. One day you are going to find that you've pushed her too far, and she'll never come back. And honestly, Mom, I have no doubt that day is quickly approaching."

Well, fuck. I get to my feet and applaud Jonah like I'm front row at a concert. "I knew I liked you," I say, not even attempting to hide my disdain for my brother's wife. I look back at my brother, more than happy to leave him to clean up the mess. "Well, this has been a huge fucking waste of my time, so I'm gonna take off."

Mae gasps at my tone, and I roll my eyes before looking back at her as her son files out with his family. "As always, Mae. It was such a pleasure seeing you again." And with that, I file out of the dining room, grabbing the other bottle of red wine, just like Harper had, and listening to Mae's overexaggerated wails as I leave.

CHAPTER 25

KNIGHT

Not having heard the sound of the front door slamming, I go searching through the house, lifting the bottle to my lips and taking a swig of the wine, and as I pass the downstairs guest bathroom, I find Harper braced against the sink, her head low as she clutches the porcelain in front of the mirror. She takes heavy breaths, her knuckles turning white from her tight grip.

I step into the doorway, pausing there as I gently knock against the open doorframe. Harper's head snaps up, her eyes wild with rage, but as she sees me here, her shoulders slump, and her fight quickly drains away.

Her gaze returns to her reflection in the mirror, and I walk in, closing and locking the door behind me. "You good?" I ask, striding up behind her and putting the wine bottle down beside her already half-empty one. I drop my hands to the sink, coming down on either side of her, caging her in, and she immediately relaxes back against me.

"I just don't get it," she murmurs, her voice so low and filled with pain that it's almost impossible to hear her. "Why does she always have to do that? Why can't she just invite me here to have a good time? And in front of the twins, no less."

I nod, my hands shifting from the sink to her waist, holding tightly. "Honestly, Harper. I have no fucking idea. I'd like to say that it's because she's threatened by you. That you shine so much brighter than she ever could. You've made something of yourself, by yourself, and you can stand on your own two feet. She's always had to attach herself to men like my brother to find acceptance. But the truth is, I don't know your mother nearly enough, nor do I feel like giving her the time of day to try and work it out."

Harper scoffs, a pleased smirk pulling at the corner of her lips. "Shouldn't you be out there enjoying your dinner?"

"What dinner?" I ask. "The party's over."

Her brows furrow. "What do you mean?"

"Your brother had your back for a change and finally stood up to your mom. He saw through the bullshit just as easily as you do, and he was pissed that she tried this shit in front of his kids. He took off while your mom started crying."

"Wow. The asshole finally grew a backbone."

"He sure did. It was incredible."

Harper laughs. "If only Elias could grow one too. I bet he was all over Mom's crocodile tears."

"He was, but don't be fooled. He knows they're as fake as her personality. He's not as fucking clueless as you think," I tell her. "He just likes playing along because a docile wife that doesn't put up a fight is a wife that can be controlled."

"No shit," she breathes, staring at me through the mirror, her eyes filled with wonder. "I never would have guessed. He seems like such a pushover, completely at the power of washed-up pussy."

My hands move over her waist, and as she lets out the softest sigh and her body relaxes further against mine, I realize this is exactly what she needs to release the pent-up frustration burning through her.

"Elias is anything but a pushover," I warn her. "He's callous and cold. The façade he puts on for your mother is just that. He likes to play women, collecting them like possessions and wearing them down until they break. Keep your eyes open around him. He's not somebody you want to fuck with."

"Oh, I have no interest in messing with that."

"I know," I say, my hand lowering down past her hip. "But just because you have no interest in being caught in his web doesn't mean that he doesn't notice you."

Her face scrunches with distaste. "Gross."

I nod, glad we're on the same page, and as my hand lowers further to cup her pussy, her gaze lifts to mine through the mirror. In a matter of seconds, the frustration and pain from earlier morphs into undiluted hunger, daring me to continue.

She immediately grinds against the palm of my hand as my other hand slips up the inside of her top, my fingers brushing against her skin and leaving a wake of goose bumps.

"We shouldn't," she groans, not even pretending that she doesn't want it.

"Oh, but doll. I really think we should."

She grins, and I don't hesitate to grip her hips and whip her around to face me. She sucks in a gasp, and as I hold her stare, I reach for her top, slowly dragging it up over her head. She doesn't say a word as I drop the small shirt to the bathroom tiles, and as that bright green gaze remains locked on mine, I reach for the front of her pants, slowly but pointedly undoing the button and fly.

I dig my thumbs into the top of her pants before pushing them down her hips, taking her thong right along with it. I kneel as I continue pushing her jeans down to her feet, and I can't help but drag my gaze over her creamy thighs.

She's so fucking beautiful.

Once the pants are on the ground, I pointedly look up at her again, waiting ever so patiently for her to step out of them. She grins and braces her hand on my shoulder before doing exactly what I want.

Straightening back up to my full height, staring down at the beautifully naked woman before me, I feel my cock hardening and straining against the front of my jeans.

"Well, you've got me naked," Harper muses, her fingers lifting to my chest as she looks up at me, those big eyes filled with a false innocence. "What exactly do you intend to do with me now?"

Rich desire pulses through my veins, and I step in closer, gripping her waist. "Didn't you hear, doll? Dinner was cut short, and I'm still fucking hungry."

Without skipping a beat, I lift her onto the vanity and drop straight to my knees, taking her thigh and throwing it straight over my shoulder. "Holy fuck," she gasps, her fingers immediately knotting into my hair.

I don't waste a single second, diving in between her creamy thighs and closing my mouth over her clit, sucking and nipping as my tongue rolls over her most sensitive parts. She leans back, her body pressed flat against the mirror, and she looks down, watching the way I eat her pussy. When I add my fingers to the mix, she lets out a deep groan, and her hips jolt, silently begging for more.

I give her exactly what she needs, my fingers splitting inside her soaking cunt, massaging her walls, and coaxing every ounce of pleasure out of her. I curve my fingers just the way she likes it, rocking them back and forth over her G-spot and watching the way she trembles for me.

"Knight," she pants. "Fuck. I need you."

Oh, she'll get me. Every fucking inch of me.

She falls apart, and within seconds, her sweet little cunt is spasming around my fingers, squeezing tight as she comes. She throws her head back against the mirror as her legs lock around my shoulders, but I don't stop, loving the way she shudders for me.

Her whole body trembles, her chest heaving, and I'd bet everything that I have that she doesn't even remember the bullshit that just went down at dinner. Not anymore. All she's thinking about is my tongue rolling over her clit.

I keep working her until she finally comes down from her high, and when her grip loosens in my hair and she lets out a breathy sigh, I pull away, slowly releasing my fingers from inside her.

"Tell me now that we shouldn't have done that," I murmur, pressing my lips to the inside of her thigh.

All she can do is stare back at me as a wicked grin tears across her face. "Do you have any idea how much trouble you are? You're going to get us caught."

"Who me? I haven't said a word. You're the one thrashing on the bathroom sink."

"Thrashing?" She scoffs. "That's a bit of an overexaggeration of your skills, don't you think?"

"Oh?" I say, getting back to my feet, unable to keep from grinning. I reach for the front of my pants, popping the button before slowly releasing the fly.

Her heated gaze follows my movements, and her eyes widen before she shakes her head. "No. Now *that* we really can't do," she says in an almost panic. "I can't be quiet with you."

My grin widens as I reach into the front of my pants, freeing my straining cock before pumping my fist up and down. She watches the way my fist moves, and the desire in her eyes is like nothing I've ever seen.

She knows just how fucking good it is with us, and there's no denying how desperately she wants it.

"Tell me you don't want it, Harper. Tell me you don't want me to take that sweet little cunt and fuck you until you scream."

She whimpers with need, and it's the sweetest sound I've ever heard, and then just as I go to step into her and lift her into my arms, a knock sounds at the door. "Knight, you in there?" Elias says from the other side of the bathroom door.

Harper's eyes widen in horror, and when I take her thighs, she starts shaking her head. *Don't you dare*, she mouths.

I pull her in, locking my arm around her waist and dragging her hips right to the edge of the vanity, the tip of my cock dragging through her wetness. She whimpers again, and I brace my hand over her mouth, keeping her silent.

Another knock sounds. "Knight?"

"I'm fucking busy."

I drag my cock through her wetness again before circling her clit and watching the way her eyelids flutter, and as my tip finds her entrance, I slowly push into her. Harper sucks in a breath against my hand, her overwhelming pleasure written all over her face.

I take her deeper, her walls stretching around me with every inch I give her.

"We need to talk," Elias spits at the door. "The fuck do you think you're doing speaking to my wife like that? Do you have any idea how upset you've made her? It's bad enough her children have disregarded her feelings. She doesn't need that same hostility from you."

Harper raises a brow and shakes her head, leaning aside until my hand comes away. "What did you say to my mom?" she whispers, but her words come out just a little too loud, and I slam the rest of the way inside of her before fixing my hand back over her mouth, just in time to catch the deep groan that tears out of her.

Harper's eyes widen, and she pants against the inside of my palm.

"The fuck was that?" Elias demands at the door. "Have you got someone in there with you? Is that Harper?"

"Harper," I scoff, taking her deep as her hungry gaze remains locked on mine. "The fuck, man? Might I remind you that's my niece. *We don't fuck family.* Now if you wouldn't mind, I'm trying to take care of business in here. Fuck off."

"Step," Elias mutters. "*Step-niece.*"

"Same fucking difference," I say for his purpose, subtly reminding him that the comments he made about Harper last week weren't okay.

Harper grins against my hand, and I tighten my hold around her waist, lifting her right off the counter before pressing her back against the cold wall and holding her there. Her arms lock around my neck, and the second she's stable, I thrust hard, bottoming out.

She tips her head back against the wall, breathing heavily, and I release my hold over her mouth, trusting her to keep quiet, but honestly, at this point, I don't fucking care if she were to scream out my name right now. Let Elias know just how deep I am inside his precious little stepdaughter.

"We're going to fucking talk about this," Elias says, referring to my treatment of his ridiculous wife.

"Not right now, we're not."

Elias mutters to himself, and not a moment later, his footsteps recede, and I can only imagine what fresh bullshit is waiting for me, but it won't matter because it'll be a cold day in hell when I walk out of this bathroom and straight into the lion's den. Both Harper and I will be escaping out the back door.

"He's gone," Harper murmurs, her nails digging into my skin. "Now fuck me like you mean it."

Well, who the hell am I to deny a beautiful woman?

My cock thrusts deep into her sweet cunt, bottoming out with every slam of my hips against hers. "Oh, fuck," she groans, gripping onto me with everything she has as I keep her pinned against the bathroom wall. "Take me, Knight."

Her body trembles, her fingers moving to knot into my hair and pulling tight. I clutch onto her hip, my other hand gripping her perfect ass as her tight little cunt squeezes my cock, fitting so perfectly.

"Shit, doll," I grunt, my jaw clenches as she brings me right to the edge.

"Don't you dare hold back on me," she murmurs, barely able to catch her breath.

My pelvis grinds against her clit, and with every new thrust, her pussy squeezes even tighter, but I give her everything I've got, my cock slamming up into her tight warmth, feeling the way she begins convulsing around me.

"That's right, baby. Let go," I grit through my teeth. "Come for me."

As if on cue, Harper detonates, biting down on her bottom lip to keep from crying out. She groans low, her body breaking into wild, frantic spasms, barely able to hold herself up against me. And as she falls to pieces, shattering like the perfect sheet of glass, I come hard, shooting hot spurts of cum deep inside that pretty cunt.

"Fuck, Harper," I groan, my hips still rocking as she reaches her climax and finally begins to come back down, gripping onto me for a whole new reason as her head falls forward, her lips against my shoulder, breathing deeply.

"What are you doing to me?" she whispers against my skin.

"Right back at you, doll," I murmur, locking my arms around her again before shifting my back onto the vanity, my cock still buried deep inside her.

She looks up at me, those sweet eyes that are usually filled with the deepest confidence, now swimming with uncertainty. "I shouldn't want you like this."

She's said it before, but it doesn't make it any less true now. "I know," I breathe, placing my fingers to her chin and gently lifting, her lips barely a heartbeat away from mine. "I want you, Harper. And not just for your body."

"We can't."

I close the distance, letting my lips briefly brush over hers. "Believe me, doll. I'm more than aware that this can't happen. But it doesn't make me want you any less."

She sighs, placing her hand against my chest and forcing distance between us. "We have to stop before it goes too far. I can't just accidentally slip and fall onto your cock every time I see you. My family . . . It's already too messed up. If my mom finds out about this, she will make it her life's mission to destroy me."

"I won't allow her to do that."

She gives me a sad smile. "You don't know my mother well enough."

"I'm not going to stop, Harper," I tell her, easing out of her. "Not when it's so clear that you and I . . . We both want this, and when I'm inside you. Fuck, doll, it's too good to deny. But if you want space or to just need to lay low for a minute, then I'll respect that. I'm not about to force you into something you're not ready for."

She nods, and it fucking kills me that this woman before me just happens to be my brother's stepdaughter. Out of all the women on this earth, why does this have to be the one I can't have?

"We need to get out of here," she finally says. "But don't think for one second that you're about to drive off into the sunset without telling me exactly what you said to my mother at that table."

Laughter pulls from my chest, and I lift Harper off the counter before placing her on her feet, not letting go until I know she's balanced. "Hungry?" I ask.

She grins back at me, her eyes dancing with happiness, and despite knowing that spending more time together is going to make all of this so much worse, all she can do is nod. "I'm starving."

CHAPTER 26

HARPER-RAYN

Fuck, Mondays come around way too quickly.

One minute I was on my back, spending my weekend ignoring the fact that I shouldn't have been in Knight's bed, and the next, I'm here, swiping my access card over the security point at the doors of the dreaded morgue.

I don't know when I started dreading coming to work. Maybe it was right at the beginning when I first realized I was being watched, or maybe it was when the two men I was dancing with showed up on my table. All I know is that this is slowly killing me. I've always loved my work. I love the challenge of pulling the body apart and scouring every inch of it. I love learning exactly what went wrong to cause a perfectly healthy person's heart to spontaneously give out, and bringing justice to victims by collecting the evidence that helps capture their killers. But lately, I've been scared to walk through the door.

When I'm not at work, I can focus my attention on Knight and pretend like none of the bullshit is happening, but the minute I walk through these doors, it always comes right back.

With a heavy sigh, I push through the door, wondering what fresh hell I'll be hit with tonight. The morgue is still buzzing with people, but it doesn't take long to realize they're all starting to pack up after their long shift.

"Ahhh, Dr. Madden. How are you doing tonight?" Dr. McKullan asks, looking worse for wear.

"Good," I say. "Ready for a busy shift."

"Oh, you better be," he says, running his hand back through his hair. "It's been a busy day, and I suspect it will be an even busier night. The criminals of Blackstone must have been out and about this past weekend."

"Oh?" I say, striding deeper into the morgue and dropping my bag on my desk while glancing toward the bodies lined up on the tables. Shit. It really is going to be a busy night.

"Had three here waiting for us this morning. Another two came in at midday, and we've just had another one an hour ago. Preliminary reports have been started on all except the last body in bay six," Dr. McKullan tells me. "If you could get started on that one, that would be much appreciated. Then once you're done there, I've organized everything into what I want prioritized. I doubt you'll get through too much, but any kind of dent you can make will be helpful."

"Sure thing," I tell him, already feeling overwhelmed by everything on my to-do list, but that's just the luck of the draw, right? "I'll get straight to it."

I don't even bother waiting for everybody to finish filing out before I crank the music and start reviewing everything that needs to be done tonight. I quickly get lost in my work, focusing on the preliminary report for the man in bay six. There are signs of injury across his knuckles, looking as though he had been involved in some kind of fight, but the injuries are a few days old. Apart from that, there are no obvious markings to determine if this was a homicide or just nature taking its course.

A thrill shoots through me. This is just the kind of case I've been needing. There's nothing I love more than a challenge, but unfortunately for me, Mr. Bay Six isn't at the top of my priority list.

I get him bagged up and deposited back into the refrigeration unit until he's ready for a full autopsy, and I have to admit, with everything else on my list for tonight, I doubt I'll get the chance to completely dive headfirst into this particular mystery. One of my colleagues will probably be awarded that honor during tomorrow's day shift. Then come my next shift, I'll be faced with a whole new array of bodies to challenge me. I hope.

Wanting to keep the ball rolling and smash out as much as I can, I jump straight into the first autopsy of the night. It's a woman, and unfortunately, she looks as though her death was brutal.

My heart breaks for her as I document the finger-shaped bruises along the inside of her thighs and the scratches left across her chest. I have a good idea what happened to her, but it's not my job to make assumptions or declarations of rape. I just report on the facts.

As I complete the external portion of the autopsy, I go to reach for my scalpel when the sound of someone swiping their access key at the door sounds through the morgue. I'm too focused to worry about freaking out, and after my stalker left me alone all last week, I'm confident that it's not him.

My gaze shifts back to the woman, and as I press the scalpel down at her shoulder, the door opens, quickly followed by the sound of the cleaning cart. A small smile lifts the corner of my lips, and I look up to say hi to Vincent, and just as the words are about to fly out of my mouth, I find the scowling face of Vincent's replacement.

"Just great," I mutter under my breath.

I give him an awkward hello and keep working, knowing how uncomfortable dead bodies made him last time, but when his eyes linger on the woman's naked body, I can't help the protective instinct that comes over me.

I shift around the woman's body, immediately covering her up. "There's nothing for you here," I tell him, moving quickly to place her back in the body bag. Last week, the janitor was here for almost an hour, and I'm not about to have her on display to be gawked at by the likes of this asshole, especially not for an hour.

He scowls at me, thankfully deciding to keep his mouth shut, and without skipping a beat, I pack up her file and notes and move on to the next item on my list.

Bay number two.

I sterilize everything before getting myself a new pair of gloves, and as I look over the body bag, I can already tell there's a man inside. My gaze shifts over the notes from Dr. McKullan's preliminary report. Male. Blue eyes. No significant markings in terms of tattoos or piercings. No identification.

Okay. I can work with that.

I confirm that steps have already been taken to identify the body with fingerprints, mouth and dental swabs, along with blood being drawn. The clothes have already been removed and bagged, leaving me an empty canvas to get straight to work.

With all the little boxes ticked, I ensure all my tools are prepped and ready before finally gripping the zipper and revealing the face beneath, only my heart stops, and agony shoots through my veins like poison.

"No," I breathe, shaking my head as my eyes immediately fill with tears. "No, no, no."

This isn't happening. This can't be happening.

Big, heaving sobs tear from my chest as my stomach twists with ugliness, unable to comprehend what I'm seeing right in front of me. My hands shake, and as I stare down at the body of one of my closest friends, I become crippled with pain.

Laith Mitchell, the one and only man I have been able to rely on over the past few years, lies dead on my table, his once bright eyes now lifeless and cold.

The tears stream down my cheeks in waves as it becomes almost impossible to catch my breath over the growing lump in my throat.

How could he be gone? Just like that.

We spoke almost every day, whether it be a call or just some stupid text to let him know I was thinking of him. Even now after letting our physical relationship take a back seat, we would still talk all the time. Just because we weren't punching holes in his loyalty card didn't mean that I didn't still crave his friendship.

He was always the best to talk to, always knew how to put a smile on my face, even in the toughest circumstances. Sure, sometimes he was a flake who would leave me high and dry, especially when he was in the middle of a case, but I liked that he put his career first just as I've always done. I respected that about him. But even then, if I truly needed him, he would do everything he could to try and make the time.

I just don't understand how he would end up here on my table. Did someone do something to him? An angry client? A family member of someone Laith had put away? It doesn't make any sense. While he was well on the road to becoming one of the top lawyers this city has ever seen, he was also one of the best people I have ever known.

Who would just hurt him like this?

The tears flow faster, and seeing that I'm not about to pull my shit together anytime soon, the asshole janitor finally decides to make an exit, not bothering to finish the job he started. It doesn't matter anyway. It's not as though he's capable of doing a good job.

Despite the agony tearing through my chest, I try to do my job, needing answers just as much as I need this moment to grieve. Then as the painful sobs rip through my body, I peel back the rest of Laith's body bag and get to work.

My gaze roams over him, knowing every inch of his body better than I know my own, and the moment I find the carvings on his chest, every last piece of me shatters.

I crash on top of him, my arms thrown around his body as the overwhelming grief tears me to shreds, realizing that I'm the reason he's gone. I'm the reason he's on this table. If we never knew each other, never got close and spent the last few years in each other's beds, my stalker wouldn't have ended his life.

He's dead simply for being someone in my life.

The grief is too much. The self-blame and loathing are already eating me alive.

I should have said something, should have told the people in my life, but I kept it quiet in order to protect myself, to protect them, but who's next? Izzy? Knight? My brother? If they knew, they would have told me I was crazy. They would have forced me to stop working just like Knight had attempted, but that's not who I am, and now I'm the one to blame.

I cry and cry, holding on to him as though that could somehow make him come back, and I almost expect him to sit up and shove me off him, telling me this is some kind of sick prank. It's not as though he hasn't joked about it before. He had a dark sense of humor at the worst of times, but so do I. It's part of the reason we bonded so well over the years. But this time, it's no joke.

Laith is never coming back.

He's never going to ask me how my day was. Never going to touch me. Never get the chance to fall in love and make a family to care for. Never earn the title of becoming Blackstone's best criminal lawyer. Never again tell me that everything is going to be okay.

And right now, nothing feels okay.

By the time I finally find the strength to lift myself off Laith, the pain has risen to a new high. The tears continue streaming down my face, and every time I wipe them away, they're replaced with new ones, so I just don't bother anymore.

Needing answers, I get to work, trying to put aside my grief to figure out what happened to my friend. My gaze immediately lands right on his chest at the carvings, and I know without a doubt there's a message here somewhere.

Taking a shaky breath, I take my pen and turn to a new page in my notebook, trying to figure out what fucking message could have been so important to get to me that it was worth murdering someone as incredible as Laith Mitchell.

One by one, I find the letters, and the further I get, the sicker I become.

YOU BROKE MY RULES
HE PUT UP A FIGHT
THE CLOCK IS TICKING
I'll GET YOU AT KNIGHT

What in the ever-loving fuck is that supposed to mean? I broke his rules? There's no way. I played his stupid game. I let him touch me at the club and went as far as to fuck him blind. I gave him exactly what he wanted and needed to fulfill his stupid game of hide-and-seek.

How can he claim that I broke his damn rules?

The grief turns to stone-cold rage as I continue looking over the message left on Laith's chest. *He put up a fight.* I can only assume that's referring to Laith. That he fought like a soldier right to the end, but as for the final two lines, I'm at a loss.

The clock is ticking. Obviously this must mean there's some kind of countdown, but as for just how much time I have left, I haven't got the slightest idea. It's that last line that's truly concerning me. *I'll get you at Knight.* It's not lost on me that there's a double meaning here.

He's warning me that he knows of my relationship with Knight, but is there more to it? Is Knight his next victim?

A part of me has hoped that he hasn't clued in on my relationship with Knight, but I'd be a fool to make that assumption, especially after Knight made the bold move to fuck me right here in the morgue for our eager audience. And yet I still hoped that for whatever reason, it could have been overlooked, and until now, it has, but not anymore.

I have to tell Knight. He has to know about this. He needs to know so he can be prepared. I can't lose him, not like this.

I focus on the rest of the autopsy, and yet my gaze keeps returning to the carvings on his chest, that is until I notice the markings on his wrist. My brows furrow, and I look a little closer. Were his wrists bound?

It looks as though he's had rope tied around his wrists for . . . shit. Parts of it appear fresh, as though it was just last night he was tied up, but the marks on other parts of his wrists appear old. At least a week old, but that's not possible. I haven't seen him in person for well over two weeks, but I have spoken to him plenty of times, especially over the last week. I FaceTimed him last weekend before Izzy and I went out, and then throughout the week we had our usual check-ins. But how could that be if his wrists have been bound for a week?

Has Laith been missing and I've been too caught up in my own world that I just didn't notice?

Has my stalker had him all week? Is that why he hasn't been by the morgue to terrify me, or why he hasn't shown up in my bedroom with another creeptastic black rose?

The tears start all over again and as my heart breaks into a million little pieces, I continue scanning over his body. There are signs of stress. His hair is dirty, and there are dark rings under his eyes, and despite how he would tease both Izzy and me about doing ourselves up, he was the definition of a pretty boy. He would never leave the house with dirty hair. His skin care routine was better than mine.

There are a few random markings, small scratches, and dirt under his nails, but just like the two men from the club, there are no obvious markers that can conclude a cause of death. I finish the external part of Laith's autopsy, and just as I go to reach for the scalpel, my hands start to shake.

I can't do this. I can't be responsible for tearing into his skin and cracking his chest. I can't hold his brain in my hands . . . his heart.

No. There are some lines that can't be crossed, some things we can never come back from, and this right here is it. When I think about him, I don't want to remember how his organs felt in my hand or the smell of his decaying body. I want to remember his smile, his heart, the way he made me come alive.

Not this.

Moving across the table, I pack up my notes and deliver them to my desk before gripping the bottom of the body bag. My gaze lingers on Laith's face, and as I slowly begin zipping up the bag, my heart breaks all over again, knowing this is the last time I will see him.

I won't return to view his body, it's too hard. Once I finish zipping this bag, it will be my goodbye.

The tears continue streaming down my face, and as his body is enclosed in the bag, every inch of me aches. I don't stop until I reach the very top, and as I carefully deliver his body to the refrigeration unit, I vow that my stalker will never get away with this.

No amount of revenge will ever make this okay, but I will never stop fighting until he has paid for what he's done to Laith, not even if it kills me.

I deliver Laith to the refrigeration unit, and as I close the door of locker number thirty-six, I know that number will haunt me for the rest of my life.

Finally reaching my desk, I crumble into my seat, and the moment my ass hits the chair, I let the grief drown me. I cry and cry, every last piece of my soul absolutely shattered. I sit here for over an hour, my face buried in my arms against the desk, and just when I'm about to pull myself together to try and get just a little bit of work done, my phone chimes from within my bag.

My brows furrow. Laith is the only person who ever contacted me this late, and it was always for a booty call. Not even Knight bothers to hit me up while I'm working. He's the type to wait for me to come to him, and more often than not, I only end up at his door when my world is falling apart.

Finding my phone in my bag, I pull it out and immediately become uneasy when I find a brand-new text from Laith, and it occurs to me, if he's been texting me as normal all week, but he's assumedly been kidnapped and bound by rope, then who the hell have these messages been from?

I have one guess.

My hands shake as my thumb swipes across the screen, and not a moment later, the text appears.

Big & Long Schlong #3: Hey tiger, working tonight? What time do you get off?

My heart races. Laith wouldn't text me that, not after we talked and he respectfully bowed out of the Dick-Me-Down Loyalty Program. He has too much respect for our friendship to risk it, too much respect for me. But my stalker wouldn't know that.

Laith and I haven't spoken about our new hands-off arrangement over text. If somebody did have his phone, which clearly they do, they would assume we were still screwing around by reading our texts.

There's no denying it. My masked murderer has Laith's phone and is using it as a connection to me, but not only that, it now gives me a direct link straight back to him.

My gaze shifts to the surveillance camera. Perhaps he doesn't know that I've seen Laith's body. Maybe he's only just tuned in to the shit show that is my night.

Uneasiness grips me in a choke hold, and as I stare down at the message, I realize that I have two choices. I can either let this asshole know exactly what I think of him, or I can play him at his own game and keep this little piece of knowledge stored safely away just in case I might need it.

With that in mind, I get busy responding to the text, hoping like fuck that I'm not screwing myself over in the process.

Harper-Rayn: If I weren't working right now, you'd probably be worried about me. Kinda wrecked though. It's been a crazy few days. Rain check?

Big & Long Schlong #3: Don't keep me waiting too long, tiger.

Harper-Rayn: You don't need to wait for me, cowboy!!! You and I both know there's a bottle of lube in your bedside drawer and a palm right there attached to the rest of your body. Get busy jerking that one-eyed meat snake and you'll be fine!

Big & Long Schlong #3: Fuck, you're trouble. Just wait until I get my hands on you.

His words have a shiver sailing down my spine, and as I put my phone down and glance back toward locker number thirty-six, I realize just how in over my head I am. This stalker has got me exactly where he wants me, and I've played right into his trap every single time.

I'm losing a game I never asked to play, and because of that, Laith is now dead, and Knight is right in the crosshairs.

I can't do this anymore. I can't be his little toy or play his deadly game.

The tears return, and I hate myself for them, feeling so damn guilty that I have the audacity to cry out of fear and exhaustion when I should be crying for Laith. I should be calling his family and offering to help them with funeral arrangements, offering to help sort out his things or simply just giving them a shoulder to cry on, but instead, I'm crying for me. I'm crying for the fear that has plagued me, the terror of walking into work and finding a friend on my table just like I did tonight, the absolute horror of knowing that Knight might be next.

I'm selfish. I'm wretched.

My mom was right about me. I'm a horrible person.

The thought has more tears falling, and I've never felt so weak in my life, and realizing there's no chance in hell that I'll be capable of pulling myself together now, I put the remaining bodies away in the refrigeration unit, pack up my things, and get the hell out of here.

Ten minutes later, I show up on a familiar doorstep, tears streaming down my cheeks and staining the top of my scrub shirt. Knight opens the door, and the moment those intense, dark eyes land on mine, he steps out into the chilly night, scoops me right off my feet, and holds me to his big chest. Then he turns his ass back around, kicking the door shut and taking me straight into the warmth of his bed.

CHAPTER 27

HARPER-RAYN

Knight's lips linger on my temple as his warm arms surround me, holding me to him as we spend the day in the comfort of his warm bed. I stayed up for hours, crying into his chest as I told him about Laith and the target now painted on his back, and after the tears ran their course, I've been feeling numb.

It's barely been twelve hours since I found Laith on my table, and despite having been the one to perform the external portion of his autopsy, I'm still in disbelief.

How can he just be gone? It doesn't feel real.

"I promise you, doll," Knight murmurs, his big hand claiming my thigh. "I'm going to find this bastard. He won't get away with this."

I attempt a small smile, but it falls flat. "I wish it were that easy, but there is no ending this. He won't stop until there's nothing more to take," I say as the numbness begins to morph into emptiness. "He's going to take and take until everything I love and care for is gone."

"I won't let that happen."

I appreciate him, I really do. But how am I supposed to respond to that? There's no doubt in my mind that Knight would go to the ends of the earth to end this thing, but I don't think catching this guy is even possible. We know nothing about him. His name. His purpose. Even why he's doing this.

He's too careful. Every scrap of evidence that's dangled over our heads is quickly taken away. It's as though the bodies he leaves behind are just part of the twisted game, used as a tool to torment me, to prove that he's always ten steps ahead.

"If something happened to you because of me," I say, my heart already breaking at the thought of Knight being next. "I . . ."

Knight takes my waist and rolls us until he's hovering over me, his hips pinning me to the mattress while he holds both my hands above my head in just one of his. "That's not going to happen, Harper," he vows, that dark, delicious gaze locked on mine, and for just a second, I believe him. "I'm not going anywhere. I'm riding this bullshit right to the end with you."

I swallow over the lump in my throat, my emotions nothing but a train wreck right now. "Why?" I breathe. "Why do you care so much?"

He shakes his head, a slight smirk pulling at his lips. "Even if I knew, I probably still wouldn't tell you."

A stupid laugh bubbles up my throat, recalling the very moment I hit him with those exact words. "You're an asshole," I tease.

Knight grins. "I'm well fucking aware, Morticia."

As I hold his powerful stare, I realize without a doubt that I'm quickly falling in love with this man. On any other day, that thought would terrify me, and I would have already raced out the door, but today, I welcome it. Love has only ever brought me pain, and sooner or later, Knight will bring the same, but I need it. I need to loathe myself, need to be punished for the lives that have been lost in my name, and what better way than to have Knight rip my soul right out of my chest?

I don't know when it happened, but at some point, this has gone from a wild fantasy to needing so much more than that. Something has changed. We're no longer just curious about one another, we're in deeper than we ever anticipated.

Lifting my chin, I let my lips brush across his. "Make me forget," I beg.

His dark gaze holds mine for a moment longer before he finally drops his lips to my neck, still holding my hands hostage above my head. I open up for him, tilting my head aside as his warm lips skate across my sensitive skin.

His hips drive between my thighs, and I lock my legs around his waist, desperate to feel him slide deep inside me. His other hand braces against my thigh, holding me so gently that I didn't even realize it was possible. Knight has always been so rough with me, not afraid to throw me around. He knows my limits and exactly what I'm willing to handle, but it never occurred to me what I'd find at the opposite end of that line.

The agony swirling through my chest immediately begins to fade, replaced with nothing but pure need and desire, and just as I feel the tip of his cock pressing against my entrance, his phone rings from his bedside table.

"Fuck," he groans, his lips moving against my skin, both of us recognizing the particular tone for the station, knowing he's being called out. "I'm sorry, doll."

"It's okay," I whisper, feeling the exact moment the desire dies inside me, allowing the pain to come soaring back.

Knight releases my hands and reaches for his phone as he rolls off me, already getting to his feet. When he answers the call, I can't help but watch him stride through his room and into the closet, already reaching for his uniform.

Knight finishes with his call, tossing his phone down on a shelf in the closet as he pulls his shirt over his head. "Active shooter situation," he explains. "I'll be gone a few hours, but I need you to stay right here where I know you're safe."

I nod, not having any plans to take off just yet. Plus, after last night, I don't know if I'll be safe in my apartment. My stalker has been biding his time, and now that there's a creepy message telling me the clock is ticking, I don't know if trapping myself in my apartment is really the smartest idea.

"Okay," he finally says, stepping up to the edge of the bed. He grips my ankle and drags me across the mattress until I'm right in front of him, his eyes locked on mine. "You call me if you need anything and I will come."

I swallow over the growing lump in my throat, hating how emotional his words are making me. "Promise."

He watches me a moment longer, and after deciding that I'll probably be fine, he turns on his heel and strides out of his bedroom, taking his tactical belt with him. His footsteps pound down the hall, and the front door opens, closes, and the lock clicks into place. A wave of loneliness crashes over me, and I scootch down into the blankets and drift in and out of sleep for the next few hours.

By the time I wake, it's almost four in the afternoon, and I let out a frustrated groan, knowing that I'll have to start getting ready for work soon. I'm really not sure that I can be at work right now, knowing Laith's body is right there in locker thirty-six—knowing one of my colleagues spent their day opening him up, cracking his chest, and looking over his body. Just the thought that someone would have had their hands wrapped around his heart . . . fuck.

My stomach twists, and I grab my phone, trying to distract myself from the pain. One thing is for sure, if this asshole has started coming after my friends and the people I care most about, then it's time that Izzy and I have a serious conversation.

I told her about my stalker the very first night I felt his presence in the morgue, but she insisted that it was all in my head, and now I have to tell her that she was wrong, but more than that, she needs to know that she could be caught in the crosshairs just from being someone I love.

Hell, how am I supposed to explain Laith? How am I going to break her heart like that? Sure, she wasn't as close with Laith as I was, but that doesn't mean that his death isn't going to destroy her just as it has me.

Blowing out a shaky breath, I bring up her number, knowing I need to do this now rather than later, and before I've even put the phone to my ear, her too-chirpy voice is coming through the line. "Girl, where the hell have you been? I've sent you like a billion messages today. I need to tell you . . . wait. I know exactly where you've been!" She laughs to herself. "Tell me you've been getting dicked down by Knight fucking Slater all day!"

"I . . ." I let out a sigh. "Iz, I . . . fuck."

There's a slight pause, and it's as if she's waiting for me to figure out what the hell I'm calling for, and honestly, I've got no fucking idea. How am I supposed to put any of this into words?

"Harper?" she murmurs, her tone shifting, clearly picking up that something's going on. "What's wrong?"

"I need to tell you something," I murmur, my heart breaking for a whole new reason. "It's important, and really fucked up, and I need you to have an open mind, but . . . damn it. I don't know how to tell you this."

"Tell me what?"

"It's Laith," I say, getting choked up. "Something—" A noise sounds from deeper in the house and my words fall away as my blood runs cold.

"Harper?" Izzy says, urgency in her tone. "What's going on? You're starting to freak me out. What happened to Laith?"

My chest heaves as the sound comes again, followed by a distinct creak of the floorboards in the hallway. Fuck.

"Knight?" I call out, knowing he wouldn't try to sneak up on me, not now. Not ever. "Is that you?"

I get no response, and just as I convince myself that I'm hearing things, heavy footsteps make themselves known in the hallway, one after another, coming closer toward Knight's bedroom.

Fear grips me in a choke hold, and I scramble off the bed, my phone clutched tightly in my shaking hand. This can't be happening. Not again. I was supposed to be safe here.

"What the fuck is going on?" Izzy demands.

"I . . . I think there's somebody in the house."

"What?"

My eyes remain glued on the open bedroom door, my pulse pounding so heavily in my ears that I can't hear a word Izzy is saying, and yet every step down the hallway feels like a vibration right through my soul.

I start backing up, my gut telling me what I already know to be true. He's come for me, and this time, he's taking no prisoners.

As if on cue, the masked stalker appears in Knight's bedroom door, a single black rose dangling from his fingers, and as I stare back at him, my hand falls away from my ear, my thumb skimming over the red button, ending the call with Iz.

The phone falls right out of my hand, dropping to the floor as a wave of overwhelming emotions plague me. Fear. Hurt. Heartbreak. But most of all, rage.

This man, whoever the fuck he is, is responsible for taking Laith's life, and I'm not about to sit back and let him have whatever he wants now. The game is over, and I don't care what I have to do to finish it. All I know is that he won't get away with this. I won't allow it.

The rage fills my veins, pulsing through me until all I see is red.

"YOU KILLED HIM!" I scream, the words tearing my throat to pieces.

The stalker lifts the rose, dragging it across the front of the fucked-up mask as if smelling it, and as he keeps that heinous stare on me, his head cocks to the side like a fucking psychopath. "You broke my rules."

"I'M NOT PLAYING YOUR FUCKING GAME ANYMORE. YOU KILLED LAITH. HE DIDN'T DESERVE THAT."

The asshole takes a calculated step forward, putting him that much closer to me and blocking any path I might have had of getting out of here. "Tsk. Tsk. Tsk. What did I tell you about screaming, little kitten? I much prefer when you're purring for me like the good little whore that you are."

Fucking asshole.

"You'll never touch me again," I spit through a clenched jaw. "You won't get away with this."

A condescending laugh rumbles through the bedroom. "Oh, sweet, naive kitten. I already have."

He takes another deliberate step, and my heart kicks into gear, racing faster than ever before. When he cornered me in my bedroom, I was all too eager to play the game in order to survive, but now that I've somehow broken his ridiculous rules, I have no idea what he's got in store for me. Is this where it ends? Have we reached the finish line of this deadly game?

"Stop. Don't come any closer."

His stare seems to laugh at me, and I realize just how outmatched I am. This man is a beast. He's just as tall as Knight, and just as broad, with obvious muscle hidden beneath his black clothes. I don't stand a chance, but I have to try. I have to get away and survive somehow. I can't let this be the end.

I inch toward the back of the bedroom, hoping to entice him out of the doorway, and when he shifts with my movements, I realize that I might just have a chance. At some point, he's going to want to get closer, and when that happens, I need to make my move. I need to be ready.

"Don't even think about it, kitten. You know what happens when you break my rules. Don't make me take somebody else from you," he murmurs. "Who shall I take next? Your little boyfriend? Or perhaps the fashion designer. Izabelle, is it?"

Fuck.

"Hmmmmm, kitten. You're running out of crutches, and soon enough all you'll have in this world is me." I shake my head, refusing to believe it. I'll die before he even thinks about taking somebody else from me. "One by one. They will all fall like toy soldiers."

"If you touch any of them . . ."

He laughs, and as he takes a step toward me, I make my move, sprinting toward the door and running for my life. My feet pound against the floor, my heart racing faster than ever before as the desperation eats me alive.

I barrel toward him, and in a flash, his hand snaps out, bracing tightly around my throat as my body crashes heavily against his. I feel his stare through the mask as I grip his hand on my throat, trying to suck in a breath, but there's no use. He's too strong.

"Oh, kitten. I'm disappointed," he murmurs, stepping into me and forcing me back, one hasty step after another until the back of my knees are pressed against the edge of Knight's bed. "You've played so eagerly up until now. *If you scream, you fail. If you run, you die.* And kitten, you will die."

My eyes widen with fear, and before I can even attempt to get away, he lifts me right off the ground, his grip on my throat like nothing I've ever felt. Then with an overwhelming show of strength, he throws me down against the mattress, releasing his grip on my throat.

I gasp, sucking in a desperate breath, the sweet oxygen burning in my lungs, and I waste no time trying to pull away, but his big hand clutches my ankle, holding me down. He reaches into his pocket, producing a thin rope, and I frantically try to get away, kicking out and throwing my body. If I could just get to my feet, maybe I could throw myself through the window and somehow get to the road before he catches me, but it's no use. I'm already a slave to his wicked desires.

He knots the rope around my ankle before tying it to the end of the bed, and when he does the same to my other ankle, I'm left to his mercy, my thighs spread wide.

Tears well in my eyes as he climbs onto the bed, crawling right over me until his big knees are braced on either side of my waist, and he simply holds out his hand with expectation.

"Play the game, kitten, and I might just spare you."

Horror rises in my chest, and I reluctantly lift my shaking hand from the mattress before gently placing it into his, terrified of what's about to happen.

"Both."

I swallow over the fear and give in, placing my other hand straight into his. Once he has both of my wrists, he pulls them behind my back and ties them beneath me, the rope painfully cutting into my skin.

"Good girl," he soothes as though his words can somehow make me feel better about this whole situation. "You belong to me. Don't you forget that."

"I'll never be yours," I spit, shaking my head. "I don't even know who you are."

"Oh, but you do," he says, digging his hand into his pocket and revealing a blade. "You know me better than you know yourself, and now . . . you'll never forget."

Horror rips through me, and I squirm beneath him desperately trying to buck him off me as the soft afternoon light streams through the window, glistening off the large blade. "No." I panic, not above getting to my knees and begging for my life. "No. Please, no."

Tears well in my eyes, and as my gaze remains locked on the blade, I realize this has to be the very same blade that tore through Laith's skin and left those despicable words behind.

"Mine," he grits.

"Never."

He reaches back with his free hand, his fingers coming down between my thighs, immediately rolling over my sensitive clit, and just like every time he's touched me, my traitorous body comes alive. My hips jolt at the sudden electricity pulsing through my core, and while the weight of his body crushes me into the mattress, he fingers the hem of Knight's shirt, pulling it up to expose my chest.

He groans, and while I expect him to dive for my tits, it's not what's got his attention. It's the space below—the blank canvas of skin over my ribs.

"All mine," he repeats as his fingers continue working my clit.

He brings the tip of the blade to my skin, slowly dragging it down my ribs and watching the way it rolls so effortlessly over my body. My gaze remains locked on the blade, terror lacing my every breath. "You're going to want to hold still, kitten," he murmurs as his fingers dip lower and push into my cunt.

My hips involuntarily jolt again as my walls automatically clench around his fingers, and when the slightest groan tears free from my lungs, I want to kill myself. How can he do this? Even when I want to gouge his eyes out with my nails, my body still responds to him as though he's the very air I need to breathe.

As his fingers split inside me, he grinds the heel of his palm against my core, and the blade finally comes down, slicing through my flesh like butter. I cry out in pain, but he rolls his fingers inside me, and the sharp pain quickly morphs into a wicked pleasure, confusing my senses. His touch alleviated the pain, making it tolerable like some bullshit from Christian Grey's Red Room.

I feel the blood roll over my side and soak into Knight's mattress, and then the blade is there again, carving out the little letters, just as I knew he would.

Tears spill over, rolling down my cheeks as my traitorous body craves more, making me sick to my stomach.

He doesn't stop working my cunt, pushing my body to its limits, bringing me right to the edge, only to pull back and do it again and again. Frustration burns through me, desperately needing the release, but the sharp sting of the blade keeps it at bay.

What the fuck is wrong with me?

He carves one letter after another into my skin, and when the blade falls to the mattress, I cry out with relief, realizing he's finished. Then as his fingers roll inside me, I can't help but look down, desperately trying to make out the little letters he's marked me with.

MINE

Seeing his handiwork on my body, he becomes mesmerized, and I don't miss the massive bulge in the front of his pants, but when my hips jolt again, it's as though he's pulled out of his own musings.

"Hmmm, hungry for more, kitten?"

I suck in a breath, absolutely repulsed by this man. Repulsed by my body's response to his touch. He took Laith's life and now his fingers are buried deep inside me. I hate that he's capable of making my body come alive like this, making me crave that touch, but never again.

There's no coming back from this. Not after everything that happened.

"Answer me, kitten," he growls.

His tone is sickening and as I remain at his complete mercy, I have no choice but to nod out of pure self-preservation. "Yes."

"That's what I thought."

He shifts over me, collecting his blade as apprehension booms through me, not knowing what to expect. His fingers pull out of me, and I hate the way my body misses his touch, but not a moment later, those fingers are replaced by the hilt of his blade, slowly pushing deeper inside of me.

I gasp, my eyes snapping up to his, not having expected this in a million years. He starts working me with it, circling the hilt inside me as he works my clit with his thumb. My body trembles and within seconds, I come, my orgasm tearing through me with a fierce intensity.

I cry out, throwing my head back against the mattress, desperately thrashing against the ropes holding me down. "Fuck," I cry out, my chest heaving, tears stinging my eyes.

This is wrong. So fucking wrong.

He doesn't work me the same as Knight can, doesn't allow me to ride it out, pulling the hilt of the blade out of my cunt and discarding it on Knight's bedroom floor. He pulls at the ropes on my ankles, freeing them, and then he grips my body and violently flips me over. He takes my hips, dragging me down the bed until my bare ass is high in the sky, and my chest is hard against the mattress.

He frees his cock, and with one brutal thrust, he's buried deep inside my cunt.

An involuntary cry tears out of me, my walls stretching around him, and as he digs his fingers into my skin, he truly starts to fuck me. Thrusting deep as he rolls his hips, taking me at every angle. My clit screams for attention, and with my hands bound at my back, I'm powerless, left to let him have me in any way he desires.

He fucks me like a wild animal, taking and taking as his fingers dig into my hips, holding me still. He's wild, untamed. Out of control, and I hate that my body loves every fucking second of it.

I'm a monster. A true fucking monster. This is the man who killed Laith and threatened to take Izzy or Knight next, and I'm here at his mercy, my body worked right to the edge.

He takes me deep and I push back against him, taking it harder like some kind of punishment as he starts to lose control.

This isn't the disciplined man who sat still and allowed me to ride him in the club. This is different. This is raw need, undiluted hunger that needs to be fed, and right now, I'm giving him exactly what he needs, right here in another man's bed.

He sinks into me again and again, driving his hips forward with brutal thrusts. Then like clockwork, my orgasm tears out of me, detonating within me like a nuclear weapon, and tearing everything to shreds in its path.

Guilt courses through my body as I cry out, my fingers balling into tight fists at my back, and not a moment later, he comes right along with me, his hips thrusting so deep I can practically feel him in my throat.

As I come down from my high, my body slumps against the bed and he simply holds my hips as he catches his breath, trying to regain just a semblance of control, but he won't find it here. Not after that.

A moment passes before he pulls back, inching that thick cock out of me until finally stepping away, and now that it's over, the apprehension soars back, unsure what's supposed to come next.

Is this when I die for breaking his damn rules?

I scramble to the farthest corner of the bed, doing my best to cover myself while my hands remain bound at my back, my eyes glued to his as he folds that monster cock back inside his black pants.

"Pretty kitty. I have such a weakness for you. Your sweet cunt might have gotten the best of me today, but break my rules again, and I won't be so forgiving."

I swallow hard, my hands starting to shake again, and not a moment later, he strides out of the room, taking the black rose with him.

The second he disappears, I let out a sigh as my eyes pool with unshed tears, and when I pull against my wrists and realize I have no chance of getting free, I let out a frustrated sigh.

"Siri," I say with deep regret. "Call Knight."

CHAPTER 28

KNIGHT

I slam into my front door, barely managing to get it unlocked before I barge in and race through my home, panic swelling in my chest. How could I have left her alone like that? I thought she was safe here.

"HARPER?" I call, my boots slamming against the hardwood floors as my gaze shoots around the house, trying to find her. Not finding her in the living room or kitchen, I grip the corner of the wall and fling myself around the corner, propelling myself down the hallway. "Harper, baby. Where are you?"

"Here," she murmurs in barely a whisper.

I follow the sound right to my bedroom, and as I rush through the doorway, I come to a screeching halt, finding blood smeared through the bed, and the blankets all but torn into ribbons.

"What the fuck?" I mutter to myself, looking the room over with a keen eye before noticing one of my kitchen knives just lying carelessly on the floor. "Doll?"

"Bathroom."

I follow the sound of her voice right into my en suite and find Harper standing at the sink with her hands braced against the porcelain, head down, with tears on her cheeks.

The sight guts me, and I immediately blame myself. I should have anticipated this. I should have known that he would search for her, but the fact that it happened in my home fucking sickens me.

I hurry into the bathroom, moving in right behind her. Every ounce of me wants to reach out and grab her, pull her into my arms, and hold her tight, but I hold back, not sure what she needs right now.

"Doll," I murmur, my voice gravelly and filled with the kind of ache I've never felt before.

Her gaze lifts to mine through the mirror, and the pain in her eyes is my undoing.

"I'm sorry, doll."

She shakes her head and turns, stepping right into my arms and allowing me to hold her, and fuck, that's exactly what I do, scooping her up into my chest. She locks her legs around my waist and knots her arms behind my neck, just allowing me to hold her, one hand around her back and the other in her hair.

"I'm sorry," she cries. "I didn't know this could happen."

"You don't have anything to be sorry for," I tell her, letting out a sigh as I reluctantly place her on the bathroom counter and pull back just an inch, needing to take her in. "Are you okay?"

She shakes her head and grips the bottom of my shirt that she's wearing, the very same one I put her in last night. She hesitates for just a moment before finally tightening her grip on the fabric and slowly lifting it over her ribs.

Horror blasts through me like a fucking bullet as I find blood smeared across her ribs and chest, and as I look a little closer, I can make out the shallow cuts. "The fuck happened, Harper?" I ask, searching her broken stare. "What did he do to you?"

Her gaze falls away from mine, and she grabs the front of my shirt, her fingers digging into the fabric. "I was on the phone with Iz when he showed up. He was pissed. Said that I broke his rules."

"Fuck."

I grip the front of her thighs, my hands firmly squeezing as if needing to remind myself that she's right here in front of me. A tear streaks down her face. "I thought he was going to kill me."

I slam into her, my arms locking around her body as I cradle her against me, her face crushed against my chest as she holds me just as tight. "What happened?"

She sniffles against my shirt. "I tried to run, but he's so fast. Like lightning. He just grabbed me and threw me down on the bed. He tied my ankles and wrists and climbed on top of me. He said I was his, and he was going to make sure I never forgot."

She pulls back from me before lifting her shirt again. "That's what this is. It spells *mine*."

The fuck?

I crouch down to get closer to her, my gaze roaming over the cuts, and as the blood continues trickling out of the wounds, I can start to make out the brutal letters.

MINE

It makes me fucking sick, and as I straighten back to my full height, I grip the counter on either side of her creamy thighs, my head dropped low between us. "This should never have happened. Not in my home," I tell her, racking my brain for any sign that she was in danger, but coming up blank. My home security system was on and active just as it always is, but I haven't had a single notification for somebody being on the property.

"There's more," she murmurs.

My head snaps straight back up, meeting her guilt-ridden stare, her blazing green eyes filled with unshed tears.

"I let him touch me," she admits, the tears finally falling down her cheeks as her eyes fill with shame. "Is there something wrong with me? I was scared and disgusted. I felt like I had no choice, but when he touched me, I didn't even try to push him away. I didn't scream for help or try to get him off me. I just . . . I let him do it and . . . fuck, Knight. Even after everything, I still came."

"There's nothing wrong with you, doll. It makes you human."

"But I'm terrified of him. Every time I see him, I become crippled by fear, but when he starts touching me, I can't . . . I can't tell him to stop. I shouldn't want it like that, especially after everything that's happened, but I do, even though I know at some point, it isn't going to end like it did today. He's going to kill me. I feel it in my bones, but there's something about the fear that just . . . It excites me."

I nod, not really understanding this, but I'm not about to tell her that she's wrong for the way her body responds to the fear.

"Are you mad?" she finally asks, glancing up at me.

A stupid smile pulls at my lips. "Fucking furious," I tell her. "But not with you. Him. You're mine, and despite what I've told you, when it comes to this motherfucker, I don't like to share. I'm going to kill him for putting his hands on you."

She arches a brow. "My oh my, Knight Slater. You're gonna kill him, huh?" she teases. "That sounds awfully possessive of you. Might I remind you that you and I are—"

"Are what?" I challenge.

She visibly swallows, and I take her hips, scooting her right to the edge of the counter. "It's just sex. Really amazing, burning-hot, might-die-without-it kind of sex. But it's just sex."

A smirk lifts the corners of my lips. "You fall into my bed every fucking chance you get," I remind her, just in case she's forgotten. "Your body trembles at my touch, and your eyes. Doll, your eyes are a window right into your fucking soul. This stopped being about sex a long time ago. Don't try and play it down. This means something."

She lifts that gaze, her eyes silently begging me not to push this. "And what if I'm not ready to admit that just yet?"

"Then I'll give you all the time you need."

"Shit," she mutters. "I think I preferred it when you were a bossy asshole."

"Don't worry, I'm still that guy."

"Oh, wonderful."

Harper takes a heavy breath, and I watch as her chest rises and falls before stepping back and giving her a bit of space. Cutting across the bathroom, I start searching for my first-aid kit in the cupboard before taking it right back over to her.

I open it on the bathroom counter before indicating the shirt covering her beautiful body. "Take it off."

Without hesitation, she lifts it over her head and exposes the wounds on her ribs, and I won't lie, my gaze can't help but skim across those perfect pierced tits and stunning tattoos. "There's too much blood. I think it might be better if I just get in the shower."

I nod, more than agreeing with her, but from what I can tell, most of the blood is just smeared from earlier. There's only a small trickle left, but nonetheless, I'm going to fix her up anyway.

She jumps down from her perch on the sink as I reach into the shower to warm up the water. As she wanders toward me, I lean back against the counter and watch her.

"What?" she murmurs, noticing my stare.

I grip the edge of the counter as I kick one foot over the other. "What is it that you like about him?" I ask. "Is it how he touches you or the fear he provokes?"

She goes quiet for a moment, stepping into the shower and letting the warm water wash the blood away. "Don't get me wrong, I don't like anything about him," she says. "But I'm starting to wonder if maybe I have some undiscovered kinks that I'm only just starting to realize. I'm not really sure, but there's something about the fear that excites me."

She falls silent as she gently rubs at her ribs, trying to clean herself up, but the crease in her brows tells me she's still deep in thought. "The first time he touched me, his hand was around my throat. He was choking me as I came, and it somehow got me there faster. There was an urgency. I knew the longer it took me, the longer it would be until I could breathe. But then today, it was different. When the blade was digging into my skin, it hurt, but the way he was touching me, it was as though he was taking the pain away, and I could just focus on the pleasure. It felt wrong, but my body liked it."

I nod. "Is that all that happened? He just made you come and then left like he did in your bedroom. Or is this more a repeat of what happened in the club?"

She cringes and my gut twists with jealousy.

It's one thing to know that another man has been fucking my girl, but to know how much her body responds to it absolutely guts me. "Like the club," she admits, barely able to meet my stare. "But it was different. He just took what he needed and then left, and yes, while I did come, it wasn't the same as when I'm with you. You make me feel things. You make my whole body come alive and leave me trembling for hours afterward. You and me, it's give and take, but with him, it's all take. It's about satisfying a raw need, and he'll take it any way he has to in order to get what he wants. It's transactional and empty. There was nothing . . . *more* about it."

I step right into the open shower door, my brow arched. "More?" I ask, gripping the shower frame above my head.

Harper grins and nods. "So much more."

I step right into the shower, clothes and all, and Harper laughs, swatting at my chest. "What are you doing?" she screeches as I grab her waist and pull her into me. "You're getting all wet."

My lips drop straight down onto hers, and if it were any other day, I'd be grabbing her ass and lifting her right into my arms, showing her just how much *more* I can offer her, but I want to give her a minute after everything she's endured today.

When she pulls back, she drops her face against my chest, letting me hold her as the hot water rains down over us. "You should run while you still can," she tells me, her voice barely a whisper. "I'm like a land mine. Sooner or later, you're going to step on me, and I'll explode into a million pieces, taking you down with me."

My hand roams over her back, wishing things could be different. "If you burst into flames, I'll be right there stepping into the fire with you. If you're burning, doll, I'm going to burn right along with you."

Her body sags against mine, and I hold her for a moment before sensing that she needs a little time alone with her thoughts. "I'll give you a minute," I tell her. "But the second you're out of this shower, I'm bandaging your ribs."

"Oop. And here I thought the bossy asshat had taken an extended vacation."

"Looks like he came home early."

Harper smirks and rolls her eyes, and I step out of the shower, dripping everywhere. Then after ridding myself of my wet clothes and drying off, I make my way into my closet to find a fresh change of clothes and grab another shirt for Harper. As I pull the T-shirt from the hanger, I realize that I'm going to eventually run out of these bastards.

Once I'm dressed, I step back into the bedroom and look over the mess left behind.

"You said he tied you with rope, right?" I call out.

"Yeah. On my ankles and wrists," she says over the shower.

I nod to myself and make my way around the bed, gripping the edge of the bloodied sheets and pulling them back. I have no idea how the top blanket ended up in ribbons. There's no sign of the rope, and it leaves me wondering if perhaps she's confused.

I finish pulling back the blankets and toss them into the corner of the room before finding the discarded kitchen knife on the ground. It makes me sick looking at it, and as I pick it up and sit on the edge of the bed, I can't stop staring at it.

Harper emerges from the bathroom a moment later, her towel wrapped around her shoulders and the open wounds staring back at me. "I'm ready," she says, pointing to her ribs.

I stand abruptly, leaving the kitchen knife on the mattress, and head back into the bathroom. Carefully avoiding her wounds, I hoist her back up onto the counter to fix her up.

She winces as I apply the antiseptic cream. "Fuck, that stings."

"Just you wait until it's a bullet wound. Now, *that* ain't pretty."

Her eyes widen. "You've been shot?"

I nod. "Three times."

She gapes at me as though only just seeing me for the first time. "Holy fucking shit," she breathes. "That means either you're always throwing yourself in front of your teammates to save their asses, or you're just really fucking bad at your job."

I grin. "I'm bad at my job."

"Bullshit."

I laugh and leave it there. Now isn't exactly the time to get into it, and I'm sure at some point she's going to find every last scar on my body and demand a full rundown of how they got there, which I'm more than happy to give. But right now, I have questions of my own.

"Those ropes," I say, watching as her body stiffens at the reminder. "When I was fixing the bed, I couldn't see anything. Are you sure it was actually rope?"

"I don't know. Maybe. I didn't exactly pause and ask him what kind of rope he was using. It looked like rope to me, but it wasn't scratchy on my skin like I assume rope would feel. Not really sure."

"Okay. And how'd you get out of them?"

I apply more cream and she winces again. "He released my ankles halfway through, but my wrists were still bound after he left. I had to rub them up against that knife after I called you. I'd only just gotten free when I heard you come through the door."

"Shit, doll."

She shrugs and glances away, letting the bathroom fall into silence as I bandage her wounds. I'm left with even more questions than before I started. I mean, fuck. Where are the ropes? There was nothing but shredded blankets on the bed and blood from her cuts, but no ropes. It doesn't make sense.

"I just have one more question, and then I swear, we can forget about it if that's what you want. Or I can order something for dinner, and we can chill on the couch."

"I'm not a fragile little petal that's going to break, Knight. I'm fine to talk about it," she says. "You don't need to freak out about asking me questions."

"I'm not freaking out."

She arches a brow, and I let out a sigh. "Okay, fine. I don't want to ask you shit about it in case it fucks with your head. But I'm not freaking out. I'm a fucking SWAT officer. I'm trained specifically to not freak out."

"Uh-huh." I give her a blank stare and she rolls her eyes. "Fine. Ask your question so the bossy asshat can go back into retirement."

"I just . . . I can't work out what happened to the blankets."

Her brows furrow. "What do you mean?"

"They were cut into ribbons, doll," I say, carefully, watching her closely. "Nothing you said in your recap explained how the blankets ended up like that, so I wasn't sure if I'd missed something, or if that had happened later."

"I . . . really don't know what you're talking about," she says, lifting her hand to my head. "Are you feeling alright? Nothing happened to the blankets."

I nod, knowing damn well what I saw in that bedroom, but after the hell she's been through today, I'm not about to push her on it. It's not uncommon for victims to block out memories of their trauma in order to protect themselves, and if that is the case, I'm sure as fuck not about to make her relive something that she's not ready to share with me.

"Okay," I finally say, finishing with the bandages before lifting her off the counter and setting her back on her feet. "I'm gonna remake the bed and order takeout, and while I do that, you're gonna call your boss and tell him either what the fuck has been going on or that you've come down with the flu. But either way, your ass is staying here tonight."

"But—"

"No. You're staying right here under my roof and on my fucking couch. We're going to watch a movie like regular people. You're not going to think about this asshole who keeps stalking you, and you're going to have a good fucking time."

She gapes at me, and I can just imagine the comment about being bossy, but I don't give a shit.

"And if I wanted to take you to bed and sit on your face instead?"

"Then I think it's important for you to know that I can be a very understanding man who cares only for giving those around me what they need most. But doll," I say, grabbing her waist and pulling her in, my tone lowering to a whispered growl. "If you're going to spend hours riding my face, then you better drop right down and fucking suffocate me with it."

Harper grins, her eyes dancing with excitement. "Well, well. Who am I to deny a starved man?" she says. "It looks like I've got some calls to make."

CHAPTER 29

HARPER-RAYN

The early-morning sun shines through Knight's bedroom window as I wake in his warm arms, never having felt more at peace than I do at this moment. Fuck everything else that's been going on; this right here is where I want to spend the rest of my life.

Yesterday was a shit show. Actually, the last few weeks have been a complete shit show. Every step I take somehow sends me back ten more. Laith is gone, and my stalker is escalating, intent on derailing my whole world, but right now, there's nothing he can do that could possibly ruin this moment for me.

This right here, this is what falling in love feels like.

Knight's arm is so tight around me that it's almost impossible to breathe, but I wouldn't have it any other way. I don't even care that his arm has been pressing up against my ribs for the last twenty minutes. I never want to leave this place.

Except to pee. Shit, I really need to pee.

I spent the night suffocating him with my pussy just as he requested, and I think my knees are still shaking. I wasn't lying yesterday in the shower. With Knight, it's just . . . more. It's as though he's in tune with my body, what I feel, and what I need. He reads me so well, and whatever gift he was given from the heavens above that allows him to please a woman is so overwhelmingly great, he uses it well.

I'd be a fool to run from him, and despite the hell that's bound to come from my mother if she ever finds out, I don't even care.

I'd risk it all just to have a life with him. If only I didn't go and make such a big speech about not being exclusive. I kinda shot myself in the foot there, and at some point, I'm going to have to find the strength to tell him point-blank exactly what I want. But until then, he'll be here waiting, and nothing has ever comforted me more.

Slipping out from under his arm, I dash into the bathroom and quickly pee before using his toothbrush and washing my face. I can't help but notice my messy hair and feel the tender skin between my thighs from a night full of riding the face of a man with stubble.

It's not the greatest feeling to wake up to, but it's one I'd happily wake up with every day for the rest of my life. I mean, shit. That man eats pussy like it's going out of fashion. And his fingers! Fuck. I don't know what training camp he went through, but whatever it was, it strived for perfection.

After freshening myself up, I slip back out into Knight's bedroom, and while the empty space beneath his arm looks more than enticing, I can't help but pad into his closet and grab one of his black hoodies from the rack. I pull it over my body and muffle a laugh, seeing just how far down my legs it goes.

Knight really is a beast of a man, and I absolutely love it. There's something about a man who can throw me around that really gets me going, and Knight is exactly that. I can almost picture him spending his free time out in the woods, living it up in a log cabin, and swinging an ax around like one of those ripped lumberjack dudes.

God. My mouth starts to water.

Creeping back out into his bedroom, I hold my breath, not wanting to make a single sound as I climb up onto his bedside table, awkwardly pausing when he threatens to wake up. I cringe, my eyes going wide, but as he settles back into a light sleep, I get into position, crouching down and making sure the hoodie covers every inch of me before fixing the hood right up over my head and pulling the strings until my face disappears behind the material.

I look like a fucking demon spawn, the perfect devil hawk

crouching on his bedside table for the most fantabulous wake-up call known to humankind.

There's the smallest little peephole to look through and when Knight doesn't immediately begin to wake, I start to regret my decision. This might take longer than I anticipated.

With my knees starting to ache from my crouching position, I slip my toe out, knocking his phone off the bedside table and making just enough noise to stir him awake. His hand immediately slips out, feeling for me on the other side of the bed, and a goofy-as-fuck grin stretches across my face.

He grumbles something in his sleepy haze before rolling over, and the moment his gaze lifts to the crouching devil hawk on his bedside table, his eyes widen. "FUCK!" he roars, reaching out and grabbing hold of me, yanking me down onto the bed as I howl with laughter.

My back crashes against the mattress as Knight comes down over me, barely bothering to hold up his own weight as he keeps me pinned. "Holy fuck, Morticia. You scared the shit out of me."

"I know," I laugh, reaching up to birth my face through the hole in the hoodie. "Wasn't it great?"

He shakes his head. "Not even a little bit."

He rolls off me, his hand braced against his racing heart, and I immediately climb on top of him, my knees straddling his hips as the hood falls back. "Oh, looks like I'm going to have to make it up to you," I say, my eyes blazing as I meet his. "Luckily I've got a few tricks you haven't discovered yet."

His brow arches, and I immediately begin scootching down the bed before showing him exactly how to turn me into the Super Soaker 3000.

An hour later, we're snuggled in bed, both of us completely exhausted, when Knight glances at the time. "I have to get ready for my shift."

"You really have to go?" I ask, grinning at him, more than ready to use his own words against him. "You can't just call in and tell your boss that you have the flu?"

He laughs. "If I thought for even a second that would work, then I'd do it in a heartbeat," he tells me as he rolls out of bed and walks that perfect, naked ass across the room. "You heading out today?"

"Ummm . . . maybe," I say, having thought of potentially getting a new tattoo. It's always worked as a good stress reliever for me, but I haven't quite made up my mind yet. "I need to call Iz after yesterday. She's probably been freaking out all night, which is totally a dick move. I should have spoken to her yesterday."

"Yeah, maybe," he says, agreeing with me, pulling those black tactical pants that I love up those toned thighs and hiding the goods beneath. "You know you can stay here if you want. There's no reason to leave, but I get it if you don't want to be alone here anymore."

"Okay. I might stay for a bit. Not really sure. It's comforting knowing you're here if something were to happen."

"Of course," he says, striding over to me and lifting my chin before dropping his lips to mine with a brief kiss. "Any fucking time, doll."

My cheeks flush; he's called me *doll* a million times over the past few weeks, and every single time without fail, it sends butterflies soaring through my stomach. I don't think I'll ever tire of it.

Knight leaves for work, and the moment he's gone, I put myself through a proper shower, washing my hair and feeling like a brand-new person before rummaging through his bathroom for just a shred of moisturizing cream.

After feeling like a normal human being, I head out to the kitchen and make myself a coffee as I try to figure out my plan. The very first thing on my to-do list needs to be Izzy. I can only imagine what state I've left her in. I need to book her a massage, some therapy, maybe get some flowers delivered and organize a mariachi band to serenade her, not that she would particularly care for all that stuff, but any apology I can muster needs to be given in a big way.

After that, I'm heading home. This bitch needs some clothes. There's only so many days in a row I can wear nothing but one of Knight's shirts. Surely he's running out by now. There's only so many shirts a man like Knight would own, and honestly, we've already flown straight past the number I would have assumed. It's starting to get weird.

The rest of my day . . . I actually have no idea. I'm making it up as I go. I don't usually wake up this early in the day. I'm a firm midday riser, especially on work nights, and I really don't know what to do with all this spare time. It's freaking me out.

With my coffee in hand, I make my way over to Knight's oversized lounge and drop down into it, cringing as I take in the thirty-eight missed calls and nineteen texts. There's even missed calls from my brother, Emily, and my mom. Izzy must have called everyone looking for me.

My heart breaks for her, knowing how worried she must have been after what she heard last night, and I don't make her wait another second.

I hit her number on my phone and lift it to my ear, and just like yesterday, it barely rings before her panicked tone answers. "Holy fucking shit, Harper? Is that you?"

"Yeah, it's me," I say, guilt tearing me into shreds.

"WHAT THE ACTUAL FUCK? What happened?" she demands. "I've called the police six times, and the bastards won't let me file a missing-person report until you've been gone for at least twenty-four hours."

And with that, I launch into my story, telling her every single detail, right from the very start, covering every last encounter with this asshole, even going as far as to tell her about the times he's forced me right into Knight's arms.

The words fall out of me with ease, that is until I tell her about Laith, and then the perfectly structured wall around my heart crumbles to the ground. I break into heartbroken sobs as Izzy tries to process everything that's happening.

"No," she tells me, disbelief thick in her tone. "That's not possible. I was talking to Laith just last night. I texted him looking for you. He responded."

"No," I rush out, feeling sick at what I have to tell her. "That's not Laith. I thought the same thing when he was texting me, but it's not him. He's gone. I saw him with my own eyes. He's gone, Iz.

It's the stalker. He's been using Laith's phone as a means of communication with me."

"No," she whimpers. "He's not dead."

"I'm sorry, Izzy."

She cries over the phone, and as she tries to process, I tell her the rest of my story, not stopping until I reach this very moment in time.

"I don't even . . . I don't know how to process all of this."

"Believe me, I know. It's a lot. It's fucked up, and it terrifies me, but you need to promise me that you'll be careful. This guy is ruthless. He's killed four people, and I can't have you or Knight being next."

"Harper—"

"No, promise me, Iz," I beg of her. "Promise that you'll be careful. Every new person that you talk to could be him. Just keep your eyes open, and then tonight, I can come to your place, or you can come here, and we can just process everything and cry."

"Cry. Yeah, I think I've already started."

"Me too," I say as tears roll down my cheeks.

"You really have no idea who this guy is?"

"Not even a little. He's like a ghost that just shows up to terrorize me and then slinks away the moment he's satisfied."

"He sounds like an asshole."

I scoff. "Yeah."

"Why do I have to work right now?" she says. "I'm sorry this is happening, Harper. I wish I had known, or that you felt like you could have told me. We were in the club and he was right there." I can almost hear the shivers sail down her spine. "We're going to get to the bottom of this, okay? He's going to have to go through me before he gets to you."

"That's what I'm worried about."

"He can't hurt me," she says. "I take Pilates, you know?"

I can't help but laugh. "Stop trying to make me feel better about it all. I'm trying to be in my feels."

"You can get lost in your feels tonight. I'll bring a bottle of wine, and we can just let it all out, but until then, you need to hold yourself together until Knight gets back and can make sure this bastard doesn't lay a horny hand on you."

"Agreed," I say.

"So, what's your plan?"

I shrug, even though I know she can't see. "I don't know. Maybe some needle therapy."

"Oooh, yes. Another tattoo to piss off your mother. Sounds perfect to me." Izzy laughs before letting out a heavy sigh. "Okay, I love you, girl. I have to go. The models have just arrived for the shoot, but try not to get yourself in trouble. And Harper?"

"Yeah?"

"I'm really sorry about Laith. I know how close you were."

A single tear rolls down my cheek, and I try to smile through the pain. "Thanks, Iz. I'll see you tonight."

She ends the call, and I just sit for a minute, needing to process everything, and as I find my heart still stable in my chest, I get up and finally get started with my day.

Twenty minutes later, I'm back at my apartment, packing a bag of clothes, my toothbrush, and my favorite shampoo and conditioner to leave in the back of my car for if and when Knight decides to eventually kidnap me. Let's be honest, it's coming. He knows it just as well as I do, and he's biding his time, hoping like fuck he doesn't freak me out, and while I'm not down to have some beast of a man demand that I move in with him, I'm certainly not opposed to him kidnapping me for a week or two.

After searching my apartment for every last one of his shirts, I throw them in the bag too, and soon enough, I'm back in my car, heading straight for my favorite tattoo parlor. We have a few in Blackstone. One is owned by a junkie, another is owned by the local motorcycle club—though I'm pretty sure they're cooking up something in the back—and the last and final parlor is a small studio owned by an awesome artist who makes killer designs and absolutely nails it every time. Harlow is always booked out months in advance, but she has a bunch of artists who work with her that can generally squeeze me in on short notice.

I park on the street just outside the tattoo parlor, and the second I make my way inside, Harlow spots me and offers a wide grin. "Hey, Harper. I was starting to think something happened to you. We haven't seen you in ages."

"It's been three months," I laugh, recalling the exact moment I saw her last because I literally fell out the door and almost broke my nose on the pavement. One of her guys took a photo of me sprawled on my ass with an ice pack against my face. The picture now hangs on their wall of shame, but I wouldn't have it any other way.

"And?" she prompts. "Three months to you is practically a lifetime."

"Tell me about it."

"So whatcha doing here? You didn't have an appointment, did you?" she asks, getting up from her station and checking her schedule, almost looking panicked that she might have accidentally double-booked.

"No, no," I rush out. "Just having a shitty day . . . Well, more like a shitty few weeks. I figured I could do with some needle therapy."

"Ahh, gotcha," she says. "That's how I ended up with the exploding watermelon on my right ass cheek."

I can't help but laugh. I've seen that particular exploding watermelon, and I've got to admit, it's pretty damn cute with its glasses and big bursty eyes. "Well, I'm not quite after an exploding watermelon," I tell her. "More like a little voodoo doll, pin cushion thing with the little X's for eyes, right behind my ear."

She arches a brow and looks at me as though I've lost my mind. "A voodoo doll?"

I nod. "A voodoo doll, indeed."

"That's not really on brand for you," she muses, making a point to glance at the rest of the tattoos covering my body, and I nod, understanding exactly where she's coming from. Every single one of my tattoos is an artistic masterpiece. Skulls hidden within butterflies and daggers and flowers surrounded by rosary beads. Every inch of me that's been covered has been done with thought and months of planning.

I don't just get random little things on my body that don't mean anything, and as I smile back at her, I know she gets it. "This one is sentimental."

"A voodoo doll?" she confirms.

I nod. "Yep, a little gothic voodoo doll. But make her cute."

Harlow grins, and I can already see the wheels turning in her mind. She glances at her watch before looking over her schedule again, and when she finally looks up at me, her brow is arched. "Fine line?"

I nod. "Of course."

"Alright. I can squeeze you in, but if you tell anyone I let you in without an appointment, I'm turning this doll into a moldy cock."

Thank fuck.

Making our way back to her station, Harlow and I get to chatting, and forty-five minutes later, I stride out of her studio with the most badass voodoo doll chick I've ever seen. Harlow only knows how to hit home runs. Failing isn't in her vocabulary.

Feeling good about myself, I make my way back to my car when somebody calls out from down the path. "Yo," a sickeningly familiar tone calls out, dragging my attention away from my car. "I know you."

I let out a shaky breath and glance up to find the new night janitor who for whatever reason has taken over for Vincent. He stands with a few friends, each of them speeding up as they move toward me.

"No, you don't," I mutter, reaching for my keys and trying to pick up my pace.

The guys crowd me, and from the stench coming off them, they're drunk and high. "Don't be such a little bitch," the Vincent wannabe says. "Say hi to my friends. They love a pretty girl."

I clench my jaw, trying to keep myself from saying what I really want to say and making this situation a million times worse. "I've got somewhere to be."

"Hey," he snaps, getting in my face. "You think you're fucking better than me?"

"I know I am."

His hand flies toward me, and I dodge out of the way, but my natural instinct has my hand shooting straight up, slamming into his larynx, and dropping the fucker to his knees.

"The fuck?" one of his friends roars from behind me, gripping the back of my head, my hair knotted in his big hand.

"Get her," the janitor says, and in the blink of an eye, the group of men are dragging me away from my car. I cry out, gripping onto the hand that pulls my hair, digging my nails into his flesh as I'm violently pulled and dragged toward the alley beside the tattoo parlor.

"LET GO OF ME, YOU PIECE OF SHIT," I roar, feeling the blood vessels in my throat burst.

The pavement burns my legs as they drag me, scratching up every inch of my skin, and as I'm thrown to the dirty ground, five men come down over me. Fists slamming against my face, boots kicking into my ribs. They grope and grab my body, pull my hair, and spit on me.

My head flies back with a kick directly to my mouth, and the pain shoots through me. Blood seeps from my split lip, and I do what I can to curl into a ball, shamelessly trying to protect myself.

"HEY!" I hear from a voice far away. "LEAVE HER ALONE. I'M CALLING THE COPS."

The men scramble, grabbing my open bag off the ground and racing toward my car, as my phone falls from my bag to the pavement. I watch in horror as the men steal my car, the tires squealing as they race away, and I do what I can to pull myself up off the bloody ground. But there's no use, I can't get my feet under me.

Inch by inch, I move toward my phone, army-crawling across the pavement, when a large man hurries toward me, snatching up my phone. "You good, girl?" he asks, scooping his arms beneath me and dragging me right back into the alley, where he sits me up against the wall.

I shake my head, unable to form a single word, and when he crouches down and swipes his thumb across the screen of my phone, unlocking it, all I can do is watch as he then lifts it to his ear. "Yo, this girl is hurt. Just got jumped in the alley by five guys."

He doesn't say anything else, just straightens up and tosses my phone down onto my aching stomach. "Sorry, girl," he says, giving me a tight smile. "This ain't my fight."

And with that, he takes off, dashing across the street and leaving me for dead as my world turns to darkness.

CHAPTER 30

HARPER-RAYN

A sudden jolt forces consciousness through my foggy mind as I wake with a gasp. I'm cramped, lying across the back seat of someone's car as they speed down the road. Pain rockets through my body, and I curl back up into a tight ball, groaning in agony.

Everything is blurry, and my head spins, but there's something familiar about this car, about the smells around me.

I press my hand to my throbbing head, and my fingers come away with sticky blood. "Wha . . . What happened?" I grumble, feeling tears on my cheeks. "Where am I?"

Bits and pieces come flashing back. The janitor from work. His hand reaching out to me. Mine splintering across the front of his throat. Everything snowballed from there.

I try to sit up, but pain shoots through my torso, making me cry out in agony, only to double over and throw up everything in the pit of my stomach.

"Fuck," a voice says from the front seat.

It hadn't even occurred to me that I wasn't alone, and I try to search the front as we speed down the road, hitting every bump and flying around the corners, jostling so much I'm almost positive I'm riding around a bumper car arena at the fair.

Consciousness comes and goes, and dark spots dance in my blurry vision as I grip my aching head, positive this is death.

"Who did this, kitten?" comes a stern voice from the front.

Fear blasts through my chest.

"No. No. No. No. No."

This can't be happening. It can't be him.

"Kitten," he growls, his tone demanding answers. "Who hurt you?"

I fade in and out, thinking back, trying to remember the faces, the people, the places, but nothing is coming to me. It's so frustrating. Only a moment ago, I could picture it so clearly, but it has fallen right out of my brain.

"KITTEN!"

"NO!" I cry. "Don't kill me. I don't want to die. I'm not ready. No! Please. Just let me go."

Visions come in and out. A back alley, faces I don't know, a man rushing across the street, but none of them help me to piece together the reason I'm hurting so badly, why my brain feels as though it's swelling inside my head. "It hurts," I cry, clutching my agonizing waist. "It hurts."

"I know," he murmurs, his tone shifting and scratching at something inside my brain. Something familiar.

I know that voice, but why? I can't work it out, can't pinpoint how I know it while my head is hurting like this. I can't even think about trying to work it out. All that matters is making the pain go away.

"Please," I cry. "Make it stop."

The driver looks back at me, and I get a flash of that terrifying mask, and I realize the man who was running across the road had grabbed my phone. He must have called someone in my contact list. Did he call Laith, only to get a direct line to my stalker? Is he responsible for this?

Tears flow down my cheeks, and I taste blood in my mouth. "You're mine, kitten," he says, a lethal chill in his tone. "I will gut the bastards who put their hands on you. Tell me who did this."

Laith. He killed Laith.

My brows crease, darkness bubbling in my vision, bringing me in and out. My eyelids grow heavy, desperate to let the pain consume me and slip away into the nothingness.

"Stay with me, kitten. Who did this?"

Why did he have to hurt Laith?

I force myself to stay awake, trying to pull the images from my brain and make sense of everything that happened. Did I get jumped? Raped? I don't know. I remember men hovering around me, someone dragging me by my hair, fists slamming into my face.

There was somebody there, somebody I knew. But why? Why would he want to hurt me?

I pull at every last memory, and with each passing second, my brain hurts more, but I need to know how this happened. Who would do this to me?

I came out of the tattoo parlor and gripped my bag, digging through it for my keys. Panic was thick in my chest, but why? My hand shot out like lightning. I felt threatened. Men standing around me. Someone dropping to the ground and screaming something.

"*Get her.*" I repeat the words out loud. "*Get her. Get her.*"

"What?" the masked driver demands. "Get who?"

"That's what he said. *Get her.* I hit him, and he said *get her* and they all—" A thick lump forms in my throat, and it becomes almost impossible to take a breath as the visions come back in screaming color.

"Who said it?" he demands.

I shake my head, and my brain instantly pounds. "I screamed at them, begged them to stop, but they just kept hurting me." I weep on the back seat of the car, struggling to hold myself still as every turn and bump in the road slings me around. "They wouldn't stop. Why would they hurt me like that?"

"Tell me who they are, kitten," he prompts, knowing time is running out, knowing it won't be long until the darkness swallows me whole.

"Why?" I cry. "Why did you kill him? Why did you kill my Laith?"

"Focus, kitten," he demands. "Picture his face. Picture his words. Tell me who he is. What does he look like? Do you know his name? Met him before? Come on, kitten. You can do this. Tell me what you know."

I think back to the moment outside my car, my hand snapping out and hitting his throat, and I replay it over and over, trying to pull the images together inside my brain. Why was I so scared? Why was I rushing to get in the car? There's an uneasiness there, the same feeling I sometimes get at work when . . . fuck.

The janitor. Vincent's replacement.

"Work," I say. "Guy from work."

"Good girl," he rumbles. "What guy? Do you know his name?"

"Janitor," I finally say, picturing it so clearly now, every moment his fist slammed into my face, every moment he spat on me, kicked and belittled me. He stole my car and left me for dead, allowing his friends to tear into my flesh like they deserved it, like my life meant nothing.

Fresh tears well in my eyes, and I feel my eyelids growing heavy again.

"That's a good kitten," the familiar voice says. "You're going to be alright now."

"Kill him," I murmur as my body gives up the fight, knowing he will do whatever it takes to make this right. "Kill him just like you'll do to me."

And in that very same breath, darkness crashes over me like a tsunami, claiming everything in its path.

CHAPTER 31

KNIGHT

After getting back to the station from a call, the boys and I collapse on the benches in the locker room. It was a rough one, and while we always come out with a successful job, that doesn't mean that it didn't push us to our limits.

We're all fucking wrecked, but this right here is exactly why we do the job. The challenge keeps us going, the adrenaline, and the knowledge that what we do saves lives.

Diesel sits forward, his elbows braced on his knees as Ace leans back against his locker. They were talking about heading out after this, but from the look on their faces, they clearly just want to go home and crash. Hell, so do I. But knowing that Harper is waiting for me in my bed sends fire blasting through my veins.

Things are changing, but I'd be lying if I said that I wasn't nervous. A part of me wonders if she's clinging to me because I can offer her a safety net against her stalker. I love that she feels safe with me, that it's my home she runs to when her world is going up in flames. I just need to know that her feelings for me are genuine, and that after this stalker bullshit is done and dusted, she's still going to feel the same.

After finding just a shred of energy, I go to get up from the bench when an incoming call draws all of my attention, and I groan, too fucking tired to be dealing with some other bullshit.

Digging into my locker, I find my phone, and a stupid smile pulls at my lips when I see Harper's name across the screen. I haven't had a chance to check over my surveillance camera yet, but as far as I know, she's still at my place. Though I guess I can't assume she hasn't gone out. She's used to the night shift, so there's a good chance she's just starting to plan what her evening will look like. If she is still in my bed, she probably wants to know that I'll be on my way home to her soon—unless this is another call to say that she's been tied up and fucked raw by another man in my bed.

Fuck. That one made my heart sink.

Accepting the call, I lift it to my ear, waiting to hear her soft tone coming down the line, only it's not hers I hear; it's a man. "Hey, is this Knight?"

"Uhh, yeah? Who the fuck is this? Where's Harper?"

Unease rips through me, and I'm immediately on edge. Why the hell does some random guy have her phone?

"I'm, uhhh, I'm a friend," he says, trying to rush through his response as though it's somehow not important. "Look, Harper's in the hospital. She—"

"What?" I demand, my hand already launching back into my locker and grabbing my shit.

"Yeah. I'm with her now. They're taking her into emergency surgery, and while she's worked with all the people here for years and knows them well, I figured it was you she'd want here when she wakes up."

How the fuck does this guy know what the hell my girl would want?

I shake my head. This bastard has skipped right over seasons three, four, and five, and skipped right to the end, not giving me a single detail. "Why the fuck is she in the hospital?" I spit, hurrying out of the locker room. Both Diesel and Ace jump to their feet, looking at me as though they're waiting for a threat. "What happened?"

My heart pounds with fear in a way that I've never felt before, not even while on the job, and fuck, I feel sick.

"I can't be too sure," he tells me, still not having explained who the fuck he is to Harper and why he has her phone. "From the type of injuries she had, I can only assume that she was jumped. I got a call from some guy telling me she'd been hurt and was left in an alley. I went and got her and she didn't look good. She'd been hurt badly. I got her in the car and brought her straight here, but . . . fuck. I don't know. She was saying some weird shit."

"What weird shit?" I ask, finally reaching my truck, diving through the door, and turning over my engine in the very next second.

I start backing out as the guy mutters something, and suddenly, all the background noise disappears as though he had walked into a private room, wanting to keep this conversation quiet. "It was weird. I've never heard her talk like this in all the time I've known her," he says. "She was coming in and out, talking about killing someone and just kept repeating the phrase *get her*. I was trying to ask her questions to figure out who the fuck hurt her and what she was talking about, but I don't know. It was fucked up. I've never seen her like that. She asked me to fucking kill someone for her."

The fuck?

A part of me can't help but wonder if this is a trap being laid by her stalker—if that's who I'm talking to right now. But I can't take the chance. If he's got her phone, that means he's also got *her*, and no matter what, I'm showing up for my girl.

"Did she say anything else?"

"Something about a janitor. Not sure. Her words were starting to bleed together at that point. She passed out after that."

"Fuck."

My head spins, trying to piece everything together, but I'm at a loss, and as I speed down the main road of Blackstone, all that matters is getting to that fucking hospital.

"My thoughts exactly," he says. "I just . . . How she was acting in the car. It was weird, man. I don't know if she had a concussion or if she was just hallucinating or something. But it's as though she thought I was someone else. She didn't even recognize me."

My brows furrow. Every word this guy says only makes me want to question him more.

"It doesn't make any fucking sense why someone would hurt her. I just don't . . ." He lets out a heavy sigh, cutting himself off.

"Look, I don't know what's going on with her lately. She's been . . . odd. I hope to fucking God that this isn't your influence, but either way, she seems to really like you, so I think it's important that you be here for her."

My fucking influence? Why do I suddenly have the overwhelming need to knock this fucker out? "She's got some other shit going on."

"Yeah—oh shit. I gotta go," he says. "Doctor's here."

"Wait. Who the fuck—" He ends the call and I sigh. "—are you?"

I stomp on the gas, racing toward the hospital as I white-knuckle the steering wheel. This isn't quite how I anticipated spending my night with Harper. I was going to go home, cook her something nice, maybe have a glass of wine, and then spend every waking second buried inside her. But apparently the world had other plans for us.

I reach the hospital in no time and get increasingly frustrated as I struggle to find a parking space. This hospital is at the top of their game, but when it comes to the whole parking situation, they really dropped the ball.

After parking crooked in a too-small space, I rush inside the hospital, reaching reception and demanding to know where the fuck she is. "I'm looking for Harper-Rayn Madden. She's supposed to be in surgery."

The receptionist takes way too long, searching the details. "Ahh, yes. She was just brought in a little while ago. What relation are you?"

"Family," I say with a cringe. "Uncle."

"Of course," she says with a nod. "Feel free to take a seat in the waiting area. She's only just gone into surgery so it could be a little wait."

"What about her condition? Do you know what happened? How's she doing?"

She gives me a tight smile. "I'm unsure," she says. "I can only offer the details here in front of me. However, you should prepare yourself. She has suffered some very serious injuries."

I blow out my cheeks, having the overwhelming need to pace in front of the receptionist, but I keep my shit together and offer her a smile instead. "Thanks," I mutter.

"I'll let the surgical team know that you're here and to give updates as they become available."

I nod before turning on my heel and stalking toward the waiting area, and as I take my seat, I can't help but look around, taking in the faces of the people around me. From the scarce details Harper has given me, none of the people here are suspicious. There's no random men just sitting by themselves, nobody lurking in shadows, or watching me like I'm some kind of threat, which makes me wonder where the fuck is the asshole who I spoke to on the phone?

The minutes tick by painfully as I sit in the uncomfortable chair, my elbows braced on my knees. Diesel and Ace both call to check in, but I can't deal with it now and give them the slightest rundown, knowing that at some point, I'm going to have to discuss this with them.

Twenty minutes eventually drags into two hours when a doctor comes through the internal hospital doors. "Harper-Rayn Madden?" he calls out.

I get straight to my feet and meet the doctor in the middle. "You're Harper's uncle?" he confirms.

I nod. "Yes, that's correct. Is she okay?"

"She is stable and out of surgery," he says. "She's suffered a lot of injuries, some more concerning than others, but she will be okay."

I shake my head, still in disbelief. "What's, uhhh, what kind of injuries are we talking about?"

"Harper suffered a great deal of internal bleeding. There was significant trauma to the liver and spleen; however, they have both been taken care of. Externally, her injuries are consistent with being beaten. She will have significant bruising and swelling that will develop over the coming days and has received multiple stitches to the face. She's in the clear, but it will be a rough road to recovery."

"Beaten?" I ask, unable to believe how anyone could do this to her.

The doctor presses his lips into a tight line and nods, placing a comforting hand on my shoulder. "She's being taken to recovery now," he tells me. "You're more than welcome to sit with her. It would be good to see a familiar face when she wakes. She will probably be quite upset and very sore and will have a lot to process."

I nod. "Thanks."

"The receptionist can help you with a room and bed number," he tells me before turning on his heel and walking straight back through the double doors.

After I visit the receptionist again, she gives me a room number, and within seconds, I'm making my way through the hospital, my desperation pushing me faster with every step. I need to see for myself what kind of hell she has suffered through.

I reach her room in no time, and as I step in beside her, my heart breaks.

Her lip is split and held together with stitches, and there's significant bruising and swelling under her right eye. Her body is covered by a heavy blanket, but I don't doubt that every inch of her skin mimics the bruising on her face.

Agony tears through my chest as I take the seat beside her bed, leaning forward and resting my arms on the shitty mattress, needing to be as close as humanly possible.

These past few weeks have made me feel as though I'm not good enough. That I don't have what it takes to be the protector she needs, and this right here just proves that I was right. I should have pushed harder for her to stay in, to take time off work and spend it in my home with me. I have more than enough vacation days saved up. I would have taken the time off with her, but she's so fucking stubborn. She insisted on going to work, and while I understand her reasoning, I can't bring myself to justify it. Same goes with her staying at her place where that asshole was able to find her and put his hands on her. But I suppose the same could be said for my home. I thought she was safe there, but not even I can offer her freedom from that man.

As I sit beside her, I can't help but go over everything that's happened over these past few weeks. I don't know if what happened today was somehow related to her stalker, but I don't believe it is. A brutal attack like this doesn't match the stalker's profile. He doesn't lose control and use his fists. He prefers to torment victims with blades while getting off. He's possessive, calculated, and vile. Harper being jumped today was the opposite of his MO: messy and opportunistic.

The moment Harper wakes and can tell me any details about her attack, I'll be looking into it, and I won't stop until the asshole who hurt her has felt exactly what she felt.

As for everything else that's been going down, I simply can't wrap my head around it.

Everything that happens leaves me with more questions. The first victim Harper found in the morgue with her name carved into his knuckles was fucked up, but where the fuck is that body? How is it possible that not a single officer in Blackstone recalls collecting the body and delivering it to the morgue, and why the hell aren't there records? That doesn't just happen.

I was willing to look past it and leave it as one seriously fucked-up situation. But then he left two more bodies with messages carved into their skin. Is it a coincidence that those bodies also went missing? When I asked around at the station, nobody could recall a double homicide. Even Dr. McKullan reported that their injuries were consistent with a car wreck.

I don't want to be the asshole who says this, but even Laith's death. Where are the crime scene photos? Who found the body and called the cops? Which detective is taking lead on the case? Who delivered the body to the morgue?

This should all be easily answered, yet I can't find a shred of information. Nobody knows what I'm talking about, and honestly, the more I ask my colleagues about cases nobody has heard of, the more I'm starting to sound paranoid.

Every single occasion that Harper has told me about has left me scratching my head. I don't want to say that I don't believe her because that would make me look like a fucking dick, and I can tell from her reactions to all of this, the fear, her trembling hands, that this is as real as it gets. But where is this guy? Why hasn't anybody but Harper seen him? She hasn't even seen his face, only the mask.

At my place yesterday, she swore there were ropes, and still, twenty-four hours later, I still haven't found them. I've searched every inch of my home, and there's not a single hint of somebody breaking in. No alarms on my security footage, and no fucking ropes.

I'm losing my mind, but that guy on the phone earlier, her friend who found her and brought her to the hospital, he said something that's been playing in my mind. He said that she didn't recognize him, that she was acting strange, saying weird things, almost like she hit her head and was hallucinating.

What if that is what this is? What if this stalker only exists inside her head?

CHAPTER 32

KNIGHT

I sit with her for almost an hour when her eyes spring open, and a terrified gasp sails out of her mouth. "Woah, woah, woah," I rush out, diving for her hand. "You're safe, doll. You're okay. Nobody can hurt you now."

Her gaze shifts to mine, and she clutches my hand as though terrified I might let go. Her eyes are big, filled with fear as though reliving everything that just happened to her, scared that she's still there in that alley.

"I've got you," I tell her, reaching over and cupping the side of her face. "I'm not leaving. You're safe now."

Harper lets out a breath, closing her eyes as she leans into my touch. Her eyes immediately fill with tears and I gently wipe them away. "How bad is it?" she croaks, her throat hoarse, and I can only assume it's from having to scream for freedom.

"It's bad, doll," I tell her, not wanting to sugarcoat it, knowing she can handle it. "You had emergency surgery and had repairs to your liver and spleen, but you're in the clear. The surgeon was able to stop the bleeding. As for everything else, you're going to be sore for a while. There's lots of bruising and swelling, and I'm sure the police will want to take a statement."

She visibly swallows, and I reach for the bottled water on the bedside table, pausing to put a straw in it before lifting it to her swollen lips. "Take a sip."

She cringes as the water makes its way down.

"Do you remember what happened?"

Her bottom lip quivers, and as she starts to cry, I get up from the chair and carefully climb in beside her, knowing this is exactly what she needs. She grunts and gasps as she's moved around, but the amount of morphine going through her body more than helps. Then the moment I'm beside her, she curls into my chest and cries, her hand still clutching mine.

"I've got you, doll," I soothe, my hand making soft circles on her back as the tears run their course.

She attempts to tell me what happened when the doctor comes in, and judging by the scowl on his face, he doesn't approve of me being in bed with her, but there's not a damn thing he can do or say that's going to pull me away from her now. She needs this more than I do, and as her tears continue to flow, I will stay here and be the rock she needs me to be.

The doctor grabs her chart off the end of the bed, making sure she's up to date on painkillers, and as he strides around the edge to look over her injuries. Only something has him pausing, his gaze flicking between me and Harper. "Uncle, right?" he asks, his gaze specifically dropping to the way her hand is clutched in mine.

I cringe. "Step-uncle," I say, as though that's supposed to make it any better.

I can only imagine the look on Harper's face, but right now, I'm too focused on the doctor. He looks at me with a deep suspicion, like I've somehow done something wrong, but when Harper shifts next to me, his gaze falls back to her.

"How are you feeling, Dr. Madden?" he asks, clearly already knowing her. "Anything I should be concerned about?"

She shakes her head. "No. The morphine has kicked in. I'm feeling pretty good, though I'm not going to say no to more. Feel free to crank it up."

He smirks at her, shaking his head in exasperation. "Watch it, Harper. Don't make me put Celia on your case."

Her eyes widen in horror. "You wouldn't."

"I absolutely would if you're not behaving yourself," he tells her. "Now, I'm sure by now you're aware that you had internal bleeding.

We had to go in and fix up that liver and spleen of yours, but everything was standard. There's some slight swelling to your organs, but nothing that wouldn't be expected in your . . . situation."

"You can say it," she murmurs, her face falling. "I got jumped."

He gives her a tight smile. "I'm sorry," he says. "I wasn't sure how much you recalled of the incident."

She nods. "All of it."

He arches a brow, and I meet the doctor's stare. "The, uhh . . . The guy who brought her in. He mentioned that she was going in and out, saying a bunch of weird things. Is it possible that she has a concussion?"

The doctor steps in closer, his brows furrowed as he looks over her chart again. "There's nothing here stating any significant injuries to her head, apart from the superficial injuries to her face," he mutters, placing the chart down on the end of the bed before moving right into her and giving a quick examination of her head. "I'm not seeing anything to be concerned about; however, we'll keep an eye on it over the coming days, and if anything alarms us, we'll get her in for a CT."

I nod and sense Harper's gaze upon me, and as I glance down at her, I find a quizzical stare in her eyes.

"What?" I say. "You can never be too careful. You went through hell today. It couldn't hurt to ask the questions."

"He's right," the doctor agrees. "Better to be safe than sorry. But either way, I'm going to make a note to keep an eye on it." He walks back to the end of the bed and scoops up the chart before scribbling something down, only to drop it back into place for the next person to come along. "Okay, if you have any questions, just let me know. Otherwise, I'll leave you to get some rest."

"Thanks, Dr. Hart," she says. "I suppose I'll be seeing a lot more of you."

He laughs. "Careful, you might just find you like it better up here than in that creepy basement."

"Hey, that creepy basement is my jam."

"Okay, now we both know you're lying." He chuckles before fixing her with a hard stare. "You know the routine. The nurses will be in to check on you soon, so try not to give them a hard time."

"I make no promises," she says as the doctor smirks and strides out of the room.

The moment he's gone, Harper's body relaxes against me, and she lets out a breath. I can't help but wonder if she was putting on a brave face for the doctor and downplaying her pain. She's always wanted to appear strong, and I suppose that's not about to change just because she's in the hospital.

"Do you really remember it all?" I ask.

She nods against my chest. "It took me a second, but once it was there, it wasn't going away."

"Do you want to tell me about it?"

She shakes her head. "Not really, but I also don't want this asshole to get away with it. He needs to be punished. I know this is Blackstone and crime is just a given around here, but he can't just be going around hurting people like that. What if there wasn't someone there to call for help? What if I didn't get here in time? I would have bled until—"

She cuts herself off, not ready to say what would have happened, but I hear the words loud and clear.

Died. She would have died, and I never would have survived it.

"Start from the beginning," I tell her, holding her tight.

She nods again and I notice how her tears have finally started to dry up, and I can't help but wonder if it's because there's simply no more tears left to cry or because there's nothing left to feel. Is she hollow inside? Empty?

"I had gotten another tattoo—"

"What?" I grunt, my head whipping down toward her, scanning over her body. Surely I would have noticed if she'd just gotten a tattoo. "Where?"

She lifts her hand to the space behind her ear, farthest away from me. "I got a cute little voodoo doll," she says. "She's gorgeous. A total badass."

"A voodoo doll?" I ask.

Nervousness flickers through her gaze, and when she lifts her chin to meet my stare, I see nothing but love shining through those big green eyes. "I got it for you," she tells me, glancing away, not able to handle the heaviness of my stare. "Because you call me doll, and every time that you do . . . I like it."

Her cheeks flush as a shy smile stretches across her lips, but when it pulls at her stitches, she cringes. "No shit, huh?" I ask, grinning right back at her. Gob-fucking-smacked.

"If you tell anybody, I'll deny it and say it's because you're obviously obsessed with me," she teases. "But it couldn't just be a cute little kid's doll. It had to be cool. Hence the voodoo part of it."

"Of course," I say, the breath completely knocked out of my chest at the fact that she was willing to put something permanent on her body that symbolizes our relationship. "I wouldn't expect anything less."

Harper rolls her eyes. "Anyway, I was coming out of the tattoo parlor, you know the one that's owned by Harlow?" I nod, knowing it well as that's where I've gotten most of mine, and she continues. "I was parked right out front on the curb when this group of guys came up to me. There were five of them, and one of them, the one who started all this shit, I know him from work. He's the new night shift janitor. He's a complete ass and always makes me feel uncomfortable, but if there's a body on the table, he gets queasy and leaves."

Why the hell didn't she tell me about this guy?

"Do you know his name?"

She shakes her head, and everything plummets inside of me, but what's one more hoop to jump through on my way to evening the score?

"He was the one calling the shots?"

She nods. "Yes. But they hurt me too. He tried to grab me so I dropped him, and then everything just blew up in my face. It all happened so quickly. They dragged me into the alley and beat me while I screamed for them to stop. They weren't going to. They would have kept going until I was dead, but someone yelled at them, and they ran."

"Shit, doll," I murmur, my heart aching for her.

She glances away. "They stole my car."

"Don't worry about your car. I'll handle that."

She arches a brow and glances back up at me. "You're gonna get it back?"

"If that's what you want?" I ask. "I'm more than happy to get you a brand-new car, but if you specifically want that one, I'll find it."

She nods. "I don't want a new car. I want *my* car."

"Then I'll get it, doll."

A soft smile pulls at her lips and she reaches for her drink again, but I beat her to it, not wanting her to move too much and pull any of her internal stitches. After having a quick sip, she holds the bottle in her hands, falling into a deep silence, and I can practically hear the thoughts storming through her head.

"What is it?" I ask, meeting her broken stare.

"Earlier you said that the guy who brought me here had spoken to you. Did you, umm . . . Did you happen to see him?"

I shake my head, my brows furrowed. "No, he called me to let me know you were here. He said he was a friend of yours, but he didn't give a name."

Her shoulders slump. "It was *him*," she says. "I was all over the place in the car. My head was pounding and I was in agony, but it was him. The stalker. He still had the mask on and everything, but there was something familiar about him. I was just . . . I was too out of it to try and put it all together or figure out how I knew him, but there was something about his voice and that car. I think I've been in that car before."

"Fuck, doll. Are you sure?"

She nods. "Positive."

"He brought you here to save your life," I muse. "Then called me so you'd have someone here when you woke up. It doesn't make any sense. Why would he do that? It's not consistent with anything we know about him. Are you sure? You saw his face . . . or that mask he wears?"

"I'm sure. He was calling me kitten, demanding to know who hurt me."

I sit back against the mattress, my mind spinning a million miles an hour, and after a minute, Harper glances up at me, her brows creasing with concern. "What is it?"

"It's just messing with my head," I tell her. "None of it makes sense."

"What doesn't?"

"This stalker," I tell her. "The first body in the morgue going missing and none of the detectives knowing shit about the case is unheard of, but I was willing to put it down to this guy playing the game. But for that to happen three more times, it's not possible."

"What are you saying?" she asks, her back stiffening.

I shake my head, not really knowing. "There have been four bodies, two of them being a double homicide. There would have been 911 calls, cops arriving on the scene, reports made. The case would have been assigned to a detective before the body was taken to the morgue, and yet no one knows a damn thing. I could have put it down to coincidence one time, maybe even called it suspicious, but four separate times within weeks of each other. That doesn't happen, doll."

She takes a breath and stares up at me as though I'm some kind of stranger, her brows furrowed. "Oh my God. You don't believe me. You think I'm making it all up."

"No, doll. That's not what I'm saying at all," I tell her, hating the pain that radiates from her broken stare. "I think your mind might be playing tricks on you. I think you believe it to be real, but there's no evidence to suggest that any of these things are actually happening."

Tears roll down her cheeks, and she just stares at me, the betrayal thick in her eyes, and I know without a doubt that I've just shattered her heart.

"You need to leave," she whispers, her voice breaking.

"Doll, you have to believe that I'm not trying to hurt you," I tell her, almost begging for her to hear me out. "You know me better than that. I just want to get to the bottom of this. I want to help you. I want to help this go away."

"No," she says, shaking her head and looking away as though she can't even stand the sight of me. "Please, Knight. Just go."

"Doll."

"Please."

I watch her for a moment, and as she refuses to look back at me, I climb off the bed, going as gentle as possible so as to not jostle her around. "I'll go, but I don't want you to be alone, not after everything you've been through today. Can I at least call Izzy and let her know?"

She shakes her head. "I'll be fine, Knight. I can handle myself."

Harper looks away again, and as I watch her, I realize there's no changing her mind. Not now, and with nothing more that I can do, I walk out of her room, leaving my heart right there in the palm of her hand.

CHAPTER 33

KNIGHT

Leaning against Harper's Honda Civic, I stare at the run-down home before me as Diesel and Ace pull up across the street, parking behind my truck.

It's a little after ten in the evening, and I don't doubt that the boys were already asleep after the fucked-up shift we endured today, but they know I wouldn't ask them to join me if it weren't important.

"What the fuck did you get me out of bed for?" Diesel mutters as he climbs out of his truck and strides across the street, not recognizing the house of the car I'm up against.

I haven't told them much about Harper or the ins and outs of our relationship, but they know she means something to me, especially after I drove her home from the bar the other night. Sure, before Harper, I was more than happy to spend the night sinking into random women, but that's all it ever was. I never cared about them, never cared how they were getting home or what their days looked like, and I sure as fuck never called it quits on a boys' night just to drive her home.

Up until right now, the boys have only been able to guess how deeply my feelings for Harper ran, and I suppose all of that is about to change.

"This is Harper's car," I tell them, tapping the car behind me and watching as they both stare at me with brows arched. "And this," I add, pointing toward the run-down shithole on the other side of the broken chain-link fence, "is the home of the asshole who stole it."

They both glance at me, and with just those few words, they know what Harper is to me. If it had been any other woman, I would have let the police or insurance deal with it, but the fact that I'm here, putting not only myself but my boys at risk, tells them everything they need to know.

"No shit," Ace murmurs, his gaze swinging back to the house, probably already trying to figure out the best way in. Though there's no point, I've more than cased the joint. I know every inch of that home and have my plan well and truly ready to go.

"Mm-hmm. Did I mention the fucker stole it after he and four of his friends jumped her in a back alley before leaving her for dead. She's fucking lucky someone called for help."

"What?" Diesel grunts, his head snapping between me and the house, his hands already balling into fists, barely able to keep still. "Aw fuck no."

Ace lets out a breath and immediately begins to pace, already pissed on my behalf. "Shit," he mutters, his jaw clenched, taking it just as personally as I have. After all, any woman of mine would be seen as nothing less than a sister to these guys, despite never having met her. "She good, man?"

I cross my arms over my chest, the vision of Harper in that hospital bed tormenting me, and I shake my head. "She had emergency surgery to repair her liver and spleen. Other than that, she's bruised up and swollen. She's going to be sore for a while."

"Fucking hell," Diesel says, stepping in beside me, his jaw clenched. "Whatever you need, you know we've got your back. No matter where this goes."

I nod. I didn't even need to ask. They've had my back from day one, but truth be told, I didn't ask them here to have my back. I can handle the asshole living in this house and anyone else who might be here as well. I simply don't have enough asses to drive both my truck and Harper's Civic back home, but if they suddenly have the overwhelming desire to jump in and teach this guy a lesson, then who the fuck am I to stop them?

This will be a piece of cake. I'm not a violent man, but something tells me I'm going to thoroughly enjoy this.

Trystin Black, the piece of shit now working as the night shift janitor. It was all too easy to get his information. After Harper kicked me out of her room, I sat outside her door for a few hours, just needing to be with her, needing to hear the steady beat of her heart rate monitor, but after overhearing the nurse say she'd fallen asleep, I was on my feet in seconds.

I couldn't just sit there and do nothing, especially while I knew she was safe, and if I was right and all of this stalker bullshit was in her head, then she was going to be okay while she slept. As for me, I was knocking on the hospital's surveillance room door the moment I could.

It took all of a few seconds to convince Carly to give up the personnel file for their newest recruit.

"Trystin Black," I tell the boys, letting them know our target. "Twenty-seven years old and lives in his deceased mother's house with his two deadbeat friends and three Rottweilers. Currently on probation."

From what information I've been able to gather, Trystin doesn't have much to live for. He's a part-time drug dealer with a rap sheet longer than the Great Wall of China. He tried his hand at growing marijuana in his earlier years, and after a stint in jail, he's back causing havoc on the street.

As for his roommates, I've got no fucking idea. But assuming they're anything like their friend, taking care of them won't be an issue.

"Three entrances," I tell them, getting in the zone and treating this like any other mission we take on. "Front door, side entrance to the east, and internal door through the garage. Kitchen and living in the front, three bedrooms down the hall."

"And the rotties?" Ace asks, nervousness in his tone. He'd never admit it, but the big fucker is terrified of dogs, and for good reason, but that doesn't mean that Diesel and I haven't gone out of our way to fuck with him because of it. For two years straight, I had him believing that I was signing him up for the K-9 program. Truth be told, he'd probably benefit from it, but that's not a fear that needs to be tackled tonight.

I nod toward the side gate, and the boys lean around me to see the three dogs, happily watching us. "They're handled," I tell Ace.

"The fuck? How?"

"I did my homework," I explain. "I bought them each a turkey sub and gave them head scratchies. We're best friends now. They won't be a problem."

Ace gapes at me. "You wasted three turkey subs?"

"Don't worry. If you're a good boy, there's a turkey sub in my truck for you too."

Ace grins, and I roll my eyes. They say a way to a man's heart is through his dick, but when it comes to Ace, if you detour past his stomach on the way to his dick, he'll be loyal until the end of time.

"Alright, let's do this."

The three of us make our way toward the house, and without a word, Diesel slinks away into the darkness, skipping over the broken chain-link fence and heading around to the side entrance.

I stop by the dogs, giving them another scratch and confirming they're not going to attempt to tear us to shreds the second shit goes down, and then I sail straight up to the front door. Ace taps my shoulder to let me know he's right behind me, and I almost grin. We don't exactly need our formal training tonight, but old habits die hard.

With Ace on my six, I slam my boot straight through the front door. The lock breaks instantly, the wood splintering into hundreds of pieces, and as we step through the open doorway, I hear Diesel breaking in through the side.

The house turns into chaos immediately.

Trystin is sitting on the couch, watching porn on the main TV with his hand down his pants, madly jerking off, and the moment we storm into his home, he scrambles off the couch, having no fucking idea where to look or where to run.

Another guy races in from one of the bedrooms with a girl on his heels, while some other asshole just stands at the open refrigerator, a slice of pizza in his hand, looking as though this is the last thing he wants to be dealing with right now.

We stand by all the exits, each of us looking like an impenetrable wild storm that's come to burn the house to the ground. As the girl squeals in fear, Diesel just looks at her and gives one simple command, his deep tone not daring to invite question. "Leave."

She slips out behind him through the splintered side door without a word, disappearing into the night. The remaining three men band together as though they have strength in numbers, and the way they attempt to size us up is almost comical. I weigh more in muscle than the three of these scrawny assholes put together.

"I . . . I don't want no part of this," Pizza Guy says, but the fresh bruises on his knuckles suggest otherwise. "Take what you want and fuck off."

I laugh, striding through the home and finding Harper's keys and bag left abandoned on the kitchen counter. I don't stop until the boys and I are evenly spaced between the three men, leaving no escape, and fuck, it already feels good.

"We're not here to steal from you," I say as though these assholes aren't already shitting their pants. "We're here to even the score."

Trystin glances around, his gaze shooting between the doors, and seeing no escape, he dives for the kitchen, scrambling toward the knife block by the fridge. I roll my eyes and step toward him, and just as he reaches for one, I slam my fist down over his hand, listening to the sweet sound of his bones snapping against the counter.

Fuck, that felt good.

Trystin roars in agony, his hand pinned under my fist as Ace, the psychotic maniac that he is, just grins, excited to get the show on the road. Pizza Guy uses the distraction to try and get past Diesel, but nothing ever gets past that bastard, and as he sprints toward the side door, Diesel's arm shoots up, grabbing him around the throat before throwing him right back.

Pizza Guy stumbles back toward his friend, crashing into him with haste.

"Woah, woah, woah," the third guy says, holding up his split knuckles while shoving Pizza Guy off him. "What's this about? I'm sure we can work something out."

"This," I say, finally releasing my hold on Trystin and watching as he falls to his knees, still clutching his broken hand, weeping in agony, "is about the woman that you fuckers left for dead in that alleyway."

Trystin shakes his head. "We didn't do shit."

I slam my foot into his chest, kicking him with such power that he skids across the kitchen floor and slams into his friends like a fucking bowling ball. I begin to stalk them, slowly creeping closer. "Are you saying that my girl is a liar?"

Pizza Guy's eyes widen, clearly recognizing a trap when he sees one. "Nah, he didn't say anything like that," he panics, nudging his friend. "You've got the wrong guys. It wasn't us."

"Trust me when I say that you don't want to find out what happens to assholes who try to bullshit me. Her car is parked right in the fucking driveway," I say. "What the fuck is wrong with you morons? You didn't even attempt to hide the evidence. Were you trying to brag about it? Showing it off like some kind of badge of honor to let all the other pieces of shit know that you were an even bigger piece of shit today?"

"You've made your fucking point," Trystin spits, clutching his hand from the ground. "Now fuck off."

I laugh, closing the distance and stepping right in front of him before crouching down and letting him see the pure evil within my stare. "You put her in the hospital, left her for dead in an alleyway with severe internal bleeding. She just spent hours in emergency surgery. She's fucking lucky to be alive, and you think a few broken bones in your hand is going to settle the score?" I laugh. "Oh no, Trystin. I've barely even begun. Let me make this clear, when I am through with you tonight, you'll be drinking through a straw for the rest of your miserable fucking life."

He clenches his jaw, glaring at me as though this scrawny piece of shit could somehow intimidate me, and I reach forward, grip him by the scruff of his shirt, and pull him to his feet.

"Now," I say as Ace and Diesel creep closer, their fists already locked and loaded. "Let's give these assholes a taste of their own medicine."

My fist slams across his jaw, coming at him with the force of a freight train, and I watch as his head violently jolts to the side. Blood sprays out of his mouth, somewhat cinematically, and before his head has even finished rebounding, I hit him again, this time from beneath his chin.

Blood spurts from his mouth, and it takes me a moment to realize that he must have bitten through his tongue, almost severing the thing, but I don't hold back, hitting him again and again, letting him feel the same agony he forced on Harper, only worse.

Diesel and Ace go hard, beating Pizza Guy and the other one in the same brutal way they attacked Harper, taking every last ounce of their dignity. I feel bones snap beneath my knuckles and skin tearing open. Blood splatters across the run-down kitchen, and with every hit, I picture Harper's bruised body, her swollen eyes, and the split straight through her lip.

Grabbing Trystin, I pull out the old chair at the shitty dining table and throw him into it. He slouches, barely able to keep himself upright. I grab his wrist, take hold of his pinky finger, and snap it with ease. "That is for even looking at my girl."

Trystin roars, desperately trying to pull away. "This," I say, taking his next finger and squeezing extra hard, "is for making her feel uncomfortable in her workplace." I bend it straight back, letting it break as well.

Tears stream down his pathetic face, but I don't dare stop, taking the next finger and snapping that too. "This is for having the fucking audacity to even approach her on the street."

Finally, I take his pointer finger and rejoice in the feel of it crushing in my palm. "This is for every fucking hair that was touched on her head. And this," I add, shifting my hold and gripping his arm, one hand at his wrist, my other braced at his elbow, and with everything I have, I slam my knee up, snapping his radius and ulna like fucking twigs. "Is for leaving her for fucking dead in that alley."

Trystin screams in agony, and I have to admit, I've done a pretty good job, especially considering his radius is now protruding from his body, and both of his hands are littered with broken bones, making it one hell of a mission to call for an ambulance.

He quickly passes out from the pain, falling straight off the chair and slumping heavily to the ground. Did I take it too far and wave my reddest flag? Possibly. But when it comes to Harper-Rayn Madden, there's not a single thing I wouldn't do, no mountain I wouldn't climb, even if it means throwing every fucking moral I've ever lived by out the goddamn window.

When all three of them are out cold, we all step back to survey our handiwork.

"Shit," Ace says, grabbing the dish towel from the kitchen counter and wiping the blood off his knuckles. "I love a good fight more than the next guy, but that one particularly felt good."

"You're telling me," Diesel murmurs, nudging Pizza Guy with his foot, double-checking that he won't be getting up anytime soon. "You, ahhh . . . You think we took it too far?"

I crouch down, looking over Trystin's face. Hurting people doesn't satisfy me. It doesn't get my blood pumping, and now is no different, but there's no denying that this bastard has been taught one hell of a lesson, and he'll think twice before ever raising his hand against another woman.

I shrug and stand to my full height before taking Harper's bag and keys off the counter. "Considering this bastard is going to have to have one of his friends hold his cock just to take a piss for the next few months, I think we took it just far enough."

Ace nods. "Couldn't agree more."

And with that, I toss him the keys to my truck, and the three of us take off, but not before Ace confirms that there really is a turkey sub waiting for him in my console.

Thirty minutes later, I pull up at the hospital, eyeing Ace and Diesel as they pull up behind me. We just dropped Harper's car back at her apartment, and not wanting to break into her home and leave her keys, I figured I'd come back here, sneak in while she's sleeping, and leave them beside her bed. But the moment I mentioned coming back here, Ace and Diesel couldn't help themselves.

They follow me into the hospital, not one of us saying a word as we stride through the long halls. Harper's keys rest in the palm of my hand, and the closer I get to her room, the more my stomach knots.

I can't walk in there, not even if she's asleep. She doesn't want me there. She made that crystal clear, and I'm not about to shit all over the boundaries she's put in place.

Reaching her door, I pause, my lips twisting into an awkward cringe. "Uhhhh," I say, glancing at the boys. "One of you is going to have to go in there for me."

Diesel's face scrunches. "The fuck?" he mutters as Ace narrows his stare. "What the fuck did you do?"

How am I supposed to explain this?

I sigh. "I might have had a theory about something and instead of keeping my fucking mouth shut—"

"You fucked a good thing right into the burning pits of hell, and now she wants nothing to do with you," Diesel finishes for me, shaking his head and snatching the keys right out of my hand. "Fucking idiot."

I nod, dropping down into the very chair I spent a good portion of the night in earlier. "Sounds about right."

Diesel looks at me as though he's never met anyone as fucking clueless in his life, and then he turns on his heel and stalks through the door of Harper's room, making intense jealousy course through my body.

"Get fucked," Ace says, hurrying after Diesel. "If he gets to meet her, then so the fuck do I."

I lean back against the wall, knowing this is about to turn into one hell of a shit show and not a moment later, his moronic voice cuts through the silence of the quiet hospital. "Well, shit. Somebody's gotta warn a man when he's about to walk into a room of beautiful women."

I'm gonna fucking kill him.

"Fuck me," Izzy's familiar tone responds, sending a ray of happiness through my chest that Harper had the good sense to call her and ask her to come. "Christmas has come early. Please for the love of all that's holy, tell me you're candy stripers who've come to give me a sponge bath because I've been such a filthy girl."

Ace chuckles, and I shake my head, willing him to keep his dick in his pants for just five minutes. He'll be eating this shit up. Izzy is exactly his type, which by default means that she's Diesel's type too.

I hear a loud smack, and I can only assume that Diesel has already had to intervene with Ace. "We're Knight's friends," Diesel says. "Just dropping off your keys."

"You got my car?" Harper asks, the soft tone penetrating right through my chest and making me wish I could melt straight through this wall and find her on the other side.

"Knight did," Ace says. "We were just along for the ride. We dropped it back at your apartment but figured leaving the keys at your front door wasn't the brightest move."

"Wow. And they say chivalry is dead," Izzy purrs, her voice shifting in the room, telling me she's moving around, probably putting herself right between my best friends. "You're both huge. It's like an Izzy sandwich. How tall are you guys?"

"Down, girl," Harper scolds. "They're the enemy."

Ace laughs, and I recognize the tone in his voice from every time he's been in a bar, working his magic on a woman. I realize that at some point, he's going to fuck that girl, which is only going to further complicate things for me. "You know what they say. Sex is always better with someone you're not supposed to want."

"Literally nobody has ever said that," Diesel scoffs before I hear the familiar jingle of Harper's keys. "The car is parked in the underground garage beneath your building. Hope that's alright."

"Thanks," Harper murmurs. "He really went and got it for me, huh?"

"Why the fuck wouldn't he?" Ace says. "He also fixed that little . . . janitorial issue you were having. You don't need to worry about him anymore. He won't be an issue. Him or his friends."

"I . . . He's here, isn't he?" she asks, making my back stiffen, wondering if she now thinks I'm a little bitch for not having the balls to come in here. I hope she realizes that I'm fighting every impulse within me that desperately wants to cross that threshold and pull her into my arms.

"Uhhhhhh," Ace says, not able to lie for shit. "He might be in the general vicinity."

"You wanna see him?" Diesel tacks on.

"No," she says too quickly, her voice almost panicked and sending a pang of agony right through my chest. "Just, ummm . . . Tell him thanks for me."

"SHE SAID THANKS," Ace yells toward the door. And I reiterate, I'm going to fucking kill him. His tone lowers again, and I can only assume he's speaking to Harper. "He said anything for you because I'm a pussy-whipped bitch, and that you should repay him by giving me this hot little vixen's number, and if not, can I at least fuck her in the disabled bathroom down the hall?"

Another smack sounds through the room, and this time Ace grunts in pain. "The fuck was that for?"

"Keep your dick in your pants," Diesel mutters before his tone shifts. "We'll get out of your hair, Harper. But uhh . . . I'm glad you're okay."

"Thank you."

"And listen," he continues. "Just know that while you're figuring shit out with Knight, you're family. If you're in trouble or you don't feel safe, whether that be at home or work, you can call."

"I appreciate that."

I can almost picture the awkward, forced smile that Diesel would offer, doing his best not to seem like the grouchy bastard that he generally is. Only that thought disappears the moment Izzy speaks up again. "Oh, don't you worry, big guy. I'll be more than sure to call."

Fucking hell. There's going to be another fight between the boys.

"You do that, babe," Diesel murmurs, and not a moment later, the boys stride out of the room, both Diesel and Ace looking far too impressed with themselves.

"Don't even fucking think about it," I tell them, knowing they each have a one-track mind.

"Fuck, you're such a thirsty little whorebag," I hear Harper scold her best friend through the thin hospital walls. "What the fuck is wrong with you? Always thinking with your vag."

"I know," Izzy murmurs. "I can't help it. I need to climb them both like trees. I've never been so worked up in my life. I'm going to have to excuse myself and take care of business in the bathroom. Holy fuck."

At that, Ace turns on his heel, more than ready to head straight back in there, but Diesel catches him by the scruff of his shirt, dragging him away from Harper's room. "Come on, Romeo. It's just you and your hand tonight."

We start making our way back down the hall, and while I know I should take off and get home to get a good sleep for work tomorrow, I can't seem to make myself head toward the exit. "You guys go ahead," I tell them, my gaze shifting toward the hall that will lead me back toward the hospital's security center. "I've got some shit I need to work out."

Their brows furrow, their gazes filled with curiosity. "You good, boss?" Ace asks.

"Yeah. Just something I need to wrap my head around," I tell them, and with that, they take off, leaving me to finally figure out what the hell has been going on with Harper lately, and as I turn to the right, heading deeper into the hospital, I prepare myself to meet with Carly for the second time tonight.

CHAPTER 34

HARPER-RAYN

Stupid fucking men. Why do they always have to ruin everything?

I sit in my hospital bed, my legs crossed on the blankets as I wait for Nurse Celia to return with my discharge forms. It's been five long days wasting away in this hospital bed, and while I've hated every second of it, I've also done everything in my power to make sure I get out of here as soon as possible.

When they told me to get up and start walking around, I all but sprang out of bed, despite the pain shooting through my body. I've pushed myself to my limits, desperate to heal from this shit and finally put it behind me.

The only thing that's been getting me down is Knight. And not only because he tore my heart into shreds, but because he took it upon himself to mention what happened to his stupid brother, who in turn told my mother.

That asshole. I get why he did it, though. He didn't want me to be alone, but is anybody ever truly alone in a hospital? There are people everywhere. Not to mention the fact that most of them are my colleagues and peers. My room has turned into the current lunch spot for the week, and while I've kinda loved getting to catch up with some of my older friends who I don't necessarily get to see anymore, all I've wanted was for that space beside my bed to be taken by Knight. Instead, it's been my mother's face staring back at me.

Apparently getting jumped can make a mother suddenly forget that she's been feuding with you for the better part of a decade, and no matter how many times I tell her that she's free to leave, her ass remains parked in that damn chair.

I let out a sigh. As much as I want to see him, I can't.

The moment he questioned me, I knew it was over. After everything that I've been going through over these past few weeks, his support is what I've needed most, and to learn that he thinks it's all in my head has killed me in a way I wasn't prepared for. He broke my heart into a million shattered pieces, and I don't know if I'll ever be able to look at him the same.

Everything hurts, and I want to hate myself for falling for him the way I have, as it only makes it harder to try and move on. I knew it was stupid to get involved with a man like Knight. It was only a matter of time before he swept me off my feet. I just wish he had been capable of catching me when I fell.

Goddamn it. That's not fair. He has caught me, time and time again. Every time I fell, he was right there to pick up the pieces. So many nights he just held me and told me everything was going to be okay. He's had my back since day one, and yet I can't forget the pain that tore through me the second I realized he didn't believe me, the second he dared to suggest that it was all in my head.

After everything, how could he possibly think that?

I was there, I experienced it all. I remember the agonizing pain as I pulled back the body bag to see Laith's face staring back at me. How could he suggest that was all in my head? I have the fucking scars spelling out *MINE* on my ribs to prove it.

This right here is why I've never allowed anyone to get this close. You let them in, you let yourself become vulnerable, and all it does is open you up to hurt.

I should have trusted my gut, should have never let him get that close.

My phone chimes on my bed, and I scoop it up, finding a new text from my mother. I let out a sigh and open it.

Mom: Just about to leave. Do you need anything?

I quickly respond before she ends up leaving.

Harper-Rayn: Thanks, but no need. I'm being discharged.

Mom: Oh good. I'll leave you to get settled at home. Might swing by tomorrow to put your place back together and make it suitable for healing. Otherwise, you're welcome to stay at my place. I can organize a nurse. I'm sure you'll be much more comfortable with me.

I roll my eyes. There's nothing wrong with my apartment, but at least she's not on my back about my career for a change. It's almost nice. Almost.

Harper-Rayn: I'll be fine at home.

Mom: Fine. I was only trying to help.

After dropping my phone back to my bed, I drag my hand down my face as I try to find just a semblance of composure. I don't know what it is about my mother, but she always manages to bring out the worst in me. That woman could just breathe in my direction and I'd lose my mind. Now that's a real sickness that Knight should be worried about.

I'm busy mulling over everything Knight Slater when a familiar face pops into my room. "Your bitch ass ready to leave yet?"

I grin at Izzy. "Almost. Just waiting for the nurse to come back with my discharge papers, and then we can get out of here."

"Thank fuck. I love you and all, but hospitals give me the creeps. I don't know how you spend your days down in that morgue. You realize how fucked up that is, right?"

"The morgue is my peace," I tell her. "Well, it usually is. Not with all this stalker shit. That's kinda fucking with my zen."

"Ya think?" she grunts.

Izzy helps me pack up all the things she brought, including the human-sized bear that's been taking up residence in the corner of the room—and scaring the shit out of me every damn night, thinking someone is watching me while I sleep.

The second everything is packed and ready, there's a soft knock on the door, and not a moment later, Celia walks in with my discharge papers just as Izzy dips out. "I'd like to say that it's a shame to see you go, but honestly, I can't wait to see the back of you," Celia tells me. "Doctors always make the worst patients."

I suck in a gasp, feigning offense. "I've been nothing less than the perfect patient."

She gives me a hard stare. "You've been a pain in my ass."

I grin, but she doesn't allow me the chance to respond. "I trust Dr. Hart has already spoken to you about your pain medication and what's expected of your healing journey? I know you're eager to get home, but I don't want to see your ass back in here, so nothing stupid. Play it smart. You're still healing, so no strenuous activity."

"I know, I know," I say, getting back to my feet just as Izzy barrels back in with a wheelchair and her eyes lighting up like the Fourth of July.

Celia shoves the discharge papers in my face before handing me a pen. "Sign here, then you're free to go."

I quickly scan over the discharge form, making sure everything looks the way it's supposed to before signing my life away. Celia disappears, leaving me in the capable hands of my best friend. "Get on," she says, her grin widening as she points toward the wheelchair. "I wanna see how fast this thing can go."

Well, shit.

An hour later, Izzy is helping me into my bed, going the extra mile by fluffing my pillows and pulling the blankets right up to my chin, and while I've done nothing but rest for the past five days, I can't help but feel tired. The trip home took it out of me. Izzy is a great driver . . . most of the time, but every corner and slight bump left me in agony.

She sets me up with my painkillers right beside the bed, along with my phone and a bottle of water. Then just when I think she's done it all, she walks out into my living room and comes back dragging my entertainment unit behind her, the TV wobbling back and forth.

"There," she says a moment later, tossing the remote onto the bed and surveying her handiwork. "That looks good."

"Have I told you that even though you're a thirsty ho, I still love you?"

Izzy grins wide. "I'm gonna fuck Knight's friends."

I sigh. She hasn't let up about it since the second they walked out of my hospital room. "Shut up and order us noodles," I tell her. "Then let's find you a Tinder date that'll work those big asshats right out of your system."

Izzy is all too happy to oblige, and forty-five minutes later, we're snuggled in my bed, eating the best noodles Blackstone has to offer while swiping through the endless choices Tinder has to offer.

Netflix plays in the background, but I don't think either of us has watched even a second of the show that's on. I don't even remember the name of it. All that matters are the faces that appear on Izzy's phone.

She's busily chatting away with someone when a text comes through on my phone, and as I glance down at the screen, all the laughter is sucked out of the room.

Knight: I'm worried about you.

I grab my phone and show Izzy, and all she can do is scoff. "That man. I swear . . ." she says, cutting herself off, not actually having an ending to that sentence.

I laugh, her supporting frustration warming something in my heart. She's always had my back like that, whether we agree or not. If I'm pissed at someone, she'll be twice as pissed at them before I've even explained what happened.

I know I should ignore his message, but I'm feeling petty and after having to spend five days in that damn hospital bed, covered head to toe in bruises and swelling, I can barely control myself as my thumb moves across the screen.

Harper-Rayn: No you're not. You're imagining it. It's all in your head.

Knight: Don't be like that, doll. We need to talk.

Harper-Rayn: Doll? Who's that? Am I even a real person? SOMEONE CALL THE ASYLUM! CRAZY PERSON ON THE LOOSE!!

My phone immediately starts to ring, and my eyes bug out of my head as both Izzy and I stare at the screen. My heart races as I gape at it. I'm more than happy to be a petty bitch over text, but I don't think I can do it with that deep tone in my ear, calling me names that make my stomach clench with need.

"What do I do?" I panic, watching as it continues to ring, knowing that the bossy version of him is waiting for me to pick up.

"I . . . I don't know," she says, just as panicked.

My brain starts to short-circuit, and in a moment of pure terror, I throw the phone across the bed, only it slips right off the edge and drops to the ground. I cringe, hoping like hell I didn't just smash my phone. After all, not having a working phone would really fuck with my recovery over the next few weeks.

"Really?" Izzy mutters, throwing the blankets back and retrieving the phone.

"I panicked."

"No shit," she says, glancing down at the phone, only to beam back at me and hold up the flawless screen like a trophy. But the moment she does, a new text comes through. "Ooop."

She hands me the phone back, and I hesitate as I swipe my thumb across the screen, not sure I want to know what he has to say anymore. But when it comes to Knight Slater, I'm a sucker for punishment.

Knight: Missed Call.

Knight: Don't make me come over there. Answer the fucking phone.

Harper-Rayn: You're not welcome here. I don't need people in my corner who don't have my back. You hurt me, Knight. I let you get too close, and that's my fault. But it's over now. You need to let it go.

Knight: The fuck I do.

I don't bother responding. All it's going to do is work me up, and soon enough, I'll end up hidden beneath these blankets with my heart torn to pieces. And honestly, over these last few weeks, I've never felt so weak in my life. It's time to pull myself back together.

Izzy and I talk shit for the rest of the afternoon, until it's time for her Tinder date, and the moment she's gone, I can't help but think about everything Knight had said about my stalker.

He's wrong. It's not in my head. I felt his fingers inside me, felt the tip of his blade cutting through my skin, felt the way his cock reached the back of my throat. Nobody can just imagine all of that, and while I want nothing to do with Knight right now, I feel as though I need to prove this man exists. I need Knight to believe me.

My head falls into my hands, having absolutely no idea how I'm supposed to prove that, but then I remember he had Laith's phone. If I could somehow draw him out, I could record him or maybe have Knight come and do some SWAT man ambush, but how? My stalker has been ten steps ahead of me this whole time. I'm his pawn to move around the board as he sees fit. But I need to try. I need to see this through. But more than that, I need to have Knight's faith.

Taking my phone again, I pull up the text chain I had with Laith, my hands already shaking. I have no idea what I'm supposed to say or how this is even going to go, and I write out a few things before immediately deleting them.

Why is this making me feel so sick?

I stew on it for an hour before finally ripping it off like a Band-Aid and hitting send.

Harper-Rayn: Thanks for taking me to the hospital. You saved my life.

It's not even a good message. Bland as plain rice on a dry piece of toast, and I immediately hate myself. What kind of bullshit message is that anyway? That's not going to help draw the fucker out.

My phone dings almost immediately, and my gaze snaps back to the screen. My heart races, but there it is, his response. This will prove once and for all that he's as real as they get.

Big & Long Schlong #3: You gave me a scare.
Harper-Rayn: I want to see you.
Big & Long Schlong #3: You and I both know that's not a good idea.

My fingers shake as I text him back.

Harper-Rayn: But I'm ready to play by your rules. Whatever you want . . .
Big & Long Schlong #3: Have it your way, Harper-Rayn. If you want to play, then we'll play.

A knock sounds at my door and my head snaps up, my eyes going wide.

Holy fucking shit.

He's here.

I sit straight up in my bed, panic storming through my chest.

I definitely didn't think this through. What am I supposed to say to him? *Excuse me, thou fucked-up stalker man. Before you attempt to take every last shred of dignity away from me, would you mind whipping off the creepy vampire mask and flashing me a pearly white smile for the camera so that my totally sexy step-uncle who hath broken thine heart can see that you are indeed not my imaginary sex slave. Mmmkay, thanks.*

Shit. Shit. Shit.

I sit on the edge of my bed, my eyes wide as I stare toward my bedroom door, not knowing what to do or how to even talk to this man. The last time I saw him, and I mean *really* saw him, was in Knight's bedroom with my ankles and wrists bound. And even now, almost a week later, I still don't know what to make of that.

There's not a single doubt in my head that he had come with the intention to end my life, and yet for whatever twisted, unknown reason to me, he decided to spare me. Which only leaves me wondering why the fuck he went out of his way to save me after finding me in that alley. If he truly didn't care for my life, he would have left me to die, but he drove me to the hospital like a madman and even called Knight to make sure I had someone sitting with me when I woke up.

None of this shit is making sense.

A knock sounds again, and this time it's followed by a pissed-off growl, the tone so familiar it makes my heart sink. "Harper-Rayn, I know you're in there. Open this goddamn door before I bust it down."

Fuck. It's Knight.

Knowing damn well that he would follow through on his threat to annihilate my door, I carefully pull myself to my feet, holding my breath as though that could somehow save me from the pain of moving around.

"If I wanted to see you, I would have asked," I call toward the door. "Go away."

"Over my dead fucking body," he says. "Door. Now."

I grit my teeth and brace my hand against the wall, using it as a support as I make my way through my apartment. There's nothing I want less than to have to deal with Knight right now, especially after the text I just sent him, which is clearly why he's here letting my whole apartment complex know my business.

Honestly, I think I'd prefer to deal with my stalker instead. At least I generally know what I'm going to get with him. He'll storm in, make some bullshit comments about rules to a stupid game I never agreed to play, and then try to fuck me in some way. With Knight, I have no damn clue. All I know is that after he told me he thinks it's all in my head, I have feared having any type of conversation with him.

He led me straight into his trap, drawing me in with that wicked grin and those sparkly eyes, promising me safety and a warm bed to crawl into. And along the way, something shifted. He wasn't just the forbidden fruit dangling in front of me, daring me to get on my knees, he became so much more. Am I in love with him? I don't really know, but what I do know is that he holds the power to destroy me and that terrifies me more than any stalker could.

It takes me a lifetime to reach my front door and it doesn't go unnoticed how despite his threat to bust down the door, he's actually extremely patient with me, not wanting to rush me.

I step right up to my door, placing my hand against the wood as though I could somehow feel him on the other side, and when I peer through the small peephole, I find him there, his hands braced against the doorframe and his head down.

"Are you done watching me through that damn hole or are you going to open the door?"

Fucking bossy asshole.

Letting out a nervous breath, I inch away from the door, just enough to unlock all the bolts and chains, and when I finally reach for the handle and slowly open the door, everything in me breaks.

I'm struck with the overwhelming need to crumble to the floor and sob, but I hold on to the tears, not wanting Knight to see just how much power he holds over me.

He stands before me, those dark, captivating eyes raking over my body, scanning me from head to toe and looking over every last bruise that mars my skin, checking how they're healing. "You shouldn't be here," I tell him.

He steps into me and I immediately back up, needing that space between us, and within seconds, he's standing inside my apartment, my back against the wall and his body barely a breath away.

He stares at me as if having no fucking idea what he's actually come to say. "You need to leave," I say, my voice shaky as my resolve begins to break down.

His gaze lingers on mine and I see nothing but heartbreak reflected in his stormy gaze. "You really think that I wouldn't catch you if you were to fall?" he asks, looking at me as though I somehow hold the power to bring him to his knees. "I've been there, Harper. Every step of the fucking way. I've caught you every damn time. When you showed up at my door, I've been there. I've held you through the night. I've bandaged your wounds. How can you accuse me of not having your back?"

I lift my hand, placing it against his racing heart as the very touch ignites a fiery blaze between us, something that's always been there, lying dormant until we touch. "Do you still believe that I'm making this all up? That all of this bullshit is just a figment of my imagination?"

I see the very moment his heart shatters, and when he regretfully nods, my heart shatters right along with his. "I would never lie to you, Harper, and I'm not going to start now in order to protect your feelings. Just give me a chance to explain everything so you'll understand."

The tears I'd worked so hard to hold back begin welling in my eyes, and I shake my head, his words hurting more than the fists that pummeled my bare skin. "Holy shit," I breathe, gently pushing him away from me, his insistence to stand anywhere but in my corner killing me, just as I knew he would. "So this is what it feels like."

"What *what* feels like?"

"What it feels like to be vulnerable with someone, to trust them and let them hold your heart in the palm of their hands, only to stand by helplessly and watch as they destroy it."

"Doll . . ."

I shake my head, hastily wiping the tears as they roll down my cheeks before reaching for the door and opening it wide. "Please go," I say, my voice shaking as my knees threaten to give out. His inability to understand and believe me is the most agonizing betrayal I've ever felt. "You and me, this is over now."

He watches me with that same agony reflected in his haunting stare, and when he steps back into me and gently drops his lips to my cheek, I want to crumble. "I'll leave, doll. I'll give you your space, but let's get one thing straight. You and me, this is far from over," he tells me, shifting toward the open door and giving me just a moment to breathe. "You can't just turn this off like we never existed. It's too deep now. Your heart beats in tandem with mine, and no matter how much you want to deny it, you can't. Not anymore. I told you once before that if you're going up in flames, that I'll step right into the fire with you, and I meant that. So when you're ready, you call me, and I'll be right here."

I can't respond over the growing lump in my throat, and I simply watch as he turns away and strides right out my door. I watch every step he takes, and the more distance he puts between us, the more the open wound right in the center of my chest begins to ache. Then as he disappears out of sight, I fall to my knees, my body completely numb as my head falls into my hands and the tears begin streaming down my face.

CHAPTER 35

HARPER-RAYN

Heavy thumping against the door has my eyes springing open into the bright sunshine of Tuesday morning, and I immediately groan, pulling my blanket up over my head and realizing that I got played . . . again.

My stalker never showed, and that's just one more time that Knight gets to say that I'm obviously crazy.

"Fucking hell," I mutter to myself, cringing as I drag my hand over my swollen eyes and press a little too hard on the lingering bruises. Though at this point, I don't really think they're lingering. They're basically a permanent fixture on my face. No sign that they're going away anytime soon. I look like Frankenstein's monster.

I spent the majority of my night crying into a tub of Oreo ice cream, and at twenty-eight years old, I can finally understand what it feels like to experience heartbreak. Sure, I had my fair share of breakups over the years, but I've always been the asshole causing the hurt. I've never been on this side of the pain before. It's a deep, soul-crushing ache, and without a doubt, I know this is the kind of pain that will leave scars.

There are so many things I could have dealt with in a relationship. Not seeing eye to eye on everything isn't a problem. It's human nature, but this was too big. Knowing that the time I was in his arms, crying against his chest as the agony of performing Laith's autopsy crippled me, he was assuming I was going crazy. Or when I was bleeding in his bathroom after having my wrists and ankles bound and a knife sliced through my skin like butter, he was wondering which asylum he should stick me in. It kills me.

I thought he was better than that.

My eyes close, and I do what I can to block out the pain. It took me all night to finally get to sleep, and when I did, I think it was from pure exhaustion, not because I was magically capable of turning off the pain. I don't think I'll ever be able to turn it off. This pain will follow me around for the rest of my life. And now at every family function, I will see him. I'll have to watch as he eventually moves past this and lets someone else in. I'll have to sit idly by as he brings her to all of Mom's ridiculous dinner parties, and then one day, I'll receive an invitation in the mail that will gut me.

Loud thumping rumbles through my apartment, and my eyes spring open again, reminding me that someone is at the door, and I groan, throwing my blanket back. It's probably Izzy coming to tell me all about getting railed on her date last night.

I pull myself up to stand, needing to brace my hand against the mattress as I get up, and as I walk through my small apartment, I can't help but notice that the pain from the surgery isn't so bad this morning. Or perhaps my heartbreak outweighs the agony of being jumped in a back alley, drowning it out.

Just my luck, right?

Making it out of my bedroom and into the living room, I beeline straight for the door, and as I reach for the bolts and chains locking me in, I realize that during my sob-fest last night, I didn't even remember to lock the door.

How fucking stupid could I be? Though if my stalker had actually shown up and taken me out, I probably would have thanked him for making the pain stop. Knowing my luck, I probably would have taken the agony right into the afterlife with me like a badge of dishonor, doomed to wallow in everything Knight Slater for all eternity.

Taking the door handle, I give a quick twist before yanking it open, fully expecting to find Izzy. Only as I stand in the open doorway, I stare up at a face I never thought I'd see again.

I suck in a breath, shaking my head, my body going weak with every passing second. "No," I breathe, my brows pinching together as my heart starts to race. It's not possible. This can't be happening.

"Holy fuck, tiger. You look like shit," Laith says, staring at me with deep concern. "Why are your eyes all red and puffy like that? Have you been crying?"

"No, you're . . . you're supposed to be dead."

"Dead? What the fuck meds did they put you on? Are you good, babe?"

He goes to reach for me, his palm aimed toward my forehead, and I spring back out of the way, fear gripping me in a choke hold. "Don't touch me!"

Laith immediately pulls back, looking at me as though I'm the one who's lost her mind, and all I can do is stare right back, my eyes wide as unease pounds through my veins.

How is he here? I did his autopsy. I cut the clothes off his body and cried against his chest, grieving for my lost friend. That agony and loss were too real to have imagined them, and yet here he is, standing before me as though not a damn thing happened.

Laith looks at me as though he's staring at a ghost, but truth be told, I'm the one staring at a ghost. This shouldn't be real. He shouldn't be standing here before me in a suit, looking as though he's about to take his ass off to work.

"Woah, tiger. Calm down," he says, inching closer again, his hands up as if to show that he means me no harm, but that's not even close to what's got me spooked. "Is everything okay? You don't seem like yourself."

I shake my head, unable to make sense of what the hell is going on. How can he be here like this, standing before me as though he didn't just die last week? As though I didn't feel the chill of his dead body. As though I didn't close up the body bag and slide him into locker thirty-six.

No. Is Knight right? Have I imagined all of this? Have I worked up some elaborate story in my head? No, it's not possible. I felt his cool, dead body beneath my fingers. Felt the sharp bite of my stalker's blade as it cut into my skin. The word left on my ribs is proof of it. So how the hell is Laith here? Has this just been some big, sick joke?

"No," I tell Laith, putting my hand up to stop him from coming into my apartment. "You're not real. You can't be here. I saw . . . I saw your body."

"What?" he says, his face scrunched with confusion. "Babe, what's going on? I just came to check on you. You've been acting weird, and I've been trying to give you space to figure out your shit with this new guy, but now you're being all flirty in your texts again, telling me you wanted to see me, so I figured that was over. I just . . . Are you good?"

I can barely make out the words falling from his mouth as my mind takes me away, swirling with endless possibilities. Laith is dead. I know it with every fiber of my soul, but this person in my doorway . . .

Is this my stalker? Is this him beneath the mask?

He goes to creep toward me, and I jump back again, terror gripping me as my head spins. "STAY AWAY FROM ME."

"Babe?"

Panic rises in my chest as I grab my car keys off the entryway table and dash right past him, too worked up to stop and grab a pair of shoes or to even close my apartment door behind me.

My bare feet pound against the cold hallway floor, every last one of my internal stitches screaming in anguish, and despite the pain, I keep pushing myself forward, knowing I'll have hell to pay later, but it doesn't matter. Not right now. I have to figure this out. I have to know that this is real.

"Harper?" Laith calls behind me, his voice sounding so real, but I know deep in my heart that it's not.

As I reach the first flight of stairs, my head whips back, staring at Laith still standing by my door, and it breaks me, but I keep running, hurrying down the stairs as my body screams for me to stop. But I won't, this is too important. Too big. I have to confirm what I already know. I have to see it for myself.

Tears well in my eyes, blurring my vision, and I hastily wipe them away, terrified of missing a step and falling right to the bottom, but

I push through it until finally reaching the underground parking structure beneath my building.

My car isn't in its normal spot, and I have to search, trying to figure out where the hell Knight parked it the night he retrieved it from my attacker's home. After taking way too long, I finally find it, hidden in the farthest row.

Within seconds, I'm in my car, one hand clutched over my aching stomach, the other pressing the engine's start button. I back out of my spot faster than lightning, and before I know it, I'm on the road, my windshield wipers flying across the glass as rain pours down over me.

The agony of the run almost has me passing out, but I force my body to clutch onto consciousness, determined to see this through. I suck in deep breaths through my clenched jaw, desperately willing the pain to fade while hoping like fuck that I haven't pulled a stitch.

I arrive at Blackstone Private Hospital within ten minutes, and after bailing out of my car, I have no choice but to slow my pace. My body is physically incapable of keeping up with my desperation. People glance my way, looking at the crazed lunatic rushing through the parking garage, barefoot and in pajamas, but I ignore every last one of them, not stopping until I make my way through the main doors of the hospital and straight to the elevator that takes me down to the morgue.

My hands tremble as I picture Laith's face. "No, no, no, no, no," I mutter to myself, shaking my head as I wait for the elevator. I can't stand still, rocking from left to right, and when my trembling hands become too much, I have no choice but to cross them over my chest and tuck them beneath my arms.

"No, no, no, no, no." I repeat it like a mantra, over and over again, knowing in my gut that Laith is gone. I saw him with my own two eyes. Felt him. Held him. That man standing at my door, that wasn't him. That was my mind playing tricks on me. It had to be. There's no other explanation. Honestly, it's almost ironic. Just last night, Knight was telling me that I was imagining things, and now this morning, I actually am.

The elevator door opens, and a bunch of nurses and doctors clamber in with me, pressing the buttons so that I don't have to worry about it. They all mind their business, not gaping at me like the people out in the parking garage had. It's not the first time someone around here has shown up in their pajamas and looking worse for wear, and it won't be the last time. It's a joke that goes around the hospital—if you haven't had a little mental breakdown at some point, are you even a real doctor?

Reaching the basement floor, I slip out of the elevator and hurry down the hall to the morgue, my feet taking me faster than my body is capable of, and just as I reach the door and automatically go for the access card that usually hangs from my scrubs, I realize my mistake.

It's lying on my entryway table, right next to where my keys usually sit.

"Fuck."

Frustration surges through me. I could race back home and get it, risk running straight into the man who I know without a doubt isn't Laith, or I could take my ass up to security and ask for a new access card. Or . . .

My fists slam against the door. "Dr. McKullan," I call out, hoping like fuck that someone's actually in there. I never actually checked the time, but it feels quite early. He might not be in yet, but I keep trying. "Dr. McKullan. Please, open up."

The door opens a moment later, and I find Dr. McKullan staring back at me, his brows furrowed as he takes me in. I've always done everything I can to appear professional in front of my boss, but right now, I couldn't care less.

I need to know that I'm not losing my mind.

"Dr. Madden?" he grumbles, his gaze sweeping over the nasty bruises still lingering on my skin. "What are you doing here? You should be home resting. You're in no condition to be working."

I cringe and barge right past him. "I'm sorry," I rush out, hurrying straight through the morgue and to the massive refrigeration unit across the back of the room. "I just . . . I need to check something. My friend, he was here. He—"

"Is everything alright, Harper?" he asks, cutting me off as he follows me deeper into the morgue, the few day shift pathologists side-eyeing me.

I shake my head, barely able to get a single thought out as I make my way down the refrigeration unit, looking for locker thirty-six. Finding it almost immediately, I grip the handle and quickly twist before yanking the door open and pulling the table right out.

Laith's black body bag stares back at me, and I reach for the zipper without hesitation.

"Dr. Madden. What on earth do you think you're doing?" Dr. McKullan demands, knowing damn well that I haven't stopped to scrub in or even bothered to find a pair of gloves, let alone a pair of shoes, but that's not important to me. I have to see Laith.

I grip the zipper tighter and pull it down, revealing the body beneath, and I suck in a loud gasp. There's a man here, tall with dark hair. He's attractive and has one hell of a nasty gunshot wound right in the center of his chest, but he's not Laith.

"Where is he?" I demand, my crazed stare snapping up to Dr. McKullan as I hastily do up the bag and push the table back inside the unit. I dive for locker thirty-seven. Maybe I made a mistake. It's rare, but it happens, and after performing Laith's autopsy, I wasn't exactly in the best headspace. Maybe I wasn't focused. Maybe I put him in the wrong unit. "The man who was in locker thirty-six. Laith Mitchell. Where is he?"

"What are you talking about?" Dr. McKullan asks, slowly coming closer as I pull out the next one and hastily check inside the bag, only to come up empty. "We don't have anybody here by that name. Thirty-six belongs to a gunshot victim, James Harding."

I stop and look back at the doctor. "No. No, that's not right. I put him there myself. The man who was in locker thirty-six," I repeat just in case he's not following. He's getting old so sometimes he forgets things. "Laith Mitchell. I performed the external part of his autopsy last Monday and put him in thirty-six. I made a note of it. That number has haunted me ever since. He was my friend. One of my best friends, and now his body is not here. I need to know where he went. Where did he go?" My gaze snaps to the girls who are trying not to gawk at me. "Did one of you move him?"

Dr. McKullan shakes his head, and I groan, diving back to the refrigeration unit and pulling out the next table as dread fills me. He can't be lost. We don't fuck up here. We can't have lost him. One after another, I search the body bags, hysteria growing thick in my chest. A lump forms in my throat, making it hard to breathe, and as I check the very last bag, the tears start to flow.

"No, no, no, no," I cry, hurrying across the morgue to the open report files. I start flicking through them, desperate to find anything on Laith. Maybe his parents had him moved. Maybe he was assigned incorrectly and was transferred. Maybe they've already claimed the body and buried him without me. Did I miss it while I was in the hospital after the attack?

Fuck!

The tears are uncontrollable, and as Dr. McKullan steps in beside me and lays his hand on my arm, I lift my panicked stare, unable to make sense of anything. "Harper, I've personally overlooked every case we've had. Nobody by the name Laith Mitchell has come through the morgue. Perhaps you've got the details wrong."

"No. I did his autopsy. I cried while I cut his clothes off him. I read the carvings on his chest, the same ones that are on my ribs. The same as the men from the double homicide and the one before that. Laith is here. He has to be. I know it."

"What are you talking about? What carvings? We've had no cases with irregular markings on the bodies, and certainly no double homicide."

"No, that's not right," I insist, getting angry that he's denying any of this. How could he? He's the one who directly looks over my work. "Two weeks ago. A double homicide came in. Two men. You concluded the cause of death as injuries sustained in a car wreck, but you were wrong, and I don't understand why you would put that in your report when it was so clearly not a car wreck. They were murdered."

Dr. McKullan watches me through a narrowed stare. "I'm sorry, Harper. I don't know what you're talking about."

I shake my head when it occurs to me that this is all the stalker's doing. Every step along the way, my stalker has been well and truly ahead of me. He took the bodies of the men in the club and the one before that. He took all the evidence and wiped it from every system it could have potentially been entered into, and apparently he wiped it straight out of Dr. McKullan's memory. So why the hell would Laith be any different? He took him as well.

I drop to my knees, barely able to feel the way my insides scream for relief, and when Dr. McKullan comes down with me, I've never felt more alone. He grips my hand in both of his as though that could somehow comfort me, but when two little words come falling out of his mouth, I realize this is how it ends.

"Call psych."

CHAPTER 36

KNIGHT

My team prepares to head out, suiting up and making sure every weapon is fully loaded and accounted for. When my phone rings, I glance down, not really having the time to deal with anything other than my squad, but seeing *Blackstone Private Hospital Security* appear on my phone, it brings me pause.

"You guys keep going," I say, already answering the phone. "I've gotta take this."

I lift the phone to my ear and hold it between my face and shoulder, freeing up my hands to holster my gun. "Now's not a great time," I say, assuming it's Carly. "Is it important?"

"Yeah," Carly says. "It's that girl from down in the morgue. Your niece."

The fuck. "The girl from the morgue?" I ask, knowing damn well that Harper is home in her bed, recovering from surgery. Hell, even if she thought she could manage going to work, it's not even close to her work hours.

"The one from the surveillance feed," she confirms. "I figured I'd call you before they shoot her up with a sedative and have her committed. I think you need to get down here. She seems to be having some kind of breakdown. She's in her pajamas, wailing in the morgue. She keeps saying something about missing bodies and carvings."

"Fuck. I'll be there in ten."

Ending the call, I shove my phone straight into my pocket before finding both Diesel and Ace staring at me. "It's Harper. I have to go," I tell them, turning my gaze to Diesel. "Can you take point?"

He nods, and I turn on my heel and run, knowing the boys will have each other's backs. After stopping by the locker room to grab my keys, I race down to the parking garage and hurry to my truck.

I wasn't there for her last time she was in trouble, and because of that, she almost died in a back alley, and I was forced to sit there and wait, hoping like fuck that she was going to be alright. But today isn't going to be like that. If she's burning, I'm burning.

My truck roars to life, and within seconds, I'm hauling ass out of the parking garage to the main road, racing to get to her through the pouring rain. I have no fucking clue how she ended up in the morgue in her pajamas. What the fuck happened between last night and this morning?

I should have stayed and taken the time off work, even if it meant just sitting outside her apartment and making sure she was alright.

I reach the hospital in just under eight minutes, breaking every fucking road rule on the way to get to her, and as I peel through the parking garage, I see her Honda and immediately want to bitch her out. She knows damn well that she's not supposed to be driving, especially while on those painkillers. But more than that, how did she get down to her car? Did she walk down all those flights of stairs herself when she can barely stand without grasping the wall?

Fucking hell.

Why does loving someone mean always being furious with them? How the fuck am I supposed to look out for her if she won't look out for herself? Damn it.

I park my truck only a few spaces down from Harper's Honda, and within seconds, I'm flying through the main door of the hospital, having no fucking clue where to find her. I head toward the reception desk when an internal door opens, and I hear her voice from down the hall. "LET GO OF ME," Harper screams. "I HAVE TO FIND HIM. I HAVE TO FIND LAITH."

Fuck.

I race through the internal doors.

"Hey, you can't go back there," someone yells from reception, but I don't bother to even glance back as my feet pound against the hospital's cheap linoleum. All that matters is Harper at the other end of the hallway.

Three security guards hover around her, holding on to her too tightly as other doctors and her colleagues stand around her, talking *about* her but not *to* her.

I reach her in all of three seconds, barging past the doctors. "Get your hands off my fucking girl," I growl, the threat clear as day in my tone, making all three of the security guards stop what they're doing and shoot their gazes straight to mine.

At my voice, Harper's head snaps up, her eyes wide and full of fear, and there's something there I've never seen before. It's as though she's not even in there.

"Knight," she whimpers as if begging me to make it all go away, the pain in her tone like nothing I've ever heard from her, and it crushes every ounce of my soul.

I step closer as the guards hastily release her, letting her fall heavily to the ground, her knees crashing into the linoleum. I grit my teeth and dive after her, not daring to let her go as I pull her back to her feet and straight into my arms, cradling her as though I'll never let go.

The guards will have me to deal with as soon as I've dealt with Harper and figured out what the fuck is going on here. Being in my job for as long as I have, I've had more than my fair share of encounters with these guys, and they know damn well that I'm about to bury their asses for even thinking about putting their hands on my girl, let alone letting her drop to the ground like that.

"What's going on, doll?" I ask, my thumb brushing over the side of her face as I hold her to my chest, her tears soaking into my Kevlar vest that I never had a chance to remove. "What are you doing here?"

She shakes her head, her voice barely a whisper now. "I have to find him."

"Find who?"

"Laith. His body is gone. I have to know that it's real."

"It's okay, doll," I tell her, wishing there were some way I could make this go away while knowing that she's going downhill fast. There is no body. There never was. Hell, there's no fucking stalker. She's sick, and I have to get her the help that she needs. "We'll find him."

She pulls back just an inch and lifts her gaze to mine. "Really?"

I nod. "Yes, but I need to get you back home and into your bed first. This is too much stress on your body. It's still healing. You can't handle all of this moving around so soon after your surgery."

She watches me closely, and for a moment, it almost looks as though she's going to let me lead her away, but when her brows pull down, I quickly realize that I've lost her. "You're lying," she says, her chest heaving, panic in her bright green stare. "You told me you would never lie to me."

"Doll, please let me help you," I beg her. "You're not well."

"I knew it," she cries, ripping out of my hold and making the guards reach for their guns, and I immediately step forward, putting myself between Harper and any potential bullets. "All of you are liars. Where's Laith? What did you do with him?"

"Sir?" a doctor says from behind me, one I've never met before. "She's having what I believe to be a psychotic break. I need to sedate her before she hurts herself or anybody else."

My gaze shifts back to Harper, and she shakes her head, having heard every fucking word. "No," she says, horror in her eyes. "No. I'm not sick. You have to believe me."

Every piece of me shatters seeing her like this, but there's no talking to her when she's like this. There's no reasoning with her. She needs help, and despite how she feels, at some point, I'm going to have to step in and take it into my own hands.

"Do it," I tell the doctor, knowing that there's going to be one hell of a big conversation when she wakes up.

Harper looks at me with betrayal, tears rolling down her beautiful cheeks, and as the guards and the doctor rush in, she hastily tries to get away, but there are too many of them. She's immobilized while frantically trying to free herself, her eyes locked on mine for every damn second of it.

The doctor quickly prepares the sedative, and within seconds, he's grasping her upper arm and injecting it into the muscle. Her chest heaves, and as the doctor steps away, her body starts to relax.

I hurry in, taking her from the guards and lifting her right into my arms, and as she watches me through her sleepy stare, she gently shakes her head, a tear still sitting on her perfect cheek. "How could you?" she whispers, and not a moment later, she gives in to the sedative, her body going limp in my arms.

CHAPTER 37

HARPER-RAYN

Heaviness sinks into my muscles as I peel my eyes open, taking in my blurry surroundings. Unease immediately pounds through my veins. Is this . . . fuck. This is the psych ward. How the hell did I end up here? Did somebody have me committed?

My brain is foggy, and as I try to sit up, something pulls me back.

My brows furrow, and I pull against my wrists, only to find them restrained to the rails on the edge of the hospital bed.

"Doll?"

My head whips around, finding Knight hovering in the corner of the room, his hands buried in his pockets and his gaze full of guilt.

"You," I breathe as bits and pieces of the last few hours come back to me. The morgue. Laith. The guards. The betrayal. "You did this to me."

He visibly swallows before nodding, and as he steps closer to my bed, I shake my head, tears welling in my eyes. "No. Don't," I cry, not prepared to hear how he thinks I'm going crazy. "Just leave."

Knight shakes his head and pulls up a chair beside me, reaching out and holding my restrained hand through the bed rails. "Push me away as much as you want, Harper, but I'm not going anywhere."

"How could you do that to me?"

"I'm sorry, doll," he murmurs, his heart on his sleeve, looking just as broken as I feel. "I had no choice. I need you to be okay, and if I took you back home, you would have just pushed me away and refused to hear me."

An overwhelming mix of rage and betrayal sneaks up on me, claiming every piece of my heart. "So you had me committed to a fucking psych ward?" I demand, pulling against my wrists. Being bound this way takes me straight back to the night my stalker tied my wrists and ankles, and my panic spikes. "Do you have any idea what you've done? What setbacks this will cause for my career?"

He nods. "I wouldn't have done this if I didn't think it was important, Harper. I know you don't agree with me, but you need to hear what I have to say. I need you to understand how we got here."

"Don't . . . Don't do this."

"I have to," he tells me. "You don't see it, but right now, you are covered head to toe in flames, and this is me stepping into them with you. You're burning, doll. Let me burn with you."

I shake my head, the weight of my situation resting heavily on my chest as I try not to cry. "I'm not crazy."

"I don't think you're crazy," he tells me, leaning right in and brushing his fingers down the side of my face in a gentle caress. "You just need the kind of help that I can't offer you."

"And you think this is where I need to be?"

Knight nods. "Just hear me out. That's all I'm asking."

"I'm restrained to a bed in a psych ward," I tell him. "I don't think I have a choice in the matter."

The guilt returns in his stare, and he eventually nods, reaching for his phone on his lap. "I don't really know where to start, so I suppose we'll just start right at the beginning," he explains, swiping his thumb across the screen to unlock it. "After you kicked me out of your hospital room last week, I went and spoke to one of the people who work in the hospital surveillance room, and after some begging and pleading, she was able to get me the surveillance feed from all the nights that you said something had gone down in the morgue."

I sit up straighter, my back stiffening. "You've seen him," I breathe, not knowing whether to be scared or relieved to finally get some answers.

"Not exactly," Knight tells me.

"What do you mean? If you have the security footage, you'll see it all."

"I do see it all, but what I'm seeing isn't what you're believing went down."

"Wha . . . What are you talking about?"

He presses his lips into a tight line and turns the phone to face me. "This is the footage of the night you first sensed someone there. I've scrolled through the whole thing, and while I can see you freaking out, there's no sign of anyone entering the morgue."

I watch the footage, my brows furrowed as all I see is myself working, but I know for a fact there was a black rose left on the autopsy table, only I don't see it here. Knight jumps ahead in the video to where I'm freaking out and eventually race out of the morgue with no sign of anybody following me.

"Okay," I say, confused why I'm not seeing a rose on the table. "How does that prove anything? I told you that night was only a feeling. I never saw the guy, I could just sense him there."

"I know," he tells me, "which is why I kept digging. This video is from when that first body came in. The one that had your name carved across the knuckles and the internal organs all messed up."

A shiver sails down my spine, as I remember it all too clearly. It had fucked with my head in a way that I'll never recover from. Even now I still remember the feel of the letters carved into the heart. It was horrifying.

Knight skips ahead in the video, only stopping when the morgue door opens and we see the coroner striding in with the body. "Wait. No, this isn't right," I tell him. "Detective Gray was there."

Knight shakes his head, putting the video in fast-forward so we don't have to replay every single moment of the night. "No, he wasn't. The coroner is the one who gives you the body and leaves. Only as you open the bag, it's not the body your head perceives it to be."

"What?" I mutter, leaning closer to see the screen better, and just as Knight said, I watch the coroner leave and get straight to work. Only as I open the bag, it's not the body I remember working on. It's an older Korean gentleman who appears to have perished in a fire. "No. No, that's not the body I worked on."

"Keep watching, doll."

My brows furrow, and I watch the footage to the end, watching as I go over the body with great detail, taking down letters and making sentences out of markings that aren't even there. "This isn't right. Somebody must have doctored the footage."

"That's what I wondered at first, but with none of the detectives, first responders, or even the people who work with you in the morgue able to confirm even a snippet of your story, it leaves too much doubt."

I shake my head. "I'm not crazy."

"I know, doll," he says, before letting out a breath. "Next up, the double homicide."

Tears silently roll down my cheeks as I go over the footage, and just like with the first body, I feel more confused than ever. I see the two bodies come into the morgue, and just as Knight and Dr. McKullan had said, they're the victims of a horrific car wreck, not the two men I had danced with in the club. They don't even look a little bit alike, and yet my brain told me they were different people all together.

I watch as I go through the motions during their autopsies, searching for secret messages and documenting my findings, only there's nothing to find.

"It got me thinking about what actually happened at the club," he tells me.

"To the two men?"

Knight nods and brings up the next video. "I needed to know that there weren't two bodies rotting away somewhere, so I got in contact with the club. I had to jump through more hoops than necessary to get the footage, but they eventually caved."

"And?" I say, not sure I want to see what he found.

"The two men you were dancing with definitely weren't the two men from the morgue."

He jumps ahead in the footage again, showing me on the dance floor, grinding against the two men, and I feel the first bit of relief, seeing that I'm not going crazy. I even grin when I see Izzy in the background hooking up with a complete stranger.

That night was wild in so many different ways.

The footage plays, and I watch as the two men eventually leave, one heading for the bar and the other hoping to meet me in the bathroom, when I begin to wander away.

"Wait," I say, knowing what comes next before realizing that if Knight has already watched it, that means that he would have also seen me with the stalker and watched as he made me come on his fingers before I pulled him away to the private booth, took him in my mouth, and then fucked him raw.

"So you saw . . ."

Knight nods. "I certainly saw something, but I don't think it's exactly what you remember."

"Huh? What's that supposed to mean?"

He cringes, and I reach for his phone, only for my wrists to pull at the stupid restraints, and then as if on cue, I see myself wander off the dance floor and step in front of a strange man. Only he's not masked, and he's certainly not tall and broad. Just some regular guy trying to enjoy his night.

Confusion plagues me. I have no recollection of this. When does the stalker come? I keep watching, waiting for him to show up. "Wha—HOLY SHIT," I gasp, watching in horror as this strange man shoves his hand up my skirt, and I start riding it like it's Christmas morning. "What the fuck am I doing?"

"My question exactly."

"That's not . . . That's not him. My stalker wears a mask, and he's much taller—like you. I'd almost convinced myself that he was you at one point."

He nods. "Just watch. It gets worse."

"Worse? How the fuck does it get worse?"

Knight skips through the awkward hand grinding, only stopping when I take Regular Joe over to a private booth and start blowing his mind before riding his cock reverse cowgirl style.

"No, no, no," I groan, hating every minute of this before realizing that this guy could have any number of diseases, and I sure as fuck didn't see him suit up. "I need to get checked for STDs."

"That you do," Knight agrees.

"Turn it off," I beg him.

He doesn't hesitate, letting his phone fall in my lap. "Do you see now, doll? All these things are happening. There are bits and pieces that are true, but your mind is distorting reality and replacing it with whatever it wants you to see. This stalker, Harper. He's not real, and the more your mind tells you that he is, the more you're at risk of ending up in a dangerous situation, and I don't want that for you. I need you safe."

I shake my head, hating this. His proof is overwhelming, but I have proof of my own, and it's fucking with my head more than ever. I don't know what to believe. I don't know what to trust.

"Laith?" I ask with shaky hands, remembering him standing at my door so clearly, but I was certain it wasn't him, and if the two men from the club are still alive, and the Korean burn victim isn't who I thought he was, then perhaps there's a chance that Laith really is alive.

Knight nods. "Laith is fine. He's alive, albeit a bit confused, but fine."

I let out a relieved breath. I'd rather admit to being crazy than to have to lose Laith all over again. "So who was I—Wait. He was confused? How do you know he's confused? Did you speak to him?"

Knight cringes. "I might have run a background check on Laith and gotten his cell number from there. But yeah, after you were sedated, I gave him a call. I figured something must have triggered your panic over needing to find his body, and he confirmed that he'd swung by to check on you this morning."

My face scrunches. "So he knows, then?"

Knight shakes his head. "No, I figured it wasn't my place to talk to him about what's going on with you. He had a lot of questions, though, so at some point, you're going to have to sit down with him and have a real conversation."

I nod, appreciating that more than he will ever know, but I'm also taking note of the fact that he's not insecure about me spending time with Laith, despite our significant history. "Okay, so if it wasn't Laith on the table, then who the hell was it?"

"A gunshot victim," he says. "I have the footage of that as well, but it's hard to watch. It's clear that you believed it was Laith. I don't know if you really want to relive that one."

"Yeah. I'll pass."

We sit in silence, and as the tears slowly roll down my cheeks, Knight holds my hand. "It all felt so real," I tell him, unable to wrap my head around it while terrified of what this might mean for me. I trust Knight, and I know he wouldn't lie to me, especially not about something like this, but I'm struggling to believe it. How can my brain just stop working like that?

"I know, doll," he says, his hand cupping the side of my face before falling to my waist, his fingers brushing across my ribs and making me stiffen. "I'm sorry you had to learn about it like this, but—"

"Wait," I say, my brows pulling down as I start to shake my head, more than ready to pull every single part of his story to pieces. "If none of this is real, then how do you explain the scars on my ribs? I didn't imagine that. Those scars are there for the world to see and will continue to be there for years to come. Somebody did that to me."

Knight nods as a distraught hollowness appears behind his eyes. "Baby, I . . . I have a theory about that, but you're not going to like it."

I watch him for a moment before understanding dawns, and I realize exactly what he's going to say. "You think I did this to myself."

Pity appears in those dark eyes, and my chest instantly starts to ache. "I do," he says, his tone shifting as though those two little words gutted him to speak out loud. "I've gone over this a million times. I've scoured every inch of my property for any sign that somebody was there. I've searched my surveillance cameras and checked the alerts. There's nothing. I come up blank every damn time."

"So you think that I just walked into the kitchen, grabbed a knife off the counter, and started hacking away at my ribs, cutting deep gouges into my body without a single care as I chatted away with my imaginary friend?"

"Don't put it like that."

"Then how the fuck else am I supposed to put it?"

He shakes his head, not knowing how to respond, and honestly, I don't even know what I'm hoping he will say. Anything will set me off right now. "I think you hallucinated the whole thing, just as you did with the bodies in the morgue. I think you went through the motions. I think you had the knife, and as you pictured your stalker touching and claiming your body, you pictured the way he would cut you. Only it was your hand making the cuts."

I shake my head, tears filling my eyes all over again, refusing to believe that I could ever have the ability to cut myself in that way. "No. You're wrong."

"Doll, I think you used the knife to cut the bedsheets into ribbons, and I think they were the ropes that you imagined."

"I couldn't have cut them myself," I tell him. "Not when my wrists and ankles were bound so tight."

"Harper," he says with a heavy breath, the heartbreak clear in his tone, probably fearing that I will try and send him away again. "I've worked in SWAT for over a decade. I have rescued countless victims in hostage situations who have had their wrists and ankles bound with rope, tape, wire. You name it, I have seen it all, and no matter what was used to keep them bound, there are always marks left on the skin. Sometimes so deep it cuts right through to the bone, but doll, there wasn't a single mark on your wrists. Not even a hint of redness."

My mind takes me back to that moment, to the fear I felt as he tightened the rope around my wrists. I felt it bite into my skin. "That's not possible," I whisper, hating every moment of this. "It was real."

"No," he tells me. "It wasn't."

His words are like a blade straight through my spine, and I sag against the hospital bed, turning away from him as the tears roll down my cheeks. I silently replay every moment I've had with my stalker. The night he broke into my bedroom and caught me in a towel. The private booth in the club. The messages left on the bodies.

It has to be real. I feel it in my chest. But Knight is adamant, looking at me with that sad stare that makes me feel as though I've somehow done something wrong, like I'm a misbehaved child who's about to be shipped off to spend the summer with her strict grandparents. Only instead of strict grandparents I'll be shipped off to, it'll be some kind of asylum.

"Please, Harper," he whispers, still clutching my hand. "Let me help you."

I don't dare look back at him, terrified of what agreeing to help will actually mean, but more than that, how can he help me if I don't know what to believe? I want to trust him. I want to pick up the shattered remains of my heart and ask him to help me put it back together, but on the other hand, I'm too scared to hand it over again, not knowing what lurks in the darkness ahead.

"Okay," he finally says when I don't respond. "I'm going to give you a minute to process all of this. Just let me know when you're ready to talk or if you just want me to sit with you, and I'll come right back in."

And with that, he gets to his feet and strides out of the little hospital room, taking my whole heart and soul along with him, leaving behind nothing but a shell of a woman restrained to a hospital bed.

CHAPTER 38

HARPER-RAYN

As the sedative wreaks havoc on my system, consciousness comes and goes, and honestly, I'm happy for it. I'd prefer to sleep through it than to have to sit here by myself, overthinking everything Knight has just dumped on me.

How could he possibly think that I would take a knife, tear his blankets into ribbons, and then cut myself? Not even if I was shot up with the most potent drugs and completely tripping would I ever do that. It's not possible.

Sure, everything else held merit. It was right there in all the footage he collected, and maybe I am losing my mind. Maybe I've been under too much stress and have been slipping into psychotic episodes and having wild hallucinations. But despite that, I feel it in the pit of my stomach. Parts of this are real. I just don't know what. What I do know is that if someone doesn't release me from these stupid restraints soon, it's not *my* safety they will need to worry about.

Knight has been gone for an hour, maybe two. It's hard to tell. I don't have my phone or even a clock in this bland room. It's just me, alone with my twisted mind, in a cold room trying to sleep off the sedative that Knight allowed them to hit me with.

I sigh. I have never been so bored in my life. This is literally ridiculous. I even consider calling out to Knight just to have him come in and tell me all over again how he thinks I'm fucked up in the head. I might even let him look at me with that pitying stare again. Gosh, wouldn't that be a blast to experience all over again?

Surely the doctor is going to come in soon to give me some big spiel about what he thinks is wrong with me. Naturally, he'd have no idea what the hell he's talking about, but at least I'd be able to ask about removing the restraints. I mean, shit. What if I need to pee? Am I just supposed to wait for someone to show up and hope they can help? It's not as though I can reach the call button with my hands buckled down by my thighs. Whoever came up with this concept really didn't think it through.

I start counting the ceiling tiles just for something to help pass the time when movement in my peripheral catches my attention. I glance across the room, and my eyes widen, fear capturing me in a choke hold as my stalker hovers by the window, leaning against the wall as though he has every right to be here.

I suck in a gasp, my hands shaking at my sides. How did he even get in here? He would have had to either scale the building and climb through the window that I'm pretty sure doesn't actually open, especially in the psych ward, or walk straight past Knight, who is hovering out in the hallway. But more than that, how the hell did I not realize he was here? I've been staring at the ceiling for at least ten minutes after my last quick power nap. Surely I would have noticed him the moment I woke up.

Fear dances through my veins like poison, and all I can do is stare back at him as my heart races. "What are you doing here, kitten?" he growls, that deep tone penetrating right through my chest, leaving me gasping.

I shake my head, knowing without a doubt that Knight is wrong. Despite all of the evidence, how could he possibly deny this? He's standing right here in front of me.

I spare a glance toward the small window in the door, seeing Knight standing in the hallway speaking with the doctor, and my eyes widen. What the fuck is going on? My stalker is right here. Why aren't they rushing in to do anything about it? Why is Knight just allowing this to happen?

Looking back at the masked man, I tell him exactly what he wants to know. "They think I'm crazy. They think I've made you up. That you're just a figment of my imagination. Not real."

He watches me for a moment, the silence in the hospital room bringing on a thick tension that sends shivers sailing across my skin, and I can't help but feel that there's something different about this. He's always terrifying, always able to make me want to run, yet some part of me feels safe enough to let my guard down. But today, it feels different. That guard's not coming down, and I realize we've finally reached the end of his wicked game.

He lets out a sigh and reaches behind him, unsheathing a large blade, his haunting stare not moving from mine for even a second. He holds the blade in front of him, his pointer finger on his other hand pressed against the blade's sharp tip as he carelessly spins it around.

"I'm going to have to kill you now," he tells me, a sadness peeking through his haunting stare. "They know too much."

"No," I breathe, shaking my head and watching as he pushes away from the wall, the blade now firmly held in his skilled hand. "No."

With every step he takes, the panic rises in my chest, knowing this time will be different. There's no indulging him with my body, no rules left to break, nowhere to run, nowhere to hide. This is it. It's game over. All this time, I assumed my body was the prize, that his goal was to have me. But I'm only now realizing how wrong I am. My body was never the prize. It's simply a placeholder for what he truly wanted all along. My life.

"No. NO!" I cry out, my wrists yanking against the restraints as he gets closer, my body bucking to get free. "Please, no. I'll do whatever you want. I'm sorry. I'm sorry."

He steps up to the edge of my bed, his blade brushing across my skin as I fret, terrified of death, of never telling Jonah how much I've loved him all these years, of never getting to see Izzy's face just one more time, never getting to say goodbye. But fuck, never getting to tell Knight how I really feel, never having the chance to make things right with him. I can't.

"It's been fun, kitten," he purrs. "But it's time to go now. Just close your eyes. I promise, it will only hurt a little."

My body violently jerks around, frantically trying to get away from the sharp bite of his blade as my vision grows blurry with tears. "GET AWAY FROM ME," I scream. "HELP! HELP! HE'S GONNA KILL ME."

The door bursts open, the hinges squealing under the force, and before it's even had a chance to rebound off the wall, Knight is storming into the room, his eyes wide and wild as he searches the room for a threat.

"Harper?" he rushes out, the doctor flying in just behind him. "What's wrong?"

"HE'S GONNA KILL ME. HE'S—" I cut myself off, the sharp sting of the blade fading to nothing at all, and as I lift my gaze back to my stalker's, confusion rips through me. He was right here, right beside me, but now he's back against the wall, his blade nowhere to be found.

How did he get there so quickly?

"Who?" Knight demands, his eyes frantic and locked on mine when he should be focused on the stalker. Why is he looking at me like this? Why isn't he doing anything to help?

"The stalker," I say, watching the masked killer across the room, refusing to look away, knowing he will strike at any time. "He's right there. Why aren't you doing anything?"

Knight glances around the room, slowly striding around the side of my bed, putting himself directly in my line of vision, turning his back on the killer behind him. "Doll," Knight says too slowly, his voice filled with a cautiousness I've never heard from him before. "There's nobody there."

The blade appears in the stalker's hand again and despite his horrifying mask covering his face, I know he's smiling. His eyes light up like Christmas has come early, and when his attention flickers to Knight, my stomach sinks.

"Come back to me, doll," Knight says as if coaxing me to focus on the sound of his voice, trying to draw my attention away from the blade-wielding lunatic behind him. "It's not real. Come back to me."

Knight inches toward me, and with every step he takes, the stalker moves with him, his blade clutched tightly in his palm.

"No," I beg, shaking my head, tears streaming down my face as I try to fight against the shitty hospital-grade cuffs on my wrists.

"Please. I'll do anything. Please, just don't hurt him. You can have me instead."

"Doll," Knight coos. "Look at me. He's not real."

"I can't," I tell him, and when the stalker raises his hand, ready to plunge his blade through Knight's ribs and straight into his heart, a petrified scream tears from the back of my throat. "NOOOOOOO!"

Something slams against my neck, a sharp sting pinching my skin and sinking deep into my bloodstream as I feel hands on my body, clutching my arms and holding me down, but I can't fight it. My body immediately goes weak, but the fear is too strong, and I keep my terrified gaze locked on the masked stalker. Only as my body grows heavier, the stalker lowers his blade and looks back at me, a sadness creeping into his eyes as if forfeiting the game I never wanted to play.

"It's been fun," he purrs, a fondness in his tone as he fades out of existence, his once-solid figure morphing into a transparent ghost. Then, as unease continues to pound through my veins, I hear the subtle tones of his deep voice one last time. "Don't be mistaken, kitten. I'll be back for you. And when I do, it'll be a game worth dying for."

Silence follows, and my pulse pounds in my ears as I stare at the empty space where my stalker was just standing, disbelief coursing through my veins.

He's gone. Just like that.

Knight was right. He was nothing but a figment of my imagination, a sick hallucination my brain had fabricated to torment me. My chest heaves, a new kind of dread sinking into the pit of my stomach, trying to work out what the hell this means for me.

I'm sick.

My gaze shifts to Knight. He's watching me with profound concern, and I realize just how much I've put him through over these past few weeks. Overwhelming emotions tear through me all at once, but Knight is right by my side before I can even draw my next breath. The stoic SWAT officer is gone, and I'm left with the man who has caught me every time I've fallen, the man who burns every time I go up in flames.

He hastily undoes the restraints at my wrists, and the moment he can, he pulls me into his arms. "I've got you, doll," he rumbles. His big hand cradles my head, holding me to his massive chest, and I let out every bit of pain, fear, and fury I've felt over the past few weeks. "It's over. I've got you."

And with that, I simply cry, knowing that I will never be safer than I am now, right here in the warmth of Knight Slater's capable arms.

CHAPTER 39

HARPER-RAYN

Call me petty, but there's nothing I hate more than having to admit when a man is right, especially when the thing he's right about has everything to do with the fact that I'm losing my goddamn mind.

It's official. I'm crazy. I'm certifiably insane. I think. Well, I don't know. It's not as though I've been evaluated by Blackstone's finest psychiatrist yet, but I'm sure that's what they're going to say. It's not as though there's a completely viable reason to hallucinate a masked stalker who's been trying to kill me for the past month.

Ugh. I can just see it now. They're going to use words like *psychotic break* and *episodes*. It's going to be awful, and what's worse is that Knight is going to insist on sitting right here by my side the whole damn time, hearing some doctor confirm that I'm a deranged nutcase. How fucking humiliating. If he didn't think I was too much to deal with before, I can guarantee he does now.

On the bright side, with the meds they've put me on, I'm probably not going to have any more sadistic hallucinations, and my nonexistent stalker can wallow away into the dark abyss otherwise known as my memories. I'll file it away right between my childhood trauma and the vivid memory of seeing Laith's body on my autopsy table.

Fuck, even knowing that wasn't real doesn't make the memory hurt less.

The only thing that really bothers me is the letters carved into my skin. Knowing that I have the ability to hurt myself in that way terrifies me. Am I only a threat to myself, or am I a threat to others? I can't be waking up in the middle of the night, assuming Knight is my stalker, and stabbing him right through the chest with a serrated kitchen knife. Once I snapped out of my hallucination, I would never forgive myself.

"You're gonna burst a blood vessel if you keep thinking that hard," Knight murmurs from the chair beside my bed, still wearing yesterday's clothes, despite how many times I've told him to go home and rest. Apparently, there's no rest for the wicked.

I've been here a little over twenty-four hours, and while I'm dying to get home and back to normal life, a small part of me doesn't want to leave. I feel unpredictable. I can't trust myself or even know what's real, and while the psychiatrist will no doubt put me on some sort of meds to keep me from completely losing my mind, how am I supposed to trust that? What if they don't work for me? What if they're not strong enough for my kind of crazy? What if I hurt someone?

"And you're gonna find yourself with a brand-new bow tie made of your own intestines if you think for one second that you get to start being a bossy asshat again," I say, crossing my arms over my chest and being grateful that the restraints were never put back on.

"An intestine bow tie, huh?" he murmurs, lifting that dark gaze to meet mine. "I'd like to see you try."

My jaw drops. Of course I don't stand a chance against him. He's a fully trained, six-foot-whatever mountain of a man. He's a complete beast. If it came down to survival of the fittest, Knight would kick my ass a million times over and still have energy to fuck after. I wouldn't stand a chance, but it'd be nice if he could at least pretend. Though I don't know why I'm surprised. Knight isn't the type to sugarcoat things. He gives it straight, and as a general rule, I appreciate that about him, but right now, it makes me want to kick his ass harder.

"You know, just because you were right doesn't mean that everything can just go back to how it was before," I tell him, hoping he doesn't have the wrong idea about what's going on here, because honestly, I haven't got a clue what I need right now. "I have some shit to work through first."

"I'm well aware, doll."

My face scrunches, and as I look at him, he arches a brow, wondering what the fuck I'm going to hit him with next.

"Why don't you call me Morticia anymore?"

Knight grins. "With everything you should be concentrating on right now, that's the question that's circling that pretty mind of yours."

I shrug. "We've already worked out that my mind is a little fucked up at the moment, so I can't be blamed for the stupid shit that comes out of my mouth," I say, knowing damn well that's a cop-out. "So hit me with it, Knight Slater. What happened to *Morticia*?"

He watches me for a moment, consideration deep in those dark eyes. "You don't like *doll*?"

I scoff. "I have a voodoo doll tattooed behind my ear. I more than love *doll*," I confirm, making sure he truly catches on to just how much I like it. "I just . . . equally love *Morticia*."

Knight gets up from the chair and leans in toward me, his hand braced on the mattress beside my thigh, his face inching toward mine until his lips drop to my shoulder, gently kissing the curve of my neck. "Morticia is well and truly alive," he rumbles, dropping his tone low. "That tends to come out when you're being the sexy little morgue freak that you are."

My cheeks flush, and I clench my thighs beneath my blankets, the idea of being his sexy little morgue freak doing wicked things to me, but considering I pulled stitches yesterday and have barely even begun to heal after being jumped and having emergency surgery, that's going to have to wait. "And *doll*?"

He takes a breath, pulling back just an inch and taking my chin between his skilled fingers, holding my stare. "*Doll* is . . . more."

I nod, understanding exactly what he's saying, and then despite my declaration of things not going back to how they were before, he closes the gap between us and gently brushes his lips over mine in the sweetest kiss.

A soft moan slips from beneath my lips, and just as he pulls back, a knock sounds at the door.

Knight reluctantly pulls away and drops into the chair as my gaze sails toward the door, watching it open slowly. A head pops into the room with a wide grin, and I immediately smile back as the rest of her body eventually follows her in.

"Oh, hey, you crazy bitch. I heard you were up here. I had to come check for myself," Amelia—one of the doctors I suffered through med school with—says as she welcomes herself in with her lunch. Her brow arches with intrigue as she notices the Adonis sitting beside me. "Goddamn. Who's the juicy man-meat?"

Knight smirks to himself, but I jump in with a response before he gets a chance. "He's just some asshole who thinks he knows what's best for me."

"Oh, tough break," she teases. "I had one of those. Got rid of him so fast, he left scuff marks on my floor. But then, he didn't look like *that*."

I nod, understanding the dilemma more than she will ever know. "Yeah, he also fucks like a god, so it makes getting rid of him a real issue."

"I can only imagine."

Knight lifts his gaze, meeting mine and conveying every last thought in that brilliant mind of his without saying a single word. "Don't think I won't bend you over and spank that sweet ass just because you have company."

A stupid grin stretches across my lips. "I'd like to see you try," I say, mimicking his earlier comments.

His eyes flash with the challenge, but as Amelia makes herself comfortable on the end of my bed and dives into her lunch, he backs down, leaving me to catch up with my friend. "Don't stop on account of me," Amelia mutters around her salad roll, shoveling it in as though she hasn't eaten for two days straight—which is highly likely. "I'm down for a show."

Knight laughs and reaches out a hand. "I'm Knight. The asshole who does in fact know what's best for her."

"Ahhh, I see," she says, taking his hand and giving it a small shake. "Dr. Levine. The asshole who likes to think she knows what's best for everyone, but you can call me Amelia."

"Nice to meet you, Amelia."

She gives him a polite smile before shifting her gaze back to me, but there's a deep curiosity in her stare that makes me uneasy. I can tell she has more than just a few questions about how I ended up here.

"Haven't seen you in forever," I say, getting in with a diversion before she gets a chance to unleash on me, knowing that at some point, she's going to be called to attend some *Grey's Anatomy* bullshit sooner or later.

"Yeah," she scoffs. "Because for some reason, you decided it would be a great idea to work night shift in the land of the dead, and everyone is too scared to go down there. You're on your own, babe. But it's a two-way street, you could always venture up here to where people actually have heartbeats every now and then."

"But the people with heartbeats also have opinions and big mouths," I mutter. "Down in the morgue it's peaceful—most of the time."

"Creepy is more like it," she laughs, shamelessly scarfing down another bite. "So, what'd ya do to end up here? Are you actually crazy or just faking it to get a mini vacation? Because if you were just needing a few days off, there are much better ways to go about it, but I applaud the efforts."

I can't help but laugh before immediately regretting it as pain shoots through my midsection. "Apparently I'm the real deal," I tell her, shrugging it off as though it's not a big deal. "At least that's what G.I. Joe over here thinks."

"Ugh, men," she mutters. "But don't worry about it too much. I had my own little menty B a few months back and wound up in this very bed. They gave me a few weeks off, some stress relievers, and after some mind-blowing sex, I was good as new."

"So, what you're saying is that I just need to get dicked down on a beach in Barcelona, and I'll be good?"

"Sounds perfect to me."

Amelia and I chat for a little while, and I'm grateful when she doesn't push me for details about what went down to land me in a psych ward, and soon enough her pager sounds, dragging her away. "Ahh shit," she mutters, scooping up what's left of her lunch. "Gotta run, but if you're still here tomorrow, I'll check in."

She barely has a chance to say goodbye before she's racing out the door, needing to get all the way back down to the trauma center to do her thing.

The door has barely finished swinging closed behind her when somebody else gently pushes it back open, a soft knock sounding on the doorframe as they enter.

My gaze snaps back to the door to find the head of psych striding into my room, a clipboard braced in her hand and a too-cheery smile on her face. Dr. Carzy, or as she's better known among the residents, Dr. Crazy. She's the best of the best, top of her field, and it's an honor to have her looking over my case, but I can't help but wonder why they feel they need to send in the bigwigs. Am I *that* messed up?

As if sensing that this is a private moment, Knight gets to his feet and offers me a small smile. "I'll grab you some lunch."

"Thanks."

He disappears a moment later, leaving me alone with Dr. Carzy.

"Dr. Madden," she says, making her way over to the end of the bed. "How're you doing? It's been a long time since I've had you on my service."

I smile politely. There's a good reason for that. I like to cut, and up here in the psych ward, we're specifically encouraging people not to play with sharp objects. "Yeah, I'm doing my residency in forensic pathology, so when I'm not vacationing in the psych ward, I'm usually in the morgue."

She immediately writes something down and it makes my stomach sink. "I see," she says.

"That . . . uhhh, that was a joke," I clarify, slightly panicked.

"Yes," she says, offering another forced smile before shifting on her feet. "I wanted to let you know how this was going to go and what you can expect. You've been placed on a seventy-two-hour hold where we are monitoring the state of your mental health and whether you are a danger to yourself or to others."

Seventy-two hours? More like a whole lifetime.

I shake my head. "I'm not suicidal, if that's what you're getting at," I tell her. "So feel free to sign whatever forms you need to sign, and I'll be on my way."

Dr. Carzy watches me for a moment before her lips pull into a tight line. "Wishful thinking. However, I'll be the judge of that," she eventually says. "For today, we'll mostly be monitoring you to make sure you don't slip back into any of these psychotic episodes, and then you'll meet with me again for a full psych evaluation to determine how your treatment plan will look moving forward."

"You make it sound so serious."

"It is serious, Dr. Madden. The brain, while beautifully powerful, is also very complex, and it's in your best interest to care for it properly," she explains before walking around the side of my bed and lowering herself into one of the chairs. "Now, I've heard reports on the events that have brought us here, but I'd like to hear your version of events."

My eyes widen. "All of it?"

"Yes, right from the beginning. And please," she adds. "Don't hold anything back. In order for me to assess you sufficiently, I need to know exactly what we're dealing with and what the nature of these episodes has been."

Crap. If she didn't think I was insane before, she's about to have a very rapid change of heart.

Taking a breath, I prepare myself to tell this woman, this colleague, that my subconscious has somehow developed a murderous fear kink that appears in the form of a sexy-as-sin stalker in a satanic mask who rails me while I try not to scream.

Fun times.

Knowing that holding back isn't going to do me any favors, I dive straight into it, giving her every sordid detail of my moments with my stalker, starting right at the very beginning from when it was just a feeling of being watched.

I tell her about the carvings in the bodies, the words left on the heart, the black roses, and the unfortunate sexual encounter at the club. I even pull up the side of my hospital gown and show her the letters carved into my skin, the very letters I somehow put there myself. I don't skip a single detail, telling her how I allowed him to touch me, how I welcomed it, even provoked it at times. How when his hand closed around my throat, it excited me. How the pain on the blade carving into my skin was alleviated by the feel of his fingers on my clit, and how despite having the clear image of Laith's dead body circling my mind, I never told him no.

"How long ago did this begin?" she asks. "Has it been slowly building for months, or is this all very recent?"

I shrug and try to remember exactly when the first shiver ran down my spine. "It started the day before my mom's anniversary dinner, so almost four weeks ago," I tell her.

"And have there been any other significant changes in your life? Work-related? Relationships?"

My gaze flicks to the empty chair that Knight vacated as the doctor walked in. "I mean, all that is new," I tell her as she follows my gaze to Knight's chair. "He's kinda my step-uncle, and if anyone finds out, it would throw both our worlds into chaos. But having said that, I don't think it's related. These *episodes* started happening before Knight and I got together."

Dr. Carzy nods. "I see, but as your relationship progressed, so did these episodes. They have escalated, become more volatile. Physical to the point of turning a blade on yourself. Now, I'm not saying that this may be the cause, or trigger, that has provoked these episodes. I believe this is more of a sexual fantasy that is manifesting. However, stress often plays a much bigger role in our mental health, no matter how big or little that stress may be. Anything can be a trigger."

I give her a blank stare. "Are you telling me that screwing my step-uncle is literally making me insane?"

"No, not in the slightest, Dr. Madden," she says. "Just that the undue stress of maintaining a sexual relationship with a partner who might not be deemed appropriate may have aided in how quickly the manifestation of this stalker came on."

"Well, shit. Do I have to stop sleeping with him?"

"I cannot help you with that," she tells me. "However, off the record, if you feel that you have a real future with this man, that he is ticking all your boxes and bringing you happiness and love, then you should hold on to that with everything you've got."

I nod as I let out a heavy breath, my cheeks puffing out in the process. I know she's right.

"Now," Dr. Carzy says, getting right back on track. "Tell me how the masked stalker would appear to you."

We talk for almost an hour, and she finally decides that I won't be a danger to myself or to anybody else and hands me a notebook along with a pencil. "Now, I know we doctors aren't always the best artists; however, I'd like you to draw your stalker, more specifically, his mask," she tells me. "In the meantime, I'm going to leave you be. At this stage, you're presenting with a mild case of psychosis. I don't believe we're looking at anything long-term with regard to treatment. However, I would like to get you started on some meds. The good news is that you can recover from this. With the right support system, regular therapy, and medication, you could be looking at a full recovery, but it is not easy. It is not a short road. You will need to put in the work. You will need to show up for yourself."

I nod, seeing that recovery far in the distance and wanting to grab it with both hands. "Whatever it takes," I tell her. "I want to put this behind me."

"Good. Now, over the next few days, I'll check in and see how you're doing and see if we can match you up with a therapist you gel with."

"Oh," I say, my eyes widening. "Don't give me Dr. Manning. He's a pretentious, cocky prick with an ego problem. Dr. Preston would be alright, I suppose. I don't know much about her, but she's always smiling. Actually, that might be an issue. Nobody is *that* happy."

Dr. Carzy laughs and jots down a note. "Okay, I'll reach out to Dr. Preston and see what her schedule is like. I don't foresee any issues, though."

"Great."

"Alright, I'll leave you to your drawing," she says, getting up from the chair and striding to the end of the bed before offering me one last smile. "You don't need to be scared, Harper. You're in good hands here. However, if you're feeling anxious or have any questions, I'm only one call away. You'll have another psych assessment at the end of your seventy-two-hour hold, and following that, you'll be free to go home."

"Thank you," I say, feeling a weight lift off my shoulders at finally getting some answers. Having the head of the psych ward confirm that you're actually mentally unstable isn't exactly the best news, but knowing for sure that the masked stalker never existed and that all that fear and grief he put me through wasn't real is a relief.

Nobody died because of me. Nobody was hurt. No lives ruined at my expense. Only my own, but with the right medication and therapy, I should be okay. It didn't go unnoticed that she never mentioned anything about how soon I can get back to normal life. Is this like when you're recovering from surgery and you're stuck on the couch for six to eight weeks? Or is it more like fill me up with meds and send me straight on my way with a smack to my ass?

Not wanting to dwell, I drop my attention to the notebook in my hands before turning to a new page. I'm really not an artist. My drawing skills peaked in kindergarten, but nonetheless, I grip the pencil and bring it to the paper and start putting down on paper every line of his mask, every slight detail, the depth of his eyes beneath and hauntingly terrifying vampire fangs that would stare back at me.

Chills sail down my spine, and yet as I pluck the details straight out of my brain, peace settles over me. He's no longer just a figment of my imagination, he's a shitty drawing in a random page of a notebook. He's nothing. He holds no weight. No purpose, and more than that, he will never be able to hurt me again.

CHAPTER 40

HARPER-RAYN

Laith stares at me from the foot of my hospital bed, and all I can do is gawk back at him. It's strange seeing his face after everything, even though I know it was in my head. It's humiliating to let my friends see me at my lowest.

"How're you doing, tiger?" he asks, his blue stare taking me in as though I'm about to break, and honestly, I can't blame him. The last time I saw him, I was barely a shell of my normal self. I was well and truly losing my mind. Hell, I was fucking crazy, screaming about him being dead while he stood in my doorway. "You good?"

"Better now," I say, my cheeks flushed with embarrassment. "I'm sorry you had to see me like that. Apparently I've been going through some things, and my mind has been distorting the truth. It really wasn't my intention to scare you like that."

"Yeah . . . about that," he says, striding around the side of the bed and dropping down into the seat that Knight usually occupies. "You wanna tell me what the fuck you thought was going on? Because I'm confused. Did you think I was dead?"

I cringe as I nod. Laith and I have always been honest with each other, but that doesn't mean that telling him about all of this doesn't make me want to slam my face against a broken mirror. However, I probably shouldn't mention that to Dr. Carzy. She might have me locked up for good.

"I've, ahhh . . . kinda been having psychotic episodes where I've hallucinated a masked stalker, and every time this stalker has appeared, his intentions have escalated and become more sinister."

His gaze narrows as he leans forward, his elbows braced on his knees. "Like?" he asks.

"Like . . . I believed he was going to kill me," I explain. "At first, it was this twisted game of hide-and-seek, and he would just show up—well, I would hallucinate him showing up. Like the night Izzy and I went to that club. One minute I was dancing, the next, he was there watching me. But it grew from that. At work, bodies were showing up on my table that I thought were messages from him, warnings, but it was all in my head. They were just regular bodies. Car crash victims, stuff like that."

"Fuck, tiger. That's rough," he says. "I'm really sorry that you've been going through all of this, but I'm failing to see how any of it had to do with me."

I cringe again. "One of the bodies that showed up in the morgue, I thought it was you," I tell him, my gaze falling away from him, shame eating at me. "When I unzipped the body bag, I saw your face, and it gutted me. I had to do your autopsy, and I've never experienced anything so agonizing in my life. I thought you were dead because of me, and it broke me in a way I've never broken in my life."

Laith immediately gets up from the chair and scoots in beside me on the bed, wrapping his arms around me as though I'm the most precious thing in his world. "I'm right here, tiger."

"I know that now," I say, resting against his chest as I stare up at the ceiling tiles. "That's why I was so messed up when you showed up at my door. I couldn't understand how you were there. My brain was playing tricks on me, trying to tell me that you were dead and in a body bag in the morgue while you were really standing right there at my door."

"After you ran out of your apartment in your pajamas, I was worried about you," he tells me. "I've never seen you like that. There was something weird in your eyes. You obviously looked like yourself, but it was as though the Harper I know wasn't in there. It was like everything behind your eyes was just blank."

"Well, that's fucked up."

"You're telling me," he mutters before brushing his thumb over my bruised shoulder. "What about everything else? You really scared me when I got to that alley and found you on the ground like that, and it killed me that I couldn't stay at the hospital and wait for you to come out of surgery, but I had to be in court. I hope that it was okay that I called that guy you've been seeing."

My head snaps up, my gaze locked on his as I push myself off him, putting just a little space between us so that I can see him properly. "Wait. That was you who drove me to the hospital?" I ask, my heart racing.

"Well, yeah. Who the fuck else would it have been?"

I shake my head. I guess I haven't really had a chance to think about it much. "I thought . . . shit. I suppose I don't know what I was thinking. I don't really remember much about that trip to the hospital. Everything was hurting, but you . . . I thought it was my stalker who was driving me, which is why I was kinda freaking out as well. I guess the trauma of what happened in the alley kind of had me slip into one of my hallucinations, but thank you. It's refreshing to know I had someone I could trust with me at that moment."

"Shit."

"Yeah."

"But you're good now, though?" he asks. "Healing? There's no permanent damage?"

I nod. "Yeah. I mean, apart from the permanent psychological trauma I'm bound to hold on to, I'm mostly good. I kinda fucked up my stitches when I freaked out and took off after seeing you in my doorway, but for the most part, I'm doing much better. The bruises still look bad and the swelling is still going down, but they're much better than they were."

"And the guy who did it? Do you know who it was? Because all you need to do is say the word, and I'll make sure he spends the rest of his life rotting in jail."

A stupid smile pulls across my face, and I snuggle back into his side. "It's all good," I tell him. "It was one of the night janitors from the morgue, but Knight paid him a little visit, and I think it's safe to say that he won't ever be a problem for me again—or any other woman, for that matter."

Laith nods, pulling me closer. "So Knight is your new hero, huh? How's that going?"

"Good enough to know that if he were to walk in right now and see you in bed with me, he'd probably want to kick your ass. And he will. He's a six-foot-four SWAT officer with more muscle than a girl knows what to do with."

Laith gapes at me, and I can't help but laugh. "Chill out. I'm kidding. Well, mostly. He is pure sex on legs, but he would never hurt anybody that I care about, no matter the circumstances. He's . . . shit. I don't know. I think I'm falling for him. Or maybe I'm already there."

"No shit, huh?" Laith mutters, impressed. "You're telling me this guy managed to thaw that cold heart of yours? I didn't think it was possible."

"Oh, shut up," I laugh as butterflies swarm through my stomach at just the thought of what Knight and I might mean to each other. "I think it might be something serious."

"Wow. I never thought I'd see the day," he tells me. "Won't lie, I'm kinda jealous. I'm going to have to go find someone else for those four a.m. booty calls. Do you have any idea how hard that is going to be?"

"Why? Because I'm irreplaceable?"

"No," he scoffs. "Because what woman would voluntarily put up with a guy who likes to fuck in the middle of the night? Don't get me wrong, you and me together. We were always great, that's not the issue. It's just that most chicks aren't spending their nights playing with dead people."

A laugh bubbles up my throat. "It was always great with us, wasn't it?"

He scoffs again. "Remember our first time?" he asks, recalling the one moment that we weren't compatible. "You were a mess, trying to put your leg in places it's got no business being."

"Me?" I gasp, gaping at him wide-eyed. "Uh-uh. That was not my fault. That one was all on you. I mean, shit. What man in his right mind asks a girl he just met to perform acrobatics during sex? It's not my fault that my foot slipped off the headboard and broke your nose."

Laith reaches up and touches his nose, shaking his head. "Sometimes when it's cold, I can still feel the pain."

I roll my eyes and shove him in the side. "You're such a loser."

"Maybe. But you'll always be a bigger loser," he laughs, pulling me back in. "I'm glad you're happy with this guy. That's all I've ever wanted for you."

"Thank you," I murmur, a small smile playing on my lips. "You know that's what I want for you too, and you'll find it."

Laith scoffs. "Oh hell no. I'm content with my single, bachelor lifestyle. I'm not looking for someone to come and screw that up. I'm just fine on my own. Don't go jinxing me with that shit."

I roll my eyes. There's no surprise that Harvey Specter has always been his idol. "You know, I hope some amazing chick comes along and really knocks you on your ass."

"Don't be ridiculous."

I laugh. "I, ummm . . . I also think now that Knight and I might be something a little more than just two people mashing their junk together, I think we need to cool it on the flirty texts. Though to be fair, when I was texting you the other day, I thought you were dead and that my masked stalker was texting from your phone, but—"

"Wait. Why are you sending flirty sex texts to your stalker?" he asks, cutting me off before his eyes go wide. "Oh, fuck! Was this stalker thing some kind of sexual fantasy? Were you getting railed by this guy? Holy fucking shit. I always knew you had some nasty undiscovered kinks. Were you holding back on me all these years?"

I press my lips into a hard line, regretting having brought up the texts in the first place. "Don't you have somewhere to be? Court? The office? Searching old dive bars for your next booty call?"

Laith laughs. "Oh hell no. Don't even try to change the topic. I wanna hear all about this freaky stalker. What did your imaginary friend do to you? Did he put it down like I can? Fuck, tiger. Give me all the filthy details."

Fuck me. This is going to be one hell of a long afternoon.

CHAPTER 41

KNIGHT

Okay, I've done a lot of stupid shit in my life, but this about tops the list.

I'm not the type of man who gets nervous, yet here I am, standing outside Harper's apartment shitting bricks. If she were ever going to beat my ass, then today would be the day.

She was released from the hospital a little over a week ago and is doing great. She's been taking her meds and has gone to regular therapy sessions with Dr. Preston trying to get to the bottom of her episodes and discover what helped to manifest such violent hallucinations. She hasn't had an episode since, and seeing the way her eyes light up instead of being clouded by fear only confirms that I did the right thing.

I hated betraying her trust like that; forcing her into a psych hold wasn't done without thought, and seeing the way she looked at me with such profound betrayal gutted me, but now that she's come out the other end and is actively getting the help she needs to put this behind her and move forward, it all seems worth it.

On the plus side, the extra few days in the hospital did wonders for her healing body. Her injuries from being jumped in that alley have dramatically faded, leaving only slight yellowing, which I'm sure will continue to fade over the next few days. She's still a little sore from her internal injuries, but for the most part, she's doing a lot better.

Though the second I walk into that apartment and she figures out what's about to go down, that's going to change.

Things have been different between us. It's as though she's waiting for me to run for the hills, but that's not about to happen. I meant every fucking word when I told her that if she's burning, I'll step right into the fire. They're not words that I say lightly, and they're sure as fuck not words that I just say to anybody.

Harper-Rayn Madden is fucking endgame for me, and I don't give a shit what she has to say about it. Fuck her bullshit nonexclusive relationship. She's mine, and it's about time she acknowledges it.

After knocking on her door, I take a step back and wait a few moments for her to spy on me through the little peephole before finally deciding that she will grace me with her presence. The door opens, and I stare down at my girl with her long black hair that's been thrown up into a lopsided messy bun. She's wearing a dirty hoodie that comes halfway down her shins while holding a tub of leftover Chinese food and a fork dangling from her mouth.

I step into the small apartment, glancing down at the Chinese food, trying to remember which day she ordered this, because I know damn well it wasn't from last night or even the night before that. "Did you even bother to reheat that shit?"

She shakes her head and pulls the fork out of her mouth. "That just seems like a waste of time."

"I really don't know how you've managed to keep yourself alive all these years."

"If I had to guess, it was those awful college years, living off ramen and beans," she says, whipping around and making her way back to her couch and getting comfortable. "I built a tolerance. I've got an iron stomach now. No form of food poisoning is gonna bring me down."

A stupid grin pulls across my face as I follow her to the couch. I take the offending Chinese container out of her hands and lean down, bracing my palms on either side of her thighs. "Listen, I'm going to need you to waltz that fine ass into the shower while I start packing up your things."

"Eh?" she grunts, her face twisting with confusion. "You're gonna pack up my what now?"

"All your things, doll," I say. "I'm moving you into my place."

Harper laughs and shoves her hand against my chest, forcing me away. "The fuck you are," she says. "I don't need some over-the-top, bossy alphahole babysitting me at all hours of the day just because he's scared that I could fall off the wagon at any given point and take a trip straight back to Crazyville."

"This isn't a negotiation, Harper," I tell her. "I haven't come to discuss it with you. *I'm telling you.* Your little pain-in-the-ass self is going to get in the shower, and then you're going to help me pack up all your shit, and then you're moving into my place."

"Oh, I see where we went wrong. I didn't realize your little caveman act came fully equipped with a tiny pea-sized brain. That's awesome, but obviously you're missing the key component of this conversation. Let me make this a little clearer for you," she says, getting to her feet and making a show of clearing her throat. "If you touch even one thing that belongs to me and try to remove it from my home, I'm going to tear you straight through the center, starting from the asshole. And if that was also too hard to understand, then allow me to dumb it down. I'M NOT FUCKING MOVING IN WITH YOU."

I cross my arms over my chest and watch her. "Are you done with your little tantrum?"

Her eyes widen like saucers. "The fuck did you just say to me?"

"Goddamn," I growl, stepping into her and capturing her waist, holding her so damn tight. "I love it when you're feisty like this."

Harper tries to push me away, but I step into her again, forcing her back until her knees hit the edge of the couch and she has no choice but to drop her perfect hoodie-covered ass back down to the cushion. I cage her in just as I had before, holding her hostage as I capture her stare with mine. "Let's get one thing straight," I tell her, my voice dropping. "I'm not moving you into my place because I think your need a full-time babysitter, I'm moving you in because the thought of not waking up to you in my bed every fucking day guts me. I'm moving you in because I need you in my space. I need to breathe the same fucking air that you breathe. I need you there because I fucking love you."

Her eyes widen, her chest rising and falling with quick, labored breaths. "You what?"

I lean in, skimming my lips over hers as I take her chin, making sure she hears every goddamn word. "You heard me, doll. I fucking love you."

Tears well in her eyes, but she doesn't dare blink them away as she shakes her head, staring at me as though she can't comprehend the words that just came flying out of my mouth. "How could you possibly love someone like me? I'm broken. I need meds just to keep me from going insane. How could you want somebody like me?"

"You're not understanding, doll," I tell her, letting her see right through to my soul as I bare it all for her. "You are my divinity. You are my God-given eternal peace. I'm not giving you up for anything."

I can almost sense the way her heart races in tandem with mine, and as she takes a breath, she lifts her hand to my chest. Her watery eyes remain locked on mine, searching them as if trying to catch me in an elaborate scheme. "You really mean that?"

I nod as a small smirk kicks up the corner of my lips. "This is the part where you finally admit that you're desperately in love with me too and send your bullshit exclusivity terms to the deepest pits of hell."

Her jaw drops, and she has the audacity to get sheepish, though I suppose now isn't the time to remind her that she doesn't need to be shy with me, especially after all the things I've done to her body. "I . . . uhhhh . . . might have some certain feelings for . . . perhaps you, my forbidden step-uncle, that may or may not be something a little more than like."

"Something a little more than like?"

"Mm-hmm," she says, holding up her fingers to show just how little.

I lean in even closer, her gaze captivated by mine, and as my lips hover just an inch from hers, she sucks in a breath. She's just as affected by my proximity as I am by hers. "Tell me what I want to hear, Morticia. Say the words that you and I both know are tormenting that pretty little brain of yours."

She lets out a sigh, her hand snaking up around the back of my neck, and I can't help but reach down and scoop her off the couch, her legs locking around my waist. Her arms loop over my shoulders as her bright green gaze rests on mine. Those eyes are like a perfect window right through to her soul. "I don't know how you've done it, Knight Slater, but I am shamelessly and irrevocably in love with you."

"There," I say, as a goofy-as-fuck smile pulls across my lips. "That wasn't so hard, was it?"

Harper rolls her eyes and closes the gap, pressing her lips to mine. "Shut up," she says, her words muffled against my lips as she kisses me. "But that doesn't mean I'm about to move in with you."

"Yeah, Morticia. You are."

She pulls back, her gaze hardening. "The fuck I am."

"I told you, this isn't a negotiation. I'm packing your ass up and bringing you home where you belong," I tell her. "Fight me on it all you want, but at the end of the day, it's my bed you'll be sleeping in whether you like it or not."

"Or what?" she grunts, shoving out of my arms and forcing me to put her back on her feet. "You'll kidnap me?"

The smirk that pulls across my face answers her question before I even have the chance to open my mouth. "If you really need clarification on that, then you don't know me well enough."

She scoffs. "That's part of the problem. I barely know you at all."

I'm not often caught off guard, but at that, I pull back and stare at her. Sure, she might not know what high school I went to or who I lost my virginity to, but I've never let anybody in the way I have with her. "What the fuck are you talking about? You know me."

Harper shakes her head. "I know that you would never hurt me or try to push for something I wasn't ready for. I know you make my body come alive in a way that nobody ever has before. I know that you have a good heart, despite being a bossy asshole. But I don't truly know you. I don't know the little things. I don't even know the names of those two guys who dropped my keys off in the hospital when you were too pussy to show your face. I don't know your favorite color. Your favorite meal. Or how the hell you managed to get shot three times."

"You're talking about superficial things," I say, feeling as though that shit doesn't matter, but the way she's looking at me makes me wonder if perhaps it means something more to her.

Harper nods, and something softens within me. Don't get me wrong, I sure as fuck haven't changed my mind. This woman will be living with me by the end of the day, but that doesn't mean that I can't take a moment to give her what she needs to be okay with this.

Scooping her back up into my arms, I stride across the small apartment and place her down on her kitchen counter, that bright green gaze locked on mine as I brace my hands on either side of her thighs, caging her in.

"My favorite color," I start, "is jet black."

Harper scoffs, interrupting before I get the chance to explain. "That's not a proper favorite color. That doesn't count."

"It sure as fuck does," I tell her, reaching up and brushing a stray lock of jet-black hair off her face.

"Why? Because it matches my jet-black soul?"

"No," I say slowly, letting her hear the need in my tone. "It's the color of your hair, and whenever I see it, I think of you, and the way I wanna curl it around my wrists and fuck you until your tight little cunt is squeezing my cock."

Her cheeks flush, and she glances away, rolling her eyes. "Okay, whatever. Jet black can be your favorite color."

I laugh but carry on. "The two guys who came to your hospital room—"

"Dumb and dumber?"

"Mm-hmm. Ace and Diesel. They've been my best friends since we were rookies, just starting out in the force. They're my brothers. They've had my back, just as I've had theirs. They're both part of my team, and now that you're mine, they're your brothers too."

She arches her brow. "They'll just welcome me with open arms despite not knowing a thing about me?"

I nod. "They know me, doll. They trust my judgment, and if you're someone important to me, then you'll be just as important to them. They will have your back, just as much as they have mine."

"Wow."

I nod again. "Anything I'm forgetting?"

"How you managed to get your ass shot three times," she reminds me.

I let out a sigh and pull up my shirt, letting her see the first scar I received from a bullet on my hip, pointing it out so she can see it among the tattoos. "Courtesy of Ace during training camp," I tell her, watching as she reaches out and brushes her fingers along the barely visible scar. "Complete accident. He was a lousy shot for a while."

"You're kidding."

I can't help but laugh. "I really fucking wish that I was."

"And the second time?"

I turn and pull my shirt over my head, pointing out the second scar high on my back. "Hostage situation gone wrong. There was one bullet left in the chamber, and it was either going to be for me or the asshole's daughter. He chose the daughter, but so did I."

Harper sucks in a breath, and I turn back to see her horrified expression. "You took a bullet for a girl you didn't know?"

I stare back at her, confused. "Wouldn't you?"

"I . . ." She lets her thoughts fall away, her brows creased. "I suppose I've never had to think about it before. I've never been in a situation that would even resemble me having to make a call like that. But I guess I would. If it was either me or a child, I would take the bullet. At least, I'd like to think that I would be brave enough to do that."

"You are, Harper," I tell her. "Doing what I do, you quickly start to learn how to read people, learn things about them that they wouldn't even know about themselves, and you would take that bullet without hesitation."

She gives me a tight smile and nods before letting her fingers dance across my hip. "The third one?" she asks in a small tone, making me wonder if she truly wants to know anymore. After all, learning about the hard realities of what I do and the risks I take every single day aren't easy.

"About eight years ago now," I say, taking her hand and brushing it across the angry scar on my ribs. "This was the closest call I've had. Punctured a lung and had me on desk duty for three months. I almost ended up on one of your tables."

"Shit," she says, sucking in a deep breath. "And you do this every day? I just send you off to work knowing you might never come home again."

"Yes," I say, not sugarcoating it because honestly, that's just the risk you take in my line of work. "But I expect you to trust that I have curated the best team members who are more than equipped to handle the situations we face daily. My team doesn't make errors. We have each other's backs, and we make sure that each and every one of us makes it home at the end of the day."

She nods before letting out an awkward laugh. "I wasn't expecting that to get quite so heavy."

I laugh with her. I wasn't either, but I don't regret sharing it with her. It's important that she has a firm understanding of this. "Is there anything else you're dying to know about me before you cave and accept that you're moving in with me?"

She lets out a deep sigh. "I really don't have a choice in the matter, do I?"

"Not even a little bit."

"Fine," she finally says, just as her apartment door flies open and Ace, Diesel, and Izzy march in, their arms loaded with boxes, tape, and snacks.

"Uhhhhhh . . . What the actual fuck?" Harper says, gaping at the newcomers who are making themselves right at home.

Izzy strides over, dropping the snacks onto the kitchen counter beside us before explaining herself. "Dumb and dumber just showed up at my place and kidnapped me," she starts, looking more than delighted at that fact. "Apparently it's moving day, but don't expect me to help. I'm here to watch as they get all sweaty and have to take their shirts off so I can get a better image for my spank bank."

Ace laughs from across the apartment as Diesel, the no-bullshit guy that he is, starts putting the boxes together, not bothering to wait to see how breaking the news went. He's here to do a job, and nothing is going to keep him from doing that.

"Well, shit," Harper says, turning her dazzling green stare right back to me. "Looks like you really were going to kidnap me if I said no to moving."

"Did you really think I wouldn't?"

Harper groans and shoves me away before jumping down off the kitchen counter. "Fine," she says, surveying the array of snacks. "I'm going to shower, but I swear, not one of you nosy assholes is permitted to look inside my bedside drawer, and if I find out that you have, all three of you will have matching testicle bow ties—and trust me when I say that I will mix and match that shit. You'll all be wearing each other's balls like one of those BDSM collars."

And with that, Harper harrumphs and stomps off to the bathroom, leaving me and the boys to move this brat into my place, her bedside drawer and all.

CHAPTER 42

HARPER-RAYN

My gaze sails around Knight's home as Ace, Diesel, and Izzy leave for the night. It's been one hell of a day, and as I try to wrap my head around it, I can't help but notice how surreal this is.

Do I seriously live here with this intoxicatingly delicious man?

One minute I was scarfing down a tub of leftover Chinese food; the next, my whole world was changing before my very eyes. Despite how much of a fight I put up, I can't help but want this. It feels so right. I won't lie; I'm terrified of what will happen if and when he gets bored with me, though he doesn't seem to think that's ever going to happen. If he wants to live in a delusional world, then who the hell am I to try and stop him? I'm more than happy to live here, to be in his arms every day and be the woman he chooses to share his life with.

Fuck. I really have fallen in love with him.

As Knight locks up, I make my way down to his closet and start putting away the last of my clothes when I find my array of sexy lingerie. I can't help but grab my favorite pieces and a pair of sleek black heels to match.

A stupid smile stretches across my face, and when I hear him making his way down the hall, I hurry out of the closet and into the bathroom, making sure to close the door behind me. Giddiness pounds through my veins, and as I stand in front of the mirror, peeling off my clothes piece by piece, I've never felt so excited.

Sure, I've worn sexy lingerie for plenty of men, but it's never felt like this.

I do my hair in a high pony, knowing how he loves to wrap my long jet-black locks around his strong wrists, and after putting on just a touch of makeup for my man, I turn my attention to the lingerie.

It's fucking stunning, and the few times I've worn the pieces, I've never felt so desired and beautiful. I fix the sheer black bra into position, my gaze shifting over the delicate design on the fabric as I adjust the way my tits sit inside the cups, making sure they look as full and delicious as possible. After all, if I'm going to do this, then I'm going to do it right.

Stepping into the matching thong, I pull the dainty material up my thighs before fixing it into place, pulling the sides up high over my hips, and adding just a little bit of shape. Butterflies swirl deep in my stomach, and as I hear Knight moving around our room, probably finding places for the last of my things, I take the sheer garter belt and clip it around my waist.

"Well, shit," I murmur to myself, taking in the sheer material covering my skin. This morning, Knight told me that I'm his version of divinity, and while I know that's an outrageous exaggeration, at this very moment, I can't help but feel as though this might be the closest I'll ever get.

Last but not least, I step into my heels, completing my outfit, and when I stand back, taking in the whole look, a stupid grin pulls across my face.

Damn. Knight is one hell of a lucky man.

"Doll, where do you want all this hair shit?" he calls out.

Showtime.

Turning off the light, I open the bathroom door and step out into the bedroom before leaning against the doorframe and coming up with the most seductive pose I can possibly think of.

Knight strides out of the closet, his gaze immediately lifting to mine, and when he comes to a dead stop in the middle of his bedroom, a wave of pride flourishes through my chest.

Hook, line, and sinker.

"Fuck me," he breathes.

He starts toward me, and I shake my head. "Uh-uh. If you want this, you're gonna have to get on your knees and beg."

He grins, his gaze raking over every inch of my body and filling with the deepest need. His eyes return to mine as he simply stands across the room, and with every passing second, the tension in the room intensifies.

That fucker. He's not about to get to his knees and beg. He's going to make me work for it.

Knight shrugs out of his shirt, putting that delicious body on display, killing me with those strong abs, pecs, and tattoos, and when he reaches for his belt and slowly unbuckles it with one hand, my mouth starts to water.

God. I'm a sucker for this man.

His belt hangs open and my gaze lingers on his pelvis, knowing exactly what hides beneath. "Come," he commands, his deep tone demanding complete submission.

I don't move a muscle, not even to smirk at him. This is my game, not his.

His gaze narrows, his jaw clenching, and when he takes the end of his belt and rips it from the loops, my whole body trembles with need. He holds the belt in both hands, his muscles bulging as he remains controlled.

"Come to me now, Harper-Rayn."

Yes, Daddy.

As if not having a single say in what my body does, I find myself pushing off the doorframe and slowly gliding toward him, desperately needing to please, desperately needing his touch.

My chest heaves as I step right in front of him, my gaze locked on his as if anxiously awaiting the next set of instructions. Knight watches me, just as captivated as I am, and when he lifts his hand and brushes his fingers down my body, starting at my ribs and ending at my hip, my skin prickles with goose bumps.

He hooks the belt around my body, gripping it hard on both sides, and hastily pulls me in so that I fall against his wide chest with both hands braced against his warm skin. He leans in as a gasp slips from between my lips.

"You want to please me, doll?"

I nod, and he loosens the belt from around my waist before suddenly cracking it against my ass, making me jump. I gasp again, my core throbbing, desperate for more, and damn it, I push back against the belt, hoping like hell he does it again.

"Knees."

I suck in a breath and within seconds, I'm down on my knees with his belt looped under my ass, my fingers gripping the front of his pants. I hastily pop the button, and just as I grasp the zipper, he takes my chin, lifting my gaze to his.

"Spread your knees."

I don't hesitate, spreading them wide, and when he groans, fire erupts deep in my body.

"Look at you, my feisty little vixen. You're starved for me."

I nod and he runs his thumb across my lip before pushing it inside my mouth. I close my eyes, rolling my tongue over his thumb, and when I open my eyes again, his stare is full of fury and lust.

"Take me in your mouth, doll, right to the back of your throat," he growls. The conviction in his deep tone demands my complete obedience. "You're not going to stop until I say so. Do you understand me?"

Hunger pulses through my veins, and as I keep my stare on his, I pull the zipper down and reach in, freeing his massive cock. My hand curls around his base, slowly trailing up and down his length. I lean in, teasing him with my tongue as I roll it over his tip, watching the way his control falters, his muscles flinch, and his eyelids flutter.

"This morning you said I was your divinity," I murmur, my lips gently brushing against his velvety skin, feeling his angry veins beneath as a teasing smile pulls at the corner of my mouth. "Now let me show you how much of a devil I can be."

Knight groans and looks at me in awe, and it's as though he can barely believe that I'm real, and damn it, I've never felt like such a woman. I don't waste a single moment, opening my mouth and taking him deep, blowing his mind with my tongue.

I grip his base, moving my hand up and down with my movements, and as if on cue, he reaches around the back of my head and wraps my hair around his wrist. "Fuck, doll."

Despite the overwhelming need to grin like the Cheshire cat, I maintain my composure, working him right to his tip before diving back in, my tongue teasing every inch of his impressive length.

His grip tightens in my hair, and he groans. "Mmm. Just like that."

I take him deep, pushing myself as far as I can take him. Sucking, nipping, teasing. He's delicious, and after I glide down his thick cock one more time, he detonates, coming hard and spurting hot pulses of cum into my mouth.

I swallow every drop, and when he releases his hold in my hair, I settle back on my heels, staring up at him with pride. He gazes back at me, his eyes shimmering with awe when he holds up his hand, using a pointer finger to indicate for me to rise.

I do so immediately, taking his hand and standing before positioning myself right in front of him. "Good girl," he rumbles, his words making something spark deep in my chest. "Now, walk this ass over to the bed."

I grin, stepping around him and slowly making my way over to the bed, making sure he gets the perfect view of my body. He watches me walk away, his dark eyes locked on my ass, and I grin to myself, having a good idea how this is going to go.

He scoops the abandoned belt off the ground, and a thrill blasts through my chest as he makes his way toward me.

It looks like someone has something special in store for me tonight, but he's kidding himself if he thinks I'm about to submit to him again. Then as he steps in behind me, his fingers brushing over my waist, a soft laugh bubbles from my throat.

"Dare I ask what's so funny?" he says.

"Oh, nothing," I say, feigning innocence. "I just think it's cute that you think you're simply going to crack that belt of yours across my ass again, tie me up, and have your wicked way with me."

"Oh," he murmurs. "I'm not?"

I shake my head, loving the way his lips drop to my shoulder and work up to the curve of my neck, making everything clench inside me. "No. I played the role of your doting little whore. I dropped to my knees without question and gave you exactly what you asked for. I played your little game, and now it's your turn."

"Really?"

"Mm-hmm. You know how strongly I feel about repaying favors," I say, remembering the exact moment I stepped right up on his bed, walked over to him, and demanded he eat my pussy until my knees were shaking. Tonight will be no different.

Knight chuckles to himself, and when his fingers brush against my shoulder and trail down my skin, leaving a wake of goose bumps, I start to wonder if my confidence might have been misplaced.

His fingers reach my palm, and just when I think he's about to give me what I want, he lifts the belt and locks it around my wrist. I suck in a breath, my heart racing as he reaches for my other wrist and works it behind my back, binding it to the other.

I fucking gulp.

This isn't quite how I thought this was going to go. I was a fool to assume I could take control of this game. The ball has been in his court the whole damn time.

With my wrists secured behind my back, Knight leans in, kissing my shoulder before wrapping his arm around my body, his hand diving between my thighs and firmly cupping my pussy. He grinds the palm of his hand against my clit, and my body trembles in his strong arms.

"It's cute that you think I haven't been thinking about devouring your sweet little cunt since the moment I got you back here," he says, mimicking my earlier words.

A soft, needy groan slips from my lips, and in a flash, his hand is gone. He takes my waist and spins me around before lifting me into his arms. A squeal tears out of me, not having hands to hold on with, but I'm secure in his arms, and as he strides across the room, my legs lock around him.

Knight puts me down in the armchair in the corner of the room, my hands squished under my ass, making sure I can't move.

My chest heaves and as his dark eyes flame with hunger, my pussy throbs with need.

He takes my legs, dragging me down the armchair before hooking each of my knees over the edge of the arm rests, opening me wide. In this position, I'm completely at his mercy, unable to move, but even if I could, I wouldn't dare try.

"There," he rumbles, looking at me laid out before him like an all-you-can-eat buffet. "This is how I expect to find you when I come home from work."

"Really?" I murmur, my tongue rolling over my bottom lip. "And what exactly do you plan on doing with me?"

A smirk kicks up the corner of his lips, and as that dark gaze burns with excitement, he falls to his knees. His fingers drop to my shoulder, slowly trailing over the fabric of my lingerie, touching me everywhere. He follows the curve of my breast down to my ribs, brushing over the *MINE* scar before dancing across my hip.

His fingers move over the fabric of my thong as I squirm beneath him, my body already so worked up, and when he pulls the dainty fabric aside, revealing my needy cunt beneath, his eyes fill with the deepest desire.

Then with my heels hanging over the sides of the armchair, Knight dives in, closing his warm mouth over my clit. I cry out, my hips jolting at the sudden rush of pleasure against my core, and he responds by rolling his tongue over my sensitive clit.

I groan as he works me, desperate to twine my fingers into his hair and pull, but I'm at his mercy, playing by his rules as he works me at his own pace, having complete control.

"Oh God, Knight," I groan, my hips rolling against his face.

His lips are like pure ecstasy working my body, and when he reaches down between my thighs and pushes two thick fingers deep inside me, I can barely hold myself together. My hips wildly jolt, and I cry out, raw, undiluted pleasure pumping through my veins.

His fingers curve inside me, splitting and rolling, massaging my walls until the intensity has my body spasming beneath him. He holds me down, his hand splayed on my waist as I feel a deep tightening in my core.

"Oh, fuck. I'm gonna come."

I throw my head back against the armchair, my eyes rolling in my head, but I need to see the way his tongue rolls over my clit, flicking and teasing, nipping and sucking.

I've never seen anything so raw, so erotic, so full of undiluted passion. The way he works me, the way he craves me, the way he worships every inch of my body. How could I ever be without him?

That coil inside me tightens until I can't possibly hold on any longer, and I explode, my orgasm tearing through me like a bomb, destroying everything that stands in its way. My body shatters, wildly spasming and jolting, and with every pass of his tongue over my clit, I fall to pieces.

Electricity buzzes through my veins as the intensity continues to reach an all-new high.

"Fuck," I cry out. "Knight!"

His fingers roll inside me, drawing out every ounce of pleasure like a twisted exorcism, like a demon calling for his willing subjects, and I'm all too eager to fall to my knees.

He gives me everything, pushing me to my absolute limits, and the moment I reach that peak and start coming back down, his precise movements become lazy, allowing me to finally catch my breath.

My body goes limp against the armchair as his warm lips move from my core to the inside of my thigh, pressing the sweetest kisses to my skin, and forcing a deep groan from between my lips.

Knight fixes the delicate fabric of my thong back into place, and I have to give credit where it's due. He's no stranger to tearing my underwear right off my body, but he managed to resist, and that right there shows an incredible display of control.

He lifts my legs off the armrests, letting me sit up on the chair properly, and as he kneels before me, I can't resist leaning forward and kissing him deeply. His hand works up to the base of my throat, gently squeezing and sending a rush of need through my body.

"You on your knees, tasting just like me. I could get used to this."

"Is that so?" Knight rumbles, pulling me off the armchair so that I fall onto him, my knees hitting the carpet on either side of his strong thighs.

"Mm-hmm."

His hand dances across my body, grabbing my ass before fingering the material of my skimpy lingerie. "This right here," he rumbles, his tone thick with desire. "This is how I want you every fucking day of the rest of my life. Just you and me, alone in this room."

"Every day, huh?"

"Oh yeah."

I roll my hips on top of him, grinding against his thick cock. "I'm not sure you could handle me every single day."

Knight grins and locks his strong arm around my waist before stepping up to his feet, my legs winding around his waist. "Oh, pretty girl, you have no fucking idea what kind of monster you just unleashed within me."

He strides over to the end of the bed before throwing me down, only before I even get the chance to gasp, he grips my thighs and flips me like a damn pancake, taking my hips and dragging me up on my knees, my chest flat against the mattress with my hands still bound behind my back.

It's eerily similar to my fantasy with my stalker, and I can't help but feel as though that fantasy is about to play out.

Knight's hand cracks against my ass and as my hips jolt, a deep groan tears from the back of my throat. "Spread 'em, doll."

I don't hesitate, pushing my knees as far as they can go as Knight grabs the belt that binds my wrists, pulling on it until I arch my back. My ass is high in the air, my cunt ready for the taking, and as his fingers dig into my hip, a wild thrill pulses through me.

"Mmmm. If only you could see yourself like this, doll. You're so fucking perfect."

I grin against the mattress when suddenly I feel his lips against my ass. He presses a gentle kiss to my skin, but when he opens his mouth and bites down, a wave of raw need crashes through me like a fucking tsunami.

As he pulls away, there's a sharp sting left behind from his teeth, and just as it starts to throb, Knight pulls the fabric of my thong aside and thrusts his fingers deep inside my cunt. "Oh, fuck," I cry out, my hips rocking back, needing more.

The pain instantly dissipates, and as he fucks me with his fingers, his brushes his other hand over the bite, and damn it, I've never wanted to tattoo something on my body more than I do right now.

He works me with his fingers, and when he pulls them back and replaces them with the tip of his massive cock, I realize I'm in for one hell of a ride.

I push back against him, wanting more, but he holds me still, controlling exactly how much I get. "You like that, doll?"

I nod against the mattress. "More."

He pushes deeper and my walls stretch around him, already trembling. "How's that?"

"Don't make me beg for it."

He teases me, inching back, only to thrust a little deeper, my body completely at his mercy. With each new inch he allows me, my walls stretch and spasm, desperately needing more. His fingers dig into my hip, my only sign that this is tormenting him just as much as it is me, and that tiny snippet of knowledge is the only thing keeping me from crying out.

Knight grunts, and the moment his resolve breaks, he thrusts deep, slamming into me until he bottoms out. "Shit, doll," he says as my walls contract around him, squeezing tight as I adjust to his delicious intrusion.

His cock flinches within me, and my whole body jolts at the sensation. "Baby," he groans. "I need to move."

I grin and look back over my shoulder as he pulls against the belt, keeping me arched. "Give me your worst."

And with that, my man truly starts to fuck me. He pulls back, his hips rolling, and as he looks down between us, he watches the way his thick cock slams into my trembling cunt. I can only imagine what he's seeing, the way his veiny cock glistens with my wetness, the way my pussy welcomes him in.

God. Just imagining it has me burning from within.

"Knight," I pant as his hips continue to roll, torturing me with every single perfect thrust, driving me wild with need.

"That's right, doll," he grits through his teeth. "See what I do to you? See how fucking perfect we are?"

"God, yes!"

He gives it to me hard, pushing me to my absolute limits as my body is pushed right to the edge. I clench my eyes, my hands balled into tight fists. I can't hold on to it any longer.

My pants turn into full-blown cries of desperation, my body coiled and ready to strike.

"Give it to me, Harper," he growls. "Show me how you come for me."

His words ignite something within me, and I let go, allowing my orgasm to rule me, shooting through my body and claiming everything that I am. My walls frantically spasm around his thick cock, squeezing him so damn tight that he can't help but come right along with me. A loud grunt rumbles through his chest as my pussy brings him to his knees.

He doesn't stop thrusting as he empties himself into me, my body violently spasming. "KNIGHT!" I cry out, sheer desperation and pleasure exploding through me, the intensity too much for me to handle.

"Keep it going, doll," he encourages. "Feel it all. Let it claim you."

"Fuck."

The overwhelming raw pleasure pulses through every inch of my body, electrifying my veins and burning me from the inside out, and when he releases my hip and reaches around, skimming his fingers over my sensitive clit, my world detonates all over again.

"Oh, fuck. FUCK. FUCK!"

Everything trembles. Spasms. Convulses. I fucking gush for him.

It's too much, but he guides me through, giving me more than I ever thought I was capable of, and as I come crashing back to earth, gasping for air, he finally releases me, undoing the belt and allowing me to crumble against the mattress.

His hands return to my hips, his thumbs caressing my skin with gentle circles as we both take a second, and as my body begins to give out, Knight slowly eases out of me and fixes my thong back into place once again.

He puts himself back inside his pants as I hear the familiar thud of his belt hitting the ground, and then not a moment later, he pulls my heels off, and I'm lifted off the mattress and pulled into the warmth of his strong arms.

"Come on, doll," he murmurs, pulling back the blankets of his bed and climbing straight in with me curled up against his chest. "Rest now, because come morning, I plan to do that all over again."

I make myself comfortable against his chest, listening to the sound of his heart, and damn it, I have never been so content in my life. He was right to have me move in here, just like he's been right about everything else. Mostly. That doesn't change the fact that he's still a bossy asshole, but truth be told, I love that about him. I love his need to look out for me, to protect me, and give me exactly what he knows I need.

Fuck, I just love him.

"Shit," I murmur. "Is it possible to die via orgasm? Because I'm not sure I can handle all that again."

Knight laughs, his hand roaming up and down my back before stopping at the garter belt around my waist and swiftly unclipping it, knowing it won't be comfortable to sleep in. "I've got no fucking idea, but death by orgasm sounds like a fucking great way to go."

"In that case," I say, lifting my chin and brushing my lips over his before adjusting myself until I'm straddled over him, his cock all but springing to life between my thighs. I reach down between us, fisting his cock and working him to the tip before adjusting myself over him and sliding down on top, filling myself to the brim. "We better test those limits and see just how far we can push them."

CHAPTER 43

HARPER-RAYN

A stupid smile pulls across my face as I stride out of the hospital morgue early on Tuesday morning. It's been a little over three weeks since my unfortunate freak-out at work, and almost a month since that asshole janitor and his friends left me for dead in that alley.

I was cleared to return to work on Friday, and after just completing my first shift back, I feel like my normal self. I was nervous to walk in there and be triggered, but it was fine.

I jumped straight back into my work and was killing it. I've kept on top of my new meds and have been to every scheduled therapy session with Dr. Preston, and while I hate being on medication and talking to people about my issues, they've done wonders for me.

My mind feels clear. There's no more paranoia about seeing a masked stalker, no more fearing that bodies will pile up with carved messages on their organs. I feel safe, not only physically, but mentally.

I feel like myself again, and that's a feeling I will never take for granted again.

Work was great. I managed to get through two complete autopsies, finished both reports, and managed to get on top of some of the work that my colleagues didn't quite finish during the day shift. Though I won't lie, there was a moment of awkwardness at the start of my shift when I walked in to find Dr. McKullan waiting for me.

He wanted to chat, make sure I was doing alright and checking that these night shifts were really in my best interest. I eagerly ensured that I was doing better and wasn't looking for any specific changes in my working hours, but he clearly still had doubts. He shouldn't, though. He made it crystal clear that he had spoken to Dr. Carzy about whether I was good to return to work, and she more than confirmed that I wasn't about to lose my mind over a corpse again. She has faith in my journey to reclaiming my mind, and she fully believes that I can overcome this, and so should Dr. McKullan.

I suppose time is the only thing that will ease his worries, especially after having a front-row seat to the infamous Harper-Rayn breakdown, but as long as he's happy to give me a chance, then that's all that matters.

Truth be told, if Dr. McKullan wanted to put me back on day shift just to keep an eye on me, it wouldn't be the worst thing. The day shift lines up perfectly with Knight's normal working hours, meaning for the most part, we'd be home together, going to bed together, and rumpling the sheets together. Though considering how often he gets called out to be the big SWAT machine that he is, I don't think it makes much of a difference.

Either way, when it comes down to it, I prefer the silence of the morgue. I prefer working alone without someone looking over my shoulder, and I prefer calling my own damn shots.

As I make my way through the parking garage, I search through the darkness, trying to remember where I parked my Honda as I feel around in the bottom of my bag, searching for my phone. It had gone off an hour ago with a new text, and seeing as how Laith has cooled his jets on the flirty texts, I can only assume it was Knight letting me know that he was on his way back home, but I was too caught up in my work to break for even a second to check it. He'd understand, though. I hope. Actually, on second thought, he might be pissed.

Knight was concerned about me returning to work, but he trusted me when I said that I was feeling better. If he's been nervous about it through the night and now I haven't responded to his text, he could be thinking the worst.

Finding my phone at the very bottom of the abyss otherwise known as my bag, I pull it out to find Knight's text, just as I had expected.

Knight: Just finishing up. Should be home in twenty. Hope there's not been any masked assholes trying to fuck you on an autopsy table.

A stupid laugh cracks out of me, and I immediately start texting back.

Harper-Rayn: The only masked asshole I've seen tonight was my reflection in the refrigeration unit, and trust me, she was definitely down to fuck on an autopsy table.
Knight: Fuck, doll. You better be on your way home, otherwise, I'm coming to you.
Harper-Rayn: Just searching for my car now.
Knight: Thank fuck for that.

I roll my eyes as I toss my phone back into my bag and grab my keys. It's a little after four in the morning, and the sun hasn't even started to think about joining us for the day. It's still dark, and one would think that after so long working night shift, I would have started parking in the same spot to avoid this bullshit at the end of every shift. Old habits die hard, I suppose.

Finally spotting my Honda, I cut across the parking garage, more determined than ever to get home to Knight and have him rail me into oblivion.

I'm only a few feet away when a chill sails down my spine, and just as I take one more step toward my car, the chill turns into sickening shivers. I pause, my brows furrowed.

Something's not right. This eerie feeling, there's something so familiar about it, yet it's different.

I swallow over the growing lump in my throat, my gaze shifting from left to right as unease leaves me shaken. I search in the shadows of the garage, trying to make shapes out of the darkness, but after coming up blank, I realize it's all in my head.

Maybe I'm not as far into my healing journey as I'd thought.

I try to shake it off and go to take the few final steps toward my car, when the darkness shifts, morphing into a person as he steps out from behind my car, the familiar mask crippling me with fear.

"No," I say, sucking in an audible gasp, terror pulsing through my veins as I clutch my keys tighter in my hand, ready to use them as a weapon if it comes down to it. I shake my head, wide-eyed as my heart races a million miles an hour. This can't be happening. I've been taking my meds religiously. I haven't missed a single dose. "No, you can't be here. You're not real."

I back up a step, shaking my head a little faster as though I could somehow shake him right out of existence. This isn't making any sense. The doctor confirmed that he was nothing more than a sick hallucination. Was she wrong? Was Knight wrong? Was all of it real?

The masked stalker laughs, only there's something different about it. His tone has changed. "Oh, sweet kitten. How easy it's been to find you."

"No." He takes a step toward me, and I hastily back up again. "No. You're not real."

He laughs again, and his tone makes me sick. "You're right," he tells me, the darkness behind his eyes filled with a sinister evil, something I never noticed before. Something that's . . . different. My stalker was always sick and twisted, but his eyes were a window into his desires. But this . . . His eyes are dead. There's no window here, nothing to see. "Your stalker wasn't real. He was a figment of your imagination, made up in that crazy little head of yours."

"Then . . . Then how are you here?" I ask, my chest heaving as my voice shakes.

"Because I am not him," he says. "I bleed just as you will when I finally make you mine."

Confusion swarms me, and I clutch my bag to my chest as though that could somehow help me, realizing this is as real as it gets. This man isn't the same one I made up in my head. This isn't the masked stalker who I thought I rode in the club, the masked stalker who took me on Knight's bed. This man before me, he's as real as I am and using my trauma to bring my stalker to life.

"Who are you?" I demand, clutching the keys so tight that they cut into my palm.

He laughs again as though truly enjoying my fear, getting off on it somehow. "It was too easy to get your notes from the good doctor. You gave her everything. His size, build. His mannerisms. You even drew me a picture of his mask. You offered up every crazy detail from that messed-up head of yours, and now there's nothing stopping me from making those little hallucinations real."

He steps toward me, and I find myself paralyzed by fear, unable to move as he closes the distance. "Why?" I say, the word falling from my mouth in a panicked whimper.

"Because I can, my sweet kitten," he says, lifting his hand and brushing his fingers down the side of my jaw before trailing them down to the base of my neck and slowly closing them around my throat, squeezing. "Because claiming you would be nothing more than a grand prize."

He squeezes a little tighter, and my knees start to shake, and when he tilts his head just a fraction to the right, I realize this man is nothing short of a psychopath. "You won't get away with this," I say, gasping for air.

Despite the mask, I just know he's smirking at me. His confidence tells me that he thinks he already has. "Haven't you heard? You're crazy," he says, his eyes flaring on the word as the satanic, fanged mask inches closer to my face. "You could scream it from the rooftops, but who's going to believe you now?"

He laughs as horror blasts through my chest, and as I hear the sharp *whoosh* of a blade being freed from its sheath, I scream.

"There's no escaping me now, kitten," he says as I gasp for air, his fingers digging into my throat. "I've got you right where I want you."

I squirm under his hold, clawing at his hand, and as my body finally runs out of oxygen and darkness dances behind my eyes, the sharp tip of his blade plunges deep into my waist.

He releases me, and I hastily gasp for air, sucking in the sweet oxygen as agony tears through my waist. I drop heavily to the dirty ground, and as blood pools around me, the masked man simply turns on his heel, wiping the blood from his blade on the thick material of his black pants. Then as he walks away, his words repeat on loop inside my head.

Who's going to believe you now?

ABOUT THE AUTHOR

Sheridan Anne is a contemporary romance author who writes about all things dark, twisted, and messed up. She lives with her wonderful husband and two beautiful daughters in the Hawkesbury region of Australia, alongside killer spiders, boxing kangaroos, and too many nope ropes to count.